* * *

To Maureen

my wife, closest companion and dearest friend

* * * * *

ALSO BY MICHAEL C. COX

* * * * *

NOVELS

Once Upon A Term

* * * * *

SHORT STORIES

Facts and Fantasies – Volume 1

Facts and Fantasies – Volume 2

Facts and Fantasies – Volume 3

Facts and Fantasies – Volume 4

* * * * *

Facts and Fantasies

An Omnibus

Michael C. Cox

MIM

Mimast Inc

Mimast Inc

This paperback edition published in 2015 by Mimast Inc

Copyright © Mimast Inc 2015,

Canadian ISBN 978-1-987926-04-0

All enquiries regarding this electronic edition to:

Mimast Inc
Edmonton
Alberta T6R 2H9
Canada
email: mimast@telus.net

Acknowledgements

Firstly, I must acknowledge a debt to the teachers who taught English language and English literature in my first five years at a Grammar school in my home town of Bristol. In spite of their efforts and best intentions, by the time I was sixteen I had acquired a taste for reading but not for writing. To be fair to those teachers, I felt at the time that I had so much to read and so little to write about.

I must acknowledge two of those teachers: Alex Mair, a Scotsman no less, and A.B. Reynolds, a somewhat eccentric Englishman. The former opened my eyes to literature by telling me to read Great Expectations by Charles Dickens. The latter opened my eyes to language by telling me to read out loud the first sentence in an exercise on syntax error: "Do not kill your wife with work, let electricity do it."

Secondly, I must thank my dear friend, Leif G. Stolee. He has encouraged me to write about people and events that have enriched my life over the past few decades. Leif's enthusiastic response to my stories has kept me at my computer and out of mischief. And I must mention here, James Stolee. He tempered his brother's enthusiasm with many well deserved criticisms of my writings.

Lastly but certainly not least, I must thank my wife, Maureen. She has always been my dearest and closest friend. She has watched over my grammar, corrected my spelling and made many constructive suggestions. Without Maureen's love and support, I doubt that I could ever have written a single word.

* * * * *

Needless to say, any mistakes in grammar and spelling, and any errors in facts used fictitiously, are my fault entirely. Nobody else is to blame.

* * * * *

THE STORIES

* * * * *

* * * * *

Author's note

In these short stories I combined, in varied proportions, figments of my imagination and actual events set in real locations. I have tried accurately to reveal the facts underlying all the stories but my memory is not what it was. Where appropriate I have also tried to conceal the identities of the people involved. If I failed to do so and thereby upset any family members, friends, colleagues or acquaintances, may I point out I never intended to embarrass and, more often than not, the law seems to benefit lawyers rather than litigants.

Eight stories (2, 3, 6, 7, 9, 11, 14 and 15) are largely biographical. Story number 6 is a fond recollection of my father and relates actual events that still have me shaking my head and thinking, "What are the chances?" Behind story number 7 are real people and events. but the consequence of my crime is fictional albeit the logically expected result of a chemical reaction.

Story number 8 describes an actual incident involving real people I knew but whose actual names I have not disclosed. If by my descriptions I have unwittingly disclosed the identities of my former neighbours, I hope they will not be embarrassed or upset by my portrayal of them.

* * * * *

Facts and Fantasies

Volume 1

Cedar of Lebanon

Michael C. Cox

Mimast Inc

THE LAWN

This story is a fiction based upon facts personally reported to me and upon events I experienced firsthand. For instance, I knew a chemist, who left a major chemical company, solved a pollution problem, published a book of walks to unusual places, brewed his own wine and who, inspired by the fall of a cast iron gutter that might have killed his son, made his fortune in PVC guttering and downpipes.

* * * * *

One secret of success in life is for a man to be ready for his opportunity when it comes - Benjamin Disraeli.

* * * * *

'I quit!'

'What?'

'You heard me.'

'But Harry...'

Dr Harold Procter stormed out of the laboratory and strode down the corridor leaving the heavy fire door to spring shut on his open-mouthed colleague.

'Hello! This is Dr Robinson. Put me through to Mr Harper.'

'I'm sorry Dr Robinson but Mr Harper is tied up and...'

'Well you'd better untie him, Pamela. This is urgent. It's about Dr Procter.'

'What about Dr Procter?'

'Just put me through. Now, please Pam!'

All that Frank Robinson could tell Donald Harper, the general manager of HG Chemicals Ltd, was that the Company's senior analytical chemist had blown his top and stormed off, saying he was leaving.

'What did he say exactly?'

'I quit,' said Frank.

'Is that all?'

'Well,' said Frank reluctantly, 'that was the last thing he said.'

'OK. What did he say before that?'

'He said… He said… Harper can stuff it! I've no idea what it was. Sorry. In the five years I've worked with Harry I've never known him to blow his top. Have you any idea what got into him?'

'It may be something that's been brewing for a while now,' Harper said hesitantly.

'Nothing I've said or done… or not done, I hope.'

'Absolutely not, Frank. Nothing to do with you at all. I'm quite sure of that.'

'He'll probably walk in on Monday morning as though nothing has happened.'

'What? Oh, yes, yes,' said Harper, putting out of his mind the clash he had with Harry earlier that afternoon. 'Look, Frank, just in case Harry doesn't come back, I'm putting you in charge of the laboratories for now, OK?'

Dr Harold Procter never did return to HG chemicals. Dr Frank Robinson became the senior analytical chemist in charge of the laboratories his predecessor had planned in meticulous detail, had equipped with the latest instrumentation and had run efficiently to the most exacting standards for the past five years. Neither Frank, who enjoyed the increased responsibility and salary, nor Donald, whose straws had finally broken Harry's back, gave any thought to how their former colleague would earn a living. That was his business. It was no concern of theirs.

* * * * *

'You're home early. Anything wrong?'

'No. Why do you say that?'

'You're never home before 5 o'clock and...'

'And...?'

13

'You've come home empty-handed.'

'What do you mean *empty-handed*?'

'I asked you to get a couple of bottles of wine to go with the meal this evening.'

'We've got plenty of wine...'

'I've told you before, Harry, I'm not serving our guests with your *home-made plonk*.'

Dr Harold Procter was very proud of his wines which never deserved to be denigrated as home-made plonk. When he didn't respond to her denigration with his usual *I'll have you know that I'm as professional about wine-making as I am about chemistry, etc., etc., etc.,* his wife was rather surprised. When Harry went quietly away and returned about forty minutes later with two bottles of Cabernet Sauvignon, two bottles of Muscadet de Sevre-et-Maine, a bottle of Harvey's Bristol Cream sherry and a bottle of Mercier Brut Champagne to drink with the pear crumble and the biscuits and cheese, Joy could not believe her eyes.

'What on earth...'

'Put these three in the fridge,' Harry said, handing Joy the Muscadet and Champagne, 'while I pour us a glass of sherry.'

'Are you feeling alright?'

'Santé!' said Harry, clinking glasses. 'Anything I can do to help?'

'Now I *know* you're not well,' said Joy. 'Go and watch the news on the telly.'

'No thanks. I've had enough gloom and doom for one day. I'll do the lawn.'

'If you really want to be helpful, perhaps you would empty the dishwasher and lay the table before you go into the garden.'

'No sooner said than done,' said Harry, draining his glass.

After he had emptied the dishwasher and set the table, Harry went outside and mowed his beloved lawn. Dr Harold Procter had three hobbies – his wife called them obsessions - which he pursued with the seriousness of a true professional. The first was Analytical Chemistry. 'Oh, no, Frank, you're quite wrong,' he once said to Dr Robinson. 'What I do here at HG Chemicals Ltd is *not* my *job*; it's my *hobby*. I'm just lucky I get paid for it.'

The second hobby was wine – making it, analysing it, bottling it and, of course, drinking it. He usually gave colleagues, including even the general manager, a bottle or two of his wine for Christmas. 'I'm glad you found the wine acceptable, Donald, but you're quite wrong,' he once said to the general manager, 'the red was not a Bordeaux; it was a blend of two separate wines: rhubarb and elderberry; the white was made from blackcurrants and over-ripe bananas.'

The third hobby was his lawn; it was his pride and joy.

Almost two hours elapsed from the time that Harry emptied the dishwasher to the time that Trevor and Dorothy Partridge rang the front door bell and he let them in. When Trevor asked Harry if they could stroll down the garden to the river's edge, Dot made a beeline for the kitchen to chat with Joy. 'Is your Harry alright? I only ask because he seemed... well... different somehow.'

Joy had sensed that something was wrong with Harry but she couldn't quite put her finger on it. He kept getting under her feet wanting to help in her kitchen; she was glad when he went out to do his lawn. When Joy asked her long-standing friend exactly how Harry had *seemed different*, Dot said, 'I don't know really. He seemed to have something on his mind. Oh, it's probably just my imagination. Trevor often seems a bit odd when he comes home late from work on Friday. Take today for instance. He was really miserable, moaning on about red-tape and a busybody inspector just out of college. But as soon as I reminded him we were coming here, he was back to his old cheerful self straight away. Funny that!'

'If your lawn didn't slope down to the river, you could play bowls on it, old man,' said Trevor. 'How do you keep it like this? Chemical fertilizers and herbicides I suppose.'

'I've told you before,' said Harry. 'It's more to do with how I prepared the ground, the seed I used and when I sowed it. As for what you usually call *those killer chemicals*, I've only once used copper sulphate; that was on a persistent bit of moss.'

'I read somewhere that per square foot of garden, a lawn takes the most time and effort; a bed of roses takes the least,' said Trevor.

'No doubt that's why you dug up your lawn to grow roses, you lazy blighter!'

'You said it. No aerating, scarifying, feeding, weeding, watering and mowing for me, thank you very much,' retorted Trevor. 'Just a bit of mulching, feeding, deadheading and light pruning now and then; that suits me down to the ground.'

'What about those aphids on the buds and that black spot on the leaves.'

'Easy,' said Trevor. 'I spray once or twice a year with systemic insecticide and copper sulphate fungicide... which reminds me... We've run into a problem at work.'

16

Trevor Partridge owned and ran Canford Mill Electroplating Ltd (CME), the company he inherited from his father and which he joined straight from school at the age of eighteen. He complemented the practical experience he gained at CME with the distance learning courses of the Institute of Metal Finishing. Trevor married Dorothy when he was twenty three. Four years and two daughters later he qualified as a Licentiate of the Institute.

'Let me guess. The Rivers (Prevention of Pollution) Act 1951?'

'That's what the young inspector kept quoting today,' said Trevor.

'I thought you stopped using cyanide complexes in your plating baths.'

'Yes, we did. Ages ago. It's nothing to do with cyanide. It's heavy metals in our waste water. According to the latest regulation, dissolved copper ought to be below 0.005 mg per litre. I've been given two weeks to deal with this. Any ideas?'

'Maybe,' said Harry. 'I've been looking at ion exchange recently and...'

'Look here Harry, I need your help,' interrupted Trevor, not really listening to his friend. 'Any chance you can get away from HG Chemicals for a couple of days?'

'I don't see why not.'

'Really? Well that would be...'

'What are friends for?' interrupted Harry. 'Let's go indoors. I think the food's ready.'

Joy was a first class cook. When Harry teased her by saying cooking was just a pastime and hobby, she rose to the bait. 'Hobby indeed! I'll have you know it's a full-time *unpaid* job satisfying your appetite, Dr Procter.' That evening the four friends enjoyed a starter of garlic mushrooms in batter followed by salmon steak amandine, asparagus tips and herb sautéed potatoes. Pear crumble followed by a choice of cheeses was accompanied by a glass of chilled champagne, made from a blend of 15% Chardonnay, 45% Pinot Noir and 40% Pinot Meunier grapes. When Dot raised her glass of the golden nectar and asked what they were celebrating, Joy said, 'I've no idea. You'd better ask Harry.'

* * * * *

On Monday morning, Harry and Jonathon, his teen-age son, left the house together as usual. Harry opened the garage door and drove off. Jonathon closed the garage door and hopped on his bicycle. When he saw his father's car turn left instead of right at the end of the road he didn't think it odd. His mind was elsewhere. When Joy was running the vacuum cleaner around Harry's study and saw he had left his briefcase on the chair behind his desk she didn't think it odd. Her mind was elsewhere.

'Trevor to reception, please,' announced the young lady over the Tannoy while Harry signed the book and clipped the visitors label to the lapel of his jacket.

'You made it then,' said Trevor hurrying down the stairs from his office; his *eagle's nest* as he called it because from there he could see almost everything that was going on in the works. 'Let's not waste any of your valuable time. Follow me and I'll show you our latest set up.' Then turning to the receptionist he said, 'Tell Joan I'm in the plant with Doctor Procter and ask her to arrange for coffee in my office at 10 o'clock.'

'Joan still looking after you and keeping your desk tidy then,' said Harry.

'Same way she looked after my dad. We couldn't do without her.'

Trevor and Harry spent the next ninety minutes in the main plating room discussing both the theory and the practice of commercial electroplating – a world away from Jonathon Procter's simple electrolysis experiments at school where he just collected two pieces of copper foil from his science teacher, connected them to a 6-volt battery and stuck them into the copper sulphate solution in his glass beaker.

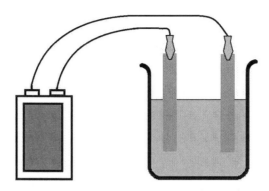

At CME all surfaces for plating had to be thoroughly degreased and cleaned. This often involved several stages and a variety of chemicals that included caustic potash (for degreasing) and special mixtures of acids (hydrochloric, nitric and sulphuric) in various proportions. After the electroplating – a process that itself could involve several stages – the surfaces would still be subjected to treatment with acid mixtures before any final washing with water. Harry was particularly interested in where the acid mixtures came from and where the final washes went.

At 10 o'clock precisely, Joan served coffee in Trevor's eagle's nest then left the two men seated in comfortable chairs facing one another. Harry came quickly to the point. 'I could solve your effluent problem and get the inspector off your back in under two weeks. It shouldn't cost much to set up and maintain. I'll give you a list of materials I'll need and start work right away.' When Trevor asked what HG Chemicals would have to say, Harry gave his friend a strange look and said, 'I don't think they'll miss me.'

For the next two weeks Harry left home in the morning and returned in the late afternoon at his usual time. He spent most of the day at CME installing and testing his ion exchange units. He and Trevor usually had morning coffee in the eagle's nest to discuss progress but they switched to afternoon tea on two occasions when Harry had meetings with his lawyer, Frederick York, of Trevanion, Oxley and York. On two other afternoons, Harry left CME early to inspect some old abandoned buildings that had served as a German prison-of-war camp during World War II.

19

'Harry, you saved my bacon. These ion exchangers you've installed remove every trace of dissolved copper. It's absolutely brilliant,' enthused Trevor. 'You should have seen the look on that young inspector's face this morning.' It was Harry's second and last Friday afternoon at CME. The two men were drinking tea in Trevor's office.

'Think nothing of it. It's the least I could do for a friend.'

'You are a friend indeed, Harry but this is also business. There's the matter of your fee as well as compensation for the time you've missed at HG Chemicals. What do I owe you.'

'Nothing at all, Trevor. Like I said, HG Chemicals won't have missed me.'

'They won't miss their senior analyst! Rubbish! Anyway, friend or no friend, you're entitled to a consultancy fee. Name your figure.'

'Trevor, I don't want a fee but if you insist on showing your appreciation, I have a suggestion.'

'Fire away.'

'Give me the exclusive contract to supply you with the acid mixtures for your plating and washing baths. I'll save you anything up to ten percent on your present costs.'

'How could you save me ten percent, Harry?' said Trevor with a frown. 'We get everything direct from ICI.'

'I know. Don't worry, Trevor, I can undercut Imperial Chemical Industries.'

'OK, Harry. I trust you. You're on. How soon can you make your first delivery?'

* * * * *

'You're home early. That's the third Friday in a row. What's going on?' asked Joy.

20

'I've got something to tell you. Come into the lounge. I'll pour you a glass of sherry. You might need it.' When they were sitting comfortably, Harry dropped his bombshell.

'You're joking. You *must be joking.*'

'It's no joke, Joy. I left HG Chemicals two weeks ago.'

'So where have you been going for the past two weeks?'

'I've been helping Trevor at Canford Mill Electroplating to…'

'So that's it. You're working for Trevor now. I hope he's paying you more than HG Chemicals. We could do with a bit extra now that…'

'No! No, Joy, I'm not working for CME. I'm on the dole. I'm unemployed.'

'You'd better pour me another sherry. The next thing you'll be telling me is that I'll have to go back to work.'

'Well I suppose that's true in a way,' said Harry. 'I'd better explain.'

Joy listened as Harry told her his plan. They would form a private company to provide Trevor with the specialized acid mixtures and chemicals CME needed. And no, they would not be messing about in her kitchen. The company would occupy the old prisoner-of-war camp. The company would buy the separate acids and chemicals at a fair trade price from Imperial Chemical Industries. Harry himself – perhaps with help from Jonathon at weekends – would mix the acids and chemicals. The company would sell the mixtures to CME at a fair mark up but for less than Trevor was paying ICI. Harry would be a director and general manager. Joy would be the company secretary and treasurer. Simple!

'Gamble, I think you mean,' said Joy. 'Procter and gamble… now where have I…'

'Droll! Very droll! You'll be turning this into a soap opera next,' said Harry.

'I don't follow you,' said Joy, genuinely puzzled.

'P&G, one of the world's largest multinational corporations, was founded in 1837 in Ohio by two immigrants; Bill Procter, a candle maker from England, and Jim Gamble, a soap maker from Ireland. In the roaring twenties, Procter & Gamble, famous for its Ivory floating soap, sponsored a series of radio programs that became known as soap operas.'

'I'm just trying to be realistic, Harry. 'You might not think it's a gamble but... well I don't think it's simple. For a start, how long does it take to form a company?'

'One day according to Freddy York,' said Harry.

'Oh, really,' said Joy. 'you've seen our lawyer. Alright. How much will it cost?'

'According to Freddy York, under £100.'

'Oh!' said Joy, taking a sip of her sherry. 'What about planning permission for the buildings; how long will that take to get?'

'Now that,' said Harry. 'is another story altogether. I rang the bell three times before anybody in the planning department came to help me. While I was waiting I couldn't help noticing the sign on the wall behind the counter.'

THERE'S NO REASON FOR IT.
IT'S JUST OUR POLICY.

'As long as it doesn't take too long,' said Harry, 'it won't be a problem because Trevor will go on getting his mixtures from ICI until we are up and running.'

'What will all this cost and what are we going to live on in the meantime?'

'Well, I was hoping you could tap Walter for a loan.'

'I wouldn't even dream of asking my father,' snapped Joy.

'I was afraid of that. So as company director, secretary and treasurer, you'd better work your charms on our bank manager.'

'I think I need another sherry,' said Joy.

Joy Procter was always the epitome of elegance even when, in her words, she was slaving over a hot cooker. When she stepped into Barclands bank, she caused heads to turn. Joy was tall, upright and slim but not thin. Her naturally black hair was neatly brushed and firmly held in a bun at the back of her head. Her makeup was skilfully applied to subtly enhance her fine features. The small jade brooch pinned at the throat of her white Victorian blouse matched the colour of her eyes; the grey of her trouser suit matched the touch of grey in her hair which, she well knew, wasn't caused by stress or worry. It was in her genes to go grey; her parents had grey hair in their early forties. Harry once explained that their melanocyte cells stopped making pigment so grey hair grew in place of the dark hairs when they fell out.

The somewhat portly manager of the local branch of the so-called *friendly listening* bank, gave Joy a reassuringly firm handshake and waited until she was comfortably seated in front of his desk before he took his own seat behind it. Joy was prepared for hostility and deafness. Instead, Thornton Metcalfe was avuncular and attentive as she presented her case for a loan and answered his questions about her company's structure, its articles of association and her business plan, copies of which she produced from her black leather portfolio case. He was particularly interested in her intention to renovate the old buildings on the site of the former prisoner-of-war camp.

'I'm sure that we can help finance your business venture, Mrs Procter, but…,' Thornton said with just the hint of a sigh, 'I fear the amount of credit Barclands can extend to your company…' He paused, placing his thumbs and finger tips together to form an arch, then continued, 'is strictly limited. You already have a first mortgage on your house.'

23

'I quite understand. It's just that…'

'Allow me to make a suggestion, Mrs Procter. Before you consider a second mortgage on your home, you might care to talk to the economic development officer at County Hall. I could give you her name. You might well qualify for a Commercial Premises Improvement and Security Grant and our local authority might well pay up to 75% of your cost of renovating that old POW camp.'

'Do you think so?' said Joy, striving to appear cool, calm and collected.

'Why not? You would be establishing a local industry and providing local employment even if it's just for you and your husband initially.'

'Thank you Mr Metcalfe. I'm very grateful for your help.'

'One other thing, dear lady,' said the manager, getting to his feet, 'you might consider selling a piece of your land for housing development.'

'Part of the old POW camp site, you mean?'

'Oh no, not that. I was thinking of where you live. You own the land freehold, I believe.'

It did take only one day to form and register H & J Chemical Distributors Ltd but it took much longer to raise the money, to obtain the planning permission and permits and to get just one of the buildings operational. Trevor and Jonathon helped at the weekends but it was Harry who did most of the renovating. According to Joy, he renovated himself with the physical effort; he lost any trace of midriff bulge and his weight fell to 170 pounds, ideal for his large frame and his height of just over 6 feet.

Joy kept a sharp eye on the cash flow but in spite of her skilful management, it became clear that the bank loan and the local authority grant would not see them through. They still had to renovate a second building and make it secure for storing the chemicals from ICI. They still had to buy a vehicle and equip it for delivering the rather dangerous acid mixtures to Canford Mill Electroplating. And they would, of course, have to pay the interest on the bank loan and the premiums on the various insurance policies; personal accident, public liability, etc. Much as she dreaded the thought, Joy would have to talk to Harry about his lawn.

'I've got something to tell you. Come into the lounge. I'll pour you a glass of sherry. You might need it.' When they were sitting comfortably, Joy dropped *her* bombshell.

'You're joking. You *must be joking*,' said Harry.

'It's no joke. This is the only way to raise the extra money we need.'

'But...'

'No buts, Harry. You'll have to sacrifice your lawn if our company is to survive.'

'I suppose you're going to sell my lawn, is that it?'

'Now that's a good point, Harry. I hadn't thought of that. Every penny helps.'

'So what's this cunning scheme of yours to do away with my lawn?' asked Harry.

'We'll gift your lawn and the land it covers to H & J Chemical Distributors Ltd. The company will sell the lawn as high quality turf - thank you for that idea, Harry – and sell the land to a builder on a 99 year lease which will bring the company in ground rent.'

'Who exactly is going to buy my lawn and our land?'

'I don't know yet,' said Joy. 'I haven't got that far.'

'Whose idea was this anyway?' said Harry. 'Trevor's?'

'No. If you must know it was something Thornton said to me.'

'Our bank manager?'

'Yes. Thornton Metcalfe.'

'So it's Thornton now, is it? Not Mr Metcalfe. Just how charming were you to him?'

'Now you're being silly. It was just his passing thought as I left his office. Anyway, I think we should sell the land for housing development – that was the term Thorn... Mr Metcalfe used.'

'I hate to admit it but you're right. I'll have to sacrifice the lawn but...'

'I said no buts, Harry.'

'*but first,*' said Harry, 'I think we should form another company.'

'Why on earth should we...'

'How about calling it H & J Builders Ltd? How does that sound to you?'

'I'm not with you, Harry. What's the idea?'

'We'll deed the land to H & J Chemical Distributors Ltd (HJCD). H & J Builders Ltd (HJB) will buy the land from HJCD on a 99 year lease and build a house on the land and sell the house leasehold at a profit.'

'So now you're going to build a house, is that it?'

'Yes my dear, that's the idea. Simple really!'

The new company was quickly formed and registered and the land quickly deeded to it. The lawn turf was quickly sold for much more than either Harry or Joy ever imagined. The plans of their existing house were quickly adapted and approved for the new house; building it was not so quick and not so simple. They do say *you get what you pay for*. Harry and Joy, as fledgling building contractors, certainly paid

26

for what they got at the hands of the tradesmen and the building supplies merchants.

'I suppose you'll be wanting wire cut facing bricks for external work and engineering bricks for below ground and damp course,' said the poker-faced brickyard foreman.

'Yes, I think so,' said Joy already bewildered by the several hundred different types of brick available.

'What are you using for your internal walls, breeze block or commons?'

'I'm not sure,' said Joy. 'Which would you recommend?'

'Commons.'

'Why not breeze blocks?' asked Joy tentatively.

'We don't make 'em,' the foreman replied sourly.

'Oh!' was all that Joy could say.

'What colour facers do you want?'

'Which colour is the most popular?'

'We make and sell about ten times more browns than any other colour.'

'Are the brown bricks cheaper to make?'

'No. All our bricks cost the same to make. Colour don't matter.'

'Oh. So why do you make and sell more brown ones? Is brown a popular colour?'

'I doubt it, but' he said, screwing up his face, 'there's no accounting for taste.'

'I don't follow you. Why do you make more brown bricks? I mean, how can you tell that builders will prefer your brown bricks to, say, your white ones?'

'The browns are half the price of t'other colours!' he said still without a smile.

Things were beginning to look up. When Trevor told one or two business associates that he had switched from ICI to H & J Chemical Distributors Ltd, they followed suit. Impressed by Harry's prices and his prompt delivery service, they recommended him to people they knew. The business was growing. Work had started on the house next door or, as Joy named it, the *Millstone*. The concrete footings were laid. The bricks, sand and cement had been delivered. The cement mixer had been hired and delivered. Everything was ready and waiting for the bricklayers.

Monday came and went. Tuesday came and went. On Wednesday morning as a result of Harry's phone calls on the previous two days, the bricklayers appeared – *the gang of three* – as Joy called them. They were still drinking the cups of tea that Joy provided when Harry left for his *Kampf in dem Stalag* (his struggle for survival in the POW camp) as he called his work in the building he had renovated.

The gang's senior member, a short, stocky, weather-beaten man in his mid-fifties, had started up the *empty* mixer to disturb the normally quiet cul-de-sac with its noisy chugging. Harry would have driven away a happier man if, *before* taking the first of their many breaks, they had put some cement, sand and water in the mixer so the mortar would be ready when they finished their tea. What a useless bunch! Luckily they were being paid for the job and not by the hour. When Harry returned home that evening, Joy handed him a large sherry as he stepped inside the door and said ominously, 'I think you should inspect the bricklayers work.'

'What in heaven's name…' said Harry. 'They've… They've…'

'It's not right, is it?' said Joy.

'How could anybody be so stupid? I mean…'

28

'I did wonder what they were doing when I took them their mid-morning coffee.'

'Did you say anything to the guy in charge?'

'Yes. I asked Doug… that's their chargehand's name… I asked him about it.'

'What did he say?'

'He said he thought it a bit odd but told me they were 'spot on' according to the plans.'

'Good morning Dr Procter. Looks like it's going to be another nice day,' said Doug.

'Only as far as the weather is concerned. You'd better take a look over here at the wall you've built.' Harry led him to the far end of the side wall, which was already about five feet high. Pointing to the base, Harry said, 'Notice anything odd about this wall, Doug?'

'Can't say I do, sir. Good bit of brick laying, is that.' said Doug.

'Take a close look… right down here at the bottom. See anything wrong?'

'D' you mean with the bricks we used, sir?'

'No. They're fine. They're engineering bricks just as they should be.'

'Ah, that's OK then. You gave me a bit of a turn, you did, sir,' said Doug.

'No, look at the bottom… the first course of bricks. Look at the last thirty inches of this side wall and all along this back wall,' said Harry in quiet voice. 'What are they on?'

'Ah, now I'm with you, sir. As I told your good lady wife this morning, I thought it a bit odd but we had to stick to your plans.'

'A *bit odd*!' Harry hissed. 'You thought it a bit odd. You had to stick to my plans! Good God, man, you've gone beyond the concrete footings and built the wall on the soft soil!'

As a scientist, Harry was used to dealing with varying units of measurement; so he took Metrication and the 1959 international definition of the yard as 0.9144 metres in his stride. It was another matter for bricklayers and carpenters; they had a different stride. Harry saw that now. The crew laying the footings for the side wall saw 12 on the plan as yards (36 feet). The *gang of three* saw 12 on the plan as metres (39.37 feet). Harry was too distraught to see the funny side of it when Doug said to him, 'Our brickwork is *spot on*, Dr Procter. It's them footings; they're *short*.'

H & J Chemicals kept Harry so busy that it was up to Joy to keep a weather eye on the tradesmen. She did her best. Each morning before he left for work Harry would give her a note of points to watch for. Each evening when he came home he would carefully check on progress. Progress was slower than they had originally hoped but, in the light of their experience, it was proving better than they might have expected. All too often life's problems are the unexpected.

'This takes the biscuit,' said Harry to himself. 'Joy! Come up here and see this.'

'What now?' said Joy coming up the stairs of the *Millstone*.

The stairs ran straight up, from the small hallway just inside the front door, to a narrow landing, at right angles to the staircase. Directly at the head of the stairs was the doorway into a small shower room. The inward-opening door was half open. Inside and to the left of the door was the toilet. Inside and against the wall facing the doorway was the hand washbasin. Inside and to the right, out of sight behind the door was the shower cubicle.

'The latest lunacy, that's what,' said Harry. 'Take a look inside the shower room.'

'What am I looking for?' asked Joy, nervously.

'You'll see. Just step inside.'

'The toilet looks fine,' said Joy. 'Oh, there's no toilet seat. Is that it?'

'No. The plumber will probably fit the seat and the cover tomorrow. Carry on.'

'The hand washbasin looks… Oh!' said Joy, as the door bumped against the edge of the washbasin. 'Is that supposed to happen?'

'No. It shouldn't. The plumber will have to move the basin a bit to the right for the door to clear it,' said Harry. 'Carry on. Take a look at the shower cubicle.'

'How am I supposed to do that?' said Joy. 'Peer around the door?'

'Of course not,' said Harry, a grin appearing on his face. 'You'll have to step inside and close the door.'

'Is this a joke?' Joy exclaimed. She had stepped into the corner of the room and tried to shut the door; it bumped against the toilet basin. 'The door's trapped between the washbasin and loo. It won't open and it won't shut!'

'Well spotted. Any thoughts?'

'Yes. We must be as crazy to have started this house as the tradesmen who are building it. How could anybody be so stupid?'

When Harry started laughing, Joy saw the funny side of it and started laughing too. They were learning the hard way that people need to communicate and cooperate. How did that shower room door come to be stuck between the hand washbasin and the toilet?

According to Harry, the plumber fixed the washbasin to the wall.

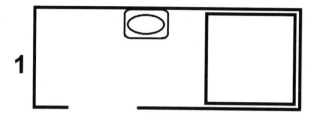

The carpenter hung the door.

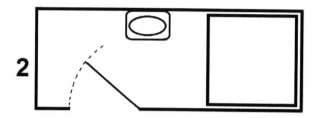

Then the plumber pushed open the door, fixed the toilet basin to the floor.

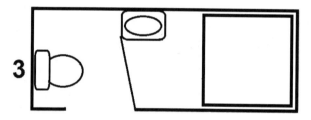

The plumber left the door open and the site foreman did not check their work.

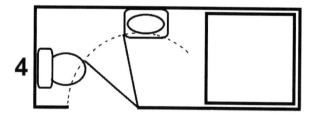

The *Millstone* was sold, the profit deposited in the bank and the ground rent was added monthly to the company's account. H & J Builders Ltd contracted tradesmen to renovate two more buildings on the old POW camp site and Harry hired Tom Matthews, a recently retired HG Chemicals laboratory technician, to help part-time in their steadily expanding Chemical Distribution business.

Using the time he once devoted to caring for his lawn, Harold Procter, B.Sc. Ph.D. wrote and published a book on the theory and practical applications of ion exchange and spent the modest royalties on the occasional bottle of sherry and on his wine making. Things were looking up. The future looked bright. But as the Buddhist saying goes *the unexpected is bound to happen; the anticipated never comes.*

* * * * *

The four deck chairs faced the river. The two men wore straw hats to shield their heads from the warm Sunday afternoon sun. Dot and Joy had gone indoors to make a cup of tea. Jonathon, Harry's only son, had gone for a cycle ride with Susan and Jennifer, Trevor's two daughters.

'Six across, eight letters,' said Harry, '*torpid company precedes mother's twisted toes.*' Trevor never understood how anybody could spend any time on crosswords, especially the cryptic crossword in the Telegraph. 'Company... that'll be co. Mother is probably ma... toes... that's an anagram,' said Harry, encouragingly. We're looking for another word for torpid.' Trevor remained silent. Just then the two ladies arrived with the teas and slices of Dutch orange cake that Joy had baked that morning. 'You'd better grab a piece of cake before the kids get back, Trevor. You know what gannets they are.'

'Have you been at my crossword again, Dr Procter?' said Joy.

'Oh, it's yours, is it?' said Trevor. 'I thought it was Harry's.'

'I was just reading Trevor an easy clue to stop him being torpid and lethargic.'

'Six across, eight letters,' said Trevor. 'A word meaning torpid according to Harry.'

'Comatose,' said Joy, after a quick glance.

'Being in a coma,' muttered Dot under her breath.

'Sounds like the kids are back,' said Harry. 'Better grab your piece of cake, Trevor.'

The four adults settled into their deck chairs to enjoy their quiet cup of tea in the garden at the back of the house. At the front of the house, Jonathon, Susan and Jennifer, put the bikes in the garage. Jonathon wanted to go straight indoors to get an ice-cream from the 'fridge but Susan said they should first tell their parents they were back. So, Jonathon followed Susan to the path at the side of the house. Jennifer, the younger sister, trailed along behind them.

Joy was listening to their faint footsteps when suddenly there was a deafening noise, the sound of metal crashing to the ground, as though a bomb had gone off, and almost simultaneously a loud scream. Then just as suddenly there was silence, broken only by the whispered gurgling of the Stour river flowing gently and unceasingly past the bottom of the garden.

Harry was first on the scene with Trevor close on his heels; their two wives were not far behind, with Dorothy slightly ahead of Joy. Both men had occasionally rendered first aid to their colleagues injured in minor accidents at work. They now had something quite different to deal with. Jonathon was lying on the path, on his back, with Susan, her head and face covered in blood, lying crumpled across his legs. Jennifer, her face ashen, her body shaking, her hands over her ears was staring down at the two seemingly motionless bodies. Suddenly she became hysterical and started to scream. Along the path and lying across Jonathon's left arm and Jennifer's left leg was a long length of cast iron guttering.

'What's happened?' said Joy, looking over Dot's shoulder.'

'An accident,' said Dot calmly. 'Trevor, take Joy and Jennifer indoors. Harry! You phone for an ambulance then get back here as quick as you can with a blanket and cushions.'

'My God!' screamed Joy, losing her usual composure. 'Jonathon! Jonathon!'

'Come on old girl,' said Trevor, 'help me get Jennifer indoors. She'll need a cup of tea.'

Before she met Trevor, Dorothy had worked as a State Registered Nurse (SRN) and done a stint in the emergency ward of the local hospital. When she checked her daughter and found no pulse or any other signs of life, Dorothy showed no outward signs of emotion. Grief was for later. During the short time that Harry was gone, she forced herself not to look at or think about her daughter Susan who was dead but to concentrate on Jonathon who was alive albeit only just.

As soon as Harry came back, Dorothy got him to help her gently lift Susan's body off Jonathon and put cushions underneath his legs to raise them ten inches off the ground (to improve blood flow to the brain) and to cover his body with the blanket (to keep him warm and improve his circulation). His breathing was rapid and shallow; his pulse was fast and weak but there was no sign of bleeding where the heavy cast iron had struck Jonathon on the head.

Harry and Dorothy waited until the ambulance had left before they went indoors to join the others. 'Jennifer,' said Dorothy Partridge, SRN, hugging her daughter, 'I want you to be brave.' Jennifer had stopped shaking and the colour had returned to her cheeks. 'I want you to be very brave.' Jennifer nodded dumbly and raised her eyes to see a look on her mother's face that she had never seen before. 'Susan and Jonathon have been taken to hospital.'

* * * * *

It rained all day. Black clouds filled the sky and it was still raining in the late afternoon when everybody except Harry and Joy had gone home. Jennifer had gone to her room as soon as they had returned from the crematorium. Joy helped Dot with the washing up in the kitchen. Harry helped Trevor tidy the dining room. When they could find nothing else to occupy their hands, the four friends sat quietly together in the lounge.

The vicar of the local church, where Susan had been a loyal member of the choir, had conducted the service with sensitivity and sincerity, exuding a genuine faith that enabled Trevor and Dorothy to take comfort from his reading of the words

> *I am the resurrection and the life,' saith the Lord; 'he that believeth in me, though he were dead, yet shall he live: and whosoever liveth and believeth in me shall never die.*

But when he began *We therefore commit her body to the ground; earth to earth, ashes to ashes, dust to dust...* and the coffin began to move slowly out of sight, Dorothy could no longer hold back her tears. She was not alone in her expression of grief.

'I fancy a cup of tea?' said Trevor, breaking the silence and starting to get up. 'Anybody else?'

'I won't say no,' said Harry.

'You sit down,' said Dot, 'I'll make it. You fancy a cup, Joy?'

'Yes, that would be nice, Dot, but we must be going soon,' Joy said, glancing at Harry. 'I'll come and give you a hand.'

'Look here, Harry,' Trevor said, staring solemnly at his friend, 'you must stop blaming yourself. It was an accident pure and simple.'

'It was not,' said Harry quietly, 'an unforeseen event without an apparent cause, Trevor. The cause was those rusty iron brackets failing to hold up that cast iron gutter. I should have foreseen that. My God, Jennifer could have been killed as well.'

'Well, we must thank God that she wasn't. What's the latest news on Jonathon?' Before Harry could reply, Dorothy and Joy came in with the tea.

At the front door, the women hugged one another, then Harry hugged Dot and Trevor hugged Joy. As he gripped Harry's right hand and put his left hand on his friend's shoulder, Trevor whispered into his ear, 'We don't blame you, old man. Please, for our sake, don't blame yourself.'

* * * * *

'Rest assured, Mrs Procter, we are doing all we can for your son. It was fortunate that there was an experienced nurse on hand at the time of the accident. She almost certainly saved his life.'

'I must apologize for my husband's outburst, doctor. He's very worried... we both are.'

'That's alright. I quite understand but he was quite correct when he said that someone who has suffered mild TBI usually becomes conscious within thirty minutes.'

'We're worried because Jonathon has been unconscious for nearly a week. My husband thinks the traumatic brain injury is severe and that Jonathon is at risk from secondary injuries caused by intracranial pressure.'

'As I tried to tell Dr Procter, there's been no sign of mydriasis or papilloedema.'

'I'm sorry, doctor, my husband may have understood you but...'

'Ah, yes, I'm sorry. Mydriasis is an excessive dilation of the pupils, one of the symptoms of severe TBI. Papilloedema is swelling of the optic disc, one of the indicators of increased intracranial pressure, a major cause of secondary brain injury. Look Mrs Procter, I know it's easier for me to say than it is for you, Jonathon's mother, to do... but please try not to worry. Your son is in good hands.'

Joy spent as much time at Jonathon's bedside as the hospital would allow. She held his hand, stroked his hair, read to him and played him his favourite music. Harry had to spend his days mixing and delivering chemicals but he spent his evenings at the hospital. Joy remained optimistic. Harry remained pessimistic, disparaging the medical science as nothing more than the art of ascribing fancy labels to sets of symptoms. He was beginning to wear Joy down.

'You're getting on my nerves,' Joy snapped. 'I wish you could go outside and mow your precious lawn,' The moment she said that she regretted it. Harry scowled, stormed out of the house and marched down the back lanes and across the fields to the Bull Inn. By the time he got there, he had calmed down. Outside in the warm sunshine, he sat on a wooden bench to sip a half pint of cider and gather his thoughts.

Jonathon was alive, albeit still unconscious, and there was nothing that he, Dr Harry Procter, could do to alter that fact. Joy was worried stiff about Jonathon and the strain was beginning to show and he wasn't helping. There was something he could and would do about that. His lawn was a distant memory; he must forget it. That piece of cast iron gutter was still lying at the side of the house; he should deal with that. 'Why on earth didn't I check and replace those rusty brackets?' Harry said under his breath. And then another thought struck him. 'Why on earth do we still use cast iron guttering? Why don't we use PVC gutters?'

* * * * *

'I didn't realize there was such a pretty walk to the Bull Inn,' said Joy. 'When did you discover it?'

'This morning,' said Harry, helping Joy over a style and taking hold of her hand again. 'Look I'm sorry I've been so thoughtless and upsetting you lately. I…'

'That's alright, Harry, I know,' she said, squeezing his hand. 'It's Jonathon. We're both worried.'

'It's my fault, I…'

'Once and for all, Harry Procter, it's not your fault. You're always telling me that what's done is done and can't be undone? It's about time you began practising what you preach.'

'You're right. Of course you're right. The brackets rusted and the cast iron guttering killed Jenny and nearly killed Jonathon. I can't undo that *but* I'll make absolutely sure it never happens again.'

After a cheese and pickle lunch at the Bull Inn, Harry walked Joy home along a different path, part of which was thought to date back to

38

Roman times. They passed a derelict water mill built in the late 18th century on the site where, Harry supposed, the Romans might have built a water mill to grind corn. The pub lunch and the walk together in the fresh air were just what they needed.

Harry held Joy's interest and kept her mind off the problems with his knowledge of local history and plant chemistry. 'The yew is evergreen and a good shrub for hedges. Its attractive scarlet berries are harmless but the seeds inside and the shrub's needle-like leaves contain a deadly poison; one of a group of compounds we call alkaloids,' said Harry. 'The caffeine in your coffee is an alkaloid.'

As they turned the corner into their cul-de-sac, Harry said, "I found out the other day that during the Second World War the German prisoners built their own camp where we've got H & J Chemicals and that the Luftwaffe strafed the camp twice thinking it was a munitions factory. After the war, a lot of the prisoners married local girls and stayed in England. There's a rumour that Merck, a German Corporation, is planning to take over HG Chemicals. Ironic! The Jerrys couldn't beat us so they're joining us.'

'I really enjoyed that little outing, Harry,' said Joy when they were back home in their sitting room drinking a cup of tea. 'You made it very interesting. We ought to do it again sometime and take Dot and Trevor with us.'

'You've just given me my second idea today,' said Harry.

'I've seen that look on your face all too often lately, Dr Procter,' Joy said. 'What now?'

'We're going to walk to a different pub each weekend. You can take notes or record what I say and we'll publish a book. We'll call it Sunday Pub Walks.'

'That was the idea I gave you? What was the other idea you've had?'

'To form another company,' said Harry. 'H & J Plastics Ltd.'

'Why? What on earth for?'

'To replace every heavy, rusty iron gutter and bracket with light, rustproof PVC ones.'

Harry was familiar with the plastic PolyVinylChloride. It was a rigid and strong polymer. It was cheap to produce and easily extruded into various shapes, like pipes and gutters, that would be five or six times lighter than their cast iron equivalent. PVC is white but it can be coloured grey; it does not discolour or deteriorate when exposed to the elements. What Harry couldn't understand was why PVC downpipes and gutters had not already replaced cast iron ones. He soon found out why they hadn't.

'So what you're saying is this,' said Trevor, 'some companies have produced PVC pipes and gutters but haven't worked out an economical way to assemble them?'

'That's about it,' said Harry. 'When cast iron replaced lead for gutters and pipes early in the nineteenth century, the joints between the sections were filled with plumbers putty and bolted together.'

'That didn't always stop the leaks though,' said Trevor. 'Putty goes brittle and cracks after a while. Have they tried using putty with plastic gutters and pipes?'

'That's probably what they tried first. They've experimented with various adhesives but with limited success. In my opinion, we've got to stop treating PVC as just a replacement for cast iron. I think I might have a solution to the problem.'

* * * * *

For almost four weeks, Jonathon remained in a coma and Joy would not even think about forming another company; her son was her priority. Meanwhile, using whatever spare time he could generate during the day, Harry converted a small building into a workshop on their company site; he still spent his evenings at the hospital and took Joy, with her pocket recorder, on a guided walk each Sunday for lunch

40

at a different pub. It was the Tuesday after their fourth pub walk that Joy called Harry from the hospital.

'Harry,' she said between sobs, 'Jonathon's... Jonathon's... He's...'

'Joy?' said Harry, trying to keep the panic out of his voice. 'What's happened?'

Since his first emotional encounter with the consultant in charge of Jonathon's case, Harry had performed an extensive search of the medical journals and was now prepared to concede that there was a little more to medical science than just applying labels to symptoms.

There was no doubt that his son had suffered a closed head injury (CHI); he had undoubtedly been struck on the head by an object that did not break the skull. There was also little doubt that his son had suffered, to use the medical jargon, a traumatically induced physiologic disruption of brain function (TBI) manifested by a period of loss of consciousness (LOC); he had undoubtedly been unconscious for a worryingly long time.

What was in doubt was the severity of the injury and the extent to which it might lead to permanent or temporary impairment of cognitive, physical, and psychosocial functions, with an associated diminished or altered state of consciousness, to quote yet more jargon. This doubt was going around in Harry's head when he found Joy, her eyes still red-rimmed, smiling and talking to the doctor in the hospital corridor.

'Ah, Dr Procter, there you are,' said the senior consultant. 'Your son Jonathon regained consciousness this afternoon and is in a responsive state. His rude awakening, if I may call it that, gave your wife a bit of a scare.'

'He frightened the life out of me Harry. Luckily a nurse was with me at the time.'

'Moaning and thrashing around, was he?' said Harry.

'And a terrible look on his face,' said Joy. 'I thought he was having a seizure.'

'As I was just explaining to Mrs Procter,' said the consultant, gripping the lapel of his white coat with his left hand and putting his right hand into its pocket, 'recovery in real life is rather different from that portrayed in TV medical soap opera, as you yourself obviously know.'

'How responsive is Jonathon?' asked Harry.

'So far he has responded to hearing, sight and touch but it's rather early...'

'to expect him to say anything that makes sense?' interrupted Harry.

'Yes, a bit too early to say but I'm hopeful that there's been little or no damage to either the frontal or the parietal regions. I expect you'd like to see him now, so if you'll excuse me, Dr Procter... Mrs Procter... I'm wanted in theatre.'

Jonathon turned his head towards the door when Joy and Harry walked into the room and over to his bed. His eyes were open but there was no expression on his face. Joy sat down on her usual chair, smiled at Jonathon and smoothed back his hair. Harry pulled up a chair and sat down beside Joy.

When Harry said *how are you, Jonathon*, he saw his son turn his head towards him. When he put his hand under his son's left hand, he felt Jonathon grip it tightly. Then Joy started saying how worried they had been; how happy they were now that he was awake; how everything was going to be alright. Harry noted that Jonathon turned his head towards Joy but still with what seemed a blank look.

'See you this evening, son,' said Harry, letting go of Jonathon's hand and standing up. 'Can I bring you anything?' His son's head moved slowly from side to side.

'I'll stay here,' said Joy. 'When you come back we can get something to eat in the hospital cafeteria, if you don't mind.'

'Fine by me,' said Harry, smiling and waving to his son. 'I'll be back as soon as I can.'

* * * * *

'Hello, son,' said Harry. 'Your mother will be here in a minute. How are you doing? OK?' Jonathon had turned his head towards Harry but there was still no expression on his face. 'I've got two liquids for you to smell. Tell me what they are, OK?' Harry took the lid off a tiny glass bottle of iso-amyl acetate and held it near his son's nose; the strong odour of pear drops caused no change in Jonathon's facial expression. Then Harry held his breath and took the lid off a tiny bottle containing just one drop of butanethiol, held it briefly under his son's nose then quickly replaced the lid. At that precise moment Joy walked into the room and saw Jonathon's face screwed up in a look of disgust.

'My God, Harry, what's that awful smell?'

'Butyl mercaptan,' said Harry smiling broadly. 'Better known as *skunk's spray.*'

'It's utterly revolting. Where's it from, if I really need to ask?'

'From H & J Chemicals. Butyl mercaptan or butanethiol, to give it its proper chemical name, is one of the industrial solvents we supply to the gas board.'

'Why on earth do they want that? It smells horrible.'

'That's the point. Our human noses can detect the smell when there's as little as 10 parts of butanethiol in 1 billion parts of air. They add it to the natural gas supply so we can detect gas leaks; methane – natural gas to you - is odourless.'

'And you brought that stuff here because…?'

'I wanted to see Jonathon's reaction.'

43

'I think I saw that. He looked...'

'Precisely! I'm delighted to say he looked disgusted,' said Harry. 'Now don't get your hopes up. It's just one simple response test and it's not in the medical books; but it suggests that his frontal lobes may not be damaged.'

'Oh! Hello!' said Harry when the nurse walked in and he saw the look on her face. 'Sorry about the smell. There hasn't been a gas leak. I was just...'

'The smell will soon go,' said Joy turning to the nurse. 'It's nothing to worry about.'

* * * * *

When he walked into his son's hospital room the following evening, Jonathon was sitting up in bed and looking more alert. Harry had two more tiny bottles of liquids; this time for Jonathon to taste. The dilute sugar solution produced no reaction but his son screwed up his face at the dilute acetic acid solution. Harry noted the response and explained to Joy that one of the results of frontal lobe damage is loss of sense of smell and/or taste. What he didn't tell her was that frontal lobe damage can affect speech.

On Friday, at Harry's suggestion, Joy took her Telegraph crossword to the hospital and read the clues to Jonathon who had still not spoken since he regained consciousness on Tuesday. Her son nodded when she asked if he would like to help her. There was no other response from him until Joy read out, '12 across... six letters... *murky after a street that smells*,' and said, 'st for street are the first two letters then...' Jonathon made a noise.

That evening Joy couldn't in all honesty tell Harry that their son had spoken intelligibly but she believed with all her heart that he was trying to say *stinky*. Neither could she say that *stinky* was a secret nickname she and Jonathon had for Harry when he brought his laboratory coat home from work for her to wash.

* * * * *

In the first few months following the tragic accident, Joy played little part in company business; she devoted herself to Jonathon's rehabilitation. Tom Matthews, now full-time, handled their chemical distribution business so that Harry could spend most of his time in solitary confinement in his workshop.

One Sunday, early in the evening, Joy walked into Dot's kitchen where her friend was making a cup of tea. Before she could start on as usual about Jonathon's progress and ask Dot her professional opinion - as a qualified nurse and not just as a friend, Dot said, 'Is everything alright with you and Harry?'

'What do you mean?' said Joy.

'You know,' said Dot. 'Is everything OK between you two?'

'Why do you ask?'

'Well, to be honest, you're not...'

'What?' snapped Joy, 'I'm not what?'

'There! You see,' said Dot. 'The Joy I once knew wouldn't have done that.'

'Done what?'

'Bitten my head off before I finished saying you're not your old self. As for Harry... well Trevor thinks...'

'What about Harry? What does Trevor think?'

'There you go again, Joy.' Dot said quietly. 'Sit down and drink your tea. I'll take the tray to the others in the sitting room and come straight back.'

The two friends sat facing one another across the small kitchen table and talked. Actually Joy talked and Dot listened. 'I'm sorry. You're right. I've not been myself since...' Dot waited while Joy wiped her eyes and blew her nose. 'I seem to be the only one worried about our Jonathon. Harry leaves the house early, often without waiting

45

to have breakfast with us; and he often comes home too late to eat supper with us. I think I told you that I have been going on bike rides with Jonathon.' Dot nodded.

'Well. One day we cycled to the building where Jonathon used to help mix the acids,' continued Joy. 'Harry wasn't in there. Tom… you know, Harry's part-time assistant… used to work at HG Chemicals… Tom told us that Harry was in his workshop. Well anyway, we went to the workshop but Harry wouldn't let us in to see what he was doing. When he came home that evening and I asked him again what he was doing, he said he was sorry but he couldn't talk about it to anyone, not even me.' Dot sipped her tea. 'We never had secrets from one another and dealing with those cowboys building the house next door… that taught us a lesson… at least I thought it did… about the importance of communicating.'

Dr Harold Procter no longer had analytical chemistry, wine making and lawn care as his hobbies which Joy had called his three obsessions. He now had just one obsession - Joy might have called it a hobby - that was his obsession with the problem of PVC gutters.

'Trevor thinks that Harry is working too hard,' said Dot.

'Trevor's probably right. It's just that… well I don't know what's got into him.'

'If Harry says he can't talk about what he's doing in that workshop, then I'm sure he'll have a very good reason. And stop worrying so much about Jonathon. He's doing very well. You'll see a big difference when he starts back to school after the holidays. By the way, we want the three of you to slum it and come to us for lunch on Christmas day.'

Jonathon helped Jennifer lay the table. Joy helped Dot bring in the food from the kitchen. Trevor carved the turkey. Harry poured the wine. Dot helped everybody to the meat, sage & onion stuffing and cranberry sauce. Everybody helped themselves to roast potatoes, roast parsnips, carrots, peas and Brussel sprouts. Trevor gave thanks for what they were about receive. They pulled their crackers, put on their paper hats and tucked into the traditional Christmas Day fare.

Joy had insisted on making the plum pudding and the brandy sauce. When Trevor pretended he'd just broken a tooth on a sixpence, everybody laughed as Joy rose to the bait. 'There are no coins in my pudding, Trevor Partridge. An awful idea dreamed up by Queen Victoria's Prince Albert when he introduced Britain to his German plum pudding.' When the men had done the washing up and they had all listened to the Queen's speech on the radio, the two families went for a walk together.

'Harry takes us for a walk on Sunday when the weather's fine. I don't suppose you'd like to join us?'

'I would,' said Trevor, 'but I can't speak for these two. When do you start?'

'We usually leave the house at about half past ten and drive to the pub...'

'I thought you said he takes you for a *walk*?' said Trevor.

'That's right. We start the walk at a pub and get back there in time for a pub lunch. The walk usually takes about an hour to an hour and a half.'

'Now *that* sounds like my kind of walk,' said Trevor.

'What about church?' said Dot.

'Ah, yes, church. We usually go to the eleven o'clock service. Oh well, we'll just have to get up earlier and attend the nine o'clock,' said Trevor, shrugging his shoulders.

Trevor and Dot spent the evening at Harry and Joy's house while Jonathon went with Jennifer to a friend's party to see in the New Year. As midnight struck, Trevor raised his glass and wished them all good health, happiness and prosperity. As they linked hands in friendship for *Auld Lang Syne*, Trevor and Dorothy sorrowed for the daughter they had lost; Joy worried about the son she still had and Harry was trying to decide if he should trust his wife and Trevor.

In the months since the accident, Harry had worked secretly in his workshop to solve the PVC gutter problem. It took less than two weeks to produce a solution *on paper*. It took much longer to get his solution off the drawing board and to produce a prototype. His idea was simple enough. Seal the joint, between two lengths of PVC gutter, with a strip of synthetic rubber and hold the joint tightly together with a clip that would also fix the gutter to the fascia board.

The difficulty was designing a clip that was strong enough to support the gutter but just flexible enough for the gutter to be pressed down into the clip.

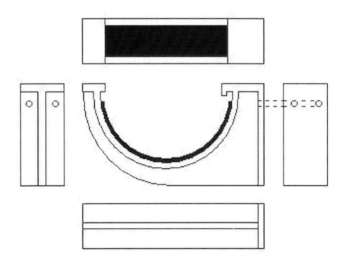

Harry lost count of the number of times he went 'back to the drawing board.' It was the morning of New Year's Eve when he locked the final plans and his precious prototype gutter bracket safely in his workshop. Joy and Trevor were still on his mind when he climbed into bed just after 1 a.m.

Harry slid out of bed just after 9 o'clock, crept downstairs to the kitchen and made a cup tea for himself and a coffee for his wife. While the tea was brewing, he tried to reassure himself that he had come to the right decision and had no other option.

'Hello Dot! Harry here. Is Trevor around?'

'Yes. Hang on a minute, I'll give him a shout,' said Dorothy putting her hand over the telephone mouthpiece.

'Hello old boy. What's up?'

'I need to speak to you, Trevor. Could you spare me an hour this afternoon?'

'Yes of course, old boy. It sounds serious. What's it all about?'

'You'll find out. I'll pop round to your place at two o'clock if that's alright.'

'See you at two, Harry.'

He tackled Joy that morning after breakfast. She listened patiently to what Harry had to say and agreed to go along with his proposals as long as Trevor didn't object.

'Harry's here,' Dot called out when she saw Harry's car pull up outside.

'Shan't be long, Dot,' said Trevor. 'We're just popping up the road.'

'I'll expect you when I see you, love,' said Dot waving to Harry through the kitchen window.

'Where are we going?' asked Trevor as he lowered his bulk into the passenger seat.

'I suppose you could say to prison,' said Harry not taking his eyes off the road.

'It's that serious then?'

'Oh yes,' said Harry.

'You're right,' said Trevor. 'This place has more security than Fort Knox.

'What do you know about patent law?' Harry asked, as he led Trevor into the workshop and securely locked the door behind them.

'Not nearly enough,' said Trevor. 'I know Dad took out the patents on some of his plating processes but he never talked about it. In fact he was secretive to the point of paranoia'

'I'm not surprised,' said Harry. 'As far as I can gather, if he had told anybody, then his inventions would not have been novel and therefore not patentable.'

'By *novel* you mean...?'

'Legal jargon for *new* to everybody except the applicant for the patent. If your dad told you about his invention *before* he applied for a patent, then strictly speaking it would not have been novel.'

'I see,' said Trevor, when he clearly didn't see.

Before bringing Trevor to the workshop, Harry had talked with Joy about forming a third company, H & J Plastics Ltd, and explained how and why he wanted to do it. He didn't tell Joy about his inventions in detail not because he couldn't trust her but because he didn't think she would be interested. Trevor was Harry's best friend and also somebody he could trust; even so, he wouldn't tell Trevor about his invention unless he had to.

'How long have we known one another, Trevor?'

'Let's see now. You and Joy were godparents to Susan Louise...'

'Eighteen years or thereabouts?' interrupted Harry.

'Yes, I'd say at least eighteen years. Why? What's on your mind?'

'Money for a start, Trevor. Quite a lot of money, as a matter of fact.'

'What's it for, old boy?'

'I'm not sure I should tell you.'

50

'I see,' said Trevor, when once again he clearly didn't. 'Just how much is *quite a lot*?'

'Ten thousand pounds to start with and anything up to two hundred thousand over the next four months.'

'That *is* quite a bit of money,' said Trevor with a whistle of surprise. 'You want a loan?'

'No. I don't want a loan. I want you to invest it in a plastics company.'

'What company?'

'H & T Plastics Ltd,' said Harry.

'Never heard of them, old boy.'

'I'm not surprised. We haven't formed the company yet,' said Harry.

'We meaning…?'

'You, me, Dot and Joy.'

'Has this got something to do with the bee in your bonnet about PVC gutters?'

'I'll answer that if you'll agree to be an equal partner in H & T Plastics Ltd.'

After the two men shook hands, Trevor listened patiently while Harry, without revealing any details of his designs and prototype, enthused about inexpensive, easy-to-install PVC guttering and downpipes not only to replace existing cast iron ones but also to install in all new housing. 'I haven't prepared a formal business plan. I'd like to leave that to you and Joy,' Harry said in reply to Trevor's question. 'Freddy York, our lawyer, will register our new company,' Harry said in reply to Trevor's second question. 'I'll be completing the rest of the designs and prototypes of the components so our company can apply for the patents,' he said when Trevor asked what he would be doing.

A month later, the four directors of the newly formed company, H & T Plastics Ltd, gathered in the workshop. Harry unlocked the safe, took out his prototype PVC bracket and showed his three partners how it would work. Trevor was impressed but Dot and Joy were less than enthusiastic.

'This is what's taken all your spare time, is it?' said Joy. 'What do you think of it Dot?'

'I don't know what to think, to be honest,' said Dot. 'Is this what our company's going to make, Harry?'

'Yes,' said Harry, 'but not just brackets. We're going to produce a complete rainwater system made from PVC.' And saying that, Harry showed them his plans for junctions to join gutters at roof corners and to seal gutters to down-pipes.

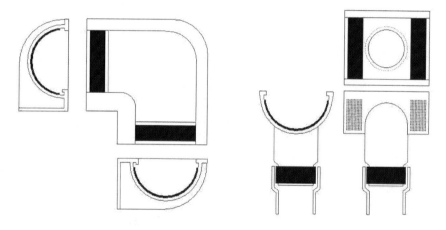

'What do you think of all this Trevor?' said Joy.

'It's a first class job. There's nothing like it on the market. It's a vast improvement on the cast iron guttering that...' He broke off when he saw the look on Dot's face.

'We've a long road ahead of us. I still have to make the prototypes for these junctions and apply for patents.'

'We've got to have the jigs, machinery and tools made,' said Trevor.

'And set up in a suitable factory,' said Harry.

'How much will all this cost and where are we going to get the money from?' said Joy.

'Quite a bit,' said Harry, 'and you'll probably have to work your charms on Thornton again.' He was right.

'How long is all this going to take?' said Dot.

'A few months if we're lucky,' said Trevor. 'but it could take two years for the patents.'

'Ah, but we don't have to wait that long,' said Harry. 'We can start production as soon as our patents are pending.'

'What do I tell Thornton when he asks what turnover we predict for the first three years?'

'One million pounds,' chorused Harry and Trevor. How wrong they were.

* * * * *

Over the next two years, whenever weather permitted, the Partridge and Procter families went on one of Harry's *Sunday Pub Walks*. Dot kept Joy company. Jennifer kept Jonathon company; he was still finding it difficult to be sociable. Trevor not only recorded what Harry said but also took photographs and asked pertinent questions.

Over those two years, as his way of escape from the pressures of business, Harry made time to publish three books of *Sunday Pub Walks* for which Trevor provided sketch maps of the walks. When Trevor refused Harry's offer of a share in the profit from the sales, Joy and Dot secretly arranged to pay the money into a trust fund for Jennifer's higher education. And in spite of his friend's objections, Harry always printed in the books his thanks to Trevor Partridge for the photographs and sketch maps.

'How old is The Crown Hotel?'

'There was probably a Crown Hotel here in Blandford as far back as the 13th century. But if you mean this building, Trevor' said Harry, 'then I'd guess it's about two hundred years old. It was probably built soon after the great fire of 1731; about the time they started making cast iron gutters.'

'Jonathon still doesn't remember...'

'No. He remembers coming back from the cycle ride but doesn't remember walking around the side of the house or being hit on the head,' said Harry.

'Changing the subject,' said Trevor, 'I still don't understand why it took nearly two years to get our patent certificates.'

'Well, for a start, the Patent Office had to do a search to decide whether our patent applications are, to use their jargon, new or obvious. That took nearly a year and wasn't cheap. They also did what they call substantive examinations of our applications to establish, for example, that someone with reasonable technical know-how could follow our descriptions and make what we are trying to patent.'

'But you never had any doubts about getting them, did you old boy?'

'No, not really. You see our inventions...'

'*Your* inventions, Harry, not ours...'

'No! *Our* inventions. Once and for all, Trevor, they belong to H & T Plastics Ltd.'

'You know what I mean, Harry. *You* invented the bracket and...'

'I know, I know. Let's not argue about it,' said Harry. 'Now, what was I saying?'

'Something about why you never had any doubts about getting the patent certificates.'

'Ah, yes. I never had any doubts because *our* inventions met the Patent Office's four crucial requirements. Our inventions were *functional* and *technical* because they related to how something works - what it does, what it is made of and how it is made. They were *novel* because we hadn't made them public in any way, anywhere in the world, before we applied for the patents.'

'So that's why you wouldn't show us your plans and prototypes until we'd formed the company,' said Trevor. 'I see... But you told Freddy York?'

'Yes,' said Harry nodding. 'and I told the patent agent Freddy recommended. The Patent Office regard those conversations as confidential.'

'I see,' said Trevor, when he obviously didn't.

'*Our* inventions also met the third and fourth requirements. They had inventive steps not obvious to someone with a good knowledge of gutters and downpipes. And, most important of all, especially where we're concerned, our inventions could be made and would have commercial and industrial uses.'

The two families ate their pub lunch at The Crown in a small private room that Joy had booked for the occasion. Trevor gave thanks for their blessings and for the food they were about to receive. Over their coffee at the end of the meal, they began counting their blessings. Joy proudly announced that Jonathon had passed his exams and was going to study chemistry at Bristol University.

Dot announced with equal pride that Jennifer, two years Jonathon's junior, had passed her exams and was going into the Sixth Form to study English, French and German. Harry quietly announced that H & T Plastics Ltd had finally received the certificates for all their patents and that the company was going to apply for US and European patents. When asked what he had to announce, Trevor stood slowly to his feet and with a solemn face dropped his bombshell.

'About two and a half years ago, I said *if we're lucky* it might take a couple of years to get those patents and a few months to get our factory up and running. Well, we weren't so lucky. It took just over two years to get the patent certificates. Never mind; we've got them now thanks to Harry. It took just over a year to start production at the factory and the capital outlay was far more than we expected. Never mind that. The bank lent us the money thanks to Joy who, if you remember, told the manager we predicted a turnover of one million pounds for the first three years. Dear old Thornton assumed, of course, that was an *annual* turnover. Never mind.

Now, according to Jim Watson, our accountant, it's almost standard practice for any new business to make a loss in the first three years. Two days ago, I had an informal meeting with Jim. As a result of that get together, I have to announce bad news I'm afraid.'

Trevor looked gloomily around the table at each face in turn. When finally his eyes met Dot's, he announced in the flattest voice he could manage, that H & T Plastics Ltd looked set to make a profit, *not* a loss. As his face broke into a grin, Dot punched his shoulder. Joy looked at Harry and they began to laugh. Jennifer and Jonathon smiled not because they really understood the implications of what Trevor had just said but simply because their parents seemed happy. When Joy asked how much profit, Trevor said, 'It's hard to say just now but I rather think Thornton Metcalfe is going to be rather upset.'

'Why?' asked Joy.

'Banks make their money from interest on loans,' said Trevor.

'Yes, I understand that" said Joy. 'So?'

'So, he won't like it when we pay off our loan after just three years instead of ten!'

'But we borrowed £250,000. Are you saying…'

'Let's not be hasty,' said Trevor. 'Jim Watson's going to prepare a provisional set of accounts next week. All I'm saying now is that our business is looking up.'

'I wonder,' said Dot, 'where we'll be ten years from now?'

* * * * *

'Colonel Jeffreys is putting the *Millstone* up for auction, Harry'

'Oh, when did Monty tell you that?'

'He didn't. I just saw them putting up a board at the front,' said Joy. 'It was so sad, his wife dying suddenly like that. It was a heart attack apparently. She loved that house you know. I can't believe they've been living there for what, ten, no, nearly eleven years.'

'It must be worth ten times what they paid us for it,' said Harry. 'I wonder who'll buy it.'

'Yes, I wonder,' said Joy.

'Lot 14, ladies and gentlemen, is a well-appointed detached residence overlooking the Stour river. The large lounge and the fully fitted kitchen look out onto the garden and well maintained lawn at the rear. Upstairs there is a shower room and four bedrooms, two of which have bathrooms en suite. There is a two-car garage and hard standing for two more cars. Who will start the bidding at twelve thousand pounds?'

The auctioneer glanced around the room and saw a dealer nod. 'Twelve thousand pounds I'm bid. Any advance on twelve thousand.' Another dealer joined in with a bid of £12,500. 'Thank you,' said the auctioneer, 'twelve thousand five hundred I'm bid.' Several more dealers nodded and the bidding reached £14,500. 'Fourteen thousand five hundred I'm bid. Any advance on fourteen thousand five hundred?'

All the dealers, except the last one to bid, shook their heads; they knew the housing market and their limit had been reached. '£14,500 once, £14,500 twice…' A slender hand was raised. 'Thank you madam. Fifteen thousand pounds I'm bid. Any advance on £15,000? Going once. Going twice. Sold to the lady at the back of the room.'

'The four friends lay on upholstered sun-loungers by the pool of the Majestic Barrière, the luxury hotel on the world famous promenade, La Croisette.

'Is this your first visit to Cannes, Trevor?'

'Oh no, Dot and I come here every year for the film festival. Come off it Harry, you know full well this is the first time I've ever been to France.'

'He wouldn't be here now if Jennifer hadn't arranged it for us,' said Dot.

'Our Jennifer might have arranged it but we're paying for it and through the nose I might add. Ouch! What was that for?' said Trevor when Dot punched his bare shoulder.

'She likes working for Thomas Cook Travel Agency then?' said Harry.

'Loves it,' said Trevor, 'and they love her apparently.'

'Jennifer was disappointed that Jonathon couldn't come,' said Dot.

'Is she still sweet on him?' said Joy.

'As far as I know, they're still just very good friends but you can never tell what the future has in store, can you?' said Dot.

'Well I think it's safe to say that Jonathon is going to have a full-time job running our chemical distribution business,' said Harry. 'Other than that, I think you're right, Dot. You can never tell what's around the corner. And why, may I ask, are you looking at me like that, Mrs Joy Procter?'

'Oh, just wondering what the future's got in store for you, Dr Harry Procter.'

With Jennifer's help, Dot and Joy had played safe; they had booked a two-week stay at the hotel. During that time, Jonathon looked after H & J Chemical Distributors Ltd and also kept an eye on the work in progress on the *Millstone*. As Trevor turned his car into the cul-de-sac where the Procters lived, Joy's eyes fixed on Harry sitting in the front passenger seat.

'What the...' exclaimed Harry, as they approached their house.

'Problem, old man?' said Trevor.

'The *Millstone*! It's... It's gone!'

'Well blow me down,' said Trevor. 'So it has.' And then with a big grin on his face, he said, 'You'll soon get rid of that fat you put on these past two weeks.'

'What are you talking about?' said Harry.

'I'm talking about the work you're going to be doing; preparing the ground, fetching and sowing the seed and restoring your lawn to its former glory.

Two summers later, the two families were standing in the middle of the new lawn around a rose bush which Harry had planted with Trevor's help. The day was the day when, fifteen years previously, the accident had occurred that changed their lives; the rose bush was planted near the spot where Susan Louise Partridge had died.

As he stood looking at the profusion of light pink roses with their delicate fragrance, Harry was engulfed by a feeling of melancholy and guilt. He was still blaming himself for Susan's untimely death. When Joy held his arm, he was comforted by the fact that cast iron gutters and downpipes were becoming a thing of the past, that the hospital, where Jonathon had been a comatose patient, would soon be getting an MRI scanner, courtesy of H & T Plastics Ltd, and that Jennifer was going to marry Jonathon and help extend the chemical distribution business to Europe.

It was Dot who interrupted his thoughts. 'I don't know about anybody else,' she said, linking arms with her husband, 'but I'm ready for a cup of tea and a slice of Joy's cake.' As the group moved off, the sun lit up the metal plate at the base of the bush.

Species: Hybrid-T rose
Breeder: George E. Adams
Registered: 1929 America
Name: *Susan Louise*

Epilogue

* * * * *

The story I have told is a fiction based upon facts that were personally reported to me and events that I experienced firsthand. For instance, I knew a chemist, who left a major chemical company, solved a pollution problem, published a book of walks to unusual places, brewed his own wine and who, inspired by the fall of a cast iron gutter that might have killed his son, made his fortune in PVC guttering and downpipes.

We withdrew from a house being built when we saw, amongst other follies, the door trapped between the washbasin and toilet of the shower room. My neighbour called me to witness that the wall of his new house had been laid beyond the concrete footings. The owner of the local yard revealed to me his brick pricing secret. The Stour still runs through Dorset, UK.

Silver coins used to be put in Christmas puddings; if you found a silver sixpence in your portion, it was supposed to bring you good luck and you were supposed to make a wish; you were not supposed to break a tooth!

All that said, the names of the characters, the companies and the bank in the story are purely fictitious.

* * * * *

THE AXE MAN COMETH

On the 12th of December 1966, Frank Mitchell absconded from Her Majesty's prison high on Dartmoor in the English county of Devon. The following story is true and as accurate as my memory permits. I have not changed the names of the people involved, so I apologise in advance to those (living or dead) mentioned herein who might feel that I have portrayed them in a worse light than I portrayed myself.

* * * * *

In August 1966 my wife and I, together with our 2-year old daughter and 4-month old son, arrived at Thirlestaine Cottages in the grounds of Cheltenham College, the public school where I was to spend nearly five years teaching chemistry. Established in 1841, this independent private school was, during my time, only for boys, most of whom were boarders and fee-paying.

Thirlestaine House had sometime belonged to Lord Northwick and had housed an important collection of old masters (I refer to paintings and not schoolteachers). The College bought Thirlestaine, but not the paintings, in 1947 for use as a house for day-boys.

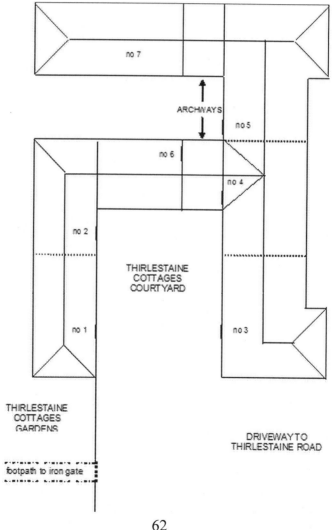

Cottage no. 1 was occupied by the secretary to the Bursar. Cottages 2, 3, 5, 6 and 7 were occupied by teaching staff. We moved into no. 4. cottage which had been vacated by Dr R C Whitfield, my predecessor in the chemistry department. The window of the lounge at the rear of the cottage looked onto a 200-year old cedar of Lebanon whose 78ft canopy sheltered a well-kept lawn.

Our front door – the only way in and out of the cottage – was within an archway. Diagonally opposite was the entrance to no. 6 cottage which was occupied by John Boulter and his wife Sally. Just beyond the archway and alongside us was the door to cottage no. 5 that housed Mike Williams and his wife Gill.

John taught French, I think. He was an athlete of distinction yet quietly unassuming about his successes, representing Britain internationally on the track in the 800 metres and the mile. Mike taught craft and design – he refused to be called the woodwork master. He was an ebullient Welshman and a man of action. Mike had a brown belt in judo. He also had an air rifle which he used on pigeons invading his allotment. The birds may well have ended their days as a roast on his dinner table along with the fruit and vegetables he grew in the Thirlestaine Cottages gardens. John, Sally, Mike and Gill were good friends as well as close neighbours.

Although I remember nothing of that first term of teaching at the College, two incidents have stuck in my mind. One occurred before term began. The other occurred in the Christmas holiday.

That doggie in the courtyard

We had just about moved into 4 Thirlestaine Cottage when our two-year old daughter, Alison, saw a large dog running across the end of the courtyard. She called out to me and pointed at it. 'That's a Dalmatian, Alison,' I said.

Later that day the four of us were invited to the home of Hugh Wright, one of the teachers and a senior tutor (called the Driver) at Cheltondale House - the boarding house of my tutees. Hugh ushered us into the lounge and offered us tea and cake. We had barely settled into our seats, when the door opened and Hugh's wife came in. With her was the large dog we had seen running across our courtyard.

The dog bounded around licking everybody in sight. Our 4-month old son, Stephen, was out of reach clinging to my wife, Maureen. Alison and I were fair game for Sam – I think that was the dog's name. Hugh's wife smiled at our daughter and said, 'Sam won't bite you. He's a nice doggie.' Alison, our two-year old, looked up and said, 'Sam's a lovely Dalmatian, isn't he?'

The Mad Axeman

Cheltenham Spa sits in a valley on the edge of the Cotswolds hills. It has been a holiday and health resort since the discovery of the mineral springs in 1716. The inhabitants are by and large respectable and affluent. The town is famous for its Regency architecture and its steeplechase horseracing. It tends to be a relatively sleepy place, especially in the warm, humid summertime. Cheltenham College (locally known as the gentlemen's college) and Cheltenham Ladies College provide an excellent boarding school education for the sons and daughters of any parents but especially of military men and statesmen often on the move. The town motto is *Salubritas et Erudito* (Health and Education). Cheltenham is a safe place to live as a rule.

Just before term ended, the newspapers, television and radio were full of the escape from Dartmoor of Frank Mitchell. In the cloistered world of the College, pupils and teachers alike were too busy to pay much attention to the news reports. Our principal concern was the end of term reports. The only escape of interest was of pupils from the demands of their teachers and vice versa. Even when term finally ended and, in the words our Head of History and Cadet Corps Commander, all was quiet on the Western Front, nobody gave thought to Frank Mitchell. Over the end of term drinks in the common room, the topic did come up in the conversation.

'The poor beggar's probably on foot,' said a geographer. 'He'll have his work cut out getting to Cheltenham. Devon and Gloucestershire counties are over 100 miles apart. Mind you, if he ran as fast as Boulter's last mile, he could be here in a day.'

'Nobody ever escapes from *the moor*,' said a young physics master in an eerie voice.

'You've been reading too many of those Agatha Christie *penny dreadfuls*,' snorted the Head of English. 'At least the Times correctly stated this fellow Mitchell absconded from the prison. He did not escape. He just walked off.'

'Why is he called The Mad Axeman?' asked another colleague.

'According to the Times,' said our Head of English, 'he was in and out of institutions from the age of seventeen. He escaped from Broadmoor, broke into an elderly couple's home and held them hostage. According to one report he made them drink tea and watch television with him while he balanced across his knees an axe he'd found in their garden shed. He never actually harmed them. Mr Frank Mitchell is said to have the mind of a child and to be given to tantrums.'

'So, he's harmless then?' said the young physicist.

'I think not,' said our Times reader. 'It seems he is a giant of a man and as strong as an ox. Certainly *not* an opponent for the holder of a mere brown belt,' he said looking at Mike Williams.

Christmas was soon upon us. We were just about ready for my parents when they arrived on Christmas Eve. They had driven from Bristol, our home town, and brought their overnight things and presents for their grandchildren. Christmas Day came and went in a blur of opening presents, overeating at lunchtime (turkey with all the trimmings followed by traditional pudding and brandy sauce) and washing up the dishes, pots and pans.

After the struggle to keep awake in front of the TV during the Queen's 3 o'clock speech to the Commonwealth, we woke up to assemble and play with various toys before overeating at teatime (sandwiches, trifle with real whipped cream followed by a slice of iced Christmas cake – no Alison, the snowman on the top is not edible). After more washing up and putting the children to bed, we collapsed in front of the TV. There were warnings about Frank Mitchell.

> *'The mad axeman is still at large. According to the police, Frank Mitchell is not armed but he is dangerous. Members of the public are advised not to*

approach him. Unconfirmed reports say that he was last seen in the Gloucester area.'

I switched off the television. We were all ready for bed. Alison and Stephen were already asleep in their room. My parents went to sleep in our bedroom over the archway. Maureen and I had our convertible bed-settee in the lounge. That night everybody slept soundly and safely in their beds.

The sound of the electric milk float at the end of the driveway and the clink of milk bottles woke me up at about 6 a.m. I slid out of the bed-settee, put on my dressing gown and made my way to the front door to catch the milkman. I pulled back the catch and peeped out.

'Merry Christmas,' I said, handing the milkman a few shillings.

'Thank you, Sir. Merry Christmas to you too.'

'Bit chilly this morning?'

'It is that,' he said, 'but at least it's dry. Not going away?'

'No. Can't afford it.'

'Have Mr and Mrs Boulter gone away?'

'Yes, I'm sure they have. Why do you ask?'

'Their front door's ajar.'

'Really? That's not like them. They wouldn't leave their place unlocked. I'll take a look.'

Sure enough it was ajar - only slightly – but nevertheless it was unlocked and open.

I retreated into our cottage to consider what I should do. *Unconfirmed reports said the mad axeman was last seen in the Gloucester area.* Thirlestaine Cottages were accessible from the main road and also through the gardens. What if Frank Mitchell was inside no. 6 cottage? What if he wasn't and instead the Boulters had let friends of Mike and Gill use it while they were away? If I woke up

66

Mike at 6 o'clock on Boxing morning (how apt a name) and his friends were in the Boulters' cottage, he would not be pleased, to put it mildly. If his friends were not using no. 6 and Mike thought Frank Mitchell was inside, he might be daft enough to don his judo kit and brown belt to try a citizen's arrest. I decided to play safe. I dialled 999.

'Which emergency service do you require? Ambulance, police or fire brigade?'

'Police, please.'

'Just one moment.'

'Police!'

It took me just a couple of minutes to give the desk sergeant my name and address, to explain why I was calling and to apologise in case I might be doing the wrong thing. Within less than five minutes of my making that call, an unmarked car came quietly to a halt at the end of the driveway and courtyard. Still in my pyjamas, dressing gown and slippers, I went outside in time to see four very large uniformed policemen getting out of the car. One was an officer, one was a sergeant and the other two were constables. I spoke to the officer in charge.

'The Boulters are away. Their door is open but doesn't look to have been forced. I've probably dragged you out on a wild goose chase.'

'You did the right thing, Sir. I just wish more people would be as alert and co-operative. Would you lead the way, please.'

I lead the way to no. 6 and showed them the open front door.

'Just stand back, Sir, if you please,' said the officer. 'Right, lads, quietly now.'

The four policemen stepped into the hallway, not noisily but not particularly quietly either. They entered two-by-two. The first two were the tallest – more than 6ft 6in plus helmet. The other two were not much shorter. I followed behind at 5ft 8in in my slippers. The door straight ahead led into the lounge. A constable pushed it open and switched on the light. The officer turned and asked me to take a look inside. I did. It was a shambles. All sorts of stuff, mostly clothing, was strewn everywhere.

'Mr and Mrs Boulter tidy people, Sir?' asked the officer in a whisper.

'Yes, they are,' I whispered back,' as the constable switched off the light.

'Right, lads! Let's have a look upstairs,' said the officer switching on the light at the top of the stairs.

Two-by-two, the tallest in the front, they walked, not crept, up the stairs. I followed in darkness – they were so tall that they blotted out the light. The five of us gathered on the landing outside the first bedroom. The door was ajar. We listened. We could hear breathing from within. In a normal voice, the officer instructed the tallest constable to take a look inside without turning on the light. He did.

'There's a baby asleep in here,' he reported to the officer. My heart sank. The Boulters didn't have any children. I was asked to take a look.

'I'm sorry. I have never seen this baby before,' I whispered when the constable shone his torch on the cot. We came out of the bedroom and moved along to the next door.

'In you go, lad,' said the officer to the constable. In he went. And in we all went. The constable shone his torch onto the couple seemingly sound asleep. Then we all stepped out onto the landing and the constable closed the bedroom door.

'That was definitely not Mr and Mrs Boulter,' I said. 'My guess is they're friends of my neighbours in no. 5 cottage. I really am sorry to have dragged you here on a fool's errand.'

'All in a day's work, Sir. You've nothing to be sorry about. You did the right thing.'

That was not what Mike Williams said to me later that morning!

* * * * *

Epilogue

The people in the cottage were friends of Mike and Gill Williams. The policemen never woke up the baby but, as I learned later, they did wake up the parents who were so terrified that they kept their eyes tight shut throughout, fearing the worst was about to happen to them.

Mike was unconvinced by my logic for calling the police and never saw any reason for telling us his friends would be staying in no. 6. Neither did he seemed concerned that his friends had not locked up properly. My parents in our bedroom over the archway and our children slept soundly through it all.

It appears that the Kray Twins (Ronnie and Reggie - Britain's notorious London East End gangsters in the 1950s and 1960s, who befriended Frank Mitchell when they were in Wandsworth prison together) masterminded his getaway from Dartmoor. They kept him hidden in London. By the 23rd of December 1966 Frank Mitchell was probably dead, shot by one the gang.

Cheltenham College is now co-educational. Thirlestaine House and the Cottages are listed buildings of historic interest. Thirlestaine Cottages have now become part of Westal House where the girls are boarded.

* * * * *

A Tick in a Box

A Canadian source defines bureaucracy as a hierarchy of authority and a system of rules, regulations and record keeping characterized by division of labour and specialization of functions. A British source defines bureaucracy as an excessively complicated administrative procedure. After reading this story, the reader will, I trust, take more care than I did when completing any official form but heed the words of Robert Frost, "If we couldn't laugh, we would all go insane."

* * * * *

Let me state unequivocally that I have never suffered from hypochondriasis. I have never been a hypochondriac. I do not have a chronic abnormal anxiety about the state of my health. Quite to the contrary, symptoms and evidence of illness or disease revealed by a medical examination do not make me anxious - they intrigue me. My wife has commented, more than once I think, that I should probably find my own death intriguing. Perhaps I shall. I am, however, in no hurry to experience that once-in-a-lifetime, not-to-be-repeated event.

In the summer of 1961, I damaged my right knee playing cricket. In the summer of 1976, I had the two wisdom teeth extracted from my lower jaw. In the late autumn of 1976, I started to see (against cloudless skies and plain white walls) numerous dark threads and spots swirling before my eyes. Then one Monday my right knee and my lower jaw started to hurt. It was time to consult my doctor. I telephoned the surgery. 'Brrrring, brrrring, brrrring.'

'Hadleigh House! Just one moment. Beep... Beep... Beep... Beep...' almost ad infinitum. 'Sorry to keep you waiting. Can I have your name please?'

'I'd like to see Dr. Fleming, please.'

'Are you a patient of Dr Fleming?'

'Yes!'

'Can I have your name please?

I gave my surname and then, as demanded, my Christian name.

'What's wrong with you, Michael?'

'That's what I expect Dr Fleming to find out.'

'Is it an emergency?'

'Is Dr Fleming in this afternoon?'

'No. He's on holiday. I can fit you in at 4:30 to see his locum, Dr Benjamin.'

'Thank you. I'll be at the Hadleigh House surgery at 4:30.'

At 4:25 I reported to the receptionist and would-be diagnostician in the white coat behind the desk of the appointments office. She ticked me off – that is my name on a list not me personally – and waved me toward a seat in the waiting area. I turned a blind eye to the ancient, well-thumbed magazines and a deaf ear to the background music accompanying the coughing and sneezing of my waiting companions. My attention was drawn to the pamphlets and posters urging me to take more exercise, eat less salt, butter, etc. and telling me what to do in the event of a heart attack or a stroke. My name was called before I could tackle the leaflet on cancer.

'What seems to be the trouble?'

I started at the top and worked my way downwards. First, the spots before my eyes.

'Those spots and threads are floaters. They're caused by dead cells or tiny spots of blood leaking into the vitreous fluid. They're quite common and nothing to worry about,' he said putting the ophthalmoscope back in its case.

'I had my wisdom teeth removed about two months ago at Poole Hospital,' I said in response to his question. 'Ever since then my jaw makes a knocking sound when I chew or yawn. It only became painful this past weekend.'

'Rest your jaw as much as possible and if you must yawn, try to keep your mouth closed. Make an appointment to see Dr Fleming if the pain gets any worse.'

'I damaged my knee playing cricket fifteen years ago. Every now and then, it swells up and the joint becomes painful. It's quite random.'

'Did they operate on your knee when you first went to the hospital after the match?'

'They aspirated two and one-half ounces of blood and fluid. Otherwise, no.'

'You've probably damaged the cartilage. Arthritis may be setting in. If the swelling and pain start to occur more often and more regularly, Dr Fleming will probably arrange for an X-ray. Anything else?'

'No, thank you, that's it for now.'

* * * * *

The following Monday morning I arrived early at school. My instructions had arrived from the Examination Board. In the office I lifted the heavy electric typewriter from the desk where I wanted to work and put it on the floor by the desk. When the bell rang for the start of morning school, I picked up the typewriter to put it back on the desk and felt a momentary twinge in my groin.

When I returned to our newly built house that afternoon, there waiting for me on the front porch were the ten laminated boards (each 8 ft x 2 ft and rather heavy) I had ordered. They would become built-in wardrobes in our new house. I carried each board separately to my workshop at the back of the garage. When I had deposited the last one, I put my hand in my trouser pocket for my handkerchief and felt a large lump in my groin. I consulted my Reader's Digest Family Medical Adviser.

Hernia – protrusion of abdominal organs through a gap in the abdominal wall. Inguinal hernia is the most common type of rupture in males. The bulge can be very large – up to 6 inches – and occurs in the groin crease.

Under the subheading *When to consult a doctor* I read that strangulation may occur and cut off the blood supply to the bowel and cause gangrene. I picked up the telephone and rang the Hadleigh House surgery.

'Dr Fleming is still on holiday. Is it an emergency?'

'Not yet but it soon could be.'

'Dr Benjamin has had a cancellation. I can fit you in at 5 o'clock.'

I reported to the receptionist behind the appointments desk and looked for that pamphlet on cancer. Just as I reached the section on birthmarks and the risk of skin cancer, my name was called.

'Michael. Room 3.'

I knocked on the door and entered.

'Lie down on the couch please.' The locum, Dr Benjamin, was sitting at a desk in the far corner with his back to the door and the couch. I did as I was told.

'Have your ankles and feet been swelling in the evenings?'

'No.'

'Any loss of breath going upstairs?'

'No.'

'What about a cough? Have you been coughing a lot recently?'

'No.'

'Have you stopped smoking?'

'Yes. No. Sorry. I never started. I'm a non-smoker. I always have been.'

'What about alcohol? Would you say you're a heavy drinker?'

'No. I might have a small glass of sherry occasionally. I don't drink beer. If we have friends in, I usually join them in a glass of wine with our meal.'

After a few more questions which seemed to me to have nothing at all to do with hernias, I blurted out, 'Excuse me! Who do you think you're talking to?' He turned to look at me lying there on the couch. I realised that I had sounded like a schoolmaster dressing down a pupil who'd had the nerve to answer me back. I rephrased the question and used a more polite tone of voice. 'Who do you think I am?'

That still didn't sound quite right, so I tried, 'What do you think my name is?' When he said Leonard Watson, I said, 'No. Mr Watson cancelled his appointment. I'm the patient you saw last Monday. You know, spots before the eyes; knocking sounds in the jaw; a swollen right knee. As a slightly strange look came over his face, I said reassuringly, 'I think I've got a hernia this week!'

* * * * *

My wife drove me to the local cottage hospital. I took with me my pyjamas, my tooth brush and paste, my electric razor and the thirty chemistry notebooks I had to mark. I signed in, changed into my pyjamas and sat on the bed to mark the books. Matron arrived in full sail.

With a firm hand and an air of unquestioned and unquestionable authority, she placed a form on the book I was marking and ordered me to fill it in immediately. I did so as quickly as possible because I wanted to finish my marking before evening visiting hour. My wife promised to return the books to my school the next day and allow me to relax for the next six or seven weeks.

The form was small (A5 = 148 mm wide and 210 mm long). The spaces on the front for me to write my name, address, etc., were very small. On the back of the form there was a question which simply required a tick in the appropriate box.

Was your injury the result of an industrial accident?   Yes ☐   No ☐

'Well,' I thought to myself, 'I was at work and I ruptured myself by picking up that heavy electric typewriter that belonged to the school.' I put a tick in the 'Yes box' and returned to my marking. That evening my wife took the chemistry notebooks away and I lay back on my bed to await the anaesthetist. When he knew I was a chemist, he was pleased to give me the details of the pre-op injection (to make me drowsy) and the anaesthetic gas (to keep me asleep). That night I slept as soundly as I always do but this time on an empty stomach.

76

The next morning I was wheeled into the antechamber. I remember counting down from 100 to 96. And then, there I was back in my bed in the ward slowly waking up to the voice of the staff nurse calling my name.

That afternoon my wife came to see me. I was so hungry that I persuaded the nurse to let me have some jelly and ice cream. It was a mistake. The picture in my wife's mind - of me losing that dessert - was not one she would want to paint for our two young children.

Early that evening, after visiting hour, I fell into my usual deep, restful sleep. At about ten o'clock, a disembodied voice was calling me. At first it was part of my dream. It was unreal. The voice kept calling my name. Gradually the dream faded and my mind slowly and reluctantly entered into the real world. The night nurse was standing by my bed.

'What is it?' I mumbled. 'What's wrong? What do you want?'

'Sit up,' she said, handing me a glass of water and a small plastic cup holding a huge white tablet.

'What's this?' I asked.

'Come along now. No fuss. There's a good chap,' she said sternly. 'Take your tablet.'

Then it began to dawn on me. 'Is this nitrazepam?' I asked.

'It's Mogadon,' she replied.

'I was sound asleep! You woke me up to give me enough nitrazepam to knock out a cart horse!'

'Matron's orders and hospital rules. You had an operation today so we need to make sure you get a good night's sleep.'

'But I was getting a good night's sleep until you woke me up!' I mumbled as she moved to the sleeping victim in the next bed. The Mogadon (trade name for nitrazepam) soon did its job. It put me to sleep and ensured that the next morning I woke with a blinding headache to go with the pain in my groin.

The breakfast trolley appeared. The food and the aspirins were just what I needed. What I didn't need after breakfast was Matron in full sail. 'Everybody up and into the lounge.' When I said that I was very sore from my operation yesterday and would prefer to stay in bed, she snorted, 'No excuses and no exceptions. This ward has to be cleaned.'

It was only when I started to plan how I might get out of bed with the minimum of pain that I noticed how far off the ground I was. A step ladder hooked to the bed frame would not have been out of place. Those old-fashioned static beds kept the patient so high off the ground that I wouldn't have been surprised if the nurses had to satisfy a minimum height requirement similar to that of police officers.

The meals in the hospital were delicious, nutritious and nicely balanced. When I left there nine days after my operation, I was a good deal slimmer than when I had entered. I had been treated well but there was no place like home especially to enjoy seven weeks convalescence on full pay and on doctor's orders not to lift even a dish cloth.

* * * * *

About a year later I was back in the hospital for repair and maintenance. Curiously enough, I had very little post-operative pain this second time. Moreover, the surgeon had followed the line of his original incision, so I actually have only one scar to show for two operations. I was incarcerated for nine days again and subject to the same Matron but in a different ward.

The food was still nourishing and the beds still frighteningly high off the ground. The nurse administered as before a Mogadon on the night of the operation. Just before I fell asleep, I was aware of noises emanating from an elderly patient. He seemed to be groaning and moaning in dire pain. His bed was nearest to the night nurse's observation window. My bed was the furthest away. Incidentally, I later learned that the nearer you were to the nurse's window the more serious was your condition.

On the first night, the patients in nearby beds were kept awake for hours by what they thought was his snoring. With each successive night, his groaning, moaning and, perhaps, snoring became more structured. A pattern developed. The noises began to rise and fall and sound like notes. It was on the eighth night that his racket began to sound like words being sung to a tune. On my last night the form, pattern and shape of his sounds became clear. The old fellow was not groaning, moaning or snoring. He was singing, albeit not very tunefully and perhaps in his sleep, the old hymn Oh God our help in ages past!

* * * * *

Several months after the second operation I received a letter from an official in the Department of Health and Social Security (DHSS) requesting my presence at the Council Building in the Civic Centre in Poole. I presented myself as requested and was led into a tiny room. The official was a pleasant lady, probably in her mid-forties (but I'm a poor judge of women's ages) and, as I recall, unmarried. We sat opposite each other on either side of a small table. The interview began.

'Full name?' An easy question to start.

'Date of birth? Present address? Occupation?' More straightforward questions.

'May I ask what this is all about?' I said politely.

'Your claim for compensation.'

'I'm sorry,' I said, 'I don't understand. What claim?'

'For the injury you sustained as the result of an industrial accident. May we continue?'

Then I remembered.

Was your injury the result of an industrial accident?	Yes ☑	No ☐

I ticked the Yes box on the back of that form Matron gave me.

'Where did you get the injury?'

'In the school office when I picked up a heavy typewriter.'

'No, sorry. Where did you sustain the injury?'

'As I just said, in the office at the school where I teach.'

'No,' she said, beginning to blush, 'where on your body did you sustain the injury?'

'It was an inguinal hernia. Would you like to see?' I asked, starting to get up and reach for the buckle of the belt holding up my trousers.

'Thank you. No, thank you. That will not be necessary,' she said, her face crimson as she hurried from the room.

* * * * *

A year must have passed before I received further instructions from the DHSS to attend another interview. This time I was summoned to a set of offices in Bournemouth. I taught my first class before driving the 9 miles into the seaside town. When I climbed the stairs and entered the large reception room, I was summoned to the desk of a rather frosty-faced young lady.

I handed her the official letter I had received. With barely a glance at me standing there, she began her questions. Name? Date of Birth? Address? Occupation? The self same questions I had already answered in the Poole Office. Fortunately, this young lady seemed to know the nature of my industrial injury and did not inquire as to its location on my body.

'Follow me.'

I followed her across the room.

'Take off your shoes and stand against the wall.'

'Why?'

'I have to measure your height.'

I did as I was told but received no reply when I asked why she needed my height.

'Stand on the scales.'

'Why?'

'I have to measure your weight.'

I didn't expect an explanation so I didn't bother to ask why.

'Put on your shoes and take a seat.'

It was nice to be able to sit down at last. Some time later, Ms Frosty, ushered me into another equally large room where I was confronted by three elderly, grey-haired men sitting behind a large cloth-covered table. The old fellow in the middle directed me to sit in the chair facing them. This chairman carefully shuffled some papers before beginning the interview.

Name? Date of Birth? Address? Occupation? All the questions I had already answered in the outer office. During this questioning I could have sworn one of his cohorts was dozing off. The other one never spoke either. And he didn't move. Had I been able to get a closer look – my chair was a considerable distance from their table – I might have seen cobwebs joining his head to the table top.

I wondered if they were medical doctors and if they would ask to see my injury. They were but they didn't ask. It was just as well. The wound had had a year to heal. The scar was barely visible. I assumed they constituted a panel to investigate the validity of compensation claims for industrial injuries. If so, I am bound to wonder if they ever exposed any frauds.

I returned to the outer office and Miss Frosty.

'Where have you come from?'

'The inner sanctum,' I said flippantly. She was not amused.

'Where did you come from to get here this morning?'

When I told her the name of the school where I was teaching, she thawed.

'Is that the grammar school?'

When I said yes, she beamed at me. 'Do you know Martin Sandel?'

'Yes, I know Boot,' I said, referring to his nickname. 'Do you know him?'

She blushed. 'Did you come by car?

'Yes.'

'How far is the round trip from the grammar school to here and back again?'

'About 18 miles.'

She multiplied 18 by 35 and gave me £6.30 travelling expenses.

Several weeks later I received an official letter from the DHSS stating that my claim had been approved. Enclosed with the letter was a £15.75 cheque and a receipt for me to sign and return to confirm that I was satisfied and accepted the payment in full and final settlement of my claim. My scar reminds me to think twice before putting a tick in Yes boxes on official forms.

* * * * *

Epilogue

My two nine-day spells in that cottage hospital were luxuries not available to hernia patients these days. Now you are usually treated as an outpatient to be cut open, stitched up before lunch and sent home in the afternoon. Of course, that may not be the case if you can afford to be treated as a private patient! As for convalescence, four weeks seems to be regarded as more than generous.

The bureaucratic machine in which I became entangled and the bureaucratic cogs whom I encountered made me ill-tempered and, on reflection, unforgivably flippant. Given the chance, I should like to apologise to those officials who were probably doing what they could to follow the rules and make the best of a poor job.

Even though those entanglements were almost 40 years in my distant past, I still have difficulty taking comfort from the words of the Pulitzer Prize-winning American poet, Robert Frost, "If we couldn't laugh, we would all go insane."

THE JOURNEY OF A CANVAS BAG

Air is a liquid at minus 200 degrees centigrade. In their research at Bristol University, chemistry students often needed liquid air for their experiments. They kept the liquid in open-necked vacuum flasks to slow its evaporation. This story is based upon an incident that actually took place on a train travelling from Bristol to Southampton around 1958-59. Apart from Bob, all the characters are figments of my imagination. Two of the characters appear in the first story in volume 2 of my collected short stories.

* * * * *

On any other Friday Bob would have slung his canvas bag of weekend clothes over his shoulder, run down University Road, jumped onto the bus to Temple Meads Station and taken a seat upstairs. Not this Friday. Today Bob held his bag upright against his chest. He walked slowly down the hill. He boarded the double-decker bus as smoothly as possible and did not go upstairs. He took the seat downstairs nearest the door. Getting off the bus and walking to the station platform, he was just as careful not to bump into people or to jolt his bag. He only started to relax after he gently placed his bag upright on the small table under the window of the 2nd class non-smoking compartment.

Before taking his window seat facing the engine, Bob cautiously unzipped his almost empty bag to check the contents and to remove a hardback edition of Organic Chemistry by Fieser & Fieser. As he carefully closed the zip he smiled nervously at the grey-haired lady in the window seat opposite. She returned his smile then quickly looked back at her knitting pattern. Bob sat down and hid behind his bag and textbook.

Daphne Millbank SRN smiled politely but did not speak. 'Quite handsome,' she thought, 'but a rather nervous young man,' His textbook and the badge on his dark blazer showed he was a chemistry student at Bristol University. She remembered the engineering undergraduate she danced with at her Nursing College Christmas Hop some thirty years ago. He had the same good looks - dark hair and soulful brown eyes.

Under other circumstances Daphne might have spoken to Bob if he had not disappeared behind his textbook and that large canvas bag. Anyway, she had a problem to solve and travellers in England keep themselves to themselves. Before Daphne could focus her thoughts, a smartly-dressed, slightly balding, puffy-faced man with a touch of grey at his temples made his entrance. She smiled. He frowned. She refocused on her problem.

* * * * *

Aubrey Pembleton-Smythe squinted into the sunshine as he left the gloomy offices of Hudson Smith, Briggs & Co. in Unity Street. He used this prestigious firm of chartered accounts to audit his accounts principally to impress the more wealthy of his clients whose investments he managed. The meeting had gone well. The senior accountants seemed satisfied with his explanations of certain entries in his books - the set of books he kept especially for them. Their final audited statements would, hopefully, satisfy the Inland Revenue. From the waistcoat pocket of his dark grey, pin-striped suit Aubrey took a silver watch and opened its case. Half-past one already! Too late for a bus! So he walked briskly the short distance to Park Street and hailed a taxi.

At Temple Meads Station Sid, a seasoned porter, materialised from the archway shadows and opened the taxi door. Aubrey handed him his dark imitation leather brief case, paid the taxi driver the exact amount on the meter and waved the porter towards the platform for the 2:15 train to Southampton. 'Smart three-piece, shiny leather shoes, lightweight briefcase, no luggage - First Class and nice tip down to expenses,' thought Sid. But when Aubrey specified a second-class compartment and non-smoking, Sid gave up any thoughts of a gratuity. Sure enough, at the door of the compartment, Sid was relieved of the briefcase and, like the taxi driver, dismissed without a word of thanks.

Aubrey frowned. Both seats by the window were occupied. And there was a large bag filling the little table where he would have put his briefcase, lid open, to hide from the gaze of that old biddy. 'Little privacy on this journey,' he thought. In his case was, as usual, his expenses notebook. But today he also had the first of two volumes by Count Egon Caesar Corti - The Rise of the House of Rothschild: 1770-1830. The second volume - The Reign of the House of Rothschild: 1830-1871 was locked away on his bookshelf in Southampton. These rare first editions, published in 1928, were English translations by Brian and Beatrix Lunn from German. First, his day's expenses. He preferred to record them while the train was stationary.

Aubrey sat by the door in the corner seat facing the engine. Resting his notebook on his briefcase he calligraphically recorded the published cost of a breakfast on the train, a lunch at the station, taxi fares including tips and a First Class Southampton-Bristol return rail fare. That done, he put away the expenses notebook, took out volume 1 and placed the case on the seat opposite. He had just opened his book when a slender young woman entered the compartment. He studied her over the top of his half-moon reading glasses.

* * * * *

Her straight fair hair was held back by two brown tortoiseshell clips. Her eyes were green behind a pair of rimless spectacles. Her skin seemed pale against her tailored dark olive jacket and skirt. The dark brown of her sensible flat-heeled shoes almost matched the colour of her real leather briefcase – a 21st birthday gift four years ago from her parents. She glanced at his imitation leather briefcase then sat down next to the grey-haired lady.

That morning, Miss Rachel Wallace, B.Econ., had visited Hudson Smith, Briggs & Co. on behalf of the Inland Revenue Investigation Office. Mr. de Veen, one of the senior accountants, had been most helpful in giving her access to their records and a quiet room where she would not be disturbed. It had been a most fruitful visit.

Stepping into the compartment she noticed the embossed letters A.P-S before she saw the owner of the case. She recognised Aubrey immediately from the flattering photograph in the file, marked *Confidential/Investigate*, given to her three days ago by her Head of Department. 'Looks younger in his photograph,' she mused, noticing his sallow podgy face, receding hairline and advancing waistline.

She put her briefcase on the luggage rack above her head and sat a short distance from the grey-haired lady. They exchanged smiles. 'A nurse,' she thought when she saw the upside-down watch pinned on Daphne's crisp white blouse. Rachel folded The Daily Telegraph, took out a pencil and started the cryptic crossword on the back page.

1. across – reduce payment this way and go directly to gaol – 3,7.

She smiled to herself as she filled in the letters. Rachel was still smiling to herself when she glanced up at the tall man standing in the doorway. His face seemed familiar.

* * * * *

Johannes van Dijk looked every inch a Dutchman – six feet tall with blond hair, blue eyes, high round cheekbones, a wide mouth and even white teeth smiling back at Rachel. Under his brown suede leather jacket and silk shirt were a pair of broad shoulders and muscular arms. 'Good afternoon everyone,' he said in a clear voice. When Aubrey glanced up from his book, Johannes, still smiling, said to him, 'Allow me to put your briefcase up here, please,' And in an instant Aubrey found his case on the luggage rack above his head.

One moment later Johannes had effortlessly hoisted his own heavy portmanteau (real cowhide leather and solid brass buckles) onto the rack on his own side and seated himself by the door opposite Aubrey. The ensuing silence was broken by the sound of doors slamming and the guard's whistle. With a slight jolt the 14:15 Southampton train started to move.

'3 minutes late,' muttered Aubrey looking at his pocket watch.

'The train is late or perhaps your watch is not good,' said Johannes.

'This watch keeps excellent time,' snapped Aubrey, 'This train is always late.'

'Not so in Holland. Our trains are never late.'

Daphne looked down at her watch and said to Rachel, ''Yes, the train does seem to be 3 minutes late.'

'What's three minutes,' said Rachel. 'The engine driver could easily catch up the time lost.'

'Most unlikely,' snorted Aubrey, as he closed his pocket watch.

'That seems a very fine watch,' said Johannes. 'May I look at it closely?'

Before Aubrey could reply, Johannes took hold of the watch. He knew it. It was a rare Paul Buhre antique - a Swiss full hunter style pocket watch. The case, almost certainly made of solid 925 Sterling silver, was about 51 mm thick and had solid rose gold hinges. Johannes opened the front cover. The ceramic dial behind the gold hands was in perfect condition. There was an inscription on the inside of the case:

Pieter van Dijk
Middleburg – 1881 tot 1911
in dankbaarheid voor uwe trouwe dienst

He frowned and said softly, 'Ongelofelijk! Hoe kan dat?'

'I beg your pardon,' said Aubrey.

'Sorry. Unbelievable! How could it be... No, I mean... is it possible you would sell to me this watch? I should very much like to have it.'

Aubrey Pembleton-Smythe was taken aback. He closed his eyes in thought. He had redeemed the watch a few years ago from a pawnbroker. A passenger getting off at Warminster had dropped the pawn ticket getting up to leave the train - this one in fact - the 14:15 Bristol to Southampton. It cost Aubrey just £17.50. He now regarded the timepiece as an heirloom of the Pembleton-Smythe family. Pure fantasy, of course, just like his name. He had been born Arthur Smith but changed his name by deed-poll to Aubrey Pembleton-Smythe to boost his self-esteem before going to college to study accounting and economics.

'This watch has been in my family a long time,' lied Aubrey smoothly. 'It's not something an Englishman would think to part with easily.'

'Yes, I understand that. No offence, you know. But, I should very much like to have that watch. I can pay cash. What cost would you consider fair?'

Aubrey took back the watch and closed his eyes again. Bob appeared engrossed in his Organic textbook but Daphne and Rachel were fascinated. Johannes smiled broadly and winked at them. 'Well? What say you? Will you sell me the watch? I can give you cash now.' Johannes took out and opened his genuine leather wallet. Aubrey lifted his lids and his eyes bulged at the sight of so many £10 notes. He

90

opened his mouth to speak just as the compartment door slid open. 'Tickets please,' demanded the guard.

* * * * *

Daphne and Rachel quickly located their tickets which the guard carefully checked and punched. The guard nodded at Bob's student pass. A somewhat flustered Aubrey eventually produced his ticket from behind the maroon silk handkerchief in his top pocket. He handed it over. The guard checked the ticket very carefully, punched it, checked again even more carefully then handed it back. Aubrey frowned but said nothing. Johannes took a ticket out of his bulging wallet. 'Please,' he said with a smile to the guard.

'When and where did you buy this ticket, sir?' asked the guard.

'I did not myself buy it. It was my secretary. She is responsible. Is it not good?'

'Oh, no, sir. The ticket is valid for this journey but...'

'But what?' frowned Johannes.

'It's for First Class, sir. You are in the wrong compartment.'

'Ah. This is because I followed this gentleman who I should think to go First Class.'

'The First Class compartment is two carriages that way,' said the guard pointing down the corridor. 'It's next to the dining car.'

'Thank you,' said Johannes, 'but I stay here. It is gezellig – cosy.'

'It's up to you,' said the guard. 'Next stop Bath Spa.'

When the door had closed, the Dutchman turned and noticed Aubrey's book – green cloth with black labels and decorated endpapers.

'What is the book you read?'

Aubrey showed him the cover.

'A rare first edition,' thought Johannes. 'Does he realise?' Then he said, 'Do you also have volume 2?'

'At home under lock and key,' replied Aubrey.

'Ah, so. Now, you will sell me that watch, yes? I have money – cash.'

These conversations had distracted Daphne. As she put her ticket back into her purse she remembered her problem. She had been invited to stay with Frank and Susan, her niece, in Bitterne for a few days. Susan was expecting her first baby any time now. On this two-hour journey to Southampton Daphne wanted to knit a pair of booties for the baby. The problem was what colour? What if she knitted a blue pair and Susan had a girl? The lady sitting next to her seemed very sensible. They had already smiled and spoken to one another. Perhaps she would help?

'Easy,' said Rachel. 'Knit one pair of each colour.'

'I'm quite a good knitter,' said Daphne, 'but I'm not sure I could knit two pairs before we reach Southampton.'

'Well then,' said Rachel, 'knit one of each colour now, When you know what it is - boy or girl - you can knit the other bootie before you visit your niece in the maternity ward. Perhaps she'll have twins – boy and girl. You'd have a pair of booties for each baby in no time.'

Bob listened to this conversation behind his textbook and wondered if he had solved his problem. Only time would tell. At least the guard had not asked him to put his hold-all on the luggage rack. And so far he'd managed to keep it upright and not to jolt it. It was tempting to check inside the bag again but he decided to leave well alone.

'What colour booties? Some problem,' thought Rachel. 'I wish my investigation could be solved so easily. I've seen the set of books he gave to Hudson Smith, Briggs & Co. He'll have his other set pretty well hidden. The guard seemed wary of him. Took his time checking the ticket. Still, he didn't query it. So he's definitely travelling on a valid Second Class ticket and not First Class as this other passenger thought. When I get to his office on Monday I'll ask for his expenses notebooks and all his actual receipts for the last six years. That should shake things up a bit.' With a smile she turned her attention to a tall blond fellow sitting nearby. His face did seem familiar.

When the train stopped, Johannes asked Rachel, 'What is this place?'

'Bath,' said Rachel. 'Bath Spa, actually. It's a cathedral city. The Roman Baths were built around the only naturally occurring hot springs in Britain.'

'This I did not know,' said Johannes.

'Apparently,' continued Rachel, looking at Aubrey out of the corner of her eye, 'in Roman times, if thieves stole a bather's money or clothes, the bather would write on a piece of metal – called a curse tablet - to the goddess Sulis Minerva asking her to punish the thieves until they gave the money and clothes back.'

'You like Bath Spa?'

'Yes, very much,' said Rachel.

'Perhaps I shall make a visit there.'

'Oh you should,' said Rachel enthusiastically. 'There is so much to see and learn.'

'When I shall go there you must come with me as my personal guide. Is that possible?'

Rachel blushed and said as the train moved off, 'Westbury is our next stop.'

'Should I make also a visit there?' asked Johannes.

'It's not at all like Bath. There's nothing to see except the Westbury White Horse. Scholars say it was cut into the chalk hillside sometime in the late eighteenth century. Locals claim the horse appeared more than eleven hundred years ago to commemorate King Alfred the Great's victory over the Danes.'

* * * * *

It suddenly occurred to Aubrey that he did not know the true value of the watch. How could he estimate it. Ah! Assume the pawnbroker knew his business. Assume the £17.50 redemption cost included a £2.50 interest charge on a loan of £15. Assume the pawnbroker lends only 10% of the value of the article pawned. That would make the watch worth about £150. Perhaps more if the £150 represents the pawnbroker's resale value – say, 60% of the actual value. He looked at the Dutchman and said, 'I cannot put a value on this watch. Perhaps you would tell me how much you would be willing to pay.'

'That's not so easy,' said Johannes. 'One should be an expert and I do not want to insult you. Furthermore I do not carry with me so much cash. Suppose I suggest £100. How do you see that? Too little?' Aubrey nodded.

'What about £150?'

'I'm no expert,' said Aubrey, 'but I imagine it's worth a little more.'

'Well,' said Johannes with a smile, 'I should like to have that watch. What would you say to £200? That is all the English money in my wallet. If that is not enough then I must give you guilders or a cheque on the Rotterdamse Bank.'

'Why do you want this particular watch?' Aubrey asked.

'I must tell you. It is possible that it is of my great-grandfather. Look here at the inscription. My name is Johannes van Dijk. My great-grandfather was Pieter van Dijk. He worked all his life in Zuid-Beveland. Middleburg is in that part of Nederland. If the watch is truly of my great-grandfather, then it should be of great sentimental value.'

* * * * *

The previous year when Johannes came to England he had lunched with Wouter de Veen, a friend from his university days, who had a senior position with Hudson Smith, Briggs & Co. Wouter had described Aubrey Pembleton-Smythe and how vain he was about his pocket watch. When he was showing it off, Wouter had noticed the inscription. When Johannes heard about the watch, he asked Wouter to let him know the date and time of Aubrey's next visit to Bristol. So on this morning, Friday the 13th March 1959, in Wouter's private office, Johannes listened to what his friend could tell him about de Mijnheer Aubrey Pembleton-Smythe.

Afterwards the two friends reminisced and swapped stories over a lunch of bread, Gouda cheese and coffee until Wouter's phone rang at 1:20 p.m. 'He's leaving now,' said Wouter. They shook hands and Wouter led the way out. At the office doorway, Wouter waved to the young Officer from the Inland Revenue Investigation Department as she hurried towards the front of the building. As he stepped into the sunshine Johannes saw the young lady climbing into a taxi at the top of the street. He would have liked to share it with her but it was already moving off and maybe it was not going to the railway station.

'Do you think that's the watch of your great-grandfather?' Wouter had asked as they shook hands again at the front door. 'Ya, I believe it,' said Johannes.

* * * * *

'Your great-grandfather's watch. I see. In that case,' said Aubrey, with a wave of his hand, 'it would be churlish of me to hold on to it. It's yours for £200. I expect it's worth more but guilders would be no use to me. And I decline most cheques even if they are in Pounds Sterling and drawn on the Bank of England in Threadneedle Street.'

Johannes smiled broadly, shook Aubrey firmly by the hand and counted all twenty £10 notes from his wallet. 'Please,' he said, handing over the cash. But before Aubrey could detach the watch from its solid silver chain Johannes said, 'It's possible the chain was also of my great-grandfather. I hope you include it in the price, yes? Thank you.'

95

With a slight grimace, Aubrey handed over the rare antique watch and solid sterling silver chain. Johannes again shook hands and settled back into his seat to study his purchase.

Pieter van Dijk, his great-grandfather, had served the Gemeente (municipality) in South Beveland as Waterbouwkundig Ingenieur (hydraulic engineer) for 35 years from 1878 to 1913. The watch had been given 'in dankbaarheid voor uwe trouwe dienst' (in gratitude for your loyal service). Much of Nederland (meaning below land or beneath sea level) would be underwater if it were not protected by the dikes designed, built and maintained by the hydraulic engineers.

Johannes realised that his great-grandfather had been held in high esteem. The pocket watch had been extremely expensive even in 1913. Now it was worth a very great deal. The pawnbroker had not known his business. Johannes estimated its value at more than £6000. What a bargain at £200! And he really did buy it for sentimental reasons. He would give it to his son when he would be Dr. Ing. Piet van Dijk.

Unaware that he could have done much, much better than a £200 return over two years on his original £17.50 investment, Aubrey settled back into his seat. He was sure he'd sold his watch too soon but was also sure Baron Rothschild would have approved. When asked how he had become so wealthy, the Baron is said to have replied: "I always sold too soon." Was this Baron Nathan Rothschild, trading in London during the Napoleonic era? Perhaps. Aubrey turned to the page where he placed the free bookmarker from George's – the University Bookshop at the top of Park Street – and continued reading.

The start of the Rothschild banking empire may be traced back to an Ashkenazi Jew called Moses Amschel Bauer who was a shrewd money lender and owner of a counting house in Frankfurt, Germany. His son, Mayer Amschel Bauer, eventually took over his father's business. He changed his name to Mayer Amschel Rothschild and in 1770 he married seventeen year-old Gutele Schnaper. They had five daughters and five sons: Amschel, Salomon, Nathan, Kalmann and Jacob. It is reputed that Mayer became extremely wealthy through a mixture of embezzlement, cunning and ruthless business transactions with various heads of state. All five sons became wealthy bankers and were made barons by the Austrian Emperor Francis I.

Aubrey was pleased to note that Mayer changed his name but envious of his ten children. At 51 and still unmarried, he had no hope of siring a Pembleton-Smythe banking dynasty. He'd been too young for the First World War and unfit for duty in the Second World War. Deep down Aubrey knew that even if he'd been wearing an officer's uniform young ladies still would not have given him a second glance. That's why he was puzzled by the looks the young lady opposite had given him.

* * * * *

4. down – Wet fields of grass – 5.

Rachel checked the answer to 1. across - *tax evasion*. So the second letter of 4. down is 'e'. The last letter is probably 's'. Ah, yes! It's 'meads' – derived from meadows. Now she remembered. Temple Meads station! That's where the Knights Templar built their Holy Cross Church in the 12th century. And there were water meadows in the Temple Parish. She looked up to see Aubrey staring at her over his half-moon glasses. Quickly looking away to her right she saw Johannes had closed his eyes. Turning to her left she saw Daphne had almost finished a pink bootie. On the other side of the table by the window the student was smiling to himself.

In 1932, after she received her master's degree, Mary Peters Atchison married her professor, Louis Frederick Fieser, who was twenty years her senior. She died in 1997 outliving her husband by twenty years. Together as co-authors, they published eight textbooks and the first seven volumes of Reagents for Organic Synthesis – known to chemists simply as "Fieser and Fieser." What fascinated Bob most was their descriptions of chemistry applied to medicine.

Diethyl ether – known by the public simply as "ether" or "that hospital smell" – was first used as a general anaesthetic in 1842. It boils at 34.6°C (below our body temperature of 37°C) and may be used to numb the skin prior to an injection.

> *Ether is highly inflammable and forms an ignitable mixture with air even at -45°C, its flash point. A refrigerator where ether was inadvertently stored exploded when the door was opened; an*

electrical spark from the interior light switch had ignited the ether-air mixture inside. The person opening the door was severely injured.

Dentists stopped using ether as an anaesthetic because their patients often woke suddenly and unexpectedly.

'Woke with a bang when the anaesthetic exploded!' thought Bob looking at the canvas bag on the table in front of him. Before he could start worrying about what was in his hold-all, the compartment door slid open. '*Refreshments. Anyone for refreshments?*'

'No thank you,' said Daphne politely. Rachel shook her head. Aubrey never looked up from his book. Johannes opened his eyes. 'You have black coffee?'

'Certainly. Sugar?'

'No thank you.'

'One and thruppence please.'

'One shilling and three pence, yes?' said Johannes, giving him a two-shilling coin.

'Thank you sir. That's ninepence change.'

'Daylight robbery,' said Aubrey. 'The railway's run by a bunch of crooks.'

Rachel couldn't suppress a laugh - Pembleton-Smythe of all people saying that!

Johannes smiled at her and said, 'Ya, it's terrible.'

'It does seem expensive,' said Rachel.

'No, sorry. I mean the coffee. It tastes terrible,' said Johannes with a laugh.

98

The train came to a halt and they heard, 'Westbury. This is Westbury. Change here for Dilton Marsh and Warminster.'

* * * * *

'Were you taking a nap just now?' asked Rachel.

'No. I just thinking with my eyes closed. This pocket watch started me to remember my family and my country.'

'Is it a family heirloom?'

'Yes, I think it is of my great-grandfather. I did not know him. He died before I was born of course. I must have known my grandfather but I don't remember him. I was very young when he died. My father is very old now but he might recognise the watch. He never spoke to me about it.'

'What will you do with it now?'

'If it *was* of my great-grandfather, then I shall keep it for when my son receives his doctorate. It should be special to him because he is an hydraulics engineer like his great-grandfather. He's a very good student. Already is he *Doctorandus*. Piet is very serious like his mother. If she were alive she would be very proud of him.'

Rachel wanted to ask him when and how his wife died but instead she said, 'Where do you live in The Netherlands?'

'So,' said Johannes, 'you do not say Holland. You know Holland is just a part of Nederland, yes? Actually it's common even for Dutch people to say Holland when they should say Nederland'

'If I remember correctly,' said Rachel, 'Holland is a province of The Netherlands.'

'Actually, North Holland and South Holland are two of the twelve provinces. Amsterdam is in the northern province. Rotterdam, where I live, is in the southern province. Have you ever been to Holland?' he asked, stressing 'Holland' with a mischievous grin.

'No, I'm sorry to say.'

'Then you must visit us and I shall be your guide in Rotterdam. That's only fair after all. You are going to be my guide in Bath Spa, yes?

Rachel blushed and said, 'What's Rotterdam like? Tell me about it.'

'Rotterdam – or dam on muddy water – was beautiful until on 10 May, 1940. That's when die Deutsche Luftwaffe started bombing to force my country to surrender. The Centrum was almost completely destroyed. Rotterdam became, as we say, the city without a heart. I shall show you Ossip Zadkine's famous statue – Stad Zonder Hart – of a person in torment with a large hole in the body. The war was terrible. The occupation was terrible. Ah, we don't talk about it.'

'Rotterdam is already being rebuilt better than before,' continued Johannes. 'We have there the largest commercial port in Europe. Now! I must not talk about business. I think you prefer history, yes? If you like museums then we have many including for architecture, art, culture, maritime, natural history and so forth. We even have a tax and custom museum.'

'You're joking, surely,' exclaimed Rachel.

'Echt waar. It's really true,' Johannes laughed. 'We have it since October 1937 but I think you would prefer our shops, yes? We'll take you to the Lijnbaan. It's a big shopping centre with streets for pedestrians only. Opened in 1953, they are the first ones in the Netherlands.'

'Listen,' he said, 'here is my card.'

'What does *Johannes van Dijk – Antiek, Kunst, Juwelen, Boeken en Horloges* mean?'

'It means I'm an old, crafty man who likes jewels and watches.'

Rachel laughed. 'No, really. What do those words mean?'

100

'Antique(s), Art, Jewellery, Books and Watches. I have a little shop in Rotterdam. Actually, I have twelve little shops – one in each province of Nederland. Please, do you have a card?'

'No, sorry,' said Rachel.

'No matter,' said Johannes, 'Please, write your name, address and telephone number on the back of one of my cards. Oh, by the way you must call me Jan.'

'The train will be stopping at Salisbury in a minute. I'll do it then.'

* * * * *

When the train stopped, Rachel wrote down her details and gave back the card.

'Thank you,' said Johannes. 'We shall correspond and make arrangements.' Then looking out of the window he said, 'Why do you say *Soulsbree* when the name is spelt S-a-l-i-s-b-u-r-y? Dutch has rules for speaking and spelling. The ij in my name always sounds the same – something like your 'ay' in 'hay'. English has no rules. In bough, cough, ought, thorough and through, the 'ough' is different every time. Sorry. I am rude. Please tell me about Salisbury.'

Salisbury Cathedral is over 700 years old. It's a masterpiece of Early English architecture. The spire is the tallest in Britain. Remembering the words on Jan's card Rachel said, 'John Constable painted the spire and surrounding countryside in some of his famous landscapes. The Cathedral has a large mechanical clock. It was installed in 1386 and is the oldest of its kind in Britain. The library has the best preserved copy of the Magna Carta, issued by King John's chancery in 1215.' Jan was staring at her.

'Am I boring you?' said Rachel nervously. Jan smiled, knowing that there was also one copy in Lincoln Cathedral and two copies were in the British Library.

'No,' Johannes replied, 'you interest me. Please, tell more,' She blushed.

'Tickets! Tickets please!' they heard the guard call out. He glanced into their compartment then continued along the corridor. 'Next stop Romsey! Romsey next stop!'

Rachel was quietly telling Jan about The Haunch of Venison – a hostelry at least 600 years old. In 1320 it housed the craftsmen working on the Cathedral spire. Aubrey was engrossed in the machinations of the Rothschilds. Daphne was trying to decide what colour to choose – blue or pink - for the third bootie. Bob was deep in Fieser and Fieser's account of the ether synthesis developed by Alexander Williamson in 1850. Then it happened.

Bob heard this sudden noise – muffled but quite loud – from his hold-all. He peeped over the top of his book. To his dismay the almost empty bag was quickly swelling up to its full size. At the same time, jets of what looked like steam or thin white smoke were pouring out of the gaps in the zip's teeth all along the top of the bag.

The jets were accompanied by a gentle whistling; it was like the sound of an elderly man sucking air between his teeth. After what seemed an eternity but was probably only a minute or two, the bag began slowly to collapse. Finally it lay flat and still on the table. Bob listened. All he could hear was the wheels of the train – diddle-dee, diddle-dee, diddle-dum – running on the track.

* * * * *

Daphne was frowning at her knitting pattern when she became vaguely aware of the noise. A few moments later a draught of very cold air ran over her legs and feet. She shivered and the expression "blue with the cold" came to mind. She reached for her blue wool. Then she looked up

102

and wondered what was happening to that handsome student's bag. The train was just coming into Romsey. She would have to be quick to finish this second blue bootie before they reached Southampton.

Rachel heard the noise and turned to see what Jan was looking at. 'Incredible,' whispered Jan, as the bag inflated, gave off steam like a whistling kettle and slowly collapsed. 'It's that student's bag,' whispered Rachel. 'He's studying chemistry at Bristol University. It's probably a Rag Week stunt. In two weeks it will be Easter and students will be on holiday.'

Aubrey nodded agreement and thought to himself, 'Students ought not to waste their time and the tax-payer's money. They should be studying.' As he went back to his book he heard Rachel explain to Jan how much money Rag Week raises for charities.

* * * * *

When the train arrived at Southampton Central, Aubrey was standing in the corridor ready to get off. Without so much as a nod to his fellow passengers, he'd left the compartment, unaware that he would have to face the Inland Revenue's Miss Rachel Wallace, B.Econ., in his office on Monday morning. Bob was still buried in his textbook when Jan and Rachel said goodbye to Daphne.

'So, Rachel,' said Jan, 'you will come to Rotterdam?'

She smiled. 'I'll write and let you know.'

When they had gone Bob smiled at Daphne over the top of his textbook. 'Goodbye young man,' she said, 'Don't work too hard.' Frank was waving excitedly to her from the platform. 'I wonder.' she said to herself. 'Have a got to knit a second pink bootie?'

When she had gone, Bob opened his bag and noticed a wet, icy-cold plug of cotton wool amongst the shattered remains of his thermos flask. 'So much for wanting to show them liquid air,' he sighed when he saw his mum and dad waiting on the platform.

* * * * *

Epilogue

After a snack lunch in the undergraduate refectory on that unlucky Friday, the 13th, Bob had returned to the chemistry department where he filled his thermos flask with liquid air. He put a loose plug of cotton wool in the open neck to prevent liquid spilling out but still allow air from the evaporating liquid to escape. He placed the flask in the middle of his canvas hold-all and kept it upright with his pyjamas. So why did the flask explode?

The cotton wool became damp and the very cold air escaping from the flask turned the moisture into ice. Gradually the space between the cotton wool fibres filled with ice until the plug became one solid block of ice sealing the flask tight shut. The air could no longer escape. Pressure inside gradually rose until the flask exploded under the strain. The 'steam' coming from the bag was a fog (tiny water droplets in the air) formed when the evaporating liquid air instantly cooled the moist air in the compartment. Fortunately nobody was hurt.

According to Bob, the other passengers in the compartment either did not notice or pretended not to notice the bag's antics. We assumed this to be an example of the stiff upper lip that had helped the British survive two World Wars in the 20th century.

I suppose our 21st century Health & Safety at Work Act Regulations would today deter Bob from taking a thermos of liquid air out of the chemistry building let alone from carrying it in a bag onto a train. Nevertheless, I like to think that our 21st century British upper lip would be just as stiff now as it ever was and that the passengers in that railway compartment would remain calm and unruffled at the sight of an inflating, steaming bag.

Incidentally, when you cool rose petals and pieces of rubber in liquid air they will shatter into pieces like glass. Bob's pyjamas luckily did not suffer that fate!

Facts and Fantasies

Volume 2

Heart of Rotterdam

Michael C. Cox

Mimast Inc

THE BEST LAID SCHEMES

My parents, like many people after World War II, did not have a car. I was fortunate. John, a friend of mine, taught me to drive his small Morris Oxford which he used for work. He was a travelling door-to-door brush salesman. John liked some of the people he met but disliked the job, so he eventually went back to work for an insurance company. He disliked that work rather less but some of his co-workers rather more. The idea for this story stems from my recollection of John's account of life as a salesman and an insurance clerk.

* * * * *

Sitting in his little car watching the sleet sliding down the windscreen, Alan White was wondering why he ever gave up his job with the Prudential Insurance Company. Their new building, on the corner of Wine Street in Bristol, opened in 1957 just a few months before he was taken on as a junior clerk. He would travel to the office by bus – a 15-minute ride – and be one of the first to sign in. His desk was in a corner next to a radiator. On a cold afternoon he could warm his outer coat before leaving the building. If his raincoat was wet when he arrived, it would be dry and warm when he left. The pay was good. With his Christmas bonus he could treat his father, Bill, to some pipe-tobacco and his mother, Ethel, to a bottle of port. So why did he quit?

* * * * *

Clerical work was dull. Little broke the daily routine. Now and then Eddie Warburton, the office comedian, might roar with laughter and read out loud from a claims form.

> *I thought my window was down but found it was up when I put my head through it.*

From time to time an attractive secretary-typist would pop in, smile and say hello as she dropped a new file on Alan's desk. On a rare occasion the senior clerk might put his head around the door and announce the opening of a new branch. This raised everybody's hopes of a change and a promotion but such hopes were short-lived. Anyway, Alan knew that even if he rose to the dizzy heights of senior clerk or assistant branch manager, he would still feel unfulfilled.

The tedious routine was a factor but only a minor one in his decision to quit. The major factor was that he fell foul of his co-workers. Alan was very serious-minded and could be rather shy. According to at least three long-serving clerks, he was also too honest for his own good. These three so-called colleagues came to their conclusion not long after Alan's mother was taken ill.

* * * * *

Rachel Wallace first met Rupert Coleman as she was leaving the Queens Road Branch of Lloyds Bank for her lunch break. He'd held the door open and stepped out in the sunshine with her. He said hello and disappeared. Later he re-appeared in the university refectory and asked if he might share her table. It never occurred to her that he wasn't a Bristol graduate or that their second encounter wasn't a coincidence. And it didn't strike her as particularly odd that he'd forgotten his wallet and let her pay for his coffee and sandwich lunch. As they stepped into University Road, he mentioned that he had two tickets for a piano recital at the Colston Hall that evening. 'Would she like to go?' She was flattered and she was free, so she said yes.

She waited for him that evening by the fountain in front of the Victoria Rooms. She had arrived a few minutes early. On the dot of six o'clock, he appeared from behind the fountain. 'Have I kept you waiting?' Before she could reply, he said, 'You look lovely.' Then he kissed her on the cheek. 'The recital starts at 7 o'clock so we've plenty of time. Do you mind walking?' Rachel, still blushing, said truthfully, 'No. I like walking.' They went along Queens Road into Park Row as far as the Christmas Steps. From there he held her hand as they walked down to Colston Street.

Denis Matthews began his recital with Mozart's Sonata in B Flat (K333) followed by Beethoven's Sonata in C Major Opus 53

(Waldstein). Rachel admired his formidable technique and prolific memory but found both works a little heavy going. In the interval over coffee, Rupert told her that the B Flat Sonata was one of a set of four that Mozart composed after his return to Salzburg from Paris in 1779. 'He may have written them for the mademoiselles Aloysia and Constanze Weber,' said Rupert, 'before he settled on marrying Constanze.'

Rachel liked the variety in the second half. She was not familiar with the six Bulgarian Dances by Bela Bartok but she knew Schumann's Kinderschenen – subtitled, according to the programme notes, *Scenes of Childhood from Strange Lands and Peoples*. When Denis Matthews was playing no.7 – Traümerei (Dreaming) and no.11 – *Fürchtenmachen* (Frightening), Rupert's long slender fingers seemed to be playing along on his knees.

As she listened to the three intermezzos and the rhapsody in E flat Op. 119/4 by Johannes Brahms, Rachel recalled the Dutchman, Johannes van Dijk, she'd met on the train to Southampton. He had sent her a picture postcard of Ossip Zadkine's statue - Stad Zonder Hart (city without heart) - from Rotterdam and promised to write her a letter.

She saw quite a bit of Rupert after that concert. They went out several times and he always walked her home. She allowed him to kiss her goodnight but absolutely refused to allow his hands to explore her body. Rachel was determined to be virgo intacto when she walked up the aisle to marry 'Mr. Right'. After her first rebuff, Rupert kept his hands to himself and seemed content with a goodnight kiss.

She enjoyed his company. He was charming, witty and fascinating when he talked about music. What she found less adorable was his readiness to borrow money and forget to pay her back. She was beginning to wonder how honest and trustworthy he was. And then one day his name cropped up during her investigations at Lloyds Bank.

* * * * *

'Open our hearts and minds, O Lord, to the knowledge and love of Thee. Amen.' intoned the Rev. George W. Stockport from the pulpit of the Baptist Church in East Street.

110

The evening sermon began like the morning service that Sunday. Alan preferred evensong and always looked forward to joining the minister and his wife at the Manse for tea, biscuits and discussions with other young people. The current theme for the Sunday sermons - and for the Wednesday evening Bible Study which Alan also always attended - was The Commandments. Alan preferred the alternative name The Decalogue which the Reverend Stockport had used at their first Bible Study on the topic. He liked the ring of the word which came from the Greek deka ten and logos word.

'My text is again taken from the Old Testament,' began the minister, 'and from the Book of Exodus, Chapter 20.' Alan opened his Bible – the King James Version. 'In the first four Commandments - *the religious commandments* - God describes our obligations to Him,' began the minister. 'First, we must worship no other god but Him. Second, we must not bow down and serve any graven image.' He paused, looked down at the congregation where a well-heeled banker was trying to keep his eyes open and said, 'Mammon – the false god of avarice.'

Alan remembered how, at Bible Study, they had distinguished between avarice and greed – two of the seven deadly sins. Greed for riches is avarice. Greed for food is gluttony. '*Third,*' continued the minister, 'we must not take the name of Our Lord in vain. *Fourth*, we must remember the Sabbath and keep it holy.' 'Amen,' murmured several worshippers.

'In the remaining six Commandments - *the ethical and moral commandments* - God describes our obligations to one another. So far we have considered four of these Commandments. We must honour our parents.' Alan thought the world of his mother, Ethel, who was at home ill in bed. 'We must not murder.' Alan didn't always see eye to eye with Bill and, after an argument, might well have said he'd like to strangle his dad but he never meant it. 'We must not commit adultery. We must not steal.'

'This evening,' said the Revered Stockport, 'we shall consider the fifth of these Commandments - Exodus Chapter 20 Verse 16 God's – *Thou shalt not bear false witness against thy neighbour.*' Alan's mind turned to his problem at work.

His dad, Bill, left the house at 4:30 every morning. This meant Alan had to get Ethel's breakfast, help her to eat it, make sure she took her medicine, help her to the bathroom and remake the bed before he tucked her back into it. Then he'd have to sprint down the road to catch the bus. Dr Pollard had confined her to bed on the Sunday afternoon. On the Monday morning Alan was almost the last to sign in. Only two people - Eddie Warburton and Jim Sparks - arrived at the office after him that day. On Tuesday, Wednesday and Thursday, Harry Davies also signed in after Alan.

The root of Alan's problem was his honesty. He always recorded his *actual* time of arrival. That first week it was around 9 a.m. The staff who arrived before him either put in false times or left their times blank. When Eddie, Jim and Harry arrived after Alan *and* after 9 o'clock, they *had* to record their times and *had* to show they were late. On the Friday of that first week, Alan arrived at 9:02. Eddie and Jim had arrived a few minutes before and put down 8:45 and 8:46. Harry arrived after Alan - well past 9 o'clock and late. When he saw Alan's time he exploded.

'What's wrong with you?' bellowed the elderly clerk. 'Why'd you have to put 9:02?

'That's when I signed in,' said Alan a little nervously.

'So? Now the boss will know we're late.'

'My mother's ill and...'

'The boss won't care,' snapped Harry. 'Now he knows we're late. That's it! You, you ...'

'I'll tell him my mum's ill. He'll understand.'

'And what'll I tell the boss?' growled Harry.

'It's not my fault you're late' said Alan, going slightly hot under the collar.

What's wrong with you, lad? You just don't get it, do you. We cover for one another here. You scratch our backs and we'll scratch yours.'

'By telling lies! Sorry, I cannot bear false witness.'

'You cannot bear false witness! Who do you think you are, you sanctimonious little twit,' Harry fumed and stormed off.

It was several more weeks before Alan's mother got better and he could catch his early bus again. During those weeks the atmosphere in the office deteriorated. He felt isolated. Even that attractive secretary-typist stopped smiling and saying hello when she brought him a file. Finally, Alan gave in his notice. He cleared out his desk and left the building for the last time on a Friday afternoon.

On the Sunday evening after church he told the Reverend Stockport what had happened. The minister was sympathetic and asked Alan what he planned to do now. 'I thought I might apply to the Bristol Baptist College to study theology and become a minister,' said Alan, 'What do you think?' George Stockport thought carefully and said, 'If you can stay out, then you should stay out. Only enter the ministry if you really must.'

When Alan told his mum and dad that he'd given up his job with the Prudential and was thinking of studying to be a Baptist minister, Ethel said, 'I think you'd make a lovely vicar, dear.' Before he could explain that the Anglican Church had vicars, the Baptist Church had ministers and the Roman Catholic Church had priests, Bill said, 'That was a cushy job you had at the Pru'. What'll you do for money now? Vicars don't earn much, do they?'

Alan grinned. Thinking of Eddie back in the office, he said, 'I heard three boys arguing about whose dad earned most. The postman's son said his father worked six days a week and earned £600 a year. The bank manager's son said his father worked five days and earned £1200 a year. The third boy, a vicar's son, said, 'I don't know how much mine earns but he only works one day a week and it takes six men to carry his wages up to him.' Bill laughed.

Ethel didn't get the joke. 'It's not funny,' she said, turning to Alan. 'Perhaps you could get a job at the Central Telephone Exchange, dear. You know, at the Bristol Exchange where the Queen and the Duke of Edinburgh were last December.' Alan explained that Bristol had been chosen for the first ever Subscriber Trunk Dialling exchange and the Queen came on the 5th of December 1958 to make the first ever S.T.D. call. 'Her Majesty called the Lord Provost of Edinburgh, 365 miles away. An electronic robot called Grace connected Her call. I don't think they'd want me now they've got Grace,' said Alan, opening the Bristol Evening Post to the situations vacant column.

WANTED
KLEENEZE SALES AGENTS
Apply NOW

* * * * *

The sleet was still sliding down the windscreen and showing little sign of stopping. Alan had dropped his two passengers at the front entrance before driving to the car park behind the building. The two of them would be in their seats and waiting for him. The thought of having to make a dash for the door reminded him of his time as a Kleeneze salesman and he began to wonder why he quit that job.

* * * * *

He sold brushes and other products door-to-door for Kleeneze but he was actually self-employed. He was his own boss and answered only to himself. When his dad became ill, he took time off to visit him in hospital. Alan himself had always been fit and healthy. At school he'd played rugby and soccer for the first teams. During his two years of National Service in the Royal Air Force he played soccer for the squadron. He also learned ballroom dancing in the RAF. When he was demobbed, he took up badminton and tennis.

Whatever the weather, he enjoyed being outdoors. He usually had a healthy-looking tan to go with his dark hair, brown eyes and white teeth. Alan's customers referred to him as Mr Kleeneze or Smiler. They liked him. He liked them. For a short while he was earning good money

- more than he was getting at the Pru and far more than he was getting now. So why did he quit?

Kleeneze wasn't the problem. It was a good company founded in Bristol in 1923 by one Harry Crook who was anything but crooked. Alan knew him to be honest, hardworking and genuinely concerned for his workers, sales force and the community. In 1938 he founded the Bristol 5 Boys Club – a Youth Activities and Education Centre – at his company premises in Chalk Road, Bristol 5. In 1959 Harry Crook he was the first in Britain to introduce the 40-hour working week in his factory. He served the City of Bristol as an Alderman, Sheriff and eventually Lord Mayor.

Alan knew Dr Crook's background: senior executive for the Fuller Company in America; returned to Britain in 1920; started a brush-twisted-in-wire business with a workbench in rented factory space; modelled himself on Alfred Carl Fuller. Alan didn't know that Fuller was a farm boy from Nova Scotia, Canada, who started his business with a small workshop in his sister's basement in Somerville near Boston, Massachusetts. Harry and Alfred were both determined to make the best brushes and sell them by direct marketing.

Harry Crook ran Kleeneze like a family business. He'd tour his factory every morning and talk with individual workers. He published a weekly bulletin, called Searchlight, to keep the salesmen informed of company progress. Alan always read it hoping to find hints and tips to improve his sales technique. Harry gave his door-to-door salesmen a 40% commission on the price of every item they sold. The more they sold the more they earned. This appealed to Alan who had never been afraid of hard work.

Harry's brother, George Crook, was responsible for sales. At his regular meetings he'd hand out song sheets and lead the salesmen in a sing-song to boost their morale. Alan had a good voice and liked singing, so he would join in but he didn't think much of the Kleeneze songs. He preferred the traditional hymns they sang at East Street Baptist Church.

At George Crook's meetings Alan often overheard old hands telling stories and offering advice.

'Watch out for dogs – they can be trouble. Keep your suitcase between them and your legs. Walk up the path like you're a friend of the family. If a dog goes for you, don't kick it. If you do, the owner's bound to see you and bang goes a customer.'

'What if he bites you?'

'You mean the dog not the customer, right?' They all laughed.

'Put on a brave face. Smile. Praise the owner for having a good guard dog. Ask the owner for a sticking plaster to put on the bite. You'll probably get a bit of sympathy. It worked for me once. The lady of the house asked me in, put the plaster on my leg and after my demo she ordered three brushes and two tins of lavender polish. Now every time I go back there she always asks after my leg.'

Alan was a bit discouraged when he heard salesmen bragging about their sales. One old hand said, 'I get through four 50-page order books every week.'

'Four books! Crikey! That's a lot. How many deliveries do you make?'

'About 200 each week.'

Alan didn't fill one book in his first month.

'Anybody ever cancel when you deliver?'

'Quite often – usually when the husband's home.'

'What do you do then?'

'Depends. Usually I ask them which brush they can manage without till my next visit.'

'That's my trick,' said another old hand from Lancashire. 'It works well does that.'

That last comment made Alan uncomfortable. When he became a salesman he'd refused to believe his job was to persuade people to buy something they didn't need and probably wouldn't use with money they couldn't afford. He didn't want to *trick* people. He wanted to earn an honest living. So far he hadn't been bitten by a dog and he hadn't tricked anybody but then he hadn't had many orders or made many deliveries. In short, he wasn't doing very well. One day all this changed.

* * * * *

Rupert had hardly been able to believe his eyes when Kate produced the tickets for the two-day weekend trip to Amsterdam. 'Happy Birthday,' she said, giving him a big kiss. What a girl and what a treat. They had flown into Schipol, Amsterdam's International Airport - eleven feet below sea level according to the brochure – and taken a taxi to the Hotel Zandberg where they booked in as Mr. & Mrs. Spencer. After unpacking their overnight bags and testing the resilience of the bed springs, they dined in a small restaurant close to the Concertgebouw.

They enjoyed the concert, especially Mozart's Symphony No. 40 in G Minor – known as the 'Great' – 'to distinguish it,' Rupert said, 'from Wolfgang's No. 25, the only other minor symphony he wrote.' Kate was sorry not to have heard Amsterdam's Concertgebouw Orchestra conducted by Bernard Haitink but thought the Rotterdam Philharmonic played very well.

The hotel bed springs were severely tested again before they turned out the light and went to sleep. After a late breakfast the following morning, they followed the advice of the concierge and took a sight-seeing trip around the canals of Amsterdam - the Venice of the North according to the advertisement - before taking a taxi back to Schipol and their plane to London Heathrow. On the return flight, it struck Rupert just how different Kate and Rachel were from one another.

* * * * *

The letter bearing a Dutch stamp and a Rotterdam postmark arrived in the morning before Rachel left for the office. She put it in her briefcase and hurried to catch the bus to Prince Street. She kept the letter to open and read it over lunch in the canteen.

Antiek, Kunst, Juwelen, Boeken en Horloges
Johannes van Dijk

Dear Rachel,

I hope that you liked my postcard to show you the statue of Zadkine. As I told you already, he made it to remember us of the bombing and destroying of the Rotterdam Centrum.

My son – Pieter – and I should like very much to show you something of Holland. So we invite you to come for a few days to stay with us. If you would take the train to Harwich and then the night boat from there we shall meet you at Hoek van Holland and bring you by auto to Rotterdam.

Please. Write me when can you come.

Greetings from

Johannes van Dijk

Rachel had been seeing Rupert – irregularly rather than regularly - for a while but with no commitment on either side. She *had* enjoyed the Dutchman's company on that train journey from Bristol to Southampton and saw nothing sinister in his invitation. And she definitely needed a break. So, that afternoon she asked her head of department for some leave and in the evening she wrote to Johannes. On the Saturday when she received a reply from Johannes, she booked her train and night ferry return ticket.

On the following Thursday she took her overnight suitcase to the office and left work promptly after lunch, taking a taxi to Temple Meads Station. At Paddington Station she took the underground to Victoria Station for the train to Harwich. She was on the deck of the S.S. Arnhem when it sailed at 10:15 p.m. The North Sea crossing was smooth and the bed comfortable but she didn't sleep very well. The cabin was rather stuffy. And, she admitted to herself, she was excited at the prospect of seeing Johannes again. The ship docked at the Hook of Holland 6:15 a.m. local time.

Friday

As she disembarked, she saw Johannes and Pieter – tall and fair-haired just like his father – smiling and waving from the quay. 'How are you Johannes,' she said as they shook hands. 'Jan. Remember I told you already to call me Jan. This is my son Pieter.' He shook her hand. 'Piet. You must call me by that name, ja,' he said. 'Please, I take your case.'

Rachel thought Piet was going to drive but then realised that the steering wheel was on the left. 'Please,' said Piet, opening the front passenger door of the pale grey Alfa Romeo grey sedan, 'you sit here.' When she was settled comfortably on the white, soft leather bench seat, he closed her door and climbed into the back with her suitcase.

'Your journey was good?'

'Yes, very good, thank you Jan,' she said. 'Is it far to your house?'

'Not far at all. I suppose about 27 kilometres – I should better say 17 miles. Actually we live in Schiedam – a suburb a few kilometres south west of Rotterdam Centrum.'

Seeing the signs for Maasdijk and Maassluis, Piet leant forward and said, 'De Maas is what you call The Meuse. It is a major river from France that comes through Belgium then Holland before it goes into the North Sea. Altogether 925 kilometres.'

'd-i-j-k means dike, I assume,' said Rachel, 'but what is s-l-u-i-s?'

'Ja,' said Piet, 'it means a *sluice* or you can better say *lock* to control water levels.'

'Oh, look, a windmill – and its sails are turning!'

'Ja, that is De Wippersmolen here in Maassluis. It's a drainage or polder mill. We call him a *draai kop molen*.'

'I know a polder is low lying land reclaimed from the sea. But,' asked Rachel, trying her best to say the name properly, 'what's a *dry cop mowlan*?'

'I may say *turn head mill* because we can turn him at the top for the wind to come at the sails. During the occupation the resistance used the windmills to send signals. The Germans didn't know we do that, niet waar, Vader?'

Johannes said, 'Ja, that's true. We could fix the sails into different positions, like + or x, and send coded messages from mill to mill.'

'Were you in the Dutch Resistance, Jan?'

'Ja, we both were,' said Piet proudly, 'even when I was only seven years.'

'You were very brave, Piet. Moeder was proud of you,' said Johannes.

'Zo, thuis,' said Piet as the car pulled up outside their house, on the corner of the Arij Prinslaan, just opposite the Julianapark.

Piet led the way carrying her suitcase. Rachel followed. Jan locked the car and caught them up. Before they reached the house, the front door opened and a young woman rushed out. She kissed Piet and said, 'Zo, hebben jullie honger. Ik heb 't ontbijt klaar. Oh, sorry, you must be Rachel, yes? May I just introduce myself. My name is Lies. I am Piet's verloofde – fianceé. You have hunger? I have breakfast ready. Please. Come in.'

On the table there were Edam and Gouda cheeses, a plate covered with thin slices of smoked meat (*rookvlees*), a bowl of hard-boiled eggs still in their shells, dishes of jam - strawberry and black currant, a basket with slices of three different kinds of bread and a dish of butter. There was a coffee pot and also what looked like an oversized purse containing a large tea pot. When they were all seated, Jan said quietly, 'In de naam van de Vader, en de Zoon, en de Heilige Geest. Amen.' Piet offered the basket of bread to Rachel and said, 'Eet smakelijk.' Jan said, 'It's how we say *bon appétit* in Dutch.'

Immediately after breakfast, Jan showed her around the house and garden while Piet helped Elise clear the table and wash the dishes. Then Jan drove them all into Rotterdam. There were so many bridges, big and small, over so many waterways. When Rachel asked, Piet confessed that even he could not always tell the differences between *kanaal*, *gracht*, *singel* and *sloot*. 'I believe,' he said, 'that *singel* comes out of Latin *cingulum* – girdle because in the beginning it was usually a moat around the city.'

When they approached the Belasting & Douane Museum, Rachel told Jan politely that she was on holiday and didn't want to think about taxes & customs. Jan and Piet laughed. Elise told Rachel they were not serious about going in there although the museum was interesting. It was the Prins Hendrik Nautical Museum they visited first before they took a luxury boat tour, run by Spido, around Rotterdam harbour – the largest harbour in Europe.

In the afternoon, after what, in Rachel's opinion, they mistakenly described as a *light lunch*, they went shopping in the Lijnbaan. This pedestrian precinct and shopping centre – the first of its kind in Europe – was opened in 1953. Jan took her to his shop where he showed her an antique Delft Blue & White brooch, 1 inch in diameter and domed, depicting a windmill scene. The ceramic was surrounded by 25 tiny intricate florets in 835 Sterling silver. The brooch was authentically signed on the back.

'Do you like this?' Jan asked. 'Zo, let me pin it on your lapel.' In a moment his large hands had expertly worked the antique T-bar hinge and wire clasp. 'What do you think?'

With a smile at Piet, Rachel said, 'It's a draai kop molen, isn't it.'

Piet smiled. 'Ja. Zeker,' he said.

'Dat is zo fraai – sorry, beautiful!' said Elise clapping her hands together.

When Rachel went to unpin the brooch Jan took hold of her arm and said, 'Please, keep it on. It is a souvenir from me for your visit to Holland.'

On the way back to Schiedam, Jan drove through Delfshaven - the oldest part of Rotterdam – to the Aelbrechtskolk and the historic church where the Pilgrim Fathers held their last service before embarking on the *Speedwell*. Piet explained that a *kolk* is the section of water between two sets of lock gates. 'It buffers between the high and low water,' said Piet.

Rachel said to Jan, 'I always thought the Pilgrim Fathers sailed in the Mayflower from Plymouth.'

Jan smiled and said, 'Ja, that is so but those people started with two ships first from Southampton. Then bad weather drove them into Plymouth Sound where they abandoned the Speedwell because it was a leaky old tub. That's what you do, ja, when something is no good for you.' She would recall his words later when she was back in England.

In the evening, after they had eaten another substantial meal, they sat in comfortable chairs and Jan poured them all a small glass of *jenever*, a traditional Dutch liqueur made from juniper berries. It was strongly alcoholic. Even a small sip burned the back of Rachel's throat. In Holland people generally did not close their curtains when it got dark. So, anyone walking by the house could look in to see the potted plants lining the window sill and the people sitting in the room drinking jenever.

'It is good that you visit Holland now,' said Jan, 'because tomorrow we have the opportunity to hear the Rotterdamse Philharmonisch Orkest conducted by Eduard Flipse in the Concertgebouw in Amsterdam.' The Rotterdam concert building was destroyed by the Luftwaffe in 1940.

Piet explained that Eduard Flipse was raising money to build a new hall for the RPhO on Schouwburgplein. 'Vader is helping with that,' he said proudly.

When she saw Rachel stifle a yawn, Elise said, 'Moe – tired? Rachel nodded. 'So, please, you should go to bed. Tomorrow we go to Amsterdam.' They all stood up and Elise said, 'Goeje nacht. Welterusten. Sorry – goodnight. Sleep well.'

Saturday

Rachel, Jan and Piet had an early breakfast on Saturday morning. Rachel helped Piet to clear the table and wash up. Jan disappeared into his study. As soon as Elise arrived, all four piled into the car for Amsterdam. Piet was a mine of information. 'I should tell you,' he said, 'that the capital of Noord Holland is Haarlem and of Zuid Holland is Amsterdam – Den Haag (The Hague) is the seat of our government. It doesn't matter to me. I prefer Amsterdam. It has 1,281 bridges and 165 canals. Many people live on the water in houseboats.' Elise told Rachel she would not want to do that and said, 'You will see such places in some moments because we are going to tour the canals with the rondvaart.'

Jan parked near the railway station and they walked across the road to the Hendrik Kade for the rondvaart (round sailing) in a long, glass-topped boat. Their guide – a student from Amsterdam university – gave the commentary enthusiastically first in Dutch, English, French and Spanish – always in that order. Often she described, in the first four languages, what to look for.

'Ladies and Gentleman, in a moment by the canal on your right you may see a bird cage outside a window of the house of Rembrandt where he worked from 1639 till 1658.' By the time she said this unenthusiastically in the fifth language, German, the boat would have gone past the canal and the bird cage. At the end of the tour the guide said in a matter-of-fact way, 'Thank you for your kind attention. I hope you enjoyed your trip. Please be aware that you are permitted to grant gratuities to the guide.' As they disembarked Rachel gave her a tip and a big thank you.

'Koffie, jongens?' said Jan indicating a table outside a café. 'Alsjeblieft,' said Piet, 'met slagroom.' Elise translated, 'Coffee, youngsters. Please – with whipped cream.' Rachel resolved to diet when she got home. After coffee they walked up the Dam Rak to the Royal Palace. Jan said, 'Buckingham Palace has more grandeur, ja?' Rachel had to agree. They took a tram to the Rijksmuseum to see Rembrandt's famous Nightwatch painting. Around lunchtime, they went on a tram back to the station for the car. Jan drove them to the Vondelpark to eat the picnic lunch Elise had prepared.

After lunch they strolled around the park – Amsterdam's largest – which was designed as an English landscape by the architect L. D. Zocher in 1864 and opened in 1865. Jan showed Rachel the statue of the most famous Dutch poet Joost van der Vondel. 'He lived from 1587 to 1679,' said Jan, 'and converted to Roman Catholicism in 1641. Many of his poems were inspired by his conversion and by his grief at the death of his wife as well as three of his five children.' Rachel wondered how Jan's wife had died.

They walked from the park to the Stedelijkmuseum to see one of van Gogh's famous Sunflower paintings. 'Look,' said Jan, 'this has fifteen sunflowers in the vase. Vincent painted them in 1889 in Arles. Altogether there are seven paintings with a vase – three with 15 flowers, two with 12, one with 5 and one with 3 flowers. All seven were painted in Arles between August 1888 and January 1889. The sunflowers he painted in Paris in 1887 are not in a vase; we call them cut flowers.'

After another so-called light meal at a Dutch-Indonesian restaurant they headed to the Concertgebouw. The Rotterdam Philharmonic Orchestra's performances of Ludvig von Beethoven's Egmont Ouverture and his Fifth Symphony were superb. The applause was long and loud. 'Odd,' thought Rachel, 'how the Dutch still dislike the Germans but like their music.'

During the interval, when Piet was telling Rachel how the first four notes of the 5th symphony matched the Morse code for Sir Winston Churchill's 'V' for victory, he saw a sudden look of surprise on her face. 'You didn't know this?'

She looked back at Piet and said, 'Sorry, Piet, what did you say?'

Jan was concerned. He'd seen her startled look. 'Are you alright?'

As she replied, 'Oh, yes, thank you Jan. I thought I saw ...' a bell warned people to return to their seats.

When they were leaving the hall at the end of the concert, Rachel seemed to Jan to be looking for someone. As he drove past along the Oude Groenmarkt, he heard Rachel gasp and out of the corner of his eye he saw her put her hand over her mouth. 'Have you left something behind,' he asked her, 'because I can turn back.' Rachel didn't hear him. Her head was spinning. Rupert, with his arm around a dark curly-haired young woman, was going into a hotel. 'So it was him I saw at the concert,' she said to herself.

Sunday

Elise joined them for Rachel's third Dutch breakfast. Afterwards Jan helped her to clear the table and wash up so that Piet could tell Rachel how Dutch Hydraulic Engineers had turned a saltwater sea (De Zuider Zee) into a freshwater lake (Het Ijsselmeer).

'From Noord Holland to Friesland we built a dijk 32 km long, 90 m wide and 7.25 m above the sea level. It took us from 1927 to 1932. We began the building from four positions – from two on the mainlands and from two artificial islands we made on the line of the dijk. The Afsluitdijk (off-shut-dike) was opened officially 25 September 1933. Of course,' said Piet, 'the Germans bombed holes into it in the war.'

Piet was just about to show Rachel technical cross-section diagrams of the dike when Jan put his head around the door and said, 'Hou op, jongen. Wij zijn klaar.' Piet smiled and told Rachel his father had just said, 'Shut up, young man. We are ready.'

It was a whirlwind tour. Rotterdam to Delft where Rachel's antique brooch originated. On to Den Haag – the seat of the Government. From the Hague to Leiden. 'We could spend a week here,' said Jan, 'and still not see everything. Rembrandt – full name Rembrandt Harmenszoon van Rijn was born in Leiden on the 15th July 1606. He was the eighth of nine children from Harmen Gerritszoon van Rijn and his wife Neeltje (little Nell or Nellie). Zoon means son. So Rembrandt was Harmen's son.'

Rachel nodded and said, 'So Rembrandt's grandfather was called Gerrit.'

Jan patted her on the back and said, 'Een knap meisje.'

Elise whispered in Rachel's ear, 'Intelligent girl.'

After coffee they drove slowly through Haarlem, the Capital of Nord Holland, without stopping. 'We shall go through Alkmaar,' said Jan, 'but the kaasmarkt - cheese market - is only for Fridays, so we cannot see men in fancy dress running about carrying those cheeses.'

When they reached the south end of the Afsluitdijk, Rachel was stunned to see the road ahead stretching out across the water. With the North Sea on their left and the Ijssel Lake on their right, Jan drove the five miles to the monument - designed by the architect W.M. Dudok. 'This is the place,' said Piet, 'where, at 2 minutes over 1 o'clock on the 28th May 1932, we finally closed the dijk to keep out the sea.'

They ate their picnic lunch there but inside the car because outside the wind was quite cold. 'We can better call the Afsluitdijk a barrier dam,' said Piet. 'It has twenty-five discharge sluices and a shipping lock at each end to control the water levels.' Rachel could see why they needed locks but not why they needed the sluices. 'Ja,' said Piet, 'because the Ijssel river all the time puts water into the lake. We cannot let the Ijsselmeer fill up and overflow.'

The journey back to Schiedam seemed quite short. Rachel remarked on the flatness of the land with so much of it divided into so many neat, orderly farms. Shortly after they passed a signpost for Hoorn, Piet said to Rachel, 'Now I think you must know that water there on our left.' When she said the Ijssel lake, she heard Jan say, 'Ja, een knap meisje.'

They stopped in Edam for coffee. Only Rachel refused the whipped cream. 'The cheese market is here Wednesdays,' said Lies, ' so we don't see it. Anyway it's mostly a show for the tourists. In a moment we shall be in Volendam. There may be some people in traditional costumes – white high-pointed bonnets, fancy bodice with full, black skirts hiding their wooden clogs – what you see on postcards. More nonsense for the tourists.'

At Volendam Jan found a little car park and they walked through the cobbled streets to the edge of the Ijsselmeer to look at the colourful, quaint wooden houses. Rachel actually saw a few elderly woman in rather drab costumes. Their gnarled hands and wrinkled faces spoke of their long lives as fishermen's wives. They seemed care-worn and oblivious of Rachel. 'They have a simple, hard life here,' said Jan. 'Let's go home.'

Before the evening meal that Elise was preparing, Rachel first packed her suitcase then looked into the kitchen. 'Can I help?' Rachel asked Lies. 'No, thank you,' said Lies, 'I shall call you in about ten minutes.' Piet was reading in a chair by the window.

Rachel knocked on the study door. 'Binnen,' said Jan. Guessing that meant come in, she went in. Jan was sitting behind his desk. He stood up. 'Please, come in.' He was holding a framed photograph in his hand.

'This was my wife.'

'When did she die?'

'I don't know exactly,' said Jan. 'The Gestapo took her and her parents away when Piet and I were not at home.' His face hardened. 'A quisling neighbour told the Germans she and her mother were Joden – Jews. It was not true but those animals took them anyway. Piet never saw his mother again.' Then he looked at the photograph and sighed. 'One day I may be able to forgive but I never forget what those Nazis did to us.' The look on Jan's face was the same one that Rachel saw when they stood together in front of Zadkine's statue – city without a heart. Just as she reached out to touch Jan's arm, she heard Elise call out, 'Eten.'

When Johannes drove Rachel back to the Hoek van Holland on Monday to catch the 11:40 p.m. night boat back to Harwich, Piet and Elise came as well to see her off. All three stood under a light on the quay so she would see them smiling and waving goodbye. They had made her so welcome. She had eaten more in those three days than she normally ate in a week. As she curled up in the cabin bed she tried to think about all the places they had seen and all the things they done. Just as she was drifting off to sleep, a picture came into her mind of Rupert and a young woman entering the Hotel Zandberg.

* * * * *

Still sitting in his car, Alan remembered his first chance meeting with Rupert. As he watched a piece of ice slither down the car windscreen, he thought, 'Slippery and sliding on a downward path to disappear when it reaches the bottom. Yes, just like Rupert.'

* * * * *

He was pretty fed up. The week had been an utter disaster. Friday already and what had he to show for his efforts. Three small orders and one pair of sore feet. Long Ashton had been a dead loss. The only thing good about the place was the Angel Inn. He decided to cheer himself up with a half of cider and a Cornish pasty for lunch. He took his food and drink from the bar and sat at a small table by a window. As usual he was feeling hard done by. He'd had no choice but to resign from his first job. Now here he was trying to sell brushes door to door. How utterly ghastly. Just as he took a sip of his cider, he heard, 'Excuse me. May I join you?'

'Suit yourself,' he said without looking up. Alan put his orange juice and ham sandwich on the table and sat down. He picked up his sandwich from the plate, looked across the table and frowned. The sandy-coloured hair, blue eyes, long nose, thin lips and dimpled chin reminded him of someone from the past – his time in the RAF perhaps. Rupert sensed Alan's stare and looked up. 'Crikey! Chalky? Chalky White?' Suddenly Alan grinned and said, 'Mustard? Well I'm blowed! Fancy meeting you here.'

'It's been a long time since anyone called me Mustard,' said Rupert, whose full name was Nicholas Rupert Spencer Coleman. 'Coleman's mustard,' he mused, 'I wonder if there's a Monsieur de Dijon in France with the nickname Moutarde.'

Alan grinned. 'Nobody's called me Chalky since I left school.' Reaching across to shake hands, he said, 'It's Alan, by the way. And you are ...?'

'Rupert but I sometimes answer to Ru. Anything but Nicholas or Old Nick.'

'What did you do when you left the Sixth Form?' asked Alan. 'University?'

'No. I tried for Maths and Physics at Bristol but didn't get a place. So I had to do National Service. What about you?'

'Straight from school into the RAF for two years. After that I got a job with the Prudential.'

'I went into the RAF as well. Signed on for three years. Got more pay and became a Personnel Selection Assessor. Absolute farce. When I finished training they sent me to the transit camp at Felixstowe. Second day there, I'm in the canteen playing the piano and the camp's commander walks in. What's your name corporal?' he says to me.

'Coleman, Sir!

"Carry on, corporal," he says and stands there listening.'

'Then what?' said Alan.

'Well, the next thing I know, he asks me to play Cole Porter's Begin the Beguine. When I finish, he says to me, "Staff dance on Saturday – 19 hundred hours sharp. Band needs a pianist." and marches off.

Alan remembered how well Rupert played the school piano for assembly and asked, 'What was that tune you used to play as we marched out of the school hall in the mornings?'

'Crikey! Mendelssohn's War March of the Priests. I haven't played that since school,' said Rupert humming the first few bars in his head.

'Anyway,' continued Rupert, 'instead of one week *in transit* I was there for nearly a year as the camp's pianist. Then we got a new commander - tone deaf! So, yours truly, Corporal Coleman, Sir, was posted to an RAF station in the middle of the Abu Dhabi desert. Half dozen tents, a million sand flies and no piano. The crazy thing was they already had a Personnel Selection Assessor – a sergeant! Two of us in the middle of the desert and nobody to assess. Actually, we did have forms from two servicemen to look at. One said he wanted to be a *gonner.* "He'll be a gonner when I get my hands on 'im" said serge. The other wanted to a *laft bincher*. We never saw him to interview so we never found out what a laft bincher was.'

'What did you do when you were demobbed?' asked Alan.

'Banking,' said Rupert. 'Lloyds Bank – the branch in Queens Road.'

'I know,' said Alan. 'next to the University. Popular with students I expect.'

'Yes,' said Rupert. 'that's how I met Rachel.'

'Your wife?'

'A girl friend. We *might* get engaged one day *if* I can afford a ring.'

'Is she a student?'

'She was. Got an economics degree at Bristol and works for the Inland Revenue now, so I suppose I've got to watch my step. What about you? A big noise in the Pru'?'

'No. It didn't suit me. I left. Now I'm a sales agent for Kleeneze,' said Alan diffidently.

'I don't believe it. A door-to-door brush salesman,' exclaimed Rupert.

'What's wrong with that?' asked Alan with a frown.

'Absolutely nothing at all, old boy,' said Rupert. 'Guess what I'm doing now.'

'Branch Manager at Lloyds in Queens Road?'

'No such luck,' said Rupert. 'No, I'm a sales agent for Betterware.'

'Not Betterware brushes?' said Alan. 'Well I'm blowed.'

* * * * *

Before she left her office for a lunch break, Rachel put the file – *Confidential/Investigate: Lloyds Bank, Queens Road Branch* – into her metal cabinet and locked the drawer. She waved to Ron, the security officer behind the front desk, as she headed for the front door of the Inland Revenue building in Prince Street. 'Out for a bit of sunshine, miss?' She looked at him with her green eyes, smiled and with a nod of her head stepped out into the street.

The sun was bright so she put on her sunglasses and turned right into Prince Street. Two engineers working on an overhead telephone line gave her wolf whistles. As she passed below their perch they looked down to see her straight fair hair held back by two brown tortoiseshell clips. As she walked away towards the city centre, they admired her slender figure dressed in a tailored dark olive jacket and skirt and whistled again. She barely noticed. She was out in the fresh air to think.

For her favourite walk, Rachel was wearing soft brown leather shoes with sensible flat heels. From Prince Street she went along Broad Quay into Colston Avenue where she paused to look at Edmund Burke – actually at his bronze statue cast in 1894 and the work of James Harvard Thomas. The replica in Washington DC was erected in 1922. She recalled that Burke - a distinguished philosopher – had been a controversial MP for Bristol from 1774 to 1780. She read the engraving on the plinth:

> *I wish to be a member of parliament to have my share of*
> *doing good and resisting evil*

With those words going around in her head, Rachel turned into St Stephens Street and headed to Corn Street where she stopped to look at the four Nails – round-topped pedestals - outside the Exchange. Merchants and traders used to place their money on those pedestals when they struck a bargain. They called it *paying on the nail*. She tried not to think about the money Rupert owed her.

She retraced her steps through St Leonards Archway, crossed St Stephens Street into Clare Street and took the shortest route back to her

131

office. Ron the security officer was still behind his desk. 'Good afternoon Miss Wallace. There was a telephone call for you,' he said, handing her a note. 'Mr Coleman.' Her heart missed a beat. 'Thank you, Ron,' she said.

* * * * *

'How long have you been with Kleeneze?' asked Rupert.

'Not long. A few months but it seems longer.'

'Same here. How's it going?' asked Rupert. Then before Alan could reply, he said, 'I've had a terrible week – month actually. This door-to-door sales lark isn't the money spinner I need.' He pulled a face at the thought of his debts.

'I've taken a few orders this week,' said Alan. 'Bit better than usual but nothing to shout about.'

'You shouldn't have any trouble. Kleeneze stuff is good - better than Betterware.'

'I thought Betterware's stuff was better – like the name suggests. If I wasn't a Kleeneze agent, I'd recommend Betterware brushes.'

A strange look came over Rupert's face. 'I've just remembered what someone said to me - Praise from your enemy is worth more than praise from your friend - and it's given me an idea.'

'Sorry? What are you getting at?' asked Alan.

'Look here. Suppose I tell people that Kleeneze brushes are better than mine – better quality and better value. Then a couple of days later you show them your brushes. I'll bet you a pound to a penny you'd get an order on the spot.'

'But your brushes are better than mine,' said Alan.

'Who cares?' said Rupert.

132

'But only one can be better. They can't both be better than the other.'

'Look, it doesn't matter. Here's the plan. First part of the week I'll tell people Kleeneze stuff is better than mine. You tell people Betterware stuff is better than yours. Second part of the week ...'

Alan interrupted him and, with a frown, said 'Wouldn't we be bearing false witness?'

'False witness? What *are* you on about? Look, I think your Kleeneze stuff is better than mine, right? You think my Betterware stuff is better than yours, right? So, who's telling lies? Where was I? Oh, yes, Second part of the week, I'll sell my stuff to your people and you sell your stuff to my people.'

'Will it work?'

'It's bound to. We'll clean up.' said Rupert. Then seeing Alan's doubtful look, he said, 'I'll tell you what - let's try it out. I'll do a house this afternoon and meet you back here at 3 o'clock. Then you go there and make your pitch. What d'you say?'

* * * * *

Rachel sat down and read Rupert's note. At quarter past two the phone on her desk rang. 'Rachel Wallace.'

'Rachel – this is Rupert. How are you?'

'Bit busy actually. Something wrong? You don't normally call me at my office.'

'No, nothing wrong. I just need your help.'

Her heart missed beat. Hoping it wasn't money again, she asked, 'What do you want?'.

'Could you be home with your parents by four o'clock this afternoon?' He then explained what he wanted her to do and, in his

133

usual smooth way, talked her into doing it. Rupert could always turn on the charm.

* * * * *

At ten past four that Friday afternoon, Alan walked up the garden path and rang the doorbell of number 48 Pembroke Road, Clifton, Bristol 8. Doris saw him and called out to her daughter, 'Rose, there's a young man coming up the path. He's carrying a suitcase. Would you answer the door. He looks a nice young man.' As Rose went to the door she said, 'Looks can be very deceptive, mother.' Doris sighed. 'I know dear.'

The young woman took his breath away. 'Um, er, good afternoon, um, miss, er, madam,' Alan mumbled. Then taking hold of himself, he started again. 'Good afternoon. I'm your local representative.'

She smiled and asked, 'Conservative, Labour or Liberal?'

'Oh, sorry. I'm not ... No, sorry. Excuse me. I'm your local Kleeneze agent. If it's convenient I should like five minutes to show what we have to make life easier for you around the house. May I come in?'

'Kleeneze you say?'

'Yes.'

'I think we can spare five minutes. Come in.'

She showed him into the living room. Alfred was sitting bolt upright in his wing-back chair near the fireplace with his back to the window - shoulders back like a soldier on parade. His strong hands gripped the arms of the chair and his shiny black shoes were planted firmly together on the rug in front of him. Doris was sitting more comfortably on the two-seater settee on the other side of the fireplace. Rose went and sat down by her mother. They all turned and looked at Alan. He put his case on the rug and knelt down facing the fire.

Nervously, he opened his case and began his demonstration. He didn't falter until he showed them the lavender polish tin. Holding out

134

her delicate hand, Rose said, 'May I see that?' He handed her the tin. She tried to open it by twisting the little lever on the side. 'Let me,' said Alan.

He was all fingers and thumbs. Suddenly the lid flew off and landed on Rose's shoe. 'Oh, I'm so sorry,' he said. Doris was smiling at him. Rose laughed and said, 'No harm done. My shoes could do with a polish anyway.'

Alan, somewhat red in the face, said, 'Actually it's furniture polish. It really does make wood shine.'

'Time for a nice cup of tea,' said Doris, easing her plump figure out of the settee and smoothing her floral apron. "Do you take milk and sugar, young man?'

'Oh, I, er, just milk, please,' said Alan.

'I love the smell of lavender,' said Rose. 'It reminds me of my late Gran. She kept little bags of it amongst her clothes in a chest of drawers. When she'd visit us, it was like a lavender bush walking in through the front door.'

Alfred laughed. 'You're right, lass. She reeked of it something awful.'

Alan couldn't take his eyes off Rose. She was radiant. She had such rosy cheeks. Alfred noticed how flushed they were and said, 'Is this fire too warm for you two?'

'Er, no sir, thank you sir.'

Doris returned with the tea tray. Alfred didn't move. Alan jumped up to help but Doris said, 'I can manage young man. Thank you all the same.' She put the tray on the table behind the settee and asked Rose to do the honours while she decided what to order from 'Mr Kleeneze', as she called him.

'Is that stuff any good?' asked Alfred, pointing a muscular forefinger at the shoe cleaning kit. Alan handed it to him.

'The brushes look well made – better than we had in the army – I'll say that.'

'I use the polish on my shoes,' said Alan. 'It keeps the rain out and the shine lasts a long time.'

'I noticed your shoes. Very nice' said Alfred approvingly. 'Done your National Service, have you?'

'Yes sir. RAF.'

'Army man myself,' he barked, drawing his finger across his trim, grey moustache. 'Face to face with the enemy we were. Dropping bombs from an aeroplane ...'

'Dad!' said Rose, looking apologetically at Alan.

'What was it like – the First World War – fighting, I mean?'

'Horrible. It's not something you forget. It was a blood bath and it was *personal*. I still remember Helmut.'

Rose handed out the cups and offered Alan a slice of home-made apple cake. 'Did you bake this?' asked Alan. 'No. Mum. It's my Gran's old recipe.'

'Delicious,' said Alan, taking a bite and making sure any crumbs fell into his case and not onto the rug. Then turning to Rose's father, he said, 'Who was Helmut?'

'Leutnant Helmut Schneider was the German soldier I met on Christmas Day, 1914, in *no-man's land* at Ypres. Only sane day in the whole war. We stood on a 30-yard patch of ground between our trenches and sang Carols. The Jerries sang *Stille Nacht, Heilige Nacht* and we sang *Silent Night, Holy Night*. Terrible singing. Some wag said he'd rather hear gunfire.' Alan laughed.

Alfred then told how the men had exchanged presents. Handing Alan a small book, he said, 'I gave Helmut my cigarette case and he gave me this Bible.' Printed in gold lettering on the black leather cover were the words Die Bibel. 'Before I ordered my chaps back to our trenches, I shook hands with Helmut and I told him his soldiers might be tougher than mine but we'd win the war anyway.'

'When Helmut said *Nein, your men - they are tougher but vee'll vin*, I thought *Praise from my enemy is praise indeed*. When Helmut saluted and said *Aufwiedersehn*, I said *Cheerio* and saluted back. That was the last I saw of him.'

Alan noticed a faded photograph between two pages. 'That's Helmut with his wife and daughter,' said Alfred. Alan pointed to four words underlined on one of the pages: *Du sollst nicht töten*. 'Thou shalt not kill,' said Alfred. 'Thou shalt not kill! - Exodus Chapter 20 Verse 13. What a waste of life. In my book, nobody won.'

'Another cup of tea?' asked Rose.

'No thanks,' said Alan, glancing at his watch. 'I should be going.'

'Not before you take Mum's order,' said Rose. 'We've heard that Kleeneze products are better than Betterware's.'

Alan beamed. When he had written out the order – the best he'd ever had – he picked up his suitcase and shook hands firmly with Alfred who remained bolt upright in his chair. Alan wondered how he'd ever managed to sit so straight and still the whole afternoon. He thanked Doris for her order and for the tea and cake before Rose showed him to the door.

'Thanks for listening to Dad's war story. He was a major in the infantry. He lost both his legs and spent two years in a prison camp – that's where he learnt German. He never complains. He says Helmut's Bible saved his life in more ways than one.'

Alan wasn't sure what to say, so he said, 'I'll deliver your order and collect the money a week on Saturday if that's convenient.' She smiled and nodded. As he walked back down the path he thought, 'I wonder if she'd like to go to a dance?'

* * * * *

Rupert arrived early on Saturday to secure a small table by the window in The Albion before the Saturday lunchtime crowd arrived. The old-world inn, renovated in 1956, was at the end of a narrow cobbled lane. Alan assumed Rupert chose the inn for their meeting because it was close to his flat in Clifton and tucked away in a quiet spot just off Boyce's Avenue.

What'll you have?' asked Alan. 'A ploughman's and a glass of red wine with it,' replied Rupert. Alan fetched the food and drink from the bar and sat down. Their lunch consisted of four large chunks of Cheddar cheese, two pickled onions and a large freshly baked cottage roll with real butter to go with it.

'Thanks,' said Rupert, 'they do a good lunch here. My treat next time.' Then he quickly scooped his onions onto Alan's plate, saying, 'Mustn't eat these. I'm seeing the girlfriend later on.' As Alan took a sip of his orange juice, Rupert said, 'So, how did it go yesterday?'

'The best order yet. You were right. It was a doddle.'

'What did I tell you? We've got it made. After lunch we'll pop around to my flat and plan our campaign for the week.'

They ate their lunch mostly in silence. Alan only told Rupert about his order. He didn't mention Rose. He hadn't been able to stop thinking about her and couldn't wait to see her again. When they had finished eating, Rupert led the way to his flat on Sion Hill. It was warm in the sunshine so they strolled under the trees along Rodney Place then turned left into Portland Street. 'Lived in Clifton long?' asked Alan, as they turned right into The Mall.

'About nine months.' They turned left into Gloucester Street. 'Nearly there,' said Rupert as they turned right into Sion Place. When they turned left onto Sion Hill, Alan saw the Clifton Suspension Bridge spanning the Avon Gorge.

Alan was surprised and impressed. Flat 5B Sion Hill was clean and tidy. The furniture was obviously fairly new and probably quite expensive. From the living room window he could see the famous Bristol landmark. The Suspension Bridge was designed by Isambard

Kingdom Brunel in 1831 but only completed and opened for use in 1864, five years after the famous architect died.

Alan wondered how Rupert could afford to live here. Then he remembered. Rupert's mother died when he was quite young. His father - a big noise in Lloyds Bank - died not long ago. 'I've put the kettle on,' said Rupert. 'Coffee or tea?' 'Tea please.' Rupert opened the refrigerator and said, 'I haven't any milk I'm afraid.' 'Black coffee then.' Alan couldn't fail to notice that the 'fridge was empty.

They stood, coffee in hand, looking down at the road map of Bristol. They had each circled their normal sales areas – Rupert's in black and Alan's in blue. 'Wait a minute,' said Alan, pointing to one of Rupert's areas, 'another Kleeneze agent covers this area.'

'Zone!' said Rupert, 'Call it a zone.'

'Alright. Zone. It's not my zone. Another Kleeneze agent does that area - zone.'

'So, we'll concentrate on this zone to start with,' said Rupert, pointing to where the black and blue areas overlapped. With that, he used a red pen to split the 'zone' in two and labelled one half 'A' and the other half 'B'. 'On Monday and Tuesday you cover 'A' and I'll cover 'B'. On Wednesday we'll swap lists. On Thursday and Friday you do my list in zone 'B' and I'll do your list in zone 'A'.'

'What if someone wants to buy my stuff when I'm in zone 'A'?'

'That's your bonus,' said Rupert. 'Just don't forget that you're in zone 'A' Monday and Tuesday to *praise your enemy* – me - who's going to call on them Thursday and Friday.'

'I understand,' said Alan.

'Right. Got to dash. Seeing the girlfriend. Mustn't be late.'

* * * * *

For the rest of Saturday afternoon and most of the evening, Alan studied the map of his area (zone 'A') and planned his route for the

139

coming Monday and Tuesday. At just after 5 o'clock, Rupert met a young lady coming out of Churchills music shop. She had dark curly-hair and an hour-glass figure. At her expense – she had just collected her week's wages - they had tea in a small café before occupying back seats in the Odeon cinema. Neither paid much attention to the films being shown. Rachel did some housework in the morning. In the afternoon she went for a walk across Clifton Downs and posted her letter to Jan. In the evening she listened to some classical music on the radio.

On Sunday Alan went to the morning service and skipped Evensong. In the afternoon he polished his shoes and pressed his trousers. In the evening he had a cup of cocoa with his mother and went to bed early. Rupert stayed in bed until lunchtime to recover from his late night. He treated himself to a Ploughman's lunch at the Albion with the money he'd borrowed the night before then returned to his flat to read the Sunday paper. In the evening he folded his trousers under the mattress and went to bed around 10:30 p.m. Rachel spent most of Sunday sifting through the documents and statements of accounts she had requisitioned from Lloyds Bank.

On Monday and Tuesday, Alan and Rupert put their plan into action. On Wednesday they met at 5B Sion Hill to exchange lists. Both had felt more comfortable not trying to sell their stuff and been quite surprised to have taken more orders than usual. Rupert had a tale to tell.

One rather attractive but not so young lady, wearing little more than a flimsy negligé, had invited him in and draped herself rather unbecomingly across a settee. When he finished his demonstration and asked if she fancied anything he had to offer, she'd said, 'Are you trying to lead me into temptation?' Caught completely off guard for once, Rupert had replied, 'No I'm trying to deliver you from evil, madam,' and hurriedly left the house. 'I put a ring around the number of her place, old boy,' said Rupert as he gave Alan the list for his visit to zone 'B'.

'Thanks,' said Alan, 'forewarned is forearmed.'

On Thursday and Friday, they carried out the second part of their plan and were overwhelmed by its success. Customers welcomed them

140

into their homes with open arms. The orders flowed. By Friday evening their order books were full and their fingers sore from all the writing. On Saturday they celebrated with the Chef's Special lunch at the Albion. 'My treat,' said Alan. Rupert did not protest.

'This week was just the start of better sales to come,' said Rupert. 'Hear, hear! To our future success,' toasted Alan, as they clinked their glasses. 'To better sales to come,' toasted Rupert. And indeed, in the following weeks their sales went from strength to strength. Alan then remembered that he had an order to deliver. 'Must dash,' he said and left, leaving Rupert to settle the bill for once.

* * * * *

'Rose, that nice young Mr. Kleeneze's coming up the path.' She opened the front door before Alan had a chance to ring the bell. They smiled at one another. 'Mum saw you coming,' she said. 'Please come in.' Alfred nodded. Doris beamed and said, 'You'll have a cup of tea?' When she came back from the kitchen, she gave the tray to Rose and said, 'Cut Mr. Kleeneze a piece of cake, Rose.' While the tea was being poured, Alan checked their order. 'Got my shoe cleaning kit, young man?' Alan smiled and said, 'All present and correct, sir.' When they had finished tea, Doris paid for her order with cash from her house-keeping purse. Alan thanked her again, said goodbye to Alfred and followed Rose into the hallway.

'Do you by any chance like ballroom dancing?' he stuttered. 'It's just that there's a public dance at the Victoria Rooms this evening. I wondered if you would like to go.' She turned and called out, 'Mum.' His mouth went dry. 'What is it dear?' said Doris from the sitting room. 'Do you need me this evening?' Doris appeared in the doorway. 'No. Why? Are you going out?' When Rose said she was going ballroom dancing at the Victoria Rooms, Doris beamed at Alan and said, 'What time does it start?'

As they walked down Pembroke Road that evening he said, 'Please don't call me Mr. Kleeneze. My name's Alan.' They danced well together. The band was good but a little loud. So when they weren't on the floor doing a Quickstep, a Foxtrot, a waltz or even a tango (Latin - I touch as Alan remembered from his school days), they sat in a quiet corner and talked.

Actually, it was the normally somewhat reticent Alan who did most of the talking. The evening flew by. Before he realised it, they were dancing the last waltz. And in no time at all they were at the bottom of the path of 48 Pembroke Road.

'It's been a lovely evening,' she said. 'Thank you for taking me. You're a good dancer.' Alan positively glowed. 'So are you. I *am* glad you came. Would you like to go again sometime?' His mouth was starting to go dry. 'I'd love to Alan,' she said. When the front door closed behind her, Alan's heart was pounding and he could still feel the touch of her lips on his cheek.

The next day he went to both the morning service and evensong. At the Manse after the evening service Mrs. Stockport nudged her husband and whispered, 'Alan seems very cheerful tonight.' The Rev. George Stockport whispered back, 'I think it's his new job with Kleeneze. He's out meeting people instead of being stuck in that insurance office.'

* * * * *

Their PYE (Praise Your Enemy) plan went from strength to strength. Every Wednesday they would meet for lunch to exchange lists and swap stories. Rupert usually had some rather salacious yarn to spin. Alan usually reported what Rupert called 'good deeds' like climbing a tree to rescue a customer's cat or taking a woman in labour to the maternity hospital. Both were increasing their commissions. Rupert could put food in his 'fridge and wine bottles in his rack. Alan could treat Bill and Ethel to something special for Sunday tea and put money into his Lloyds savings account. He might have saved more but somehow he always seemed to be landed with the Wednesday lunch bill.

On Saturday morning, one week after he had taken Rose dancing, Alan rang the bell at 48 Pembroke Road. Doris answered the door. 'Oh, hello Alan.'

'I just called to make sure you were satisfied with everything you ordered.'

'Everything's fine. Alfred's really pleased with his shoe cleaning kit and I just love my brushes and polish.'

'That's good. I've made a note to call when you might be running out of polish, if that's alright?'

'Were you hoping to have a word with Rose? She's out doing some shopping for me.'

'Well, I did wonder if she would like to go dancing again.'

'I'm sure she would, dear, but not tonight. She's going out.' When she saw his face, she said, 'Why don't you call her tomorrow? I'll just go a write down our telephone number.'

As he walked away with the number in his pocket, he wondered where Rose was going then told himself it was none of his business. Suddenly a thought struck him. Doris had called him Alan – not Mr. Kleeneze!

Since her visit to Holland, Rachel and Jan had corresponded regularly and frequently with picture postcards of cultural and historical interest. They were pen pals and friends - good friends but nothing more. Rachel's cards were about Bristol but she promised to send cards from Bath and Salisbury one day. Jan's cards came from all over the Netherlands as he travelled to each of the twelve provinces to visit his antique shops.

In the weeks following his weekend in Amsterdam with Kate, Rupert noticed a change in Rachel. He was sure Rachel didn't know about Kate whom he was seeing regularly and more frequently than her. He wondered if Rachel's increasing coolness and reluctance to see him had anything to do with her investigations at his former bank. If it was, then he couldn't stop seeing her until she finished at the bank and he knew he was in the clear. As it happened, she had already connected the name Nicholas Spencer to certain dubious accounts. It was only a matter of time before she identified Rupert as Nicholas Spencer.

* * * * *

On Sunday Alan telephoned as Doris had suggested. 'Hello.' His heart skipped a beat and his mouth went dry. 'Hello, is that you Rose? This is Alan. How are you?'

'I'm fine, thank you Alan. How are you?'

'I'm fine.'

'Mum said you called in yesterday. I'm sorry I wasn't here.'

'So was I – sorry you weren't in I mean. Did you have a nice time?'

'If you mean last Saturday with you, then yes I did. I really did.'

'Would you like to go dancing next Saturday?'

'I'd love to but on one condition.'

'What's that?'

'You let me get the tickets. If you don't then I won't go. Pick me up at 7 o'clock.'

At two minutes to seven, Alan walked up the path and rang the bell. Doris opened the door and called upstairs, 'Alan's here Rose.' As she came down the stairs she looked radiant. 'We won't need your car,' she said, 'we can walk to the Vic' Rooms.' Alan was a little puzzled because he knew that it was a University Student Hop and wondered how Rose managed to get tickets. He was too polite to ask.

When he walked her home after the dance he asked if she would go out with him again. 'I'd love to Alan,' she said. 'Would you like to see Quo Vadis? It's showing at the Gaumont cinema next week.' He beamed and said, 'On one condition – I get the tickets.' She laughed. 'See you next Thursday then.' She kissed him on the cheek and went indoors.

All the way home in his car he was ecstatic. He had already seen Quo Vadis – *whither goest thou* – but he would enjoy seeing it again. Peter Ustinov as Nero won a Golden Globe for best supporting actor. At the ticket kiosk, Alan chose two seats together in the middle of a row near the back of the cinema. When they were seated, he handed Rose a small box of Rowntree's Black Magic chocolates. 'Oh, thank you,' she said. 'I love dark chocolate.'

She opened the box and offered it to Alan. 'No, you first.' She took an orange cream. He had a caramel. Just in time. The lights went down and the film started. When they left the cinema, Alan took hold of her hand as they descended the steps and didn't let go until they reached 48 Pembroke Road. This time on his way home he treasured the touch of her lips on his.

In the weeks that followed, Alan and Rose met regularly not just to go the cinema or ballroom dancing. They visited the museum and art gallery. They went to a concert at the Colston Hall and an opera at the Hippodrome. They took walks across Clifton Downs. They took a boat ride up the river to Keynsham for afternoon tea. It was just after their last outing – to the Theatre Royal in King Street – that things started to go wrong.

They saw the Bristol Old Vic production of John Steinbeck's Of Mice and Men. As they left the two-hundred year-old theatre building, Alan recalled that the title of the play was taken from Ode to a Field Mouse - a poem by the Scottish poet, Robert Burns. 'Yes, you're right,' said Rose. 'it's from the seventh verse.'

> But Mousie, thou art no thy lane,
> In proving foresight may be vain:
> The best laid schemes o' mice an' men
> Gang aft agley.
> An' lea'e us nought but grief an' pain,
> For promis'd joy!

* * * * *

The sleet had turned to hail. The icy beads danced on the front of the car and glittered in the beam from the security lamp over the rear

145

doorway of the church. The hailstones on the car roof provided a kind of musical accompaniment to the ballet of the bouncing ice. Alan knew he couldn't stay in the car much longer but his mind filled with the thoughts of those two life-changing weeks as he recalled the words from the Church of England Book of Common Prayer – The Burial of the Dead

> *Man that is born of woman hath but a short time to live, and is full of misery. He cometh up, and is cut down, like a flower; he fleeth as it were a shadow, and never continueth in one stay.*

* * * * *

When she entered the living room, Bill seemed to be asleep in his chair with his hands resting on the newspaper. Ethel saw his pipe lying on the floor at his feet and knew straight away that something was wrong. 'It was a heart attack,' Dr Pollard told them. 'It probably happened when he was taking a nap. He went peacefully.'

Alan arranged for the Rev. George Stockport to conduct the simple service at the crematorium and invited the few relatives and friends present to come back to the house for a cup of tea and a sandwich. Needless to say, on Monday and Tuesday of that week Alan did not cover his zone 'A' and on Wednesday he told Rupert why not.

'My condolences, old boy. How's your mother bearing up?' Then after what he thought was a suitable pause, he said, 'Here's your zone 'B' list for tomorrow.'

The same week that Bill passed away, the phone rang in Rachel's office. 'Good afternoon. May I speak with Miss Rachel Wallace please.'

'Speaking. Who is this?'

'Rachel? That is you?'

'Yes.'

'This is Lies. I am speaking from Schiedam.'

146

'What is it Lies? You sound upset. What's wrong?'

After a silence that seemed to last an eternity instead of a few seconds, Elise sobbed, 'It's terrible. Piet en zijn vader hebben een ongeluk gekregen.'

'Lies, I don't understand. What's happened?'

'Oh, ja, sorry. Piet and Johannes had a car accident. Piet was driving. Now he is in the hospital. His leg is broken and our hearts are broken.'

'What about Jan? Elise! Is Jan alright?'

The small 17th century Dutch Reformed Church overflowed. Close and distant relatives. Friends and neighbours. Members of the World War II resistance. People with whom he did business. People from the many charities he supported. People whom he befriended. All his employees from the twelve provincial antique shops – closed for the day. Everyone present was there to pay homage to the man they admired, loved and respected - Johannes van Dijk.

Piet hobbled into the pulpit and delivered a heart-rending eulogy. Elise gripped Rachel's hand as their eyes welled with tears. Flying out of Schipol airport back to England that evening, she opened the package Piet and Elise had given her. Inside was an envelope on which was written *for Rachel* in Jan's handwriting. Tears filled her eyes when she opened the envelope and saw the eleven postcards of Vincent van Gogh's Sun Flower paintings.

Rachel spent Friday in her office finalising her report on her investigations at Lloyds Bank. She was now saddened not only by the passing of her dear pen friend but also by the evidence of Rupert's role in the unscrupulous misappropriation of funds. There were those skilfully changed cheques:

Eight Thousand Pounds £8000
changed into
Eighty Thousand Pounds £80000

There were all those mortgages and account statements for people whose names she'd traced to old headstones in Arnos Vale cemetery. And there were those transfers to Swiss accounts in the name of Nicholas R. Spencer. The theft was large scale and bound to carry a heavy prison sentence. She would have to give her head of department the report on Monday. She locked it away in her filing cabinet and left the office for the weekend.

* * * * *

Alan gave what time he could spare to the list Rupert gave him for zone 'B'. Almost every visit he made yielded a substantial order even though his thoughts were elsewhere. On Saturday morning, he delivered his previous week's orders as quickly as possible then headed to George's Bookshop at the top of Park Street.

He said he'd come but Kate knew he might not. She stayed behind the counter and skipped her lunch break for fear she might miss him. She'd told him today was his last chance. She had just finished serving a customer when Rupert walked in. Kate rushed from behind the counter.

Through the window of George's bookshop Alan spotted Rupert, a short distance down the hill on the other side of Park Street, entering Churchill's Music Shop. He paid for his two books by John Steinbeck – the Grapes of Wrath and East of Eden – then hurried over to the music shop.

As he stepped inside and closed the door, he saw the dark-haired shop assistant kiss Rupert on the cheek and lead him across the showroom to the piano – a Steinway & Sons Concert Grand according to the display panel alongside it. 'Play something for me,' said Kate. 'This is your last chance. When we close at five, they're loading this piano and delivering it to the maestro's home before he's back from his Amsterdam recital.'

Rupert sat down and played a few bars of Rodgers and Hart's The Lady is a Tramp. She laughed and playfully slapped his arm.

148

Alan walked briskly over to the piano and in a clipped tone barked, 'Begin the Beguine if you please, Corporal Coleman,'

Rupert grinned at him, played two bars then stopped. 'Sorry,' he said, 'bit rusty.'

Kate took the music from the Chappell & Co. Ltd. display in the window and put it on the piano stand in front of Rupert, saying, 'No more excuses, Ru. Here's the score.'

After the four bars of introduction, Alan, standing to Rupert's right, started singing, 'when they begin the Beguine...'

'Nice voice,' said Rupert without taking his eyes off the music. Kate, standing to Rupert's left, smiled at Alan and at the appropriate moment leant across and turned the page.

'I'm with you once more under the stars,' Alan sang.

Kate gave Rupert an adoring look as she leant over to turn the page. He smiled and winked at Alan as the music changed to the minor key.

'And there we are,' sang Alan, 'swearing to love for-ever...'

Customers gathered to listen. Rachel had entered the shop just as Kate turned the second page. She remained partly hidden behind three or four customers standing at the door. When she saw the curly, dark-haired, buxom girl kiss Rupert as she leant over to turn the third page, Rachel frowned and bit her lip.

'That's the girl I saw with Rupert at the Concertgebouw in Amsterdam,' she said to herself. When Kate put her arm around Rupert's neck, Rachel turned and left the shop as quietly as she could.

Out of the corner of his eye Alan saw the door open. He turned to look. As the door closed he got a glimpse of Rachel's long, fair hair as she left the shop. '... till clouds come along to disperse the joys we had tasted ...'

149

At the end of the song Alan held the final note for the full four bars and Rupert finished with a flourishing glissando. The two men bowed to acknowledge the applause and Kate gave Rupert another big hug and kiss.

* * * * *

As she left Churchill's music shop and headed up the hill to George's Bookshop on the other side of the road at the top of Park Street, she knew what she'd have to do. The main window displayed a collection of books by John Steinbeck. Two books caught her eye and drew her into the shop. 'I'd like these two, please.'

'Oh,' said the assistant, 'Of Mice and Men. Wasn't that on at the Old Vic recently? Ah, I see this is the book. We do have the three-act play if you'd like that as well.'

When he checked the price on the other book, he said, 'Once There Was A War – it's Steinbeck's latest. I found it fascinating. It's a collection of humane and hard-hitting dispatches he filed for the New York Tribune in the Second World War. I'm sure you'll enjoy them.'

She smiled. 'I'm sure my father will. The book's for him.' He put the books and her receipt in a bag.

As he handed her the bag and her change, he said, 'Well you'll enjoy Of Mice and Men.' She smiled again and said, 'That's for my boy friend.'

Kate planted a parting kiss on Rupert's neck and went back behind the counter leaving him talking to Alan. 'Did you pick up plenty of orders this week from that list I gave you?'

'Yes. Even more than last week. What about you?'

'Same here. Another good week. You know which zones we're doing this coming week?'

'I think so. Zones 'A5' and 'B5'. Yes I'm sure.'

'That was good thinking, Alan – marking and labelling all the zones in one go.'

'Must be off. See you for lunch next Wednesday.'

When Alan had left, Rupert strolled over to the counter. 'What time this evening?'

'About half past six. I want to wash my hair first.'

'Why not do that at my place?'

'You haven't got the shampoo I use.'

'That's a poor excuse. Suit yourself. See you at six thirty.'

Rupert spotted Rachel coming out of George's and hurried to catch her up. When she heard his voice, she stopped and turned around. The first thing she noticed was the patch of red lipstick on the left side of his neck. He knew something was up when she didn't return his smile. 'Been buying me a present?' he asked. She didn't even nod or shake her head. 'Fancy a cup of tea?'

This time she nodded. 'Better get it over with,' she thought to herself. They found a table in the corner of the café & pastry shop in Queens Road. When the lady behind the counter asked what they wanted, Rachel said, 'You'll have to pay today, Rupert. I've just spent all my spare money on books.' Then seeing the notes in his bulging wallet, she said, 'By the way, I think it's about time you paid me back the money you owe me, don't you?'

When they left the café, Rachel turned left and walked towards the Victoria Rooms. Rupert turned right and headed back down Park Street. She was relieved, relaxed and considerably richer. He was anxious, tense and considerably poorer. She would have no qualms about handing in her report on Monday. That was the last they would see of each other.

When Kate saw Rupert that evening, she learned about his involvement in shady dealings at Lloyds and about Rachel. Love can turn so easily into hate. He could steal. He could take her hard-earned

151

money. He could be fickle. Kate didn't care. But he could not tell her he'd been seeing another woman and then pretend this Rachel meant nothing to him. Kate stormed out of his flat and that was the last she saw of Rupert.

First thing on Monday morning, Rachel handed her report to her boss – the head of the Inland Revenue Investigation Department in Prince Street. 'Everything alright?' he asked. 'Never felt better,' she replied.

First thing on Monday morning, Alan took his mother to Temple Meads station to catch the train to Torquay. 'I don't like leaving you on your own, dear,' Ethel said. 'A few days by the seaside will do you the world of good, Mum,' he said. 'Don't you worry about me. Safe journey and give my love to Aunty Ruby.'

On Monday and Tuesday Alan did zone 'A5' without having to worry about his mother being in the house on her own. On Wednesday he met an unusually subdued Rupert at the Albion for lunch. 'Cheer up,' said Alan, 'it may never happen.'

'I'm afraid it already has, old boy.'

'What are you talking about?'

'No time to explain now. It's just that... well to be honest, I'm packing in this sales lark.'

'What! Why? It's going great guns.'

'Like I said, can't explain now. I've got to go away. Get away from here.'

'Why? Where are you going? How long are you going for?'

'Not sure where I'm going yet. Don't know how long for either. Might not be up to me.'

'Well that puts the tin lid on it.'

'Sorry, old boy, if this puts you in a spot.'

'The best laid schemes of mice and men gang aft agley,' murmured Alan

'What? Oh, yes – Rabbie Burns.'

'Anyway, what'll you do for money?'

'Bit of luck there. An uncle died and left me eighty thousand quid.'

'Crikey,' said Alan, '£80,000! You lucky blighter.'

'Look,' said Rupert, handing Alan a fiver, 'lunch on me today. It's been nice knowing you. Look after yourself and don't do anything I wouldn't do.'

Alan guessed that was the last he'd see of Rupert.

Early on Saturday afternoon he met Ethel at the station. She looked well. 'I'll make us a nice cup of tea, dear,' she said as they stepped inside the front door. Alan took her suitcase upstairs then joined her in the kitchen. 'Everything alright, dear?'

He took a deep breath and said, 'I'm packing in Kleeneze, Mum.' Ethel smiled and said, 'I'm sure you know best.'

Alan said, 'Yes, Mum, I do,' and smiled.

'Are you seeing your young lady this evening?'

Alan relaxed. 'Yes, Mum, I am. Is that alright? You won't mind being on your own?'

She sighed and said, 'No. I'll be fine. I've lots to do. Bill wouldn't want me sitting around moping. I'll miss him, you know, but I've got photos to look at and lots of lovely memories. You go on and enjoy yourself. You're only young once.'

* * * * *

'There's that young man of yours coming up the path,' Doris called out.

'It's Alan,' said Alfred. 'Go and let him in Doris. I'd like to show him my book.'

As she opened the door, Doris called out again, 'Rose, it's Alan. Get a move on or your dad will keep him talking for ages.'

He just had time to wave hello to Alfred before Rose rushed down the stairs and hurried him out of the house. 'You look more beautiful than ever,' he said.

'So do you,' she said with a laugh.' Alan loved the way she laughed. Nothing false about it. It was a sincere laugh. The laugh of a lovely and loving woman.

They first found a quiet corner away from the band where they could talk when they sat out a dance. Alan usually did most of the talking and realised that Rose knew far more about him than he about her. She knew, of course, he was a door-to-door salesman but he didn't know what she did for a living. She never talked about her work.

He knew she'd been in the Sixth Form at The Red Maids' School – Doris had shown him a photo of her in her red uniform – and had taken English and History. Alan took Latin and English. This evening he resolved to hold his tongue. 'Something to drink?'

She smiled. 'Let's have some wine this evening.'

When he arrived back with two glasses of wine, white for her and red for him, there was a small parcel on the little table. 'It's a present,' she said.

'Wine and now this. What's the occasion, Rose?' The band started to play.

'Open it in a minute,' she said. 'Let's dance.'

Back in their quiet corner, she raised her glass and said, 'To the future!' They klinked glasses. 'To the future,' said Alan. 'Now what's going on?'

154

The band struck up and she said, 'In a minute. I'll tell you in a minute.'

During the dance Alan told her that he was leaving Kleeneze. He told her about Rupert and his Praise Your Enemy plan. He told her how well it worked but how uneasy he felt about it. Then he said, 'If it hadn't been for Rupert and his PYE plan I may never have met you, Rose. I shall always be grateful to him for that.' The music stopped and they went back to their seats.

'May I open my present now?'

'Yes, dear, of course. I hope you like it.'

'Of Mice and Men – and it's the book not the play. Thank you so much, Rose.'

'Please Alan, would you mind not calling me Rose? My parents call me that because my middle name is Rosina – my grandmother's first name. I prefer my first name.'

'Sorry, I never realised you didn't like to be called Rose. So what do I call you?'

'Rachel. Please call me Rachel.'

'Not Rupert's girl? Surely not?'

'Once upon a time I may have imagined I was his girl friend. But he was never really my boy friend. And I *never* belonged to him – *not ever*.' Then for the first time in her life she was telling him things she had never told any young man, all the while afraid she might drive him away.

She did Mathematics as well as English and History at Red Maids; three A-levels not just two. '*Een knap meisje*.' She went to Bristol University and graduated with honours in Economics. '*Ja, een knap meisje*.' She worked for the Inland Revenue and had been investigating criminal activities at Lloyds Bank.

155

When she paused for breath, Alan, wide-eyed said, 'Crikey. In Queens Road? Rupert worked there once. Was he involved?'

'I'm afraid so but I can't discuss it.' Then the band started playing. 'Oh, Cole Porter. It's a tango.' As she got up from her seat, she said, 'Alan, it's only fair to tell you. I've fallen deeply in love.'

Alan put his right arm around her waist. Rachel took hold of his left hand. Then off they went, moving together as one to the rhythm of the music. Tango, tangere, tetigi, tactum – Latin to touch. Tangimus – We touch. As they danced, Alan sang softly into her ear, 'Strange dear, but true dear, when I'm close to you dear, the stars fill the sky...'

Then Rachel joined in. 'So in love with you am I.'

* * * * *

The sleet hadn't stopped when Alan opened the car door and made a dash for the back door into the church.

* * * * *

The evening service began as usual with a bidding prayer.

Let us pray. Let us pray for the needs of the whole world.
Let us remember those who have lost a loved one this year.
May they know peace that only You can give. Grant that our
prayers draw us closer to You and closer to those for whom we
pray. We ask this in the name of Thy Son, Jesus Christ Our
Lord. Amen.

The congregation sang the first hymn and then sat down to hear the notices. The organist played the introduction to the second hymn. The congregation rose and began to sing as the minister walked slowly up the steps into the pulpit.

The hymn ended and the congregation settled into their seats. 'In the name of the Father, the Son and the Holy Ghost,' said the minister. 'Amen,' everyone said. 'My text for this evening is taken from the New Testament. Matthew - Chapter 22 - verses 36 to 40.'

"Teacher, which is the greatest commandment in the Law?" Jesus replied: " 'Love the Lord your God with all your heart and with all your soul and with all your mind.' This is the first and greatest commandment. And the second is like it: 'Love your neighbour as yourself.' All the Law and the Prophets hang on these two commandments"

The Reverend Alan 'Chalky' White paused and surveyed the congregation filling the church. When he saw Rachel Rosina, his beautiful, intelligent, pregnant wife, sitting alongside Ethel, his widowed mother, Alan smiled and began his sermon.

* * * * *

Epilogue

None of the characters bears an intentional resemblance to anyone living or dead – and that includes my friend John. I first created Rachel Wallace and Johannes van Dijk to appear in my story The Journey of a Canvas Bag. Like their thoughts, words and deeds, all the characters in this story are imaginary.

The geographical locations in which I have set their fictitious actions and the history, literature and music are real but they are drawn from memory and therefore liable to errors for which I accept full responsibility.

The bronze statue of Edmund Burke is still there in Bristol - my home town. His marble statue, at the south end of Westminster Hall in the House of Commons in London, is by William Theed. The Inland Revenue may no longer have offices in Prince Street and may never have had an Investigation Department with powers to pry behind the mighty doors of Lloyds Bank Ltd – now Lloyds TSB Bank Plc.

The Victoria Rooms housed the Student Union when I was at the University of Bristol. The Baptist Church was on the corner of East Street. There was a manse in Ackerman's Road and The Reverend George W. Sterry was a major influence on my life. It was George who advised John to stay out of the ministry if he could.

Pembroke Road and Sion Hill are real places in Bristol but the numbered locations given for where Rachel and Rupert lived are imaginary. The same goes for the home in Schiedam of my fictitious character Johannes van Dijk.

I was about to begin a year of post-graduate research in the Netherlands when I first saw Ossip Zadkine's statue Stad Zonder Hart in Rotterdam. I was moved by the statue and took the following photograph on the 14th of August 1954.

158

Eduard Flipse, the director of the Rotterdam Philharmonic, laid the first stone for the concert hall on the Schouwburgplein on the 9th July 1962. The first concert was performed there on the 18th May 1966. Flipse died in Breda on the 12th September 1973.

WHAT ARE THE CHANCES?

Certain people and chance events change our lives. They make us reconsider our beliefs, discard our old habits and gain a new sense of purpose and direction. This true story is about my father and an event that achieved quite the opposite. It gives credence to the adage 'Old habits die hard' and, dare I say it, to the adage 'You can't teach an old dog new tricks.' In regard to the first, I fear that I follow in my father's footsteps. Incidentally, on the North American continent a petrol cap is called a gas(oline) cap.

* * * * *

Saturday

After lunch my dad told us he was going to see the 'Robins' at Ashton Gate. The kick-off was at three o'clock. Bristol City FC (Football Club) was known locally by their nickname because the players wore bright red jerseys when they were playing at home. *Up the Robins* in those days was not derogatory but a loud shout of support. The 'City Ground' was about a mile from our house in Greville Road – a 20-minute walk away. Dad did not ask me to go with him. He knew I did not like football or walking.

At Merrywood Grammar School For Boys, I was ordered onto a soccer pitch every Wednesday afternoon, every winter and spring term, for five years. *Mens sana in corpore sano*! In my football shirt, shorts, socks (with shin pads tucked therein) and boots, I would take up my position as 'right back' and hope the ball never came my way. Whenever it did, I booted it to the other end of the field. Dad admired my strong kick but not my unwillingness to run around and get my boots muddy.

Dad loved football. In his youth he played in a league and his team were champions one season. I still have his inscribed silver medal:

KEMP BROS
UNION ST BRISTOL
B.T.S.L.
CHAMPIONS
R.M.I. DIV II
1925-6
C.H.COX

Dad always came to see me play cricket for the school – I gained my colours as a Junior, Under-XIII and 1st XI – and as captain for the Bristol Schools XI. Looking back, I'm sure he would have preferred to watch me play football for the school. And to my regret, I'm sure he would have liked me to have gone with him to see the match that Saturday.

'What time are you leaving, Charlie?' my step-mother, Rose, asked.

'2 o'clock. Why?'

'Just wanted to know,' she said, giving me a conspiratorial look.

As soon as he was out of the front door, Rose said, 'What time do you think he'll be back?'

'I don't know. Match starts at 3 o'clock and lasts 90 minutes. There's an interval of 15 minutes. 10 minutes to get out of the ground and 20 minutes to walk home. I suppose he could be home by a quarter past five.'

'Play safe. Say 5 o'clock. We've got three hours.'

'What for?' I asked, guessing it was her 'royal we' and the three hours were mine alone.

'To clear out that cupboard,' she said, pointing through the window of our back room.

'Dad's junk hole in the conservatory?'

'Yes. I've got hold of some empty cardboard boxes. Put the rubbish in those and put anything worth keeping back in the cupboard. If we wait for your dad to sort out his junk, we'll be here till kingdom come.'

What my dad had in that cupboard was, as I recall, mostly junk. It is sixty years ago since I opened that cupboard on that Saturday afternoon. I remember it was full when I started and almost empty when I finished. One shelf groaned under the weight of tobacco tins filled with assorted nuts, bolts, nails and screws – all mixed in together! There was a collection of old rusty tools; several different saws, pliers and hammers – one was a panel beater's hammer which I am sure my dad never put to its intended use. I specifically remember an old spokeshave. It was blunt, very blunt, but this small two-handled plane did not get that way by my dad making wooden chair legs or spokes for a farm cart.

Another shelf was bent under the weight of paint tins whose contents varied from nearly full to practically empty. With few

163

exceptions, the contents were solid and unusable. One or two jars were filled with brushes whose hairs were locked in a permanent embrace with the viscous linseed oil stuck to the bottom. In addition to the spokeshave, I remember quite specifically a grease gun, an oil can and a petrol cap for a car.

Rose put her head around the conservatory door and hissed, 'Quick. Your dad's back.'

'Just finished,' I said, 'closing the cupboard door.'

'Good game?' we asked. Our first mistake. He knew we weren't interested in football.

'We won for a change.' Then my dad saw us looking at one another. 'What have you two been up to?'

'Nothing, Charlie. Nothing. Fancy some bacon, egg and sausages for tea?'

'You've been up to something, I can tell.'

'I'll make a cup of tea. Would you lay the table, please, Mike?' she said, hurrying into the kitchen.

Dad took off his coat and hung it on the hook out in the hallway. When he came back into the room he must have seen, through the window, the boxes in the conservatory. The next we knew, he was out there opening the door and finding his cupboard almost empty but very tidy. Then he went for the cardboard boxes. Rose took him out a cup of tea and said, 'I asked our Mike to tidy that cupboard and throw away the junk. Don't get worked up. Drink your tea while it's hot.' Dad drank his tea, put his cup and saucer on the window sill and opened one of the boxes.

'This isn't junk,' he said, 'taking out a shiny black petrol cap. Nothing wrong with this. It might come in handy one day.'

'C.H.,' I said, 'we haven't got a car. You don't want a car. According to you, we can't afford a car. And even if we could, you reckon we couldn't afford to run it.'

164

'Yes, I know. But there's nothing wrong with this petrol cap. It's as good as new.'

'Dad, anybody who's got a car – a black car that this petrol cap will fit – can afford to buy a petrol cap if they lose one. Anyway, it's a screw cap, so who's going to lose one?'

'Food's ready,' called out Rose. Dad put the petrol cap in his cupboard and we went back into the house to eat.

Sunday

Dad spent the morning in the conservatory unpacking the cardboard boxes and putting most of his stuff back in his cupboard. I spent the morning in my room studying. Rose cleared away and washed up the breakfast things then read the Sunday paper before getting lunch. Early in the afternoon from my little study/bedroom I heard the front door bell. Shortly afterwards, Rose called up the stairs to say it was Jane at the door.

When I came downstairs, Jane was telling Rose and Dad that she had passed her driving test. This Sunday was the first time she had been out in the car on her own. Her father was usually with her because he taught her to drive. It was his car she was driving. We all trooped outside to see the 1939 Ford Prefect – licence plate GGK 446.

The car was black and shiny, in immaculate condition inside and out. It was brand new when her father bought it just before we declared war on Germany. It still looked brand new. The mileage on the clock was low because they hadn't been able to drive it during the war – severe petrol rationing – and because her father now only used it for pleasure on Sundays or holidays.

'So,' I said, 'this is your car now, is it?'

'No,' said Jane, 'it's my dad's. I couldn't afford to run it even if I could buy it off him.'

'Is he selling it then?

'Yes. He's had it long enough. He wants a new one.'

'How much does he want for it?' I asked.

'Why? Do you want to buy it?'

'I'd like to. I passed my test last year and I'm hoping to go to the States next year. I'd like to keep in practice.'

'I'd have to ask but I'm pretty sure my dad wants ninety pounds.'

To cut this long story short, Rose and I persuaded my dad to share the cost with me - £45 each. At this point I should mention that my dad was a very good and very experienced driver. He drove for a living. He began by driving a small oil lorry (or truck as it's called in North America). Then for many years he drove double decker buses. So, Jane had no hesitation in letting my dad drive us all to her house. Her mother made us a nice cup of tea while we made whatever arrangements were necessary with Jane's dad to pay for the car.

Monday

By the lunchtime, GGK 446 was parked in the road outside of our house in Greville Road. It was my dad's pride and joy. He cleaned and polished it. I looked forward to driving it to the university. I should mention here that traffic was very light in those days and parking not the serious problem it is now. That evening when my dad walked home from work – actually from the bus stop at the top of the road - we walked around our car with, I believe, a certain pride of possession. It was sixty years ago, so I cannot say for certain who spotted it first but I think it was my dad. 'The petrol cap's gone! Somebody's pinched our petrol cap!'

The rest of the story I'm sure, dear reader, you can guess. The petrol cap that my dad had taken out of the cardboard box of junk and put back in his cupboard was a shiny black petrol cap. It was also a screw cap. And it fitted GGK perfectly! From that moment on, there was nothing Rose could say to persuade my dad to throw away anything.

* * * * *

166

Epilogue

When I got married, my wife and I lived upstairs above my parents in Greville Road. We had converted my little study/bedroom into a kitchen and the front bedroom into a lounge. I bought dad's share of the car and we kept it locked safely away in a small garage at the top of the road. One year after we were married, my wife and I took GGK to Holland for a three-week camping holiday. When I took up a three-year appointment as a lecturer in educational research at Aberdeen College in Scotland, we sold the car – complete with the self-same petrol cap that dad once hoarded - in part-exchange for a newer model.

When my dad retired, he and Rose moved to the outskirts of Weston-Super-Mare to a small bungalow with its own garage. His cupboard of junk went with them. When my dad died, Rose asked me to sort out my dad's garage – she never learnt to drive – so it was my dad's garage, not theirs. The cupboard was full – mostly of junk that needed to be ditched. The problem was that I had inherited my dad's hoarding habit. With a sad heart and a head full of memories, I gritted my teeth and did Rose's bidding.

The spokeshave and any other half-decent woodworking tools went to a neighbour who would clean them and put them to good use. The tins of assorted nails and screws went to my garage. I left them behind, sorted and labelled, when we moved to Canada. The grease gun and oil can? They are sitting on a shelf in our garage in Edmonton, Alberta, patiently waiting to be used. Old habits die hard, dear reader.

A MIXED BLESSING

This story is a confession of a crime I committed out of false pride and in a moment of weakness more than forty years ago. By now both the statute of limitations and the statute of repose have probably run out and the long arm of the law in England is unlikely to reach across the Atlantic Ocean to Canada but, to be on the safe side, I ask you to believe the name of my victim and the associated geographical details to be pure fiction.

* * * * *

My father left school when he was fourteen. My mother left my father and me when I was ten. Her parting shot, when I determined to stay with my father, was that I, like him, would never amount to anything. So you can imagine my father's pride when I passed the eleven-plus examination to go to a grammar school. For most people, 1945 meant the end of World War II. For my father it meant the beginning of my seven years at Merrywood Grammar School For Boys.

To prove my mother wrong and to make my father proud, I worked hard and was more successful than I might otherwise have been. Every year I was awarded the class prize for academic achievement. Every annual speech day my proud father was there in the audience to applaud as I went onto the platform to collect my book. At my seventh speech day I was called onto the platform twice; first to receive the chemistry prize and secondly to receive the award of a University Open Scholarship.

Three years later, on the platform of the Great Hall, the Dean of the Faculty of Science in all his academic finery said, "Mr. Vice-Chancellor, I present to you Candidates to whom the Degree of Bachelor of Science has been duly awarded with Honours." The Vice-Chancellor, Sir Philip Morris, KCMG, CBE, MA, LLD, FRCS, ARCVS, replied, "By the authority of the University of Bristol, in virtue of the power vested in my office, I admit the Candidates so presented to the Degree of Bachelor of Science with Honours."

When I stepped onto the platform, wearing a rented mortar board, hood and gown which incidentally hid my dark suit – my one and only suit of any colour that I didn't rent but actually bought for the occasion - it was my father's proudest moment and the last time he would see me on such a platform.

A British Council Scholarship allowed me to undertake my first year of post-graduate research in The Netherlands in the van't Hoff Laboratorium of Utrecht University. It was there that I met Ron or, to give him his proper title at that time, Dr R H Ottewill. He was on a sabbatical term from the famous Colloid Science Laboratories at Free School Lane in Cambridge.

During our lunchtime strolls along the Catharijnesingel, a waterway near the laboratory, I learned that Ron had gained a First Class Honours degree and a Ph.D. at London University before moving to Cambridge University on a Nuffield Foundation Research Fellowship. He left London as *Doctor* Ottewill and, with another chemist - his wife Dr Ingrid Ottewill – arrived in Cambridge as *Mister* Ottewill.

Allow me at this point to explain the difference between a *proper* doctor and a *real* doctor. Ron was a *proper* doctor. He had been admitted to the degree of Doctor of Philosophy at the University of London. He was *not a real* doctor. He was not a Bachelor of Medicine registered with the General Medical Council to practice medicine. He could not sport an unbuttoned white coat, hang a stethoscope around his neck and scrawl illegible prescriptions for the sick. He was not one of the many GPs (General Practitioners) we customarily and traditionally address as Doctor even though they are not *academically* entitled to be so addressed.

Ron *was* entitled to be called Doctor Ottewill. If Ron had been a *real* doctor he might have been pleased to be called Mister Ottewill in Cambridge. Why? Because he would have joined the ranks of the medical elite and become a consultant surgeon entitled to wear a three-piece grey pin-striped suit, entitled to scare hospital registrars (junior doctors) by peering at them over half-moon spectacles and entitled to cause all female nurses – with the exception of matron – to blush whenever he appeared in their ward.

Ron was by nature modest and unassuming. Nevertheless, it rankled him to be addressed as Mr Ottewill just because he had a PhD from London and not a PhD from Cambridge. Ron soon discovered that his research as a Nuffield Fellow could, subject to *certain conditions*, form the basis of a doctoral thesis. And indeed it did. After three years at Cambridge, Ron acquired his second doctorate and became R H Ottewill BSc PhD (London) PhD (Cantab).

One of those *certain conditions* required him to live in approved accommodation and to be in by 10:30 every evening. So for three years Ron and Ingrid lived in a rented flat (apartment) which the university inspected and approved. And during those three years Ingrid, officially designated Ron's landlady, was responsible for seeing that he was not out after 10:30 p.m. 'That was the only period in our lives when I was *officially* in charge and could tell my husband what to do,' said Ingrid.

Ronald Harry Ottewill went on to become an eminent chemist and Fellow of the Royal Society. Professor R H Ottewill, OBE BSc PhD PhD CChem FRSC FRS - Ron to me, to his friends and to his colleagues - died on the 4th of June 2008 at the age of 80.

Inspired by Ron to become a proper doctor, I completed my second and third year of research in Bristol where I submitted my doctoral thesis. My Viva Voce examination was conducted the day before I sailed for the USA where I remained for one year. To my father's bitter disappointment I was still in California on a Fulbright Travel Scholarship when the Dean of the Faculty of Science might have said, "Mr. Vice-Chancellor, I present to you Michael Charles Cox, Bachelor of Science of this University, to whom the Degree of Doctor of Philosophy has been duly awarded." Instead, he actually said, "Mr. Vice-Chancellor, I commend to you [*at which point he read out names from a list that included my name*] to be admitted 'in absentia' to the Degree of Doctor of Philosophy." My father was denied the opportunity to applaud his son stepping onto the platform as Mr Cox and stepping off as Dr Cox.

What, you may ask, has all this got to do with confessing my crime? It is, as a defending barrister might have submitted, '*the background needed to establish the state of mind of the defendant at the time when the crime, with which he has been charged, is said to have been committed.*' From the age of eleven I was encouraged to work hard and be proud of my achievements. At the age of twenty-five, after fourteen years of study, I was awarded a PhD and entitled to be called Dr Cox. I was a *proper* doctor and *proud* to be one.

* * * * *

At the end of my year of post-doctoral research at the University of Southern California in Los Angeles, I returned to Bristol to take the University's one-year post-graduate course in education (PGCE), to become a qualified teacher, to get a job and to get married. My fiancée was already qualified and in her first year of teaching in Bristol when

172

Roger Wilson, the Professor of Education and my tutor, asked me if I should be interested to teach at Bristol Grammar School. I smiled when I said yes because at the tender age of eleven and to the bitter disappointment of my father and myself, I failed the preliminary entrance exam for that ancient school founded in 1532!

One Friday morning in the autumn of 1959, the headmaster, Mr John Garrett, MA (Eng. Lit. Exeter College, Oxford) informally interviewed me from behind his large desk in his large oak-panelled study. He addressed me throughout as *Mister* Cox and frequently drew attention to my *provincial* background. 'The young fellow I shall be seeing this afternoon was, unfortunately, born and bred in Cornwall but fortunately had the good sense to be educated at Cambridge,' Mr Garrett confided.

When the interview was almost at an end, Mr Garrett asked me if I had any questions to ask him. My task that weekend was to compose my first full-blown essay as part of the PGCE course, so I asked what in his opinion were the aims of education. He slumped back in his chair, clapped his hand to his forehead and exclaimed, 'I should have asked you that.'

I listened carefully hoping for some useful points for my essay entitled, as you have no doubt guessed, *The Aims of Education*. When he finished I stood up to leave.

'Well,' he said, 'Have I passed?'

'No!' I replied, looking down at him still slumped in his large leather chair behind his large desk.

'No!' he said incredulously. 'Why not?'

'You didn't answer my question. You talked about the purpose of a grammar school. I asked you for the aims of education. The two are not the same.'

As we shook hands at the door of his study, Mr Garrett warmly complimented me on my tie. When I explained that it was hand-woven in pure wool in Scotland and a gift from my fiancée, he seemed to sigh as he queried, 'From your fiancée?'

'Yes,' I replied. 'We are getting married when I have completed my PGCE course. Next August as a matter of fact. On Saturday the 6th of August 1960 to be precise.' I may be mistaken but I thought the life-long bachelor seemed somewhat crestfallen at my news.

When I re-entered the headmaster's study the following Monday morning to be offered the post of assistant chemistry master, Mr Garrett said, 'Do you know, *Mister* Cox, what that wretched Cornishman asked me last Friday afternoon when I asked him if he had any questions?' I shook my head. 'He wanted to know how many points up on the Burnham scale his salary would be!' I gave Mr Garrett my best look of sympathetic horror and made a mental note to rectify my ignorance. I had never before heard of this Burnham Scale and during my interview, the question of salary had never entered my head. I also mentally concluded that my PhD would never cut any ice with *Mister* John Garrett.

After our marriage (reported in the Bristol Evening Post in a small column carrying my wife's photograph under the caption *Doctor's Bride*) and our honeymoon in Paris, my wife and I returned to Bristol, our home town. Maureen started her second year as a full-time teacher and I began my first of three years as a chemistry teacher at The Grammar School. Actually I was obliged also to teach some physics which I knew something about, to teach some biology about which I knew very little and to umpire, often on a wet and windy day, some hockey or rugby; two games which I have never understood and still have no desire to play.

When I joined the staff in September 1960, Mr Garrett, still a bachelor, had retired and been replaced by Dr John Mackay (DPhil - Merton College, Oxford); a charming man with a charming wife called Margaret. The second proper doctor on the staff was David Dickinson, the Head of Mathematics. The third and only other proper doctor was myself.

Discipline was never a problem for anybody at the school but I do believe my being referred to as *Doctor* Cox by the headmaster, the staff

174

and the students was a factor in helping me maintain a calm atmosphere in my classroom and laboratory. I seemed to command respect from my students even though I never wore a three-piece pin-striped suit nor glared at them over half-moon spectacles. And I was, to be honest, getting quite fond of hearing *doctor* in front of my name. The PhD was beginning to be a blessing. However...

At some point during my first year of teaching, I and my colleagues were obliged to attend a parents' evening. This was a strictly formal occasion. We all wore academic black gowns and colourful hoods over our best suits. Our nameplates were mounted high on the oak panelled walls of the great hall and we sat beneath them to await any parents who might wish to see us. The high vaulted ceiling, the stained glass windows and the hushed voices around the hall created a religious atmosphere more befitting a state funeral being held in a cathedral.

While waiting patiently for my first parent, I tried unsuccessfully to eavesdrop on the whispered conversations of a nearby senior colleague. I hoped for some tips on how to conduct myself. Suddenly I became aware of a well manicured, expensively dressed lady, perhaps twenty years my senior, standing in front of me at a distance of about twelve feet. She looked up at my nameplate, looked down at me, crept to within two feet of me and peered closely at my face. She frowned.

She stepped back and once more studied the nameplate above my head. She crept forward again and whispered, '*Doctor* Cox?' I nodded. Her eyes widened. She took several steps back and shrieked at the top of her voice in a broad Yorkshire accent, 'Ee! You're just a young lad!' The Great Hall fell silent. Senior colleagues looked down their noses and junior colleagues smirked at the dent in the young *Doctor* Cox's ego.

* * * * *

After three years at the Grammar School, I applied for and was offered the post of Lecturer in Educational Research at the College of Education in Aberdeen in Scotland. I was given a three-year contract to conduct research into the latest educational innovation - Teaching Machines and Programmed Learning. Although the other candidates had the advantage of being Scottish and experienced teachers, they did not have the research background and title that came with my PhD – a blessing that outweighed my being English and inexperienced as a teacher.

After three years of marriage and full-time teaching, Maureen and I had accumulated very little in the way of furniture or money even though we lived on the upper floor of my parents' house for a modest rent. My salary when I left The Grammar School was £1050 per annum! On my new salary of £1700 per annum as a lecturer, I qualified for a mortgage on a small semi-detached house in a cul-de-sac on the edge of the city of Aberdeen.

Unfortunately before we could move in, my wife and I had to endure a very cold, very wet August month. At first we shivered in our little tent. Later we dried out and warmed up in a small caravan courtesy of the kindly Mr & Mrs Davidson, the farmer and his wife who owned the camp site and took pity on us. We were their only campers. The weather was so bad everybody else had gone home.

When the day came for us to move into our house, Mrs Davidson gave us a dining table and chairs. *'Och awa wi' ye, Doctor. Dinna thank me. We're aboot t' tak 't oot the byre tae the midden the noo. We've nae mair use for 't.'* The misinformed and prejudiced Sassenachs (we English south of the border) often portray the Scots as canny and tight-fisted and the Aberdonians as permanently bent double looking on the ground for a coin somebody may have dropped.

I did not always understand what the people north of the border were saying but I almost always found them to be friendly and generous to a fault. The exception was the couple who sold us their house. They kept postponing the completion date of our purchase. When we were eventually able to move in, there were no curtains at the windows, no carpets on the floor and no electric light bulbs anywhere! The previous owners had taken them all away.

'Good morning! My name is Dr Michael Cox. I should like an appointment to see the manager.'

'May I ask, Doctor, why ye'll be wanting to see himself?'

'I have just arrived in Aberdeen to lecture at the College of Education and I wish to open an account with your bank.'

'Certainly, Doctor. Would tomorrow morning at 10 o'clock be suitable?'

'Yes that would be fine. What is the manager's name?' I asked, before I put down the telephone.

It proved a simple matter to open an account at the Union Street Branch of Lloyds Bank and to transfer our meagre funds from our local branch of Lloyds Bank in Bristol. It also proved a simple matter to arrange an encounter with the manager. However, although my proper title gave me quick access to Alistair MacTightfist – not the manager's real name but it will suffice – it did not gain me access to his safe.

'And why would you be wanting to borrow £200, Doctor?'

'My wife wants money to buy some carpet and curtains.'

'This £200 would be in addition to your mortgage of £3250, Doctor?'

'Yes.'

'And your salary is to be £1750 per annum I believe, Doctor?'

'Yes.'

'Then I'm afraid, Doctor…'

I could detect no trace of fear in Mr MacTightfist's voice or demeanour as he confirmed the adage that *banks only lend you an umbrella when the sun is shining*. When I stepped out of the granite building into Union Street and into the rain, I had only enough cash in my pocket to buy some light bulbs. I was left with no other choice. The carpet and curtains would have to be on hire purchase (HP) – or on the never-never as my father disparagingly called it. In view of the exorbitant interest charged by the lender, I think of HP as *higher* purchase.

'Yes certainly, Doctor. Just sign here. The carpets will be delivered and fitted next week.'

'If you're going to be away for a whole week attending a conference in Oxford, I want a television set to keep me company,' said Maureen, firmly leading me from the furnishing store into a large radio and television shop in Union Street.

'Good morning, sir. May I help you?'

'Yes. My wife and I are looking for a television set.'

'Certainly, sir. Please follow me.'

The salesman led us downstairs into the basement to a bewildering array of sets. When we eventually chose a modestly priced set – a small, black & white (monochrome) CRT (cathode ray tube) television in a fake teak case – the affable salesman asked how I wished to pay. When I whispered hire purchase, he produced the necessary application forms and, without any loss of affability, prepared to fill them in. When I announced in a normal voice that I was Doctor Cox, an elderly, white-haired gentleman, seated at a desk near the foot of the stairs, looked up from his ledger.

With the paperwork completed and a delivery date agreed, my wife and I headed for the staircase. As we approached it, the white-haired gentleman was struggling to his feet. Bowing his head in my direction, he said in a reverential voice, 'Guid afternoon, Doctor.' I nodded, smiled and hurried up the stairs. I did not look back to see if he tugged his forelock. It was in Aberdeen that the penny dropped: the Scots were treating me with the respect they reserved for *real* doctors.

The tradition of medical training in Scotland began over 500 years ago and bachelors of medicine from the ancient universities of Aberdeen, Dundee, Edinburgh and Glasgow are rightly respected the world over. In Scotland itself, respect for real doctors seemed tantamount to worship. This reverence for medics was bolstered by Dr Finlay's Casebook, a popular television series broadcast by the BBC from 1962 to 1971 and by ITV from 1993 to 1996.

Dr Finlay was junior partner to Dr Cameron in his practice held in fictitious Arden House in the equally fictitious town of Tannochbrae. The two doctors were played by four celebrated Scottish actors; Bill Simpson and Andrew Cruickshank for BBC; David Rintoul and Ian Bannen for ITV. The series was based on the writings of the Scottish author, A J Cronin. When Maureen and I arrived in Aberdeen (just four months before Dr Who made his first appearance on our small screen), Dr Finlay's Casebook had been on the TV for almost a year.

* * * * *

Our first journey from Bristol to Aberdeen, a distance of approximately 500 miles (800 km), took us two days in our little black two-door 1954 Ford Anglia. Nowadays, the journey could take less than 9 hours driving most of way on the M4, M5 and M6 motorways at 70 m.p.h. However, in those days, we had to drive slowly on the narrower trunk roads such as the A6, through towns and villages often congested with traffic. So, when we saw the sign *Poplar House Bed & Breakfast* in the early evening of the first day, we were about four miles north of Penrith. We had driven just over 250 miles. We were tired and hungry.

I remember little of that first sojourn at Poplar House other than the name of the lady in charge and the names of the two villages not more than 6 miles north on the A6. The lady's name was Mrs. Heskett. I still have her card.

Mrs. Heskett

Poplar House,
Via Bowscar,
Penrith.
Tel: Plumpton (Cumberland) 230

The villages, part of the civil parish of Hesket, were (and still are) called High Hesket and Low Hesket presumably because High Hesket is about 150 feet higher above sea level than is Low Hesket.

Given the vagaries of English spelling in former times, I surmised that our hostess was descended from a long line of Hesket(t)s whose distant, foreign invading ancestors had pillaged and plundered the surrounding area from the indigenes. I gave little weight to the view that *hesket* is derived from *eski* – Old Norse meaning a place overgrown with ash trees. In my book Mrs Heskett was descended from landed gentry. She was not named after a tree. Poplar House was her country seat in Cumberland and I was determined it would be our resting place on the journeys to and fro between Aberdeen and Bristol.

'Good morning! Is that Mrs. Heskett?'

'Yes! Who is that speaking?'

'This is Doctor Cox, Mrs. Hesket. I am telephoning from Aberdeen.'

'Ah, yes. Good morning *Doctor*. How are you today?

'I'm very well, thank you, Mrs. Hesket. How are you?'

'Well enough *Doctor*. I mustn't grumble. How is your wife?'

'She's in the pink. Our daughter, Alison, is four weeks old now.'

'Please congratulate your wife for me.'

'Thank you, Mrs. Heskett. I shall. Now, may I book a room for...'

It was in the summer of 1964 that we made our first journey back to Bristol and our second visit to Poplar House. We were now a family of three. We had exchanged our small two-door Ford Anglia for a brand-new dark-green Ford Cortina. It was an estate car big enough to accommodate our daughter, all the paraphernalia a new-born baby needs - carrycot-cum-pram, bedding and clothing, feeding bottles, steriliser, innumerable nappies, etc. – and our own luggage. And as I recall, compared to the Anglia, the Cortina gave us a smoother ride and took less time to get us to the scene of my crime.

During our first year in Aberdeen, my wife was becoming increasingly concerned at the way people seemed to be taking me for a real doctor. She worried that I might be called upon to assist in some medical emergency. What would I do then? I supposed that I could, if called upon, apply my scant knowledge of first aid; I did have an old copy of the St. John's Ambulance *First Aid Manual* somebody had given me. In truth I had never really studied it or taken any course based on it and I no longer have it; but I do still have the *Traveller's First Aid Handbook*, A Reader's Digest guide to emergency treatment at home and abroad. This covers all major emergencies including gun shot wounds, poisoning and stab wounds. Unfortunately I only acquired it in 1985, twenty years after our last fateful visit to Poplar House when, in a moment of weakness and out of false pride, I committed my crime.

I remember there was one occasion when we did not have bed and breakfast with Mrs. Heskett. I drove from Aberdeen to Bristol in one day and took two days to recover. It was a journey none of us wished to repeat. After that we always stopped overnight at Poplar House but I do not remember exactly how many times. I do know that with each visit my wife grew progressively more unsettled by what she felt was a gradual and subtle change in Mrs Heskett's manner towards me. It was something about the way Mrs. Heskett called me *Doctor*.

'Does she know you're not a *real* doctor?'

'I don't know,' I said. 'Probably not.'

'Couldn't you get into trouble impersonating a doctor?'

'I don't *impersonate* a doctor. I *am* a doctor.'

'But you're not a *real* doctor. Mrs. Heskett thinks you are.

'I don't know what she thinks. I'm not a mind reader as you must know by now.'

'One of these days, *Doctor* Cox. One of these days...'

Before I describe *one of those days*, I should point out that the law, whether civil, common, criminal or statutory, is complex. In the UK it is mainly the Medical Acts of 1858, 1860, 1983 and 1991 that provide the statutory laws governing the medical profession, the protection of title and the right of practice. In particular, Section 49 of the 1983 Medical Act states

> *'... any person who wilfully and falsely pretends to be or takes or uses the name or title of physician, doctor of medicine, licentiate in medicine or surgery, bachelor of medicine, surgeon, general practitioner or apothecary, or any name, title, addition or description implying that he is registered under any provision of this Act, or that he is recognised by law as a physician or surgeon or licentiate in medicine or surgery or practitioner in medicine or an apothecary, shall be liable on summary conviction to a fine not exceeding level 5 on the standard scale.'*

Level 5 was £5000 when the 1983 Act came into force. It was probably less than that when I stood for that last time in the kitchen at Poplar House.

My wife waited in the doorway with our daughter in her arms as I approached Mrs. Heskett and reached out to put my money on wooden table top. 'Ee, Doctor,' said the elderly lady, placing her hand gently on my outstretched arm, 'I've been meaning t' ask you...' At that point I saw, out of the corner of my eye, Maureen flee with our baby daughter down the corridor. 'I wanted to ask you...'

'What, Mrs. Heskett?'

All of us have moments in all our lives when we are faced with a choice. We are at a junction or crossroad, if you will. Which path should we choose? Which road do we take? Such critical moments of decision often remain crystal clear in our memory and, upon reflection, are seen to be turning points in our lives. That moment, on that morning in the kitchen of Poplar House, is still fresh in my mind.

'It's my feet, Doctor. I'm having trouble with my feet.'

'Don't tell me,' I said. 'Let me guess. At the end of the day, your feet ache. They're tired. They feel hot and sore. They itch between the toes.'

'Ee, you're right, Doctor. You're quite right.'

'I'm not surprised, Mrs. Heskett, especially if you're standing on them all day.'

'Could you…'

'I interrupted with, 'I suggest you go to the local pharmacy and buy a very small amount of permanganate of potash. In the evening put one tiny crystal – just *one tiny crystal* – into a bowl of hot water. The water will turn pale pinkish purple in colour. Soak both feet in the water for about fifteen minutes. Have the water as hot as your feet can stand but be careful not to scald yourself. Try that for a while.'

'Permanganate of potash, you say, Doctor?'

'Yes. The pharmacist may call it potassium permanganate. Remember! One tiny crystal in a bowl of hot water so it's just a pale pink colour.'

'Ee, thank you, Doctor, she said.

I hurried to the car and drove away from Poplar House for the last time. My wife wanted to know what went on in the kitchen. I told her. When the judge and jury sitting alongside me in the passenger seat said that I was a criminal and should be locked up, I said in my defence, that all I did was tell Mrs. Heskett how to prepare Condy's fluid, a traditional remedy for athlete's foot – a fungal infection – and that I never once told her I was a real doctor. When my wife demanded anxiously to know what would happen to the lady's feet, I was bound to say, 'She'll have the healthiest feet in Cumberland but…' I paused and my wife gave me a worried look. '… since French polishers use Condy's fluid to stain wood, Mrs. Heskett may also have the brownest feet in the whole of Hesket!'

* * * * *

Epilogue

A J Cronin was an outstanding scholar who, in 1914, at the age of 18, entered Glasgow University to study medicine. Although his studies were interrupted by a year of naval service, Archibald Joseph Cronin became a real doctor in 1919 and a proper doctor in 1925 for his doctoral thesis on The History of Aneurism. In 1930, at the age of 34, during a three-month period of 'rest' to recuperate from a duodenal ulcer, Dr Cronin wrote Hatter's Castle, his first novel which was published by Gollancz in 1931 and made into a film in 1941. For the remaining fifty years of his life, Dr Cronin gave up practising medicine to become the celebrated novelist and dramatist A J Cronin.

Albert Schweitzer, already a celebrated organist from an Alsatian family of talented organists, began his theological studies at the University of Strasbourg in 1893, at the age 18, and six years later became a proper doctor, obtaining a PhD for his dissertation on The Religious Philosophy of Kant. In Strasbourg, as Dr Schweitzer, he preached at the church of St. Nicholas, worked as an administrator at St. Thomas Theological College and published his famous book The Quest of the Historical Jesus and other books including a biography of Bach. In 1905, at the age of 30, Schweitzer began studying medicine. When he became a real doctor, Schweitzer went as a medical missionary to French Equatorial Africa where he founded a hospital in Lambaréné. In 1952 he was awarded the Nobel Peace Prize; he used the money to start a leprosarium.

In 1963, on the 23rd of November, the English actor William Hartnell starred in the first episode of the BBC Television science fiction series Dr Who. Thanks to his regenerative ability as a Time Lord, the fictitious Dr Who has already been portrayed by eleven different actors. The series ran continuously until 1989 and was regenerated by BBC Wales in 2005. The twelfth Dr Who appeared in the eighth series that started in August 2014. There seems to be no end in sight for Dr Who but the fictional Dr Cameron and Dr Finlay are long forgotten. Sadly I suspect that most people today will know more about the fictional Dr Who than they do about those two real and proper distinguished doctors, Archibald Cronin and Albert Schweitzer.

I am still Dr Cox, a proper doctor, but to avoid any risk of lawsuits I always explain to new acquaintances that should they faint and fall to the ground, all I could do is to jump over them and fetch a real doctor.

THE LAWNMOWER

This is a true story. By that I mean I have described a real incident to the best of my ability and memory. However, I have not disclosed the names of the real people involved. Any former friends and neighbours who think they recognise themselves and take exception to being excluded or included will, I trust, accept my apologies and neither strike me from their Christmas card list nor add me to their to-be-sued list.

* * * * *

'It's probably nothing,' she said with a look on her face that suggested she thought otherwise. 'Anyway, I'm playing safe and reporting to you, Colonel.'

Ours was a quiet little horseshoe-shaped cul-de-sac of nine individual dwellings in a quiet little village barely three miles from the Dorset coast. My wife and I lived at number 2 for fifteen years before I retired. During that time, the only reported incident was a quiet break-in at number 3 when thieves quietly jemmied the rear patio door and quietly stole Joyce's jewellery. In point of fact there were two incidents because, true to form, the thieves returned to number 3 just after the rear door was repaired and quietly stole Martin's collection of silverware.

Just after I retired, I was unanimously elected to organise a neighbourhood watch for our cul-de-sac and to be its representative. Gerald Thompson, the wag at number 5, gleefully christened me Colonel of the Watch! He may have been thinking of his prize possession, an original cartoon - signed by the cartoonist, Sir David Low himself - showing Colonel Blimp naked, save for a towel around his waist, and spouting nonsense in a Turkish bath. Then again he may not have had Blimp in mind. I'm not bald or fat. I do not frequent steam baths. And I consider myself neither pompous nor reactionary. That said, Mrs Margaret Drummond at number 6 would be quick to knock me sideways with a quote from a poem by her countryman, Robert Burns:

"O wad some Power the giftie gie us, To see oursels as ithers see us!"

So, here I was retired and Colonel of our Neighbourhood Watch. What was I supposed to do? Well, first of all I had to persuade the local authority to install an official sign:

> **THIS IS A**
> **NEIGHBOURHOOD**
> **WATCH AREA**

In the fullness of bureaucratic time, it was installed without pomp or ceremony high up on our street lamp. It is still there as far as I know.

188

Does it deter would-be burglars? Perhaps! However, they would need better eyesight than Don Grant at number 9 who never saw the sign until Barry Whiteside, at number 7, pointed it out. And of course they would have to take the road into our cul-de-sac and not quietly sneak down the lane at the back of numbers 3, 4 and 5.

What was left for me to do once the sign was installed? Listen from time to time to the recorded telephone messages from the local police station and pass the information to the residents in our cul-de-sac.

A bicycle has been stolen from a garden shed in Clarendon Close. Residents are advised to keep sheds locked and any windows covered to conceal the contents from prying eyes…

Apart from those two quiet burglaries at number 3, which occurred before we formed our neighbourhood watch and before the local authority workman put up our sign, nothing untoward happened until that fateful Saturday morning when Mavis Birch from number 4 rang my doorbell.

* * * * *

'Is that the postman?' inquired my wife, Maureen, from the kitchen.

'No, my dear. It's Mavis.'

'Who?'

'Mavis Birch from number 4.'

'I'll be out in a minute.'

'Don't bother, dear. It's neighbourhood watch business. I shan't be long.'

'Hello Mavis,' said my wife, brushing past me. 'I'm just making coffee. Fancy a cup?'

'That would be lovely. Thanks.'

'Black and no sugar?'

'Please.'

'Come on in and make yourself at home. Michael! Take Mavis into the lounge. I'll fetch the coffee.'

Mavis had barely dropped her sparse, bony frame into the contrasting ample, soft padding of my favourite easy chair when Maureen appeared with the coffee and biscuits. 'Michael! Come away from the window and offer Mavis a biscuit while I pour the coffees.' I did as I was told. 'Try the one wrapped in foil, Mavis. It's milk chocolate with an orange-cream filling.' For one moment I thought I was going to lose my favourite biscuit as well as my chair but true to form, Mavis shook her head and muttered something about watching her weight. As far as I could tell, she was the last person who needed to do that but I admit I was grateful for her watchfulness.

I extracted my chocolate biscuit from its protective foil, took a bite and waited for a lull in their conversation.

'What did you come to report, Mavis?' I interjected at the least inconvenient moment.

'Oh, it's probably nothing really,' she replied. 'It's just that…'

'Something suspicious?' Maureen said.

'Not suspicious. Just a bit odd, I suppose. A bit unusual...'

'Well, go on,' said Maureen. 'Tell us all about it.'

'It's Martin's lawnmower.'

'Martin Lake at number 3; his lawnmower you mean?' I asked.

'Yes,' said Mavis, turning again to look at Maureen. 'You know Martin? He and Joyce live right next door to me. Lovely couple! They were very sympathetic when Aubrey left me.'

'What about Martin's lawnmower, Mavis?' I asked, seeing her eyes starting to well up and fearing the effect a loss of even a few tears might have on her body weight.

'Oh, yes. Sorry!' said Mavis, dabbing the corner of her eyes with a lace handkerchief. 'I heard its engine running but it didn't sound right.'

'What do you mean, Mavis?' asked Maureen. 'It didn't sound right.'

'The engine was making a loud, high-pitched noise. I think,' said Mavis, looking at me,

'Sounds like it was racing,' I said.

'Racing? I don't know what you mean?' said Maureen, looking at me.

'Revving an engine so it's running too fast for the gear it's in,' I said looking at my wife. 'It's what set your father's false teeth on edge when he was trying to teach your mother to drive.'

Mavis gave a sympathetic glance in Maureen's direction then said, 'It's not just that the engine was racing. The mower wasn't cutting the grass. It was just standing there.'

'Sorry, but you've lost me, Mavis,' I said. 'Standing where?'

'I think you should come and take a look.'

* * * * *

We finished our coffee and followed Mavis into the cul-de-sac and up the steep drive to the front of number 3. As we climbed the steps to the terrace and front door we could hear the high-pitched whine of the lawnmower. The noise was coming from the side of the bungalow. When we reached the metal gate barring the way to the path to the rear garden, we saw the screeching mower belching smoke for all it was worth. It was alongside the wide-open door of Martin's garden shed.

191

'It was just like this twenty minutes ago, Colonel, before I came to make my report.'

'So it's been running for at least twenty minutes?'

'More like thirty minutes. I only came to look after I finished hanging out my washing.'

'Joyce probably called Martin indoors for some reason or other,' I said. 'lost track of time and forgot that he'd left the engine running. Did you ring their front door bell?'

'Actually, no I didn't. I was afraid they would think I was being nosy. They probably wouldn't think that if the Colonel of our Neighbourhood Watch rang their bell'

Maureen and Mavis studied the pots of flowers and shrubs on the terrace whilst I rang the front door bell. There was no response. I rang several times. There was no sound of movement inside the bungalow. I peeped through the letterbox. The place seemed deserted. I opened the side gate – normally padlocked shut – and walked to the back of the bungalow and peered through all the windows. The place was deserted. I returned to the front terrace to find that Don Grant, from number 9, had joined Mavis and my wife.

192

Don was, as usual, dressed in his one-piece blue work overall, the embroidered insignia, BEC, on the left breast pocket identifying his former employers as the Bradford Engineering Company. On his head was a red hard hat to which was clamped a pair of large, yellow ear defenders. Below the rim of the hat, his long, collar-length, swept-back grey hair was held in place by the elastic strap of the safety goggles that protected his steel-rimmed prescription spectacles. Around his nose and mouth I could see the marks of the formidable dust mask that now hung under his chin. The shiny black industrial gloves protruding from the sleeves of his overalls and the matching industrial boots peeping from beneath the trouser legs completed the picture of a worker ready for any eventuality.

'Good morning, Don. Nice morning,' I said pleasantly.

'Something up?' said Don curtly, fixing me with his doubly protected beady eyes.

'It's Martin's lawnmower,' said Mavis. 'It's…'

Don didn't wait for Mavis to finish. He hurried to the side of the bungalow and pushed open the gate. The three of us followed.

'Martin should know better than to rev the engine like this. Bad for the cylinder.' said Don, delicately adjusting the throttle until, like a tuner preparing a grand piano for a concert, he was satisfied with the note.

'Well done,' said Maureen. 'You've certainly cut down the noise. Martin will be pleased.'

'He might,' I said with little conviction in my voice as I tried to imagine my reaction if Don had fiddled with my lawnmower without so much as a by your leave.

'You won't get any more soot on your washing now, Mavis,' said Maureen.

'Right,' said Don, turning towards the gate. 'That's that problem solved.

'Actually,' said Mavis, hesitantly, 'that was only part of the problem.'

'The fact is,' I said, 'Mavis, found the lawnmower running full blast thirty minutes ago and reported to me. The three of us came to investigate and as far as we can tell the bungalow is deserted. There's no one at home.'

According to his wife Mary, Don Grant didn't actually retire several years ago. BEC made him redundant. Mary, Don, his mother Edie and his large parrot, Cracker, left Bradford as soon as they could to set up home in the small bungalow – at number 9 - in our cul-de-sac in Dorset. Over the years, Don extended and modified their detached double garage until, from the outside, it looked less like a garage and more like a larger version of their bungalow. The garage now held his old car, a boat that had never been on the water, two large workshops equipped with an assortment of industrial machinery and a large wood-burning stove to keep everything warm and dry in winter.

Each day Don behaves as though he had never stopped work. He walks the few steps from his home to his place of work, his garage, where he puts on his overalls and safety gear before checking the daily job sheet on his clipboard. The jobs vary from designing & installing a system for collecting & storing rainwater to trimming the leylandii hedges. And all these jobs, including trimming the hedges, he does with an engineer's precision – to the nearest thousandth of an inch. Suffice it to say, Don is a confident, practical man with a down-to-earth approach to life's problems.

'Where's Don off to?' said Maureen.

'I imagine he's going to ring the door bell, peer through the front and back windows to check for himself that the bungalow is empty.'

'There's no one home.' said Don, 'I checked.' I gave Maureen a look to stop her saying I'd told him that. 'The front and back doors are locked so I couldn't go in to check the back room where the curtains are still pulled.'

194

'Why would you want to do that?' asked Mavis nervously. 'What are you thinking?'

'Well,' said Don, 'let's face it, Martin's not very practical. Perhaps there's been a gas leak and the two of them are lying in bed unconscious, maybe even dead.'

'Oh dear, do you think so?' said Mavis, looking at me.

'I didn't smell gas when I looked through their letter box,' I said. 'I'm sure there's nothing to worry about. They've probably just popped out and Martin forgot all about the lawnmower.'

'What's going on?' Why are you all up here?' It was Don's wife, Mary.

'Martin's lawnmower was making a racket alongside the house and there's no sign of Martin or Joyce.' I told her.

'They've gone out,' said Mary.

'How do you know that?' Maureen asked.

'I'm pretty sure I saw Joyce drive down the road this morning,' Mary replied.

'Joyce was driving?' I asked. 'Not Martin?'

'Yes, I'm pretty sure it was Joyce.'

'And Martin was in the passenger seat?' I queried.

'Oh, well I'm not sure about that. Joyce was definitely driving. Martin might have been sitting alongside her. I don't know. He is tall but he's got very long legs. With his short body he could have been hiding behind Joyce.'

'It's a bit odd if they were both in the car but Joyce was driving,' I said. 'When they go out together, Martin usually drives.'

Martin and Joyce were the oldest retired couple in our neighbourhood watch. Martin had been a highly respected senior orthopaedic surgeon. Joyce was a highly qualified State Registered Nurse (SRN) who served for many years as matron in a major hospital. Contrary to what Don had said, Martin was a fairly handy man but in his own unorthodox way. For example, I remember an occasion when I saw Martin on his hands and knees doing something at the base of a very large but dead tree. I walked up the drive to see what he was doing. Don quickly joined me.

'What are you up to now, Martin?' I asked

'This tree has had it. I'm cutting it down.'

'With that miniature hacksaw?' asked Don, in utter disbelief.

'Yes, why not?' said Martin with a wicked smile.

'You need my chain saw,' said Don.

'No thank you,' said Martin. 'I can manage perfectly well with this. I just scrape away the soil, find a root and amputate it with my hacksaw. I grant you it's a bit slow and tedious but when I've cut all the roots, the tree will fall down.'

We left him to it. An hour or two later, to Don's chagrin, the dead tree fell over. Personally I shouldn't have been surprised if Martin had used his surgeon's scalpel instead of that mini-hacksaw. Needless to say, at Martin's request, Don returned later with his chain saw, cut the tree into logs and hauled them away for his stove.

* * * * *

While we were waiting at the top of the drive for Don to try unsuccessfully to look into Martin's garage to see if one of their cars had gone, Mavis's neighbours, Brenda and Gerald Thompson joined our group.

'Morning Colonel,' chirped Gerry, giving me an exaggerated salute. 'Laying siege to number 3, are we?'

'As a matter of fact,' I began, 'we are…'

'We're worried about Joyce and Martin,' said Mavis. 'Don thinks they may have been gassed.'

'How terrible!' said Brenda. 'How did it happen?'

'Look here,' I said, trying to take control of the situation. 'That's not quite what Don said. He said there may have been a gas leak and Martin and Joyce may be lying in their bed unconscious.'

'Have you called the police, Colonel?'

'No! I haven't, Gerry, because…'

'Shall I call them?' asked Gerry, producing his mobile phone from the leather case attached to his belt.

'No! Definitely not,' I said. 'There's been no gas leak. Nobody's unconscious. It's just that Martin and Joyce are nowhere to be found and…'

'I think they've popped out to the shops,' said Mary. 'They usually go shopping on Saturday morning although I can't think why now they're retired. Monday's much better. It's less crowded.'

'Yes but the vegetables are often fresher on Saturdays,' said Maureen authoritatively.

'I agree,' said Brenda.

'Look here,' I said, trying again to take control. 'The fact is Martin's lawnmower was left running at the side of the house, we can't find Martin or Joyce and Mary thinks she saw Joyce drive down the road but she's not sure if Martin was in the passenger seat.'

'I saw Joyce's car go down their drive about half an hour ago,' said Brenda.

'Joyce's car? Not Martin's?' I asked.

'I think it was Joyce's,' said Brenda.

'Was Martin with her?' Maureen asked.

'I've no idea,' said Brenda.

'The point is,' I said, 'if Martin was with Joyce, why wasn't he driving?'

'And why was she driving Martin in her car?' Gerry chipped in.

* * * * *

For no particular reason, other than perhaps the thought in the back of my mind that Martin and Joyce might return at any moment and not be pleased to see the seven of us barring the way to their garage, I started to walk down the drive. The others followed me across the cul-de-sac to gather outside Don and Mary's house. Mrs Margaret Drummond probably saw the procession from her kitchen window. She hurried down her drive to be joined by Barry and Sheila Whiteside from number 7.

When Margaret married, she moved with her husband to the Midlands where he launched what was to become a very successful business. She had four children, three boys and a girl. When the oldest boy was eleven years of age, Margaret's husband died. She was left to bring up her four children and to run the business. When she retired and came to live in Dorset, her daughter had become a State Registered Nurse and her three sons had graduated from Oxford University, one becoming a barrister, another becoming a surgeon and the third becoming a mathematician.

None of us knew Margaret's age. Her thick, well groomed white hair gave her the appearance of the senior she probably was but her boundless energy was that of someone much younger. She did her own gardening and the results put us all to shame. She changed her car regularly because she drove thousands of miles each year visiting family and friends and dealing with business matters. She employed an accountant to handle her financial affairs so that she could voluntarily

198

manage the local Citizens Advice Bureau. Mrs Margaret Drummond was a formidable lady.

'Might I ask what's going on?'

'Good morning Mrs Drummond,' I said. 'Nothing is actually going on. It's just that Martin Lake's lawnmower was left running at the side of their bungalow and Martin and Joyce are nowhere to be found. Mary says she saw Joyce drive down the road this morning and Martin may have been in the passenger seat. If Martin was in the car, we're wondering why he wasn't driving.'

'Presumably,' said Mrs Drummond, 'because he wasn't fit to drive.'

'Bit early in the morning for Martin to be hitting the bottle wouldn't you say?'

'That's not what I meant, Mr Thompson,' retorted Mrs Drummond. 'Mr Martin Lake is certainly a connoisseur of fine wine but he is certainly not given to overindulgence at any time of the day or night.'

'What did you mean, Mrs Drummond, when you said Dr Lake, sorry, when you said Mr Lake may not have been fit to drive?'

'That he was unwell. Taken ill, if you prefer.'

'So where was Joyce taking him?' Barry Whiteside asked.

'Hospital!' stated Mrs Drummond in a matter of fact voice. 'Where else?'

At that, separate little conversations broke out. Mavis recounted to Barry the events of the morning, including Don's theory that Martin and Joyce may have been overcome by a gas leak. Brenda admired Mrs Drummond's sweater and discovered that it actually was from Fair Isle and was hand-knitted by a man or woman in the Shetland Isles. Gerry pulled Don's leg by asking him if he really needed all this protective gear just to replace a washer on a tap. Brenda, Mary and Sheila discussed the pros and cons of vegetable shopping on Mondays instead of Saturdays.

'Mrs Drummond could be right, you know. Joyce could have rushed Martin off to hospital,' I said, drawing Maureen aside.

'Why do you think that?' whispered Maureen.

'Well, I know Martin is slim and looks as fit as Barry Whiteside who's probably 15 years younger and always playing golf with his wife and Tony and Josie. But, I do know Martin's been on the receiving end of the surgeon's scalpel quite a few times in the past.'

'Really?'

'Oh yes! And,' I confided, leaning forward to whisper in Maureen's ear, 'he suffers from arrhythmia.'

'Meaning?'

'A dicky ticker, old girl.'

'So Martin might have had a heart attack. Is that what you're saying?' Maureen asked.

Before I could reply, someone tapped me on the shoulder. It was our neighbour, Ray, from number 1. His wife Pat had joined Brenda, Mary and Sheila to discuss Saturday grocery shopping.

'Hello Ray,' I said, smiling. 'What brings you out of the house?'

'Pat and I wondered what the gathering's all about. Anything to do with the mess the Council has made of our road and footpath?

'Well, no. As a matter of fact…'

'Damn disgrace.' said Ray. 'They did a first class job when they resurfaced our road and pavement, right?' I nodded in agreement. 'But then what? Days later, the Electricity Board dig holes everywhere. They're no sooner gone than the Gas Board comes and dig more holes.'

'Terrible!' said Maureen. 'You'd think that…'

'After the Gas Board we had the Water Board digging more holes. God only knows why. Last week British Telecom dug their holes. It wouldn't be so bad but not one hole was filled in properly. One of these days one of us is going to trip and break something. Then who's to blame? We'll never be able to prove who dug and refilled the hole we tripped over. And you can forget taking the Borough Council to court. It just would be a waste of time and money. All because someone in the Highways Department can't arrange for our road and pavement to be resurfaced after these idiots had dug their holes. Why if I had my way…'

'Ray! Have you heard? Martin Lake's in hospital.' It was Ray's wife, Pat. 'Don Grant thinks he may have been gassed.'

* * * * *

Things were definitely getting out of hand. There was now quite a crowd outside the Grant's bungalow. Apart from Martin and Joyce Lake, the only people missing were Josie and Tony Small from number 8. Just as that was going through my mind, their black BMW tore around the corner into our cul-de-sac, its sudden appearance and speed being enough to make anybody standing in the road jump onto the footpath and form a line along its edge. Maureen exchanged raised-eyebrow glances with Sheila; they frequently feared for the safety of their Persian cats that often sat in the middle of the road preening themselves in the sunshine.

I didn't want Tony and Josie being fed any misinformation, so I hurried to meet them as they came to join the throng.

'Quite a get-together,' said Tony. 'Have you called a meeting, Colonel?'

'No, not at all. It all started when Mavis came to tell me about Martin's lawnmower.'

'Sawbones Martin?'

'Mr Lake,' I said loudly, hoping Mrs Drummond hadn't overheard Tony, 'has disappeared. Joyce might have taken him to hospital.'

'Do we know what's wrong with him?' Josie asked.

'We don't know there's anything wrong with Martin,' I said. 'It's just a theory.'

'So what's this got to do with his lawnmower?' Tony asked.

'Mavis found it standing alongside Martin's garden shed. It had been left running at full throttle and belching smoke. The shed door was wide open and the metal gate was unlocked. We rang their front doorbell and looked in all the windows but the bungalow was deserted. There was no sign of Martin or Joyce anywhere.'

'Well, you're in charge,' said Tony. 'What are you going to do?'

I was about to confess that I had no idea what to do, when Barry shouted out, 'Your boy's goats are on the loose again, Gerry.' Sure enough, two goats were heading across the front lawn towards number 6. Young Stanley Thompson was in hot pursuit of his pets. A cheer went up when the teenager grabbed their collars just before they reached Mrs Drummond's garden. 'I thought your dahlias were done for this time, Margaret,' said Barry, with a grin all over his face, obviously impervious to the scowl she gave him.

'I'm surprised that you are allowed to keep goats or any other livestock on your land, Gerald,' said Mrs Drummond. 'Our land is subject to a restrictive covenant. It dates back to Lord Shaftesbury's time. If we're not allowed to keep caravans here, I cannot imagine the Council allowing your goats and chickens or Don's parrot.'

'Actually,' said Gerry, 'They're not my goats. They're Stanley's. Anyway, Lord Shaftesbury's been dead awhile, so I really don't think he'll be bothered. And unless somebody complains, I don't think the Borough Council will be bothered either.'

Before Gerry and Mrs Drummond could say any more to one another I stepped in and asked how Stanley was doing now he had left school. Brenda told us that during the day he worked at the wholesale animal feed company on the quayside and that in the evenings he was studying hard to retake his exams and improve his results.

'Good for him,' said Mrs Drummond. 'Any idea what he wants to do afterwards?'

'Breed goats,' said Gerry, shaking his head in disapproval. 'That's why he's got this pair.'

'Perhaps he'll change his mind when he passes his exams and goes to university.'

'If he passes.' said Gerry. 'And if he decides to apply to university.'

'Has he thought of reading veterinary science?' asked Mrs Drummond.

'Unfortunately,' said Gerry, 'he dropped sciences in favour of English and History.'

* * * * *

We were all so distracted by Stanley's pair of rare Bagot goats that we nearly didn't notice Joyce's car turn into the cul-de-sac and drive slowly past the line of people. As she went by, everybody started waving and smiling. She looked completely bewildered. I imagine she thought we'd all gone mad. She didn't stop. She just drove up her drive and parked in front of her garage.

'Where's Martin?' someone asked.

'He wasn't in the car.' said someone else.

'I think you should go and have a word with Joyce,' said Maureen. 'Find out what's happened.'

'Yes, go on,' said Gerry. 'You're our leader. Ask her where Martin is.'

'Somebody looking for me?' It was Martin Lake. He had walked unnoticed into the cul-de-sac and joined the end of the line.

'Good Lord, Martin!' I said. 'Where have you come from? Are you OK?'

'We've all being terribly worried,' said Maureen.

'Don thought you and Joyce might be dead, gassed in your bed,' exclaimed Mavis.

We all gathered round while Martin explained what had happened. Joyce wanted to go shopping in the town. He wanted to change his library book so Joyce gave him a lift into the village. It was a nice morning so he decided to walk home.

'What about your lawnmower?' asked Don. 'Did you know you left the engine running?'

'Oh yes,' said Martin. 'I didn't want to put it away in the shed for winter with fuel still in the tank. Wouldn't want to risk a fire.'

'But you could have ruined the engine,' said Don.

'I doubt it!' said Martin. 'I've been doing this for the past ten years without much damage as far as I can tell.'

'Why did you leave your side gate and shed unlocked?' I asked.

'Why not? There are only a few old garden tools in the shed - nothing worth stealing. Besides, if thieves can break into our securely locked bungalow and steal our valuables, they'll make short work of a padlock on a shed door.'

After the crowd had dispersed, I expressed my relief that he had not been rushed into hospital on account of his arrhythmia. Martin gave me a somewhat superior kind of look, one that a surgeon might give a young student doctor, and said in a matter of fact voice, 'There are many types of arrhythmias. Mine are premature atrial contractions - early extra beats that originate in the atria or upper chambers of the heart. They're quite harmless and require no treatment. Now if you'll excuse me, Michael, I'd better go and help Joyce unload the shopping.'

* * * * *

204

Epilogue

In 1982, the United Kingdom of Great Britain and Northern Ireland saw the launch of satellite TV, the start of the Falklands War and, in the sleepy village of Mollington near Chester, the formation of the first neighbourhood watch. One of the villagers brought back the idea from a visit to the USA and Canada.

In April 2009 in the UK there were 133,195 neighbourhood watch schemes registered for Public Liability Insurance (PLI) and covering more than 7½ million households. It is estimated that schemes not registered for PLI would increase the number to more than 170,000 neighbourhood watch groups with over 10 million members.

We did form a neighbourhood watch in the cul-de-sac in Dorset where we lived and thereby encouraged a greater neighbourliness and a closer community spirit. I was called the 'Colonel' and my neighbour did leave his lawnmower running and cause us all great concern.

David Low, the political cartoonist and satirist, was born in New Zealand in 1891. He came to London in 1919. Colonel Blimp, his most famous character, was created in 1934 to represent a pompous, reactionary, ultra-nationalistic person. David Low was knighted in 1962 and died the next year.

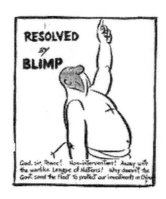

The caption in this cartoon is: "Gad, Sir, There! Non-intervention! Away with the warlike League of Nations! Why doesn't the Gov't send the Fleet to protect our investments in China?"

Stanley Thompson – that's not his real name – did keep a pair of goats and intended to breed them but they may or may not have been Bagot goats, a breed in existence since 1380 and named after the family then living in Blithfield Hall, Staffordshire. However, Stanley retook his exams after he left school, went to university and obtained a degree in English and went on to study law. He is now a successful barrister living in London.

Facts and Fantasies

Volume 3

Cognac – l'eau de vie

Michael C. Cox

Mimast Inc

DECEPTION AND A DEADLY SWITCH

The truth underlying this story is the foolish unsecured loans that two colleagues and I made to a former colleague and his brother in 1991. The name of the school, the names of the two companies and the names of the characters, apart from my own, are fictitious. I definitely lost money. I believe I was deceived. I think it best not to comment further.

* * * * *

The two men shook hands and parted. I saw them as I happened to glance out of the window of my classroom, on the upper floor of the school, overlooking the car park. What, I wondered, was Cyril Rainsthorp doing shaking hands with a dubious former member of staff? Even with senior colleagues such as myself, our Head of Classics refused to shake hands in order to minimise the risk of contagion – one of his favourite words derived, as he never hesitated to declaim, from the Latin verbs *tangere*: to touch and *contingere*: to touch on all sides or pollute.

My thoughts were interrupted by the bell to end morning school. As I reached the foot of the staircase, Cyril came through the main door into the foyer. The cold wind had brought a pinkish colour to his sallow cheeks and made his white hair even more dishevelled than usual. We walked side-by-side down the corridor to the staff common room.

'I thought I saw A Simpleton in the car park just now getting into a new red Mercedes.'

'Sorry, I'm not with you, old boy,' replied Cyril, giving me a sideways squint.

'Anthony Simpleton. Unfortunate name for a schoolmaster. Left here about three years ago to set up his own computer business.'

'Oh, I didn't know his first name was Anthony,' said Cyril, unconvincingly.

'Tony! Most of us called him Tony.'

'Oh! I didn't really know him. What did he teach?' he asked, seemingly without interest.

'Physics and mathematics.'

'Ah! I see. Bit of a boffin then? Clever chap was he?'

'Tony always thought so. Probably still full of himself.'

'I'm surprised a clever chap like that hasn't changed his surname by deed poll.'

'He seemed to take a perverted delight in his name,' I said. 'Did you know his middle name is Simon?'

'A worthy name. Two of the Apostles were called Simon.'

'True. Unfortunately, some of our rather less worthy pupils favoured the association of Simon with the nursery rhyme: *Simple Simon met a pieman going to the fair...*' I said, tailing off, not knowing the rest.

'*Said Simple Simon to the pieman, Let me taste your ware,*' continued Cyril. '*Said the pieman to Simple Simon, Show me first your penny. Said Simple Simon to the pieman, Sir, I have not any.*'

'Bad enough that our wretched pupils nicknamed him Simple Simon,' I remarked, 'Do you recall how quick our colleagues were to draw attention to his initials when the draft timetable was posted on the notice board.'

'His initials? Oh, good gracious!' exclaimed Cyril as the penny dropped. 'ASS! But...'

'Indeed. Fortunately our beloved headmaster had them changed to TSS. The mind boggles at what the Upper Fifths might have made of ASS.

It was in 1983 that Tony Simpleton began his five-year teaching career at Lytchett Upper, our minor league independent boarding school for boys. During that period, Dr Trevelyan Wynne Evans, our fiery headmaster and former Welsh Rugby International, would from time to time ask me as chairman of the staff common room and Head of Science what I thought of Tony as a colleague and teacher. Trevelyan and I were a similar age and hoping to retire early. The staff saw us as the elderly bastions of the old school, being of one mind on the subject of *discipline* (masters were paid to teach and pupils were required to learn) and *uniforms* (blazers and badges for the boys; suits, ties and gowns for their masters).

Tony did wear a suit. It may have been a good fit once upon a time. We only ever saw the coat buttoned up at Sunday morning chapel. Tony's considerable bulk was a possible benefit when he was on the field in rugby kit but the bulge around his middle (courtesy of the ale he drank at the local village tavern) was an unequivocal deficit when he was straining his voice and the buttons of his suit in the staff pews.

Over the summer holiday between his first and second year at the school, Tony grew a thick beard. Staff opinion on it was divided. The geographers, grammarians and scientists said he grew it to compensate for his advancing alopecia. The classicists, historians and linguists said he wanted to hide his youthful features. A small minority which included myself and, I suspect, Dr Evans, believed he grew the beard to make it hard for us to tell if he was wearing a tie.

According to the few Oxford and Cambridge graduates on our staff, England has only two universities. Those of us who graduated from civic universities, such as Bristol, Exeter and Southampton were equally disdainful of the *New Polytechnics*. Tony emerged from a *Poly* somewhere in the Midlands and was offered a post at our school chiefly because he was the sole applicant but also because he claimed to share our headmaster's enthusiasm for rugby. He became a fairly competent teacher of mathematics, physics and rugby in spite of his antics much frowned upon by senior staff and, if truth be told, by the more intelligent of his pupils. Tony would prance around in his rolled-up shirt sleeves, perspire profusely and bellow at the pupils to get stuck in. Such a performance and such urgings may have been appropriate on the field but in the opinion of his heads of department there was no place for them in the classroom or the laboratory.

As far as one could tell, Tony had few if any friends on the staff. His principal enemies were the non-smokers who took great exception to the foul-smelling cigarettes of Turkish shag tobacco he rolled in a little machine and smoked in the corner of the common room. He did acquire a small following amongst the younger pupils when he formed a computing club which convened two evenings a week to write programmes and play games on the early machines such as Sinclair's ZX Spectrum, Commodore's Commodore 64 and Acorn's BBC Micro.

When the mathematics department introduced computing science into the curriculum, Tony was asked to teach it. When a computer room was set up for use by the mathematics and science departments, Tony was called upon to maintain it. When computers were introduced into the school office, Tony was asked to train the office staff and to service their machines. Tony became our computer expert. So nobody was surprised when, after five years as a perspiring teacher, he resigned his post to set himself up in business.

'How's his business doing these days?' I asked Cyril as we entered the common room.

'Rather well,' said Cyril. 'He's just formed a second company in point of fact.'

'Was that what you two were talking about in the car park?'

'Yes it was in point of fact,' said Cyril with a *mind your own business look*.

'Want you on his Board of Directors, does he?' I asked wryly.

'In point of fact,' retorted Cyril, catching sight of the slightly sardonic look on my face, 'he's looking for investors.'

'I see. He touched you for a loan.'

'Not at all. He's offered me a short term investment opportunity with a return of 13%.'

'Are you the first one he's approached?'

'In point of fact,' said Cyril, yet again uttering his favourite phrase, 'in point of fact yes, I am.'

'You're what?" asked Christopher Lovell, our Head of Music, who overheard.

'He's the first one that Tony Simpleton has touched for a loan,' I said.

'An investment,' snapped Cyril. 'He's asked me to invest in his new company.'

'Office Developments (International) Ltd? Is that the company?' Chris asked.

'Yes, I think that's the name,' replied Cyril.

'Then you're not the first. He's already asked me,' said Chris.

'How much does he want you to invest?' asked Cyril, somewhat crestfallen.

'Five thousand pounds. Is that what he asked you for?'

'Yes,' replied Cyril, 'with a return of thirteen percent.'

'If that's 13% per annum,' I said, 'perhaps I should put in £5,000. I'm only getting 7% on my building society savings.' In hindsight, what I should have said was *Thirteen percent sounds too good to be true; so what's the catch?* but I fell victim to the cardinal sins of envy and greed. Pride and wrath were to follow later.

* * * * *

We had no difficulty finding the place. A SIMPLETON'S COMPUTER SUPPLIES was printed in large letters high up on the long wall of the warehouse bordering the car park. The front entrance into the warehouse was equally easy to find, set as it was in the short wall and beneath the word ENTRANCE printed in the same large letters. The pair of thick metal security doors were wedged back to allow customers access to a carpeted foyer and a pair of glass doors.

A small, simple logo was frosted onto the glass of each door and a larger version, printed in black, dominated the centre of the foyer carpet.

Tony designed the logo himself and put it everywhere; on letterheads, supply notes and invoices, the stock, the goods and packaging, the employees' overalls and company sweaters, even the washroom towels; nothing except the toilet paper was spared.

Cyril led the way into the tiled reception area. Chris and I followed. A barren counter, facing the entrance and running the width of the area, was roughly divided into three unequal sections by the signs hanging from the ceiling above. Cyril ignored the RETAIL and the TRADE sections and led us to ENQUIRIES.

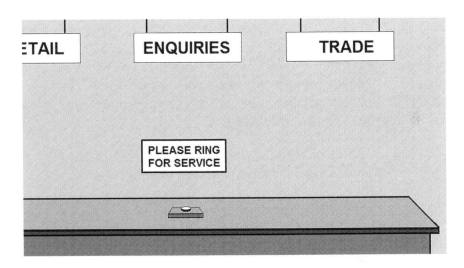

I braced myself for his invective against enquiries – it should be *inquiries*; *inquire, inquiry*, from the Latin *in* – in and *quaerere* – to seek – but his mind was elsewhere. Cyril was intending to put at risk, without his doughty wife's approval, a significant proportion of his retirement nest egg.

There was an open doorway in the wall behind the counter. Voices echoed through it but nobody appeared until Cyril, in response to the *notice please ring for service*, pressed the button on the counter. There was something familiar about the face of the young fellow who responded to the bell but I couldn't for the life of me think what it was.

'Good morning sir. What can I do for you?' he asked Cyril pleasantly with an accent suggesting he hailed from somewhere in the Midlands.

'These two gentlemen and I wish to see Anthony Simpleton.'

'Is he expecting you?'

'In point of fact, yes,' said Cyril, 'we have an appointment for 10 o'clock this morning.'

The young chap was solidly built and made the dark blue company sweater bulge in all the right places, giving a certain dignity to the quirky company logo on his chest. His auburn hair, neatly combed and parted down the middle, was starting to thin. He had a clear, healthy complexion and clean, white teeth which he displayed in a pleasant smile that he preserved even when Cyril suggested he change the notice from *please ring for service* to *please push for attention*. 'I am not,' said Cyril, 'a motor car requiring an oil change. Neither am I a bride wishing to be wed nor a corpse wishing to be buried.'

When he picked up the telephone in his left hand, I noticed that the young man was wearing a wedding ring, that his fingers were unstained and that his fingernails were clean and short. A thought crossed my mind as he spoke into the telephone with a definite Midlands accent, 'Tony! Mr. Rainsthorp, Mr. Lovell and Dr. Cox to see you. Will you come down or shall I bring them up?' After a short pause, he put down the phone, joined us on our side of the counter and said, 'Please follow me.'

He opened a door marked Private and led us up a wooden staircase to an uncarpeted corridor along which the four of us clattered until we reached a door whose upper half was panelled with glass bearing the inevitable logo. Without knocking, the young man opened the door and led us into a sparsely furnished room. It was Simple Simon's office.

Tony hauled his bulk out of a large, plush-leather swivel chair and waddled from behind a large desk to greet us, his dark blue company sweater bulging in all the wrong places. He extended his podgy hand first to Cyril who was still wearing his soft leather driving gloves; the redoubtable Mrs Rainsthorp would no doubt sterilise them on his return home. As I gripped Tony's surprisingly limp, clammy hand with its nicotine-stained fingers, I recalled what scientific research had established; that one hundred different hands could yield more than

4,500 different species of bacteria and that one typical hand could be home to about 150 different species. A shiver went down my spine as I wondered what corrupting or harmful influence (or contagion as Cyril would say) Tony was spreading.

'Would you organise some coffee, Reggie,' Tony said as he waved us into three wooden foldaway seats arranged in a semicircle with their backs to a four-drawer metal filing cabinet. We took our somewhat uncomfortable places and waited. As Tony returned to his soft leather chair, I noticed that he had lost more hair in the three years since he had left our school; he was thinner on top and his beard was now quite neatly trimmed; it was too short to hide even the top of the polo-neck shirt he was wearing under his company V-neck sweater. When Tony was seated, I studied his desk.

Although the ashtray in the centre of the desk was empty and appeared unused, a smell of stale Turkish tobacco hung in the air and began to impregnate the clothing of we three non-smokers. The three trays (in, pending and out) at one end of the desk seemed as unused as the ashtray; in point of fact, as Cyril would say, they were empty but not necessarily unused. At the other end of the desk there was a bright red telephone and a polished granite pen holder. The ashtray and pen both bore the company logo.

Tony produced a box file, presumably from a drawer in his desk, like a magician pulling a rabbit from a hat, and flipped open the lid. I half expected a white dove to fly out. 'I've assembled some information about our new company and the product it will be launching internationally,' he said, handing each of us a rather glossy brochure. 'Perhaps you'd like to look it over while we're waiting for the coffee.'

To my untrained eye the document Tony handed us looked quite professional. The pages were securely bound by a hard plastic spine. The glossy appearance was achieved by one clear plastic sheet atop the front cover which bore the company logo and the words *Offering Memorandum issued by Office Developments (International) Ltd.* The first few inside pages set out the details of this offering in what I supposed was a legal format. The narrow left-hand column bore short titles (The Issuer, Name, Head Office. The Offering, Securities offered, etc.) associated with the sections and individual paragraphs in the wide right-hand column.

On the first page, one paragraph in particular caught my eye. It occupied more than one third of the length of the wide column and consisted of just one sentence which was sprinkled with words such as debenture, heretofore, non-convertible, notwithstanding, redeemable, retractable and unsecured. The later pages included sections on financial statements and business plan details that were just as obscure. My head was still spinning when I came across the management biographies section. Just as I saw the photo of Reginald Stephenson alongside Anthony Simpleton's picture, Reggie walked into the room with the coffee.

* * * * *

'More coffee?" asked Tony, addressing the three of us. We shook our heads. 'If you'll clear away the coffee cups, Reggie, I'll set up the overhead projector,' said Tony, as he conjured up the machine from behind his desk. While he was adjusting the focus of the company logo projected onto the wall we were facing, Tony informed us that his younger brother, Reggie, would explain the business side of the new company. When I turned to the two pictures in the biographies section of the *Offering Memorandum* and saw the brotherly resemblance, I asked Tony why his brother had changed his name to Stephenson.

'Reggie's second name is George. When he was a boy his hero was George Stephenson who invented the first steam locomotive to run on railway lines.' When Chris said it was called *The Rocket*, Tony immediately corrected him with, 'No! It was the *Blucher* in 1814. That was the first steam locomotive. George and his son Robert built *The Rocket* fifteen years later when they invented its multi-tubular boiler.'

Reggie returned and stood by the overhead projector, cutting short any further discourse on the topic of steam locomotives. He introduced himself as Tony's brother and outlined his intention to explain their offering memorandum, the structure of their new company and their business plan. We learned that Office Developments (International) Ltd was a private company owned jointly and solely by Tony and Reggie. Only the three of us – Tony's former colleagues – were being privileged with the opportunity to invest in their new company by purchasing a corporate bond; to *get in on the ground floor* and so share the company profits.

Their business plan was to build a network of independent distributors, starting with the UK and then extending overseas. When I asked Reggie what the company was going to distribute, Tony replied with, 'It's called *Ink-Up*. I'll tell you all about our product in a minute.' Reggie continued by displaying overhead transparencies of various projected sales charts and ended with a titillating table of anticipated profits to swell our retirement nest-eggs.

'What *exactly* is this corporate bond of yours?' asked Chris.

'It's actually a debenture,' said Reggie confidently.

'From the Latin phrase *debentur mihi* – there are due to me,' said Cyril, giving us the correct literal translation.

'So it's an I.O.U. and you are asking for a loan,' said Chris.

'The £5,000 debenture is a non-convertible, non-redeemable, non-transferable, unsecured, fixed term, fixed interest, *corporate bond*,' recited Reggie a little less confidently.

'In other words, a loan,' said Chris.

'Is the fixed term three years and the fixed interest thirteen percent?' I asked.

Tony nodded.

'Is that thirteen percent *per annum*?' I stressed the last two words.

Tony nodded again.

'So that means after three years you'll pay me back my five thousand pounds plus three times 13% of £5,000, correct?'

'That's a good point,' said Chris, nodding at me and then looking hard at Tony.

'When we repay your principal on the debenture's redemption date, we were thinking...' Tony tapped the keys of a calculator he had conjured from his desk drawer and mumbled, 'nought... point... one... three... times... five... nought... nought... nought...'

'Six hundred and fifty pounds?' I questioned rhetorically.

'Um, yes. £650. That's it,' said Tony.

'Per year that's about £217...,' I said, taking out my calculator. 'Actually two hundred and sixteen point six recurring... or four point three recurring per cent per annum,' I stated, having divided the 216.66666 by 5000. When I continued crisply with, 'My building society gives me 7% on my safe as houses, risk free savings account. So...' Tony hastily cut me off.

'No! Sorry. My mistake. It is 13% per annum, of course, and you would get...' He tapped his calculator keys again. 'You would get a return of £1950 on your principal.'

'I can't speak for Cyril and Michael,' said Chris, 'but I'd want the interest paid monthly.'

'So should I,' said Cyril.

'Same here,' I said. 'Could you pay it directly into my bank account?'

'Certainly,' said Tony without batting an eyelid. 'That can be arranged. Just give Reggie your bank account details and he'll do the rest. OK. If there are no more questions, it's my turn. I'm going to tell you about *Ink-Up*. It's a bit technical but I'll try not to blind you with science.' Tony then treated us to a lecture that was gratifyingly short and, I had to admit, most interesting.

The *gunsmiths* E. Remington & Sons produced the first Type Writer (as they called it) over 139 years ago in America; Christopher Scholes and Carlos Glidden invented it. They made and sold fewer than five thousand but they started something which was to lead to the modern typewriter and dot-matrix printer. Incidentally, they patented the QWERTY keyboard (now called the *universal keyboard* and used on all modern computers) which they designed to space apart the most widely used letters in order to minimise the clash (or sticking together) of a pair of typebars. Now even if Remington sold only 5000 Type Writers, they would have sold thousands more type writer ribbons.

Scholes made his ribbon from cotton. Later ribbons were made of silk. When the cotton and silk was needed in World War II, nylon was used but the ribbons were stiffer than the silk ribbons, held less ink and produced printing that was less sharp. Even silk ribbons do not last forever. The ink eventually runs out and we throw the ribbon away. Last year Western Europeans threw away more than 160 *million* ribbons – about twelve thousand tonnes in weight and worth about £600 *million*!

Ink developed in China more than five thousand years ago was a mixture of soot, oil and gelatine from animal skins. In the 15th century when Gutenberg turned a wine press into a printing press, an ink was developed (from soot, turpentine and walnut oil) that would stick to the paper but not blur the letters. Modern ink is a complex colloidal mixture whose ingredients are designed to control the viscosity of the liquid, the speed at which the ink dries and the appearance of the ink when it is dry.

'This is where *Ink-Up* comes in,' enthused Tony. 'I have scientifically developed and tested an ink that we can spray, from a non-pressurised environmentally-friendly canister, onto typewriter and printer ribbons so they can be used over and over again. The canister is made of aluminium and is recyclable. A canister of Ink-Up retailing at £12.95 will save the customer at least 90% of the cost of buying new ribbons.' Tony paused for breath and would, I suspect, have conjured up his Turkish cigarette making machine had he not been facing a trio of anti-smokers. 'Any questions?' When we shook our heads, Tony led us downstairs and through another doorway into the warehouse proper. Reggie followed along behind us.

The large area seemed half empty to me but probably half full to Tony. Occupying one half of the floor space were several long lines of tall metal shelving on which boxes of various sizes and colours were stacked. The other half of the floor space was empty save for a small rectangular building about 10 feet long and 6 feet wide. It was made of bricks and mortar. Its flat metal roof with its 6 inch metal lip seemed to be clamped down, onto the four brick walls, the way the metal lid clamped down on Tony's tobacco tin to provide an airtight seal. The brick shed – for that's what it really was – had a solid metal door in the short wall but there were no windows.

Tony flipped the two switches on the outside wall, explaining that he was putting on the extractor fan, in the small end wall, to remove any fumes that just might be inside, before putting on the fluorescent light that ran down the middle of ceiling. When Cyril asked why, Tony explained that the fumes and the air could form an explosive mixture that arcing in the light switch might detonate. *Arcing in the fluorescent light could also detonate explosive mixtures*, I thought to myself, especially since Tony didn't allow much time for the fumes to be extracted and since there seemed no way for fresh air to be drawn into the hut he called his *laboratory*.

After a few moments, Tony opened the door for us to look inside. Down the right-hand wall was a bench supporting odds and ends of scientific equipment (a balance, several measuring cylinders, and some funnels), various bottles, a machine that looked like an oversized kitchen blender and a few empty aluminium canisters. Down the left-hand wall were stacks of plain cardboard cartons which, we were told, were packed with *Ink-Up* canisters ready for dispatch. When I asked Tony why his logo was not on the boxes, it was Reggie who answered me.

'*Ink-Up* is produced and distributed by ODI - Office Developments (International) Ltd, an entirely separate company from SCS - Simpleton's Computer Supplies.

'So you're saying the two companies have nothing to do with one another?'

'That's right,' said Reggie, 'they are separate legal entities/'

'But you and Tony own both companies, don't you?' I said.

222

'Yes, that's right,' said Tony, butting in, 'but the two companies are quite separate.

'Which company owns this brick hut?' I asked

'SCS.' Said Reggie. 'ODI just pays SCS a *nominal* rent to use it.'

The three of us left by the deliveries entrance and found ourselves in the car park close to Cyril's Ford Fiesta. It was raining so we dashed for the car. Once inside, we gave some thought to our encounter with Tony and Reggie. Cyril seemed to have the most doubts about parting with five thousand pounds. Chris pointed out that Tony was really asking for an unsecured loan but willing to pay a high interest for it.

I recalled that our Head of Economics, commenting upon the adage *low risk low gain, high risk high gain*, said that investments with a high return may be risky but investments with a low return need not be safe. With inflation running at 12%, a safe investment in the bricks and mortar of a building society deposit account yielding 7% would be losing value. Then I remembered my father used to say *a faint heart never won a fortune* when he went to post his football coupon; it was his version of the saying *a faint heart never won a fair lady*. When the three of us finally agreed we should lend Tony the money, I said rather prophetically, 'Nothing ventured, nothing gained.'

* * * * *

The school year of 1990-1991 was memorable for several reasons. Our robustly fit headmaster, Dr Wynne Evans, fiddled his retirement on the grounds of ill health and left at the end of the Michaelmas Term. The Second Master took temporary command and held the fort for the Hilary Term. On the basis that my salary as a senior master could pay for two young teachers able to coach sports, I persuaded the new headmaster to let me go. I did think it diplomatic to refer to my two possible replacements as *young* rather than *inexperienced*. So, I took early retirement at the end of the Trinity Term.

Chris Lovell, at least ten years my junior, also left that summer to become Head of Music in an International School somewhere in the Far East. Cyril Rainsthorp was destined to remain at the school for a while

223

longer until his teaching career came to an abrupt end. At the beginning of the Summer holiday, Chris, Cyril and myself handed over our cheques to Reggie Stephenson and collected our £5000 debenture bonds.

On the 23rd of September 1991, a credit of £40.62 appeared on my bank account. It was from Office Developments (International) Ltd. I thought it should have been £54.17 until I remembered that ODI had to withhold £13.54 as a tax to be paid to the Inland Revenue. When I saw that £40.62 + £13.54 = £54.16 I realised that Tony and/or Reggie had rounded 54.16666 *down* to 54.16 and *not up* to 54.17 thereby robbing me of 1 penny. Then I chided myself for being niggardly. What was one penny out of 5,417 pennies? The money was rolling in.

A year passed. During that time I occasionally heard from Chris extolling the benefits of working in an American-run school, being paid in Hong Kong dollars, and teaching so many beautiful girls. With his keen musical ear he had little difficulty coping with the four tones of Cantonese and soon learned to speak the language; the reading and writing of Chinese was another matter altogether. The 56,000 or so complicated characters were bad enough but when they all occupy the same space and run together on a page so you have to work out where each word starts and finishes, well who but the Chinese would bother. Chris was on a five-year contract; he planned to return to England before the island's sovereignty transferred in 1997 to the People's Republic of China under the Sino-British Joint Agreement. He was rather blasé about his monthly credit from ODI.

Cyril, by contrast, was like a cat with the cream. I saw him at the school's 1991 Christmas concert to which I was an invited guest. 'How are you, old boy,' said Cyril, beaming broadly but taking care not to offer me his hand. 'Pleased with our monthly return on our corporate bond, are we?' At my cautious *so far so good response*, he tut-tutted and said, 'Still have reservations, do we?' I still felt it too good to be true but I simply asked Cyril what his wife thought about it. 'In point of fact,' he replied, 'I haven't mentioned it to Marjorie yet. No need you see.' I didn't see and I rather suspected that Cyril also feared the venture might be too good to be true.

In September 1992 on the anniversary of the first payment, the thirteenth deposit of £40.62 appeared on our accounts. October and November saw two more such credits. The money usually appeared in the first week of each month. On the 22nd of December, a damp and chilly Tuesday, I telephoned my bank.

'No, I'm sorry, sir, there's no mistake. The cheque received from Office Developments (International) Ltd was not honoured.'

'What do you mean,' I asked, 'not honoured?'

'It failed to clear.'

'What do you mean,' I said, 'It failed to clear?'

'There were no funds in the account to cover it.'

'In other words,' I gasped, 'it bounced.'

'I'm afraid so, sir. Merry Christmas!'

'Cyril here. Is that you old boy?' whispered the voice when I answered my telephone.

'Yes, Cyril, it is,' I said. 'How are you? Ready for Christmas?'

'Look here,' whispered Cyril, 'I thought I'd better ring you about ODI.'

'What about ODI?' I asked as if I couldn't guess.

'They haven't paid me this month's interest. Have they paid you?'

'Yes and No,' I said.

'What do you mean, yes and no?'

'My bank got the cheque as usual but it bounced.'

'Oh, no!' said Cyril loudly. Then more quietly and in a calmer voice to his wife, 'No Marjorie, sorry my dear. Nothing's wrong. I'm on the telephone. Be there in a minute.'

'Let's not panic, Cyril,' I said. 'Leave this with me. I'll find out what's going on.'

Chris Lovell said he was probably coming home to spend Christmas with his parents, so I rang their number. Mrs Lovell confirmed he was back for Christmas but said he had gone out to do some last minute shopping. I left her my number and made it clear that I wanted to speak to her son as soon as he came in.

'Hello Chris. Thanks for ringing.'

'Mother thought it sounded urgent. What's up?'

'Have you checked your bank account today?'

'I've just drawn heavily on it but otherwise no, I haven't checked it.'

'Do you know if you got your monthly payment from ODI?'

'Now you mention it, I didn't,' said Chris, not sounding concerned.

'Neither did I and neither did Cyril. The cheques bounced.'

'Oh dear. I'll bet our classicist is in a flap.'

'That's putting it mildly. Any chance you could come with me tomorrow to find out what Tony and Reggie have been up to?'

'Tomorrow? Wednesday? Yes why not.'

'Thanks. I'll pick you up in the morning. 10 o'clock OK?'

'10 o'clock is fine with me. See you then.'

I parked near the warehouse delivery entrance, next to a familiar Ford Fiesta, and we walked around the building to the front entrance.

The security doors were wedged open as before. Through the glass doors we could see Reggie behind the TRADE section of the counter. He was smiling pleasantly to a tall white-haired fellow with his back to us. We entered and the glass door closed behind us. Reggie looked in our direction and asked, 'Have you come to see Tony?'

'Hello Cyril,' said Chris. 'Three minds with but a single thought.'

'I thought you were in Singapore,' said Cyril who seemed to have aged ten years since I had seen him just a few days before at the 1992 School Carol Service.

'Hong Kong, Cyril. Hong Kong,' said Chris.

'I don't think Tony is in yet,' said Reggie, reaching for the telephone.

'I should like to see for myself,' said Cyril heading towards the door marked private.

Reggie hurried from behind the counter and dashed ahead. When we entered the office, Tony was hurriedly trying to clear his desk of a mound of paperwork and what looked like account books. The ash-tray overflowed with cigarette ends and there was an unfamiliar sickly odour mingling with the smell of Turkish tobacco smoke in the hazy blue atmosphere.

On a small trolley alongside the leather chair was a computer whose monitor was displaying a complicated spreadsheet. Tony was red-faced and flustered. As he struggled to close an account book with his left hand and switch off the monitor with his right, he appeared to me like a second-rate magician unsuccessfully trying to perform a new trick. Cyril probably saw him as an overweight schoolboy whom he had caught red-handed in the act of some mischief.

'Sorry,' said Tony. 'I wasn't expecting you. I'm rather busy right now. Could…'

'I didn't get my cheque this month,' barked Cyril. 'I'd like to know why not.'

227

'Could you organise some coffee, Reggie,' said Tony regaining some composure.

'What's going on?' asked Reggie.

'Coffee, Reggie, there's a good chap,' said Tony.

'We haven't got any coffee. Sorry,' said Reggie apologetically to us, before turning to face his brother again. 'What's this about Mr Rainsthorp's cheque?'

'It's not just my cheque, young man,' said Cyril. 'It's all our cheques. They bounced!'

'They bounced?' said Reggie. 'I don't understand.'

'It's just a bit of a mix up. It's a cash-flow problem. I'm sorting it out now.'

'I wrote those cheques myself,' said Reggie. 'They shouldn't have bounced.'

'I don't care who wrote them,' said Cyril angrily. 'They bounced. I want to know why.'

'So do I,' said Reggie, glaring at Tony. 'What have you been up to?'

Sensing a family row brewing, Chris and I dragged a protesting Cyril out of the office, down the stairs and through the door into the warehouse. It was neither half full nor half empty; it was at least seven eighths empty. There was only one line of metal shelving and there were very few boxes on the shelves. The brick laboratory stood out like a tiny oasis on the concrete desert of the large warehouse floor. I guessed correctly the switch for the extractor fan then made my fellow creditors wait a few minutes before I switched on the light and opened the door. There were bottles and equipment on the bench and a stack of cardboard cartons against the left-hand wall much as before. We stepped inside.

The smell of paint thinners and other flammable liquids was almost overwhelming; so much for the efficiency of the extractor fan. I suspected that the door hadn't been opened in quite a while. I wondered what might have happened if I'd switched on the light first. One large bottle bore a label *Acetone – Highly Flammable* on which was a red diamond with a 3 in the middle, indicating on a scale from 0 to 4 a *serious fire hazard*. When I unscrewed the stopper, Cyril said, 'That smells like Marjorie's nail varnish remover.'

'That's just one of the minor uses of this stuff, Cyril.'

'Is it dangerous?'

'This large amount in this confined space is very dangerous. Acetone has a very low flash point; minus 20 centigrade.' Seeing the blank look on his face, I explained that a mixture of acetone vapour and air above minus 20 centigrade could explode. 'If memory serves me, as little as ten percent acetone in the air could blast this brick hut to rubble.'

'I don't much like the sound of that,' said Cyril. 'Marjorie has a bottle on her dressing table. I think I should...'

'I don't think there's much chance of Marjorie blowing up your house. You should be more worried about the toxic effects of acetone.'

'What do you mean, toxic effects?'

'If you inhale a large concentration of acetone vapour, it could damage your central nervous system and cause nausea, headaches and dizziness. You could become unconscious and fall into a coma.'

'I don't think I should like to get trapped in this hut with that stuff in the air,' said Chris who had just opened one of the thirty cardboard cartons. Then he changed the subject by saying, 'Look what's in this box, you chaps.'

The cardboard carton held two dozen full *Ink-Up* canisters. Based on its weight, we judged the other twenty-nine cartons also held two dozen full *Ink-Up* canisters. So, altogether we reckoned that there were 720 canisters for sale at £12.95 each.

'This lot is worth £9,324,' Chris said. 'That's £3,108 apiece if we each take 240 canisters and sell them for £12.95 a canister.'

'Don't forget we have already had £609.30 in interest,' I said. 'So £3,108 plus £609.30 equals...'

'What are you two babbling about,' interrupted Cyril. 'I'm an investor not a salesman. I want to know what they've done with my money.'

'Judging from Reggie's reaction to our news,' I said, 'I rather think the question is *What has Tony done with our money?*'

'He did seem pretty upset,' said Chris, stepping out into relatively fresh air of the warehouse. 'Let's come back tomorrow and have a word with him.'

'With Tony?' said Cyril.

'No, Cyril. With Reggie,' I said, closing the laboratory door and switching off the light and extractor fan.

'Let's speak to him now,' said Cyril, striding off towards the door behind the enquiries, retail and trade counter.'

* * * * *

Reggie was captain of soccer at his school and almost made the England National Under-17 team. At the age of eighteen he was given a trial by Wolverhampton Wanderers FC but he really wanted to be a mechanical engineer not a professional footballer playing for Wolves. He managed to get a place at Wolverhampton Poly on the strength of his modest A-level examination results but he eventually dropped out because he couldn't cope with the mathematics.

His clean-cut appearance and pleasant personality secured him several jobs which he failed to hold down. He was working as a sales assistant in a TV and electronics store when Tony persuaded him to join his private limited company Simpleton Computer Supplies. He soon learned what *private limited* and *join* meant; the company was limited to Tony, the sole director, and young Reggie had *joined* as an underpaid employee of his older brother.

When Tony was going to form Office Developments (International) Ltd, he persuaded Reggie to buy into the company – ten thousand shares at £1 per share – and become an equal partner. Reggie expressed concern at the cost but Tony had reassured him that he would get his money back in three years from dividends and his share of the profits. So Reggie gave Tony his savings and raised the rest with a bank loan. That was a couple of months before the three of us had parted with our money. So the question in the minds of the four of us was *What did Tony do with £25,000?*

'Can you get hold of the books?' I asked Reggie.

'The books?'

'The company accounts,' said Chris.

'Yes, I suppose so.'

'I saw a spreadsheet just now on the computer in Tony's office,' I said to Reggie. 'Can you get a backup of all the data files from that computer?'

'Yes, I suppose so,' he said again.

'Good. I'd like those books and files by tomorrow.'

'That's Christmas Eve,' said Reggie.

'Well spotted,' said Chris. 'Merry Christmas.'

Cyril Rainsthorp looked a ghastly colour by the time he reached his car. Although he assured me he was fine, I was worried about him, especially when I saw the way he drove out of the car park and I heard the squeal of brakes; he had pulled out without checking that the main road was clear. He was lucky; the driver of the oncoming vehicle applied his brakes in the nick of time.

231

Before I turned the key in the ignition to start my car, I asked Chris what he thought of the whole business. He didn't seem all that concerned about the possible loss of his £5,000 and twenty-one months interest at 13%. 'There's no gain without risk,' he said. 'Anyway, it's not over until the fat lady sings.' I wondered where that expression came from.

Chris was sure it had nothing to do with large females ending operas with an aria. 'It's a popular but unsupported theory,' said Chris. 'Not all operas end with a solo from the heroine and not all female opera singers are fat. It might stem from the popular saying *Church ain't over 'til the fat lady sings*; quite a few church choirs in the Southern States of America are falsely reputed to consist of generously proportioned females.' When I asked Chris what he thought was the origin of the saying, he replied, 'I like the Kate Smith theory. She was a very large woman who popularised Irving Berlin's song God Bless America and had her own late-night TV show. The station always closed down for the night immediately after her last song.'

The next day, in the afternoon of Christmas Eve, Reggie showed up at my house with various documents, account books and computer disks. After we had left the previous day, Tony apparently dodged all Reggie's questions. One thing led to another and they had a terrible argument that might have ended in blows if Tony had not stormed out of his office. 'That was the last I saw of him,' said Reggie. 'I closed up the building at 9 o'clock and went home. When he never appeared this morning, I grabbed all this stuff you said you wanted and here I am.'

'Are you any good with accounts and spreadsheets,' I asked Reggie.

'To be honest, I haven't a clue. Tony handled that side of the business.'

'But you wrote and signed the cheques, didn't you?'

'Yes, I did,' said Reggie sheepishly but that was all. 'I looked after the warehouse and dealt with the customers. I'm not really much good with figures but I get on well with people. Tony's the opposite. He's very good at mathematics and computing.'

'I know someone who'll help me make sense of these books and spreadsheets,' I said, thinking of Quentin Frobisher, my former colleague and Head of Economics.

'Can I hang on to all this for a while?'

'The warehouse is closed now until Monday the 4th January. My wife and I are going back to Wolverhampton for Christmas to see our parents. Tony's supposed to be coming too. We should all be back on Sunday the 3rd January. I usually open up the building in the morning, so I'll pop round here first thing Monday morning if that's alright with you.'

'That should be fine, Reggie. Thanks. If you're back early on the Sunday, give me a call. Perhaps you could come and see me then.'

* * * * *

My luck was in. Quentin was at home when I telephoned after Reggie had left. I told him that I had some accounts and needed his help. I didn't go into details and I didn't bring up Chris or Cyril's name. Quentin Frobisher was, like myself, one of the old school who believed in uniforms for the boys and gowns for the staff. He was a formidable and highly respected teacher. Many of his pupils gained Open Scholarships to Oxford or Cambridge.

Quentin himself obtained a First at LSE (The London School of Economics and Political Science, to give it its full name). Before he entered the teaching profession at age forty, he trained, qualified and worked as an accountant for a prestigious firm in London; he eventually became a Fellow Of The Institute Of Chartered Accountants In England And Wales. He did not suffer fools gladly.

I believe that all his pupils would remember the first time he spoke to them. They would see standing in front of them a tall, slender gentleman, wearing a white shirt and bow tie with a matching silk handkerchief cascading from the top pocket of his dark grey, three-piece, pin-striped suit. They would see beneath his dark, furrowed eyebrows a pair of piercing blue eyes looking over the top of a pair of gold-rimmed, half-moon spectacles balanced on the end of a thin nose.

They would see his hair precisely parted down the middle, brushed back from his forehead and matching in colour the steel grey of his neatly trimmed moustache. And they would hear him say, 'Good morning, gentlemen. You are about to embark upon a two-year journey of discovery in the complex and difficult world of Economics. I am here to teach. You are here to learn. It may reassure you to know that I shall expect from you neither more nor less than I expect from myself.'

I arrived at Quentin's house on Sunday, the 27th of December, at 10:30 in the morning and was welcomed inside to the aroma of freshly ground coffee.

'Black would be fine, thank you,' I said, knowing that my host frowned upon anyone spoiling the taste of coffee by adding milk or, God forbid, cream. 'Your wife…'

'Elouise has gone to church to pray for our souls.'

'You don't go?'

'Not during the holidays, except for midnight mass on Christmas Eve. The knees of my trousers get enough wear and tear every Sunday morning during school term.'

'I hope you don't mind my…'

'If I had minded, dear boy, I'd have said so when you telephoned last Thursday. So, what's the problem?'

'I think I've been had.'

My telephone rang on Tuesday morning at 9:30 a.m. at precisely the time Quentin said he would contact me. One hour later, Elouise opened the door and led me through the house to their sunny conservatory. As she poured me a cup of freshly ground Douwe Egbert's coffee, Quentin put aside his Times newspaper and looked at me over his half-moon glasses.

'You have been had, dear boy, and quite cleverly at that.' It came as no surprise but it still upset me to hear him say so. 'I see he's taken our resident classicist and our musical émigré for a ride as well.' I

234

nodded. 'I shouldn't imagine Christopher will lose much sleep over it. £5000 will be pocket money compared to his salary and perks in Hong Kong.'

When I said that our former music teacher hadn't seemed all that bothered, Quentin said, 'You never can tell. None of us likes to be robbed and even the mildest mannered soul can turn nasty. There was a case in the paper recently of a 76-year old grandmother who put a young mugger into hospital when he tried to steal her handbag.' When I deplored the fact that the old lady had been charged with assault, Quentin punctiliously quoted Mr Bumble in *Oliver Twist* by Charles Dickens: *the law is a ass*. When I asked him how he thought Cyril might react to being robbed, he said, 'That, my dear boy, is a very good question.'

When we had finished our coffee, we retired to Quentin's study. There were two leather armchairs facing the fireplace. The wall on either side of the bay window was hidden from top to bottom by solid oak shelves filled with books; many were leather bound and many, I should guess, were first editions. Behind the door and against the wall opposite the fireplace was a wooden roll-top desk; on it's pulled out writing section were Tony's account books. Alongside the antique desk was a modern metal trolley holding a printer and computer whose monitor was displaying one of Tony's spreadsheets. Quentin sat in his swivel chair. I sat by him on a chair he had fetched from the dining room. Before he even uttered one word, I asked myself why I hadn't consulted him *before* I gave Tony my money. Experience teaches even fools; *experientia docet stultos* Cyril would have said.

'So we've been had?'

'I'm afraid so.'

'How?'

'Quite simple really,' said Quentin. 'You lent money to Office Developments Ltd which transferred your money to Simpleton Computers Ltd, a company heavily in debt.'

'But ODI and SCS are *separate* companies. How could that happen?'

'Ah, now that's the clever bit. Firstly, SCS raised ODI's rent.'

'But Reggie said...'

'Tony's naïve brother, Reginald Stephenson?'

'Yes. He said that ODI just pays SCS a *nominal* rent for that brick laboratory.'

'I should hardly call £12000 per annum *nominal*.

'A thousand pounds a month. Why the...'

'Secondly, SCS charged ODI £250 per annum for lighting and heating and £400 per annum for cleaning.'

'Cleaning! What cleaning? You could plant seeds in the dust on the lab bench.'

'Thirdly, ODI paid SCS £12000 per annum in management charges.'

'Management charges?'

'ODI hired its staff from SCS.'

'What staff?' I asked but I knew the answer before Quentin replied.

'Anthony Simpleton and Reginald Stephenson, of course,' said Quentin.

'But... But...' I stuttered, 'Those two were joint sole owners and directors of ODI. How can they charge themselves for hiring themselves to themselves. It doesn't make sense!'

'Ah but you see, dear boy,' said Quentin. '*They* were not doing the hiring and charging. Their companies were. And they and their companies are separate legal entities.'

'What else did their *companies* do?'

'They paid their directors salaries, of course,' said Quentin.

'Salaries?'

'SCS paid Mr Anthony Simpleton, its only director, £1250 per month.'

'What about Reggie?' I asked. 'What did SCS pay him?'

'Very little I expect. He was an employee of SCS, not a director. Mr Stephenson is, however, an equal partner in ODI, the company which owes you money, but if these accounts are anything to go by, I believe your friend Reggie is worse off than you.'

'Why do you say that?'

'He and his brother are equal partners and directors of Office Developments (International) Ltd so they are equally responsible for its debts. Unlike Simpleton Computer Supplies Ltd, ODI did not, as far as I can tell, pay its directors a salary or any dividends on their shares. So, your friend Reggie has not been paid for his work and he stands to lose the £10,000 he paid for his shares which, being private shares, he cannot sell and which look to become worthless.'

'The rotten crook.. We'll have the law on him.'

'Unfortunately, dear boy, Mr Anthony Simpleton has not done anything illegal. So PC Plod will not be tapping his truncheon on Anthony's head let alone his front door.'

'We'll sue him then.'

'Waste of time,' said Quentin in his matter of fact voice. 'He's broke and being the crafty scoundrel his surname belies, he will no doubt shortly file for bankruptcy.'

'Poor old Reggie,' I said, beginning to feel genuinely sorry for him.

'He may not be that poor,' said Quentin. 'It looks as though both companies had directors share protection and life insurance in place.'

'What does that mean?'

'If a director/partner were to die, share protection insurance provides cash for the company to buy the shares of the deceased from their beneficiaries. In the case of Office Developments (International) Ltd, if Mr Simpleton were to die then Mr Stephenson would, for all practical purposes, collect on the insurance.'

'How much might that be?' I asked.

'£100,000.'

'One hundred thousand pounds! I wonder if Reggie realises this?'

'You might ask him the next time you see him, dear boy. Anyway, Let me take you through these accounts.'

For the next hour Quentin showed me how to read company accounts and distinguish between a profit & loss statement and a balance sheet. He explained that both basically deal with *assets* (what a company owns) and *liabilities* (what a company owes) but the P&L covers a period of time (3, 6 or 12 months) and the balance sheet gives the financial position on a given day.

As we looked through Tony's accounts Quentin bandied terms such as fixed and current assets, net asset value, EBITDA (earnings before interest, tax depreciation and amortisation) and operating profit. He was in danger of losing me when he introduced *liquidity ratio* (current assets divided by current liabilities) and calculated the value for Simpleton Computers. When I asked somewhat naively what it meant, he said, 'Anything less than 1.0 is bad news. This value of 0.006 is extremely bad news.'

* * * * *

'One hundred thousand pounds? Are you sure?' gasped Reggie.

'No, Reggie, I'm not sure but it should be easy enough for you to check. Look for the policy document. It's probably somewhere in Tony's filing cabinet.'

'So according to your friend, we've been had?'

'Good and proper, Reggie, and there's nothing we can do about it.'

'I'm not so sure about that,' he replied giving me a strange look as I got up to answer the front door bell.

'Chris! Cyril! Come on in. Reggie's already here. Find yourselves seats. I'll be with you in a tick.' As I returned with a tray of coffee and biscuits, I heard Cyril's raised voice.

'That brother of yours has robbed me of my savings. He's a crook and should be in gaol.'

'Careful, Cyril, that's slander.' I said as I handed out the coffee. 'Quentin assured me that Tony has done nothing illegal.'

'We should sue the scoundrel,' said Cyril, lowering his voice a little.

'Waste of time. According to Quentin, Tony's broke and will probably declare himself bankrupt.'

'We cannot just do *nothing*. We can't let him get away with our money,' fumed Cyril.

'What do you suggest?' said Chris. 'Turn him upside down and shake the coins out of his pockets?'

'I don't think any money would fall out,' said Reggie, 'but the contents of his tobacco tin might be of interest to the police.'

'Look here,' said Cyril, 'I don't want the fellow locked up on a drugs charge. I just want my money back.'

239

After we had all felt suitably sorry for ourselves, that meeting on the 3rd of January 1993 broke up. Cyril left first in a huff and drove down the road even more erratically than before. He worried me. In spite of our advice and what he had heard, he was determined to have it out with Tony. As I gathered up the coffee cups I heard Reggie asking Chris if he knew anything about electrical wiring. 'A bit,' said Chris.

He was being unduly modest. Chris knew a lot. He completely rewired the stage sound and lighting; he saved Lytchett Upper a small fortune. When I returned from the kitchen, I heard Chris say, 'Tomorrow morning then. Eight o'clock at the warehouse. I'll bring a couple of screwdrivers. We shouldn't need anything else if it's just a couple of wall switches you want looked at.'

After lunch I sat down and read my Sunday newspaper. The sorry state of the world and the desperate plight of others helped to put my relatively small financial loss into perspective. Quentin had pointed out that the £5000 wasn't a complete write off. I had received £609.30 in interest payments and I could set the £4390.70 loss against my capital gains. Even though I had no capital gains, I appreciated Quentin's trying to cheer me up. I put all thoughts of Tony's skulduggery out of my mind and settled down to the Telegraph crossword.

Monday the 4th of January 1993 came and went quickly. Although I was only in my second year of retirement, I was already routinely wondering where the days went and how time flies; tempus fugit as Cyril would probably say in his retirement; a state he was not destined to achieve. I cannot remember what I did that day but I recalled that Chris was to see Reggie in the early morning and to catch his 12-hour flight out of Heathrow in the late afternoon. It was just after breakfast on Tuesday the 5th of January when I answered the telephone and heard Marjorie Rainsthorp's voice.

'Marjorie! *Marjorie.* Calm down. I can't understand what you're saying.'

'It's Cyril,' she sobbed. 'There's been a terrible accident. He's dead.'

'Dead? Are you sure?'

'Yes. The police have just been here. They looked the same age as my own children. The young woman police constable… Oh dear! Was that right? Are they still WPCs? She was very sweet…'

'*Marjorie*! Tell me what happened? Was any other vehicle involved?'

'Vehicle? What do you mean, *vehicle*?' said Marjorie. 'I don't understand?'

'It was a traffic accident involving his car, wasn't it?'

'No. It was nothing to do with his car. I know he's been a bit… not reckless exactly. No, not reckless. Careless perhaps. He's had a lot on his mind lately but he wouldn't tell me what was bothering him. Do you know what it was? He said he came to see you last Sunday… I thought perhaps…'

'Marjorie,' I said in a firm, quiet voice, 'how did Cyril die?'

'The policeman said he was…' she started to sob, 'they said he'd been killed.'

> *…and our political correspondent reported the rumour that in the forthcoming budget, the Prime Minister, Mr John Major, intends to replace the controversial Community Charge, a Poll Tax introduced under Margaret Thatcher in 1990, by a Council Tax.*
>
> *Turning to local news… An explosion occurred today in a warehouse on an industrial estate. At least one person is believed dead. Nearby buildings are undamaged. Police and the fire brigade are on the scene. The cause of the explosion is as yet unknown.*
>
> *Now over to the weather centre for the latest forecast.*

It was several days before a more detailed report appeared in the newspaper and I read that the explosion had occurred inside the A SIMPLETON'S COMPUTER SUPPLIES warehouse and that the bodies of two men had been identified, that of Cyril Rainsthorp, Senior

241

Classics Master at Lytchett Upper and... 'Two policemen to see you, dear,' said my wife, showing the uniformed men into my study.

'Good morning, sir,' said the inspector. 'My name is Trustcott. This is Sergeant Preston.'

'We're conducting inquiries into the explosion at a local warehouse. You may be able to help us. Do you mind if my sergeant takes notes?'

'No, not at all, inspector,' I said shaking my head. 'How can I help?'

'I understand that you knew the gentlemen who died in the explosion.'

'Yes, I did,' I said. 'They were colleagues.'

'Can we start with Mr Rainsthorp? How well did you know him?'

'Well, he and I were heads of departments at the same school for over ten years...'

'That would be Lytchett Upper?' said the sergeant.

'Yes, that's right. He was Head of Classics and I was Head of Science.'

'You are a chemist, is that right Dr Cox?'

'Yes. My Ph.D. was in Physical Chemistry.'

'I understand,' said the inspector. 'My son's doing chemistry at Bristol. He hopes to do a Ph.D. in Organic chemistry. Anyway, getting back to Mr Rainsthorp. I gather from Mrs Rainsthorp that her husband came to see you last Sunday. Is that right?'

'Yes.'

'How did Mr Rainsthorp seem to you?'

'How do you mean?' I asked.

'Did he seem upset? Was anything bothering him, would you say?'

'Cyril was… Look, I don't believe he told his wife this… He was in a flap because he had just discovered that he had, in his words, been swindled out of money he'd put aside for his retirement. When he left here he was extremely agitated.'

'Have you any idea how much money, sir?'

'A little over five thousand pounds,' I said thinking of the twenty-one months of interest we wouldn't get as well as the £4390.70 loss we could set against capital gains.

'Can you think of any reason why Mr Rainsthorp would be at that warehouse at the time of the explosion?'

'He could have been looking for Tony Simpleton.'

'Ah, yes. Mr Anthony Simpleton, the owner of the warehouse. You knew him I believe.'

'Yes. He taught for five years at Lytchett Upper before leaving teaching to start his own business.'

'And Mr Rainsthorp thought that Mr Simpleton had swindled him?'

'Yes.'

'And why should he have thought that, sir?'

At this point it seemed easier to explain how Tony had borrowed Cyril's money and used it to pay off some of his debts. When the inspector asked if I had visited the warehouse, I said that I had. When he asked why, I explained the reasons. When the sergeant asked if I had seen the brick hut and been inside it, I nodded.

'We think it was some kind of laboratory. Would you agree, sir?'

'That is what Tony, sorry Mr Simpleton, called it, inspector.'

'Could you tell us what was in it?'

'A bench with bits of equipment on top and various bottles of liquids underneath. That was on one side. There were cardboard boxes stacked on the other side. They contained aluminium canisters of ink for spraying on printer and typewriter ribbons.'

'Were these canisters pressurised?'

'Not in the usual sense of *pressurised*,' I said, 'but the ink contained volatile liquids and the canisters were capped. So…'

'They might explode under certain circumstances?'

'Yes. They might very well,' I said.

'What about the liquids in the bottles under the bench; do you know what they were?'

'I think they were the volatile liquids Mr Simpleton used to make his special ink.'

'Dangerous, were they sir?'

'Yes, sergeant. One or two were highly flammable and therefore very dangerous.'

'One last question, sir,' said the inspector. 'In your professional opinion, how safe do you think the laboratory was?'

'Let me put it this way,' I said, 'any decent Health & Safety inspector would have closed him down like a shot.'

As soon as the two policemen had left, my first thought was to call Chris in Hong Kong but then I remembered we were eight hours behind in Britain and realised my fellow creditor would be asleep in bed. I telephoned the next day; he was out. It was five o'clock in his afternoon when I tried again on Sunday the 10th of January.

I was just in time. He was getting ready to go out, to a restaurant and then to a *Music for Christmas and New Year* concert, at St. John's Cathedral, with the Hong Kong Chamber Orchestra conducted by Jerome Hoberman. 'Pity you're not here,' said Chris. 'They're doing The Christmas Oratorio by Bach; Handel's Messiah: A Sacred Oratorio, Part 1 and the Hallelujah Chorus from Part 2, ...'

'Sorry to cut you short, Chris, but I've some terrible news. It's about Cyril Rainsthorp.'

'What about Cyril?'

'He's dead.'

'We've all got to go sometime, old chap. Heart attack was it?'

'No. He was killed.'

'Car crash?'

'No. An explosion in Tony Simpleton's warehouse.'

'You still there Chris?'

'Yes, I'm still here,' he said after what musicians call a *lunga pausa*. 'When did it happen?'

'Early last Tuesday morning.'

'Any idea how it happened?' Chris asked in what seemed a nervous voice.

'The police are investigating. They were here on Friday asking me what I knew about that brick hut Tony called his laboratory.'

'What did you tell them?'

'I told them what was inside the hut and that it did not comply with the Health & Safety at Work Act,' I replied. 'I should simply have told them it was a death trap.'

245

'Poor old Cyril. What a way to go,' said Chris in a strange voice.

'It was quick, I believe, and he didn't die alone,' I said. 'The police identified the bodies of two men at the scene.'

'Who was the other... Was it Reggie?'

'Why do you think the other man was Reggie?'

'I just thought... Didn't Reggie say he was always first there, to open up the warehouse early in the morning.'

'Yes, he did. In point of fact,' I said, thinking of Cyril, 'it was Tony.'

Perhaps I was mistaken but I thought I heard Chris utter a sigh of relief, especially when I told him that I thought the police were treating the deaths as accidental. At the mention of Reggie, I realised that I had not seen or heard from him for a week; curiously, the police hadn't asked me if I knew him. 'Look, I don't want you to be late for your concert but may I ask what you and Reggie were talking about last Sunday?'

'I don't rightly remember?' Chris replied unconvincingly.

'Sounded to me like he was picking your brains. Something to do with electrical wiring?'

'Oh, yes. That's right. He wanted my help to fix a switch.'

'Not the two switches on the outside wall of that brick hut, by any chance?'

'As a matter, it was. He wanted me to check the wiring. Something about the extractor fan not always coming on. He thought the switch might be faulty.'

'Was it?'

'No. It looked OK to me. We checked the wiring in the light switch while we were at it.'

246

'Reggie watched you dismantle those switches and put them back together again?'

'Yes he did. He seemed very keen to learn. I was surprised that he had never in his life wired a switch and didn't know how to shut off the power at the fuse box. Come to think of it, he didn't even know where to find the mains switch.'

'That's what he led you to believe anyway,' I said. 'Very interesting. I'd better let you go. You'll be late for your meal. I assume you're not dining alone.'

'No, not alone. I shall be enjoying the company of a colleague; charming young lady who is, as Eddie Duchin wrote *Lovely to look at, delightful to know*.' As he rang off, I had a vague recollection that the line continued with *and heaven to kiss*; but I could be wrong.

* * * * *

It was the 1st of April. I remember because I was skimming an article in the paper about a legal action, brought in the European Community, against British Gypsum Ltd and BPB Industries plc who were, according to their accusers, the Commission of European Communities, supported by the Kingdom of Spain and Iberian Trading (UK) Limited, monopolising the supply of plaster and plasterboard in contravention of Article 86 of the EEC Treaty governing competition. Just as I was coming to the conclusion that the article was not an April Fools Day joke, the front door bell rang. It was Reggie Stephenson.

'I'm sorry not to have been in touch,' he said. 'The past three months have been rather hectic as you can imagine.' I hung up his tailored overcoat and waved him into a chair. He looked the picture of health sitting there in his smart corduroy two-piece suit. His polo-neck shirt was woven from a fine, cream-coloured wool – pure cashmere I believe – that was not blemished by a logo of any kind. His socks and shoes matched the rest of his outfit in colour, style and, no doubt, expense.

After my wife had brought in the coffee and closed the study door behind her, Reggie said, 'I really did mean to get in touch sooner but

247

what with one thing and another.' I sipped my coffee and waited for him to continue. 'How did Mrs Rainsthorp take her husband's death?' I lifted my shoulders, tilted my head and took another sip of coffee. 'It's all my fault you know. He should never have died like that. It was my fault... all my fault.'

According to Reggie, his brother came in very early on that Tuesday to work on the books. Cyril arrived shortly afterwards and brushed past Reggie who was wedging open the metal security doors. He heard Cyril shout at Tony. When Reggie looked round, he saw his brother dodging behind the counter and Cyril following him. Reggie was in the car park by his car when he heard the explosion. He ran back to the front entrance to find the foyer carpet covered in shards of glass. An acrid smoke was billowing through the open doorway behind the counter. He put a handkerchief over his nose and mouth and managed to dial the emergency services from the telephone at the enquiries end of the counter. The worst moment was when they brought out the two badly burned bodies.

'Why do you think Cyril's death was your fault, Reggie?' I asked quietly.

'I shouldn't have let him in. I could see he was in no state to tackle Tony.'

'What do you think caused the explosion?'

'All I can think is that Tony dashed to his laboratory to get away. Mr Rainsthorp ran after him. In the rush Tony probably didn't give the extractor fan enough time to work.'

'Or perhaps he switched on the light first,' I said.

'Oh, he wouldn't have done that. Tony knew which switch was which and he was always careful to put on the fan first. Mind you, it had been playing up. I asked Mr Lovell to take a look at the switches for me but he said the wiring was fine.'

'The police recorded the deaths as accidental, I believe.'

'Yes. They did. They were very thorough. They asked me a lot of questions about the stuff in the laboratory that I couldn't answer. I hope you didn't mind but I said that you might be able to help.'

'I told them what I could, Reggie. I think they were satisfied.' As I said that, a terrible question came into my head. Did I screw the stopper back on that bottle of acetone?'

As Reggie was leaving, he shook my right hand and placed an envelope in my left. When his red Mercedes was out of sight, I returned to my study to find my wife gathering up the coffee cups. 'He seemed a nice young man,' she said. 'Wholesome. Yes, wholesome.' When I picked up my souvenir of Paris letter opener, my wife said, 'What have you got there?' I slit open the envelope and handed it to my wife. 'Goodness me!' she exclaimed.

My first phone call was to Hong Kong. Chris had just finished his evening meal. 'What's that, old boy? Speak up. It's not a very good line.' He listened carefully to my question then said, 'Hang on a minute, I haven't actually seen today's post.' I heard the sound of an envelope being torn open and then a loud whistle. 'Hello! You still there, old boy?' When he knew I was still listening, he said, 'What a stroke of luck. Did you get one as well?'

My second telephone call was to Cyril's widow. 'Hello! Marjorie Rainsthorp speaking,'

'Hello Marjorie,' I said. 'How are you? Bearing up?'

'I'm as well as can be expected.' She was obviously still missing Cyril.

'Marjorie, did a smartly dressed young chap drop in to see you today?'

'In point of fact, yes. He said he was a friend of Cyril. I'd never seen him before.'

'No, you probably wouldn't have done. He was just somebody Cyril and I knew. He was really just a casual acquaintance.'

'It was odd, you see. He didn't tell me his name and he wouldn't come in. He just handed me an envelope and said it was what Cyril would have wanted me to have. I couldn't believe my eyes. Is it genuine? I mean it is April Fools Day.'

'I'm sure it's quite genuine, Marjorie. It's not every day somebody gives us cheques for ten thousand pounds.'

* * * * *

Epilogue

Two colleagues and I were foolish enough to lend a former colleague £5000 each. We did receive interest for fifteen months and we did set our net loss against capital gains; but we still lost more than £4000. At the time of writing, only one of my two colleagues is still alive; the other died of natural causes. I did teach for five years in an independent school but I was never Head of Science or chairman of a staff common room. There was a brick shed, located in a warehouse and subject to various charges. There was also a product for re-inking typewriter and printer ribbons but it was not called Ink-Up.

There were, I confess, moments when I should have liked to do away with the rogue who relieved us of our money but deep down I knew that if I were to commit such a crime and I were able to evade the law, I should not escape the judgement of my own conscience and the inevitable punishment it would inflict upon me for taking the life of another.

The London School of Economics and Political Science is a specialist single-faculty constituent college of London University and the only one of its kind in England. The LSE, located in Westminster and near the Courts of Justice and Temple Bar, is a world leader in research and the teaching of social science. It probably has the most international student body of any university in the world today.

The are several clichés in sports such as baseball, basketball, football and hockey that imply one cannot be sure of the result until the final whistle. Not all invoke a fat lady singing. Their origins are variously attributed to Ralph Carpenter, Dan Cook, Bill Morgan and Yogi Bera. Kate Smith, who helped to popularise Irving Berlin's God Bless America by singing it at the start of many hockey games, was fat. She once weighed 235 pounds.

Acetone is used as nail varnish remover and the hazards mentioned in the story are true. It is very volatile and its vapour does form an explosive mixture with air, the percentages ranging from 2.5 to 12.8 by volume of vapour; a static discharge could detonate it. Acetone should never be stored in a refrigerator with an interior light switch.

A GORILLA IN THE CUPBOARD

This story concerns a real event I witnessed and a likely consequence I imagined. I have not named the school where this occurred or used the real names of the teachers and pupil concerned in order, hopefully, to avoid costly legal actions. To any former colleagues who were also witness to the event and who might think themselves unfavourably portrayed in my story, may I assert that the names and characters are the product of my imagination and any resemblance to actual persons, living or dead, is entirely coincidental.

* * * * *

During the time when I was a pupil and subsequently a teacher in England, the school year of about 38 weeks was divided into three terms by the Christmas, the Easter and the Summer holidays. Each term - winter, spring and summer - was usually split into two by a one-week break at approximately mid-term. To anyone who has never taught classes of up to 30 or so pupils at a time, teachers might seem to have a cushy life. Indeed, I had a friend who took great delight in asking me when I was going to get a proper job. He worked for a commercial company, 8-hours a day, 5 days a week, with a 3-week summer holiday and just a few days at Christmas, New Year and Easter.

I shall not attempt to argue a detailed case for teachers here. Suffice it to say, my salary was much lower than my friend's salary, I received no Christmas bonus or overtime pay, and I took work home evenings and weekends. Anyway, the point I wish to make is that my colleagues and I worked hard and were always glad when the last day of the summer term arrived.

'Settle down. The final bell hasn't gone yet. Make sure you clear everything out of your desks. Anything left behind may – I say *may* – end up in lost property. Problem?'

'Are you going on the French trip this summer, sir?

'*Peut-être. Je ne suis pas certain.* Desk lids open, gentlemen.'

'Sir, could I ...' The rest of his sentence was drowned by the loud final bell and the even louder noise of thirty boys banging down their desks lids and hurrying to the door.

When the last of my charges had disappeared, it took me a few moments to adjust to l'état de calme. It was almost twenty past two. Enough time for me to sort and file away various papers, tidy the books on my shelf and clear the top of my desk before the cleaners started their rounds. It was ten minutes to three when I walked into the staff common room to check my pigeon hole for any last minute memo from the Second Master and to scan the notice board. The invitation was still pinned up.

The High Master is pleased to invite all teaching staff to join him for sherry at 3 p.m.

As I entered the study, I was offered the statutory small glass of Jerez de la Fronteira 'Fino'. I prefer their 'Oloroso' but in the headmaster's opinion, nobody with a decent palate would countenance such a tipple. At precisely 3 o'clock, we were all present and as correct as we'd ever be. On the first chime of the clock in the college tower, Dr Anthony Saint-John Howard (pronounced 'sinjun' in the best circles) and his acolyte, the Second Master, entered. They circulated separately - the pair were nothing if not discrete - to exchange a few pleasantries.

'Looking forward to the French trip are we?' I was, as it happens, but the question was rhetorical. The good doctor had moved on before I could raise a faint smile. At 3:15 p.m. precisely, we turned to face the large, antique desk - in old oak to match the panelled study walls and bookcases - for the annual speech of thanks and congratulations for our jobs well done. At 3:30 p.m. precisely, we raised our glasses and drained the few remaining drops of sherry in support of the Second Master's reply on our behalf. The formalities over, we trooped back to the common room to start our long summer holiday.

'Listen up, chaps,' said Alan 'Jock' Crawford, 'we've organised a 100-yards staff dash for a bit of fun. We're starting at 4 o'clock.'

'I'm game,' said one of the new young members of staff. 'On the track near the 1st XI cricket pavilion?'

'*Gaudeamus igitur iuvenes dum sumus*!' quoted the Head of Classics. 'Therefore let us rejoice while we are young!'

'Come on,' said Jock, 'it's handicap race. The older you are the bigger the handicap.'

'Sorry, old boy, but my body is already my biggest handicap. I shall be happy to join the spectators. If I may quote Horace, '*Eheu fugaces labuntur anni.*'

'Alas, the fleeting years do slip by,' said Jock who taught Latin and ran the 1st XI cricket.

'Count me out,' I said, pulling a face, 'I've got a doctor's note for my arthritis.'

After some repartee from the master i/c rugby and a rather more erudite comment from the Head of History, Jock said, 'It's for fun. No running kit or running shoes allowed. We'll fire the starting gun at 4 o'clock sharp. Don't be late.'

That's how it started. A half-dozen took part. A few of us cheered them on from the pavilion steps. The rest of the staff went home. The following summer a few more took part. One of the runners wore a floppy sun hat. Another had a red bandanna around his forehead. A few more stayed behind to watch. One of the housemasters brought some cans of beer. At the end of the race, most of us stood around chatting for a while. Before we knew it, the summer end-of-term staff dash had become the excuse for us to gather and unwind over a bottle of beer or a glass of wine.

We'd put money in a kitty to cover the drinks and to buy the hamburgers which the Head of business studies would turn into burnt offerings on the barbeque. Some participants transformed the race into a costume parade. Straw hats. Coloured braces (suspenders in America) holding up baggy trousers. Bowler hat and umbrella. T-shirt from the Canary Islands. Even a pair of striped pyjamas. It was, after all, just a bit of fun. Clearly, however, with each successive year, the members of that merry band of runners were trying to outdo one another. Just when we thought the limit of this absurd competition had been reached, one of the least likely of our colleagues surprised us all.

* * * * *

It has been my lot to have taught boys only. It has been my further my lot to have taught in schools and colleges with highly qualified staff and extremely intelligent pupils. It has also been my experience to have encountered more than my fair share of eccentricity amongst both the staff and the boys.

In the five or six years leading up to what I shall call, with apologies to William Shakespeare, the summer of our content, the Head of music was fortunate in having an extremely gifted young pianist as a pupil. Indeed, this boy's solos in the school concerts were a delight. Moreover, his sensitive playing – always from memory – was of such a high standard that a senior colleague, who reported on the concerts for the school magazine, always wrote as though he were the Times music critic analysing the performance of a celebrated professional.

Now according to my tutees, it was well known to everybody except the Head of Music that this young pianistic prodigy was in the habit of borrowing a large number of long-playing classical records for the summer holiday. My sources told me that he would raid the music cupboard when the final bell had rung and the Head of music had gone to the common room. On the first day back - at the start of the winter term – I was assured he would return the records to the cupboard, sneaking into the music department early before anyone was about. In all previous summers, his visits to the cupboard had been uneventful. This time there was a surprise in store – in the music store to be precise.

* * * * *

The final bell had sounded. My papers were filed away. The books on my shelf were in ordnung. My desk was clear. The High Master's invitation was on the common room notice board as usual. His speech was as dry as his 'Fino'. His second-in-command's reply was as sweet as a Jerez 'Dulce'. The staff dash was all set for 4 o'clock. There was plenty of time to complete a few last minute chores in the common room. On my way there I thought I heard two noises. The first sounded like a grunt and the second like a scream. Both seemed to come from the music room. I probably should have investigated but I was suffering from end-of-year fatigue and just couldn't be bothered.

The department appeared to be deserted when Jeremy Fitzgibbon, our young pianist entered. As he approached the door of the large music cupboard, he was playing loudly in his head the piano part of *L'Éléphant mouvement* no. 5 - for double-bass and piano - from the musical suite *Le Carnaval des Animaux* by Camille Saint-Saëns.

The French composer's *groupe zoologique* had lions, hens, roosters, asses, tortoises, elephants, kangaroos, cuckoos, an aquarium, an aviary, a swan and even fossils. Ironically, it had no primates in any shape or form. Jeremy was still playing the waltz-like triplet figure on the piano and hearing the double-bass humming the melody - all in his head - when he reached the cupboard.

When he opened the door and stepped inside, his thoughts were on the records he would borrow. From within the darkness there was a muffled grunt. Jeremy switched on the light and screamed – out loud – and not in his head.

* * * * *

It was one of those hot, dry days with which the summer holidays rarely began. The aroma from the BBQ was already filling the air. The spectators assembled on the pavilion steps near the finish line. The gaily bedecked competitors were assembling at their handicapped positions in the distance. The starting pistol was raised.

'On your marks!'

'Get set!'

Before the gun could be fired, a gorilla lumbered into view and posed on the start line.

'I say, chaps, there's a gorilla on the track,' exclaimed a biology teacher.

'That's no way to speak of... crikey! You're right,' said one of the chemists.

'*Fallaces sunt rerum species*, as Seneca would have said,' quoted the Head of Classics. 'Old Seneca was right,' I thought, 'the appearances of things are deceptive. Who is that in a gorilla outfit?'

'*Vestis virum reddit,*' said our classics scholar, quoting Quintilianus.

'*Clothes maketh the man* is hardly appropriate, old boy,' said Jock. 'It's a gorilla suit.'

A mathematician started to tick names off a staff list to identify the gorilla by the method of elimination. The Head of History and former guards officer who ran the school cadet corps raised his pistol for a second time.

'On your marks!' he barked.

'Get set!'

The shot he fired into the air made the gorilla jump and take off.

'It's our music master! It's Tudor Williams!' exclaimed the Head of Mathematics. 'No one else on the staff has such uncoordinated legs. And the way his arms are moving, I'd say he's still conducting the school orchestra.'

All eyes were on the gorilla. He was going to be last but clearly not least. He was stealing the show. As he got closer to the finish line, his legs seemed to become progressively more uncoordinated. His last few yards to the line was a sight to behold. His arms and legs thrashed wildly and independently in different directions. He reached the finish line and then, to everyone's surprise, he staggered onwards for ten more yards and then collapsed.

It was a wonderful performance. He came in last but in a grand style unsurpassed to this day. We were all laughing and cheering even when he was on his back, all his limbs still thrashing wildly. Then Howard, the Head of Biology, grabbed me and said, 'Something's wrong.'

'We've got to take his head off,' said Howard.

'Shall I fetch a saw from the workshops?'

'This is no time for flippancy. He's in trouble. Help me with this zip.'

'What the ...?'

'He's hyperventilating. Help me get him into the pavilion.'

When we removed the head of the gorilla we recognised the face of Tudor Williams but only just. He might have been an astronaut in a rocket accelerating out of the earth's atmosphere, except that he was in a gorilla costume lying on his back on the school running track. His skin was waxy and grey in colour. It was stretched so tightly against his high cheek bones that it looked translucent. His cheeks were rippling and pulsating. His mouth was held open in a grimace. His lips were rapidly vibrating and noisily sucking in great gulps of air. I helped Howard lift him to his feet and heave him into the pavilion where, to everyone's relief, he recovered quite quickly.

'What were you thinking of?' we asked.

'I saw this outfit in the window of our local costume and fancy dress shop. I thought it would be a bit of fun.'

'It was fun until you fell over and we realised you were in difficulties.'

'Looks like I made a bit of a fool of myself, didn't I?'

'Nemo risum prebuit, qui ex se coepit,' said our elderly classicist quoting Seneca again.

'I beg your pardon,' said Tudor.

'Roughly translated,' said Jock, 'nobody is laughed at, who laughs at himself.'

'Fancy a hamburger?' asked Howard.

'Just give me a few more minutes and time to get out of this outfit. I'm boiling in it.'

'Fine!' said Jock. 'See you at the barbeque.'

'Tudor, old chap,' I said, 'when did you put on this costume?'

'Straight after the final bell.'

'Where did you put it on? Here in the pavilion?'

'Oh, no. I didn't want to be seen until the race was about to start. That would have spoilt the surprise.'

'So where did you put it on?

'In my music cupboard.'

'Did you hide in the cupboard till 4 o'clock?'

'Yes. It's the perfect place. Nobody goes there after the bell, do they?'

'No,' I thought, 'and young Fitzgibbon certainly won't be going there again in a hurry.'

* * * * *

Epilogue

There was a music master who put on a gorilla costume and hid in his music cupboard. There was a pupil who was in the habit of borrowing LP recordings from that cupboard for the summer holidays. It is, therefore, highly probable that the pupil encountered a gorilla in the cupboard.

There was a staff dash after school on the last day of the summer term. The music master did run in a gorilla costume on a hot, dry day and hyperventilate. And his appearance was much as I described. I did assist the Head of Biology that day but I taught Chemistry, not French.

For the record, hyperventilation (sometimes called overbreathing) is rapid, deep breathing leading to low levels of carbon dioxide in the blood. It is often caused by anxiety or panic. The overbreathing may exacerbate the anxiety and lead to a vicious circle of panic and hyperventilation.

WATER OF LIFE

The Bristol-Bordeaux family-to-family exchange began in 1947 with one teacher and twenty-seven pupils from Fairfield Grammar School. The scheme rapidly expanded. In the Easter of 1951, more schools – my own included – were involved and more than one hundred pupils took part - myself included – even though I was no longer studying French. In April 2007, the exchange scheme celebrated its 60th year jubilee.

* * * * *

In July 1950, we all sat at desks in the school gymnasium of Merrywood Grammar School For Boys to take what we called *the school cert*. It was the culmination of our five years of study. One incident stands out in my mind. As Roger and I entered the gym for the three-hour chemistry paper, I wished him good luck. My friend grinned and said he would leave as soon as the supervisor would let him.

Roger hated chemistry as much as I loved it. My best subject was his worst. From my seat near the back, I could see Roger at his desk near the front and on the far side of the gym. Whenever I happened to glance in his direction, he was writing and, to my surprise, he was still writing when the supervisor told us to put down our pens.

As soon as we were outside the gym I rushed over to Roger eager to know which six of the ten questions he'd tackled.

'Didn't do any,' he said.

'But you were writing for the whole three hours, weren't you?'

'No, not really,' he replied.

'But I saw you.'

'I wasn't writing,' he said with a grin. I wasn't answering any of those chemistry questions, if that's what you think,' he said with an even bigger grin on his face.

'So what were you doing if you weren't writing?'

'I was using the exam paper to play book cricket!'

Our exam results, which included a distinction in French for each of us, persuaded the school to admit us into the Sixth Form and persuaded our parents to bear the financial burden that entailed. In September 1950, Roger began the two-year Advanced Level course in French and, I believe, in English and Latin. I took chemistry, physics and mathematics. During that first winter term, James G Clark, the master i/c the Sixth Form and the language teacher, suggested it might be good for us to go on the Bristol-Bordeaux Exchange.

Mr. Clark – a Scotsman better known to us by his nickname 'Angus' – had tried to persuade me to do French and Latin, claiming they were my best subjects. I resisted by saying that I could learn languages in my own time but not chemistry and physics which required a laboratory for the practical work. Whether or not French was my best subject, I had enjoyed it and I was delighted when my parents let me go with Roger on the exchange.

For the last few weeks of the winter term and for all the weeks leading up to Easter, 1951, I could not rid myself of a very bad cold. I always walked to and from school with Roger and other friends. The school was at the top of a hill and reached by more than a hundred steps. When I arrived at the top I would be wheezing and coughing fit to die.

I felt bad. The fact that my face was covered in blackheads and boils made me feel worse. Our family doctor, Dr John Pollard, a delightful, elderly Irishman with a hearing aid as defective as the ear it was supposed to help, tried a range of medicines on me without success. The acne and acne vulgaris even resisted his three-week course of *arsenic*!

The infection on my chest and/or lungs may, or may not, have been bronchitis or pneumonia – *tis a mystery to be sure it is, that's what it is, a mystery* - but whatever it was, I still had it when the time came to depart for Bordeaux. Throughout the journey by train and cross-channel boat, I stifled my wheezing and coughing in a handkerchief and buried my ugly face in Dr Phillip Frank's biography of Albert Einstein. Roger, by contrast, in the pink of condition, dilly-dallied from Bristol to Bordeaux with young ladies from a variety of schools.

* * * * *

Our first unforgettable smell and taste of France was at a Youth Hostel in Paris. It was at breakfast (*le petit déjeuner*) - *l'arôme et le goût du café et des baguettes*. We drank the coffee from a large bowl. The bread was fresh from la boulangerie. Long and thin, crusty on the outside and soft inside, it was still warm enough to melt *du beurre* but not to affect *la confiture d'orange*.

265

That coffee, bread and marmalade was the best I have ever tasted. Although I have been back to France and to Paris (but not that hostel) since then, I have never managed to recapture the magic of that first breakfast. We were probably shown la *Tour Eiffel, l'Arc de Triomphe, le Sacré Cœur* and Napoleon's tomb at *les Invalides*. I have long forgotten. But I can still smell that coffee and taste that bread and marmalade.

The train journey from Paris to Bordeaux took most of the day. I had probably finished Einstein: His Life and Times by the time we arrived. Roger had probably filled his pocket notebook with names, addresses and telephone numbers. As soon as we were out of the train and assembled, we were introduced to our French *correspondants*.

'Bonjour. Je m'appelle Michael.'

'Bonjour. Je m'appelle Louis.'

My *correspondant* was two years younger and a few centimetres shorter than myself. His hair was dark and very curly. I envied the clear, sun-tanned skin on his face which, to judge from the dark fuzz on his upper lip and around his chin, had not yet felt the touch of a razor blade. He had been adopted by Madame Escary and lived with her at 146 Avenue de la Libération *au banlieue*, which I discovered meant in a suburb (called *le Bouscat*) on the outskirts of the town. We went there by tram.

En route, I practised my French and discovered that Louis spoke little or no English. Mme. Escary greeted me warmly in French – no English there either – but spared me the traditional embrace and kisses on the cheeks. My wretched skin and hacking cough had something to do with that I suspect.

'Tu veux manger quelque chose?' she asked.

'Non, merci Madame,' I replied with the best pronunciation my hacking cough would allow. 'Je n'ai pas faim.' I was tired not hungry.

'Mon Dieu! Tu est malade, n'est-ce pas?' she said.

I nodded. I was sick. I was sick of this hacking cough and infection for which Dr Pollard had found no cure. She disappeared into another room and returned to the kitchen, where Louis and I were sitting, carrying a large tumbler full of a pungent, golden brown liquid.

'Bois!' she said, handing me the glass. I took a sip. It had a horrible taste.

'Allez! Bois tout!'

I did as I was told and drank the lot. Some of Dr Pollard's remedies had been worse.

'Tu est fatigué, oui?'

'Oui, Madame,' I said honestly. It had been a long journey and I was ready for bed.

Louis led me outside the bungalow and into a kind of outhouse where I was to sleep. I do not remember much about it. On reflection, I think it may have been a wooden summerhouse. What I do remember vividly was the bed. At home I had a small, single bed. The kapok-filled mattress was thin and firm. I slept between cotton sheets under a blanket. This French bed was large. The mattress was very thick and filled with feathers. On top was *le duvet* - equally thick and also filled with feathers. I changed into my pyjamas and crawled under *le duvet* and onto *le matelas*.

* * * * *

When I woke up after what turned out to be 12-hours of sleep, I just could not believe it. I had slept on my back and I had not moved. I was no longer coughing and wheezing. I was delighted. As I started to get up, I found that my pyjamas, the mattress and the duvet were saturated with my perspiration. I was less delighted by that discovery. How would I explain this and apologise to Mme Escary? French in a classroom in England amongst English-speaking schoolboys and French in a home in France amongst French-speaking people proved to be two different languages.

'Bonjour, Madame. Bonjour Louis.'

'Bonjour, Michel. Ca va? Tu as bien dormi?'

'Oui, merci, Madame.'

Yes, thank you, madam. It was a totally inadequate response to 'How are you?' and 'Slept well?' But my mind was elsewhere. I may have perspired away litres of water in the night but I still needed to go to the lavatory. At my first attempt (*Où est le cabinet?*) to ask where it was, Louis showed me a large cupboard filled with coats hanging on hooks. At my second attempt (*Où est la salle de bain?*) he showed me a room with a bath and shower but no toilet. At my third attempt (Où est la toilette?) we were back to the cupboard again.

All subsequent attempts led to this large cupboard. Finally, Louis took me inside and pointed to a hole in the ground in the corner. That was my first - but not my last - encounter with *des sanitaires français*. I do not remember what form of sanitation was in that Paris hostel. Whatever it was - or whatever they were (the term in modern usage - *les toilettes* - is plural) – it would not have been an elaborate toilet roll holder cum musical box from Switzerland. When I pulled off my first piece of tissue paper, the holder played Franz Lehár's Merry Widow Waltz!

At the breakfast table I managed to explain and apologise for the damp bed. *Ca ne fait rien!* I was glad it did not matter but I was embarrassed all the same. Then I endeavoured to discover what the medicine was that she had given me to drink.

'Excusez-moi, Madame. Qu'est-ce que c'était ce médecin que vous m'avez donné hier soir?' Louis was grinning from ear to ear.

'Quel médecin?' she asked.

She was justifiably puzzled. I had asked her what was *that doctor* you gave me yesterday evening! So, I tried again substituting that *medical science* (*cette médecine*) for that doctor. Finally, I got it right.

'Qu'est-ce que c'était ce médicament que vous m'avez donné?'

'Médicament? Ce n'était pas de médicament,' she said with a laugh and went to fetch the bottle.

'If it wasn't medicine,' I thought, 'then what was it?'

She returned and handed me a large bottle, saying, 'C'est l'eau de vie.'

I translated this literally - the water of life. Then I looked at the label on the bottle. I had consumed a tumbler full of Cognac Brandy!

* * * * *

Epilogue

Sometime in the summer term of 1951, 'Angus' told Roger he was not working hard enough and should choose between his studies and his piano playing. He chose. He closed his desk, walked calmly out of the classroom and never came back. He became a very successful professional pianist, conductor, arranger and composer. At the time of writing, details of his life and work can be found online. Sadly it fails to mention that my friend died some time ago. J. G.(Angus) Clark collapsed and died many years ago on supervision duty in the school playground.

Our school cert was the last of the First School Certificate Examinations. The following year it became the General Certificate of Education (GCE). Today it's the General Certificate of Secondary Education (GCSE). I shall not debate here the relative merits and standards of the education that I received as a schoolboy for those five years and that I delivered as a chemistry teacher for thirty years. I shall simply say that I relished those five years of schooling that prepared me for the last school cert. I still have my old 1950 examination papers. They challenged me then. I confess they challenge me even more now.

WHAT THE EYE DOES NOT SEE

My wife and I once owned some timeshare at Castillo Beach Club, a resort on the lower slope of a hill overlooking Caleta de Fuste on Fuerteventura in the Canary Islands. The reception, bar and restaurant were in the main area known as Lake. The other area, known as Moon, was on the other side of the Calle de Virgen de Guadalupe. There are still squirrels on Chipmunk Hill. The supermarket (El Supermercado) and restaurant (El Papagayo) may still operate. I am not sure. The characters and events in this story are pure fantasy but the settings are real enough.

* * * * *

'Good afternoon ladies and gentleman. We shall shortly begin our descent into Fuerteventura. At this time we ask you to return to your seats and fasten your seatbelts. Please place any hand-luggage in the overhead lockers or under the seat in front of you. All electronic devices must be switched off, tables should be stowed and seatbacks should be in the upright position.'

The Boeing 737 had taken 4 hours and 15 minutes to fly from a cold, damp England to a hot, dry island off the west coast of Africa, a distance, as the crow flies, of 1,719 miles from London Heathrow to Aeropuerto de Fuerteventura. Its passengers were mostly British. They would find no crows on the island and, for that matter, few other birds but they would find plenty of cats roaming wild. Only twitchers and cat lovers amongst these holiday makers would be interested. Their main concern was to tan their white bodies to the leathery brown of a well-worn horse saddle unaware, in all probability, of the pros and cons of sunbathing. Over-exposure to sunlight increases the risk of skin cancer. Under-exposure increases the risk of vitamin-D deficiency, leading to rickets in children and less resistance to skin cancer in adults.

'Where's my bottle of water, Florrie?'

'In your bag, Ernie. Under the seat in front of you by your big feet.'

'How did it get there?' asked Ernest.

'I put it there when you were keeping everybody awake with your snoring,' said Florence.

'Since when do I snore? You're a fine one to talk, you are ...'

'Oh shut up. We're landing in about twenty minutes. D'you want a boiled sweet?'

'No thanks. I'll pinch my nose and blow hard to unblock my ears,' said Ernest.

'The pilot said it was thirty-two degrees, clear skies and sunny in Fuerteventura.'

'What about the wind? I'll bet it'll be windy. It has been windy for the last five years,' snorted Ernest.

'He said nothing about the wind. You'd better have your hat handy. Keep the sun off that bald head of yours. I don't want you burnt on our first day, same as last year.'

The cabin crew made their final rounds. They collected earphones and newspapers. They held open black plastic bags for garbage. They checked that all seatbelts were fastened, that all seats were in the upright position and that all luggage was properly stowed in the overhead lockers or under the seats.

'Janet! ... Janet! ... Wake up, dear.'

'What ...? Oh goodness! I hope I wasn't snoring, Geoffrey?'

'We're starting our descent. Put your seat upright. I've stowed your table.'.

'How long was I asleep?' Janet asked.

'Most of the flight,' said her husband.

'Four hours? Did I really sleep for four hours?'

'No, probably not. More like three I suppose. Anyway, you needed the rest.'

'I was tired and these business class seats with their extra tilt... *so* comfortable,' said Janet stifling a yawn.

'Hear that? Sounded like the landing gear. We'll soon be on the ground,' said Geoffrey.

'What's the weather going to be like?' Janet asked.

'The pilot said it's very warm and sunny so everybody'll be wearing sunglasses.'

'I'm so glad we're going to Castillo Beach Club again, Geoffrey, I really am.'

Geoffrey Walters couldn't remember the last time he travelled economy class. He was tall and his long legs needed the extra space. And he could afford to pay the five times as much for his seats that Florence Broadbent had paid for her economy class seats. He, Geoffrey J. Walters, was after all a successful business man with an unwavering faith in the old Yorkshire adage *where there's muck there's brass*.

Geoff (as he was known to his Yorkshire parents) left school at sixteen and was apprenticed to a local plumber. One day they were called out to unblock a drain. It was in fact a sewer. The wily old plumber stood well back smoking a cigarette while the young plumber's mate, Geoff, tackled the job and became more than just wet behind the ears. That evening as he soaked in a hot bath and his father burnt his overalls at the bottom of the garden, Geoff recalled his encounter with that sewer.

To cut a long history short, Geoffrey J Walters completed his apprenticeship, worked hard, saved his money, bought his own van and specialised in clearing drains and sewers. Before he and his parents knew it, *Fast Drain Clear Ltd* had grown into a major franchise across Yorkshire, Lancashire and other parts of the North of England. G.J., as he was known to the members of the company who worked closely under him, became rich.

'That's the undercarriage opening, Florrie.'

'What?'

'I said that's the wheels coming down. Didn't you hear?'

'No I didn't, not above all the other noise going on. At least *your* ears are unblocked and your hearing's not impaired,' said Florence.

'No, I'm not *deaf* if that's what you mean. Got to be grateful for small mercies. Ears like a bat ... and *no*, they're not big and sticking out, thank you,' said Ernest.

'You said it, Ernie Broadbent, I didn't.'

'No, but the way you've been acting lately, I wouldn't put it past you, Florrie Broadbent.'

'We've not landed yet, have we?' Florence asked.

'Course not! Open your eyes and look out the window.'

'You're right. Silly me. We're still in the clouds. I hate landing.'

'And you hate taking off. Just relax and stop worrying,' said Ernest.

'Easier said than done. I'm not like you. I'll be alright once we're on the ground.'

'I hope so. You've been on edge ever since we left the house. Is it me?'

'No, Ernie, it's not you. I've just had a lot on my mind recently,' said Florence.

* * * * *

'Good afternoon ladies and gentlemen. Welcome to sunny Fuerteventura in the Canary Islands. The outside temperature is thirty-three degrees. Please remain in your seats with your seatbelts fastened until the plane comes to a complete stop and Captain Jackson switches off the seatbelt sign. Take care when opening the overhead lockers in case any luggage has shifted during the flight. Would anyone needing assistance please remain seated until the other passengers have deplaned. On behalf of Captain Jackson and the rest of the crew may I thank you for choosing Zipjet Airlines. We wish you a pleasant holiday and look forward to serving you again.'

'What was that you said Ernie?'

'I said what's wrong with disembark or just get off? Deplane! Another Americanism! What with spelling aluminium *aluminum* and sulphur *sulfur* I don't know where it's all going to end.'

275

'Oh for goodness sake stop moaning. We'll be getting off in a minute,' snapped Florence.

'There, you see. You said *getting off*. You didn't say deplaning!'

'Everything alright Mrs. Broadbent?' asked Melanie, one of the cabin crew – Ernest disliked the term *cabin crew* and preferred to call them stewards and stewardesses.

'Yes thank you,' said Florence.

'Do either of you need any help?' Melanie asked.

'No thank you, Melanie, we can manage. We're just waiting for everybody else to get off. Not much point in standing up. We'll have a bit of a wait for our luggage, won't we?'

'Very sensible,' agreed Melanie. 'I can never understand why everybody stands up before we open the doors or why they're in such a rush to get off.'

'Could you get my wife's bag down for her, Melanie?' said Ernest smiling ingratiatingly and making a mental note that Florence and the stewardess had said *get off*.

'No problem,' said Melanie. 'Which one is it?'

'It's the tartan wheel along case,' said Florence.

'Here you are Mrs Broadbent.'

'Thank you, Melanie,' Florence said. 'Come on Ernie, it's time for us to *deplane*.'

Fuerteventura airport at El Matorral was opened in 1969 for flights between the Canary Islands and European destinations. As the tourist trade grew, so did the airport. It now has an extended runway to cater for long-range aircraft annually ferrying more than four million passengers to the island.

The airport boasts a variety of shops, places to eat, an observation deck and a children's play area. It does not boast about the delays through passport control and customs or of the long waits at the luggage carousels now all too prevalent at international airports. And *El Aeropuerto* does not accept any responsibility for the lethargic taxi and shuttle services outside the terminal, let alone boast of them.

'Taxi, Señor?'

'Si! Quisieramos ir al Castillo Beach Club, por favor.'

'What was that you said, Geoffrey?'

'I said we should like to go to Castillo Beach Club, please,' said Geoffrey without a trace of his boyhood Yorkshire accent.

'Would you ask the driver his name?' said Janet.

'Cómo se llama Usted?'

'I am Alejandro Carlos Ramirez, Señor! Señora!'

'Do you speak English?' Janet asked.

'Yes. I learn at school. Do you speak Spanish, Señora?'

'No, I'm sorry, I don't but my husband does.'

'You learn at school, Señor?'

'Si! Clase nocturna,' replied Geoffrey rather casually.

'I too go evening class. You have good accent, Señor.'

'Gracias!' said Geoffrey deigning not to comment on Alejandro's English pronunciation.

Florence and Ernest Broadbent were last off the plane, last through passport control, last through customs and last to collect their luggage. When they joined the end of a rather long queue for a taxi, Ernest was considerably hot and not inconsiderably bothered. Florence was doing her best to remain calm.

'Taxi! Taxi!' yelled Ernest in his blunt Yorkshire accent.

'He heard you the first time, Ernie. Keep your hat on your head. Stop waving it about.'

'Buenas tardes, Señor! Señora!' said the driver smiling at Ernest and then Florence.

'Do you speak English?' Ernest asked unnecessarily loudly and in the worst tradition of the Englishman who assumes Europeans are deaf if they don't understand him.

'Si, Señor! I speak English.'

'Yo hablo español pero mi marido no habla español, Señor!' said Florence.

'What did you say?' Ernest asked his wife.

'I told him I speak Spanish but my husband doesn't.'

'Your wife speak Spanish very good, Señor. Where you are going?'

'Castillo Beach Club, por favor,' answered Florence.

'Very nice place, Señora. First time?'

'No, we have been before. ... Do you want to sit in the front, Ernie?'

'No. I'll get in the back and hold on to my flight bag. You can get in the front and practise the lingo.'

The airport was about three miles from Puerto del Rosario, the capital of Fuerteventura, and just five miles from the resort where Ernest and Florence would spend their week's holiday *if* they survived the taxi ride. Florence put on her seat belt and made sure Ernest did up his. The driver only ever bothered with his seat belt when *la policia* were around. He drove with his left arm hanging casually out of the window and the thumb of his right hand hooked loosely onto the bottom of the steering wheel. When he took his dark brown eyes off the road to look at Florence, she wished she hadn't asked him a question.

'Cómo se llama?'

'My name is Esteban, Señora. What is your name?' said the driver.

'Mi nombre es Florence Broadbent,' she said. And then she turned to Ernest and said,' Our driver's name is Esteban. Isn't that interesting?'

'I heard! What's so interesting about Esteban?' asked Ernest.

'Esteban is Spanish for Stephen. It's our son's name in Spanish,' she said to Ernest. Then turning to look at the driver, she said, 'Stephen es mi hijo. Stephen – inglés. Esteban – español.'

'Ah, I understand. Now I call myself Stephen. Is good?' said Esteban.

'Muy bien, Esteban. Mi hijo prefiere Steve.'

'Did you tell him to call himself Steve?' asked Ernest. 'What's wrong with Stephen?'

'No!' said Florence. 'I told him our Stephen prefers to be called Steve.'

'Mi marido se llama Ernest pero prefiera Ernie.'

'Ha-ha! Is funny, Señora Broadbent,' said Esteban.

'What did you say to him this time, Florrie?'

'I told him your name is Ernest but you prefer Ernie.'

'So? What's funny about that? What's wrong with Ernie?'

'Nothing. It's just that... well, why can't our Stephen be Steve if you can be Ernie?'

'We arrive, Señor y Señora. Castillo Beach Club! I bring your luggage.'

'Gracias, Esteban. ... Adios!' said Florence, paying the fare and including a nice tip.

* * * * *

The glazed terracotta tiles of the steps and path leading down from the road shone in the bright sunlight and would have been dangerously slippery if, in the extremely unlikely event, rain should fall on them. The red of the tiles contrasted sharply with the thick white walls of the building but not with the purples and reds of the thorny bougainvilleas bordering the entrance to *La Recepción*.

'Hola!' said Ana Maria, the pretty dark haired, dark eyed *recepcionista*.

'Buenas tardes, Señorita. Mi apellido es Walters,' Geoffrey said fluently.

'Buenas tardes, Señor Walters.'

'Hable inglés, por favor. Mi esposa no habla español,' said Geoffrey

'Of course. I'm sorry, Señora Walters,' Ana Maria said to Janet. 'I didn't realise you do not speak Spanish like your husband.'

'That's quite alright. I like to hear Geoffrey speaking Spanish,' said Janet.

'Please may I see your passports, Mr Walters?' When she had checked the passports, she handed them back to Geoffrey and said, 'Gracias Señor.'

'Which apartment are we in?' asked Janet.

'You are in apartment 46, Señora Walters,' Ana Maria said. Then she turned to Andrés, a tall, muscular sun-tanned fellow with blond hair and blue eyes who probably descended from the Guanches – the original natives of the Canary Islands. 'Las maletas, por favor. Apartamento cuarenta seis.'

'Gracias, Señorita,' said Geoffrey

'De nada, Señor. Here are your keys and TV remote. Please follow Andrew.'

Esteban, their dark-haired, dark-skinned, thick-set taxi driver, hurried ahead with their suitcases while Ernest held onto his wife's arm and used his stick to help him negotiate the tiled steps and path from the road down to the entrance and reception. Once inside the building, Florence wanted her husband to sit down but he refused. He stood alongside her while she spoke to the young lady behind the desk.

'Hola!' said Ana Maria.

'D'you speak English?' asked Ernest curtly before Florence could speak.

'Yes, of course, Señor. Good afternoon. Welcome to Castillo Beach Club. Your name is?

'Broadbent. Dr. and Mrs. Broadbent. We were here last year. Don't you remember?'

'Ah, si! Señor y Señora Broadbent. No, sorry. I am new here,' Ana Maria replied.

'Ah! I thought I didn't recognise your voice. What's your name?

'Ana Maria, Señor.'

'What a lovely name. If I'd had a daughter I might have called her Anne Marie,' said Florence before Ernest could say any more. 'Here are our passports.'

'Thank you, Señora.'

281

'What's our bungalow number then, lass?' Ernest asked.

'Your apartment is number 47, Señor.'

'And where's that exactly? Lake or Moon?'

'It is here on Lake, Señor,' said Ana Maria, smiling at Florence.

I hope it's not next to that noisy bar.'

'No, Señor. It is at the other end. On the corner facing the pool,' Ana Maria said.

'That sounds lovely, doesn't it Ernie?'

'Better than last time when we were next to the bar and that blooming racket.'

'Here are your keys and remote for the television, Señora.'

'Gracias, Ana Maria.'

'De nada, Señora. Andrés!' said Ana Maria, turning to the young porter, 'Las maletas, por favor. Apartamento cuarenta siete.'

'Now what?' said Ernest to Florence.

'Please go with Andrés, Señor. He will take your cases to the villa. Enjoy your stay.'

The door into *La Recepción* from the road faced north. The door opposite and facing south, led to the apartments and pool area. When Ernest, holding onto his wife's arm with his left hand and holding his stick in his right, stepped into the open air and the blazing sun, he felt as though he had just put his face into an oven.

'What's your name again?' said Ernest.

'Andrés. His name's Andrés. Andrew in English, Ernie,' said Florence.

'You speak English, Andrew?' asked Ernest rather loudly.

'Si, Señor. A little,' Andrés answered modestly.

'I gather you've got the remote control for the television,' Ernest said in a slightly more normal voice.

'Si, Señor.'

'Waste of time! What would I want with television specially since it's all in Spanish.'

'No, is not all Spanish, Señor. Six English. Two German. Two Italian,' said Andrés.

'Six English? I'll tell you something, Andrew. Those six *so-called English* channels will be one English - BBC World News I'll bet you a pound to a penny. The other five will be American! Four minutes of adverts - one minute of rubbish! Complete waste of time.'

'Give over, Ernie,' said Florence. 'and mind the step!

Like all *los apartamentos* at Castillo Beach Club and probably at most of the other resorts on the island, *apartamento* 47, had thick walls, to keep the interior cool. They were painted white on the outside to reflect the sun's rays. The roof was not pitched but flat because it was cheap to build and rarely rained upon. Apartments 46 and 47 formed one unit and shared an inner dividing wall. A narrow terrace of red terracotta tiles ran across the front of the entire unit. A thick hedge of bougainvilleas divided the terrace into two and on each half stood a white plastic table and four white plastic chairs.

Andrés unlocked the glass-panelled wooden door, pulled back the curtains keeping out the sun and carried the suitcases into the bedroom. Their holiday bungalow, as Ernest called it, consisted of three rooms.

The door from the terrace – the only door in and out of the apartment – led directly into the largest room comprising the kitchen, living room, dining room (identified by the presence of a square pine table and four chairs) and spare bedroom (identified by the two-seater couch that could convert into a bed).

283

The second, much smaller room was the main bedroom. The third, even smaller room, was the bathroom. All the walls were white. All the floors were tiled. There were one or two framed abstract prints on the living room and bedroom walls and a mirror on the bathroom wall over the washbasin.

'Oh, this looks very nice,' said Florence.

'It's cooler in here than outside but it smells a bit musty to me, said Ernest.

'For goodness sake, Ernie!' snapped Florence. 'Cheer up! We're on holiday.'

'Where are the suitcases?' Ernest asked.

'I put them on the bed, Señor, so you not fall over them,' the porter said.

'Gracias, Andrés,' said Florence, handing the young man a tip.

'De nada, Señora. Muchas gracias, Señora! Adios Señor!' said Andrés.

'Right!' said Florence. 'I'd better go to the supermarket. I don't suppose you want to stretch your legs and come with me, Ernie?'

'No thanks. I'll stay here and unpack the cases.'

'Alright. I won't be long. Stay out of trouble,' said Florence.

'What's that supposed to mean?'

'You know *very well* what I mean, Ernie Broadbent.'

Next door, at number 46, the Walters had already settled into what Geoffrey told Janet was *nuestra casa de las vacaciones* – our holiday home. When Janet tried to call their apartment a villa, Geoffrey patiently explained that *casa* means *house* or *home* but *villa* is Spanish for *town*.

'I've unpacked the cases, Janet. Will you be alright if I pop to *el supermercado*?'

'Yes, dear. I'll sit out here on the veranda until you get back.'

'I won't be long. I'll just get some milk and coffee. D'you fancy anything?

'A Danish pastry would be nice as long as it's fresh,' said Janet.

'Right! See you in a minute,' said Geoffrey, kissing his wife on the cheek.

'Bye!' Janet said, content to feel the sun on her slender legs.

* * * * *

Meanwhile, in the bedroom of number 47, Ernest Broadbent BSc PhD, restless as ever, was talking to himself as he tackled the suitcases that Andrés had put on the bed.

'Right! Let's see if I can get these cases unpacked before milady gets back. This must be hers. Oh, for God's sake! Why does it always weigh a ton? OK. Hangers. Where are the hangers? One, two, three, four five, six, seven, eight. There's got to be more than that. Ah, at the other side of the wardrobe. Nine, ten, eleven, twelve. O.K. That's one, two, three, four for me and one, two, three, four, five, six, seven, eight for milady. Now where's my one and only summer suit from Burtons? Ah, here it is. My God, why did I let Florrie drag me into that outfitters for this? It cost me a bomb and I had to listen to that twerp of an assistant into the bargain.'

> *'Nice fit, if I may say so, Sir. What do you think, Madam? D'you like the colour? Just feel the quality of the cloth, Sir. Lightweight. Crease-resistant. It's also stain-resistant. The perfect suit for formal and informal occasions. Would Sir like a shirt and tie to go with it? I can recommend this silk tie and Mackay 100% cotton shirt. ...'*

'Whoops! Now where's that hanger gone?'

When Geoffrey left apartment 46, he was wearing a pale beige short-sleeved shirt and white tailored shorts. His straw hat matched his shorts and his leather sandals matched his shirt. Even in his holiday attire the 6 ft 4 in tall Mr G J Walters looked every one of his inches the successful businessman. He strolled around the pool, trying to think in Spanish as he headed south for the gate leading to *Calle Virgen de la Caridad del Cobra*.

Geoffrey crossed the Virgin of the Charity of the Cobra street and ambled along in the shade. He took his time down the steep steps between *los apartementos* to *Calle San Francisco* and yet more steep steps to *Calle Virgen del Carmen* and *el supermercado*. It had been a short walk - 350 yards to be exact – from apartment 46 to the supermarket situated on the corner of Virgin of Carmen street. Geoffrey had timed his arrival to coincide with the supermarket being open at 5 p.m. after the traditional 3-hour siesta. Florence walked into el supermercado sometime later.

'Right! Let's see what I can get his nibs for supper,' thought Florence. 'Eggs still look reasonable. Mushroom omelette with chips and tomatoes. Yes. Bread rolls seem fresh. Butter. Where's the butter? Cheese. Ah! Real fruit yoghurts. Breakfast cereals. Corn Flakes and Rice Krispies. Milk? Full cream? No. Ah, 2%! Yes. *Marmelada*'s a bit steep. Oh well, we're on holiday. Strawberry jam for me. Croissants? No. I'll pop back tomorrow morning when they're in fresh. Bottle of red wine? Still cheaper here than in our local wine shop back home.'

> *'I'm sorry Mrs. Broadent. It's the Government taxes you see. They're driving us out of business. I couldn't believe it myself when I was in Majorca. The wine was so cheap there compared to here. No wonder so many Brits get drunk abroad. Not you or Dr. Broadbent of course. It's all these young soccer hooligans. We have an Amontillado on special today. '*

'What a hypocrite! The Wine Barrel go out of business with her running it? Fat chance. Whoops! I'd better get back and see how his nibs is coping with the unpacking.'

* * * * *

'Hola!' said Juanita Diaz, the maid as she approached apartment 46.

'Hello! Who are you?' said Janet

'Servicio de habitación, Señora?'

'D'you speak English?' Janet asked.

'Inglés? No. Lo siento. Necesita un rollo de papel higiénico, Señora?'

'I'm sorry. I don't understand. I do not speak Spanish,' apologised Janet.

Juanita shrugged her ample shoulders, put a spare toilet roll on the veranda table then waddled off towards number 47. She worked hard all day cleaning the apartments in readiness for the new arrivals. Checking on the supply of toilet paper and clean towels was her final task that afternoon. Her *adios*! as she left number 46 fell on deaf ears.

'I'm back, Janet. Everything alright?'

'Yes - but some woman came by and spoke to me in Spanish about something or other.'

'There's a toilet roll on the veranda table.'

'Oh!' said Janet.

'Any idea how it got there?' asked Geoffrey.

'No ... unless that woman was the cleaning lady and she put it there.'

'That's probably it. So, shall we walk down to *El Papagayo* and get some supper?'

'Lovely, Geoffrey. Give me your arm and tell me what the restaurant's called in English.'

'The Parrot. *Papagayo* is Spanish for parrot,' said Geoffrey.

Juanita Diaz was short and plump. Put less kindly but more accurately, she was fat. She had a large bosom and, as Ernest might have said, plenty to fall back on. Not surprisingly, she perspired a great deal. Put less kindly and more accurately, she was sweaty.

'Hello! That you Florrie?' said Ernest when he heard footsteps.

'Hola! Servicio de habitación, Señor,' said Juanita Diaz poking her head around the bedroom door of number 46.

'D'you speak English?' said Ernest rather loudly as usual.

'No, Señor. Lo siento. Necesita un rollo de papel higiénico, Señor?'

'No speak Spanish! No comprendez!' said Ernest just as loudly.

The journey from England to Fuerteventura was tiring enough. The walk back from the supermarket, most of the way uphill, carrying two bags of shopping made Florence even more tired. She was perspiring and feeling a trifle irritable when she entered number 46.

'What's going on?'

'Florrie? You're back,' said Ernest with relief.

'Yes, I'm back. Who's this woman. What's she doing in our bedroom with the curtains closed?' snapped Florence.

'I don't know. She just walked in. I thought it was you at first.'

'Buenas tardes, Señora. Servicio de habitación. Necesita un rollo de papel higiénico?'

'Si. Gracias,' said Florence, becoming calmer.

'Adios, Señor! ... Señora!'

'That was the maid, Ernie. She brought us a spare toilet roll.'

'Oh, the maid,' said Ernest. 'I asked her if she spoke English. All I caught was 'No, *senior* and something about *Sorrento*.'

'No, *Señor. Lo siento.* She was saying No, sir. Sorry!'

Florence pulled back the bedroom curtains. She was surprised that Ernest had managed to unpack and put away most of his clothes but not surprised to see that her suitcase still lay unopened on the bed.

'Here! Change into this short-sleeved shirt and shorts. I'll finish the unpacking.'

'I've put my stuff in the top drawer and I've hung my suit up,' said Ernest.

'Yes, yes! Hung it down more like. Go and sit outside. There's a chair on the veranda – on the left outside the door. I'll call you when supper's ready. Do you want your iPod?'

'Not now. I might take a nap,' said Ernest with a yawn.

'For goodness sake *be careful*. Don't put your bare feet on that black grit out there.'

'That black grit, as you call it, is *volcanic ash*. It's a mulch to keep the plant roots moist,' said Ernest who, as a non-gardener but a retired chemist, was quick to pass on his theoretical horticultural knowledge.

'All I know is it's sharp and you'll cut your feet like you did before, remember?'

'That was two years ago,' retorted Ernest. 'Two years ago!'

'The veranda's on the left outside the door,' said Florence

'I know, I know. I heard you the first time,' said Ernest.

'And don't walk into the bougainvillaea covering the screen between us and next door. You know how sharp its thorns are,' Florence snapped as her husband headed to the door.

* * * * *

'Are you going to stay in bed all morning?' said Florence.

289

'What time is it?' Ernest asked sleepily.

'It's half past eight. I've laid the table for breakfast on the veranda.'

'I didn't hear you get up,' said Ernest rubbing his hand over his bald head as though he were polishing it.

'You were out to the world. It's a wonder you didn't wake the entire resort with your snoring. I can never understand why snorers don't wake themselves up,' said Florence.

'Have they finished cleaning the pool yet?' asked Ernest.

'Yes. They finished more than half an hour ago. The pool's available from 8 am to 9 pm. You go and have your swim while I pop down to the supermarket for some croissants.'

The sun was already up but there was a breeze to move the air which was still quite cool. Florence wore sunglasses, a wide-brimmed hat, a long-sleeved blouse and white slacks to protect her fair skin. She liked walking and wore a pair of flat-heeled canvas shoes to cope with the uneven paths and roads all too common on the island. Florence left apartment number 46 for *el supermercado* just a few minutes before her neighbour left number 47.

'Janet! Where are you Janet?'

'In the bathroom, Geoffrey.'

'Everything alright?'

'Yes. I'm just putting on my bathing suit. What time is it?' asked Janet.

'Just gone half past eight,' said Geoffrey glancing at his Rolex wristwatch.

'I've done the best I can to lay the table for breakfast on the veranda.'

'So I noticed,' said Geoffrey. I'm going to fetch some croissants from *el supermercado* while you have your swim. Will you be alright?'

'Yes, of course, Geoffrey. Don't worry. I'll be fine. The pool's only outside the door.'

The supermarket on the corner of Virgin of Carmen street was certainly too small to be called *el hipermercado* and too big to be just *el mercado*. Florence collected a cart and went towards *la entrada*. The lady assistant, sitting behind the check-out at *la salida*, spoke first.

'Buenas dias, Señora. Cómo está?'

Florence smiled and responded to the *Good morning, Madam, How are you?* with, 'Muy bien y Usted?'

In response to Florence's *Very well and yourself*, the assistant smiled back and said, '*Bien, gracias!*'

Florence made a beeline for *la panaderia* to see if the croissants were fresh. Had she looked behind her she might have seen Geoffrey Walters collecting a cart and exchanging pleasantries with the attractive, dark-haired woman behind the check-out counter.

'Buenas dias, Señora. Cómo está?' said Geoffrey, politely doffing his straw hat.

'Muy bien y Usted?

'Bien, gracias. Hay croissants frescos?'

In response to his asking if the croissants were fresh, she pointed to the far left corner and replied, 'Si, Señor. Por aqui!'

The pool outside apartments 46 and 47 was narrow and oval in shape. It was connected to a larger, square-shaped pool by a small waterfall kept running continuously by a hidden circulating pump. The water was cool bordering on cold. The water should have been kept warm by solar heating.

According to Dr Broadbent, there were at least two obvious methods. The inexpensive method was to cover the white reflecting tiles on the bottom of the pool with thick black mats that would absorb the sun's rays and heat the water. The expensive method was to install solar panels in line with the circulating pump.

'Brrrr. When are they ever going to make this a heated pool?' Ernest thought to himself as he slid off the side into the water. 'With all the sunshine they get here off the African coast, how hard can it be to install solar heating. Well at least I get the place to myself this time in the morning. Now how many strokes was it to the other end. ... Ow! D**mn it! O.K. Fifteen not sixteen. ... Oh, no. Now what?'

'Hello. Good morning. What's the water like?' said Janet as she gripped the handrails of the steps into the pool.

'Cold. Blinking cold,' said Ernest.

'Is it alright if I join you?' asked Janet.

'Why not? I'll keep to this far side if you don't mind.'

'Oh, you're right. It's not very warm, is it? I thought it was a heated pool.'

'Wouldn't that be nice. You'd think with all this sunshine it would be warmer.'

* * * * *

'Perdone, Señora.'

'Geoffrey! Geoffrey Walters!'

'Qué tal, Florence?'

'How long have you been here?'

'About five minutes,' said Geoffrey putting his hat back on his head.

'No, I mean how long have you been in Fuerteventura?'

'Flew in yesterday afternoon on Zipjet flight 197 same as you.'

'Ah, you were sitting right at the front in business class, weren't you?' said Florence.

'Yes. You walked right past me. You looked very tense,' said Geoffrey.

'I'm sorry. It's just that... Well I'm not very keen on flying.'

'Worried about taking off and landing?'

'Yes. They say that's when we're most at risk,' said Florence.

'You should read *The Polar Bear Strategy: Reflections on Risk in Modern Life* by John Ross. On second thoughts, perhaps you shouldn't.'

'Why? Why shouldn't I read it?' asked Florence.

'You've heard people say that aeroplanes are safer than cars. Well, according to John Ross that's not quite true,' said Geoffrey.

'Thank you very much. That's not what I wanted to hear,' Florence said.

'No, you should read it, Florence. You'd enjoy it. Anyway, you're not accident prone, are you?'

'No, I don't think so. Not like somebody I know,' said Florence rather sadly and thinking of her husband having his morning swim.

Unlike Geoffrey Walters, Ernest Broadbent went to a grammar school and from there to university where he studied chemistry. He gained a First Class Honours degree and after three years of research obtained his PhD. In his final year of post-graduate research he was interviewed by a scout and offered a post with Imperial Chemical Industries. He would still be working if it had not been for the laboratory accident.

'Ouch! That's the second time I've done that,' exclaimed Janet.

'You alright? What did you do?' asked Ernest.

'I hit my hand on the edge of the pool.'

'Not looking where you were going?' asked Ernest.

'You might say that,' said Janet.

'What were you doing? Back crawl?'

'No. Just breast stroke,' said Janet.

'Got water in your eyes then I suppose,' said Ernest. 'You should wear goggles.'

'I'm afraid that wouldn't help much,' said Janet ruefully. 'Anyway, didn't I hear you shout out just now.'

'Yes. Just after you got in. I bumped my head.'

'So you weren't looking where you were going either,' said Janet.

'Actually, said Ernest, 'I thought I needed sixteen strokes for the length of the pool but it's only fifteen. ... I'm Ernie, by the way.'

'I'm Janet.'

When Florence arrived with her croissants, she found Ernest sitting on his towel on a chair on the terrace in the sunshine. His hair and his swimming trunks were still wet but the rest of him had dried in the sun.

'You'll never guess, Ernie.'

'Guess what?'

'Who I bumped into at the supermarket. Mr. Walters.'

'Who's he when he's at home,' Ernest asked.

'He's in the same evening class as me – Intermediate Spanish - at the Tech.'

'Handsome, good-looking fellow, is he?'

'Now you mention it, yes, I suppose he is in a way.'

'Anyway, how did you get on? Have a nice swim?'

'Water was cold as usual. Why they can't ...'

'Oh, don't start on again about solar heating. Go and get yourself dressed. I'll put the kettle on. Breakfast on the terrace in five minutes,' snapped Florence.

When Geoffrey arrived with his croissants, he found Janet relaxing on the couch inside the house. She had showered, dried her short dark-brown hair and changed into a short-sleeved blouse and culottes.

'Have a good swim, Janet?'

'Yes, thank you, Geoffrey. The water was a bit cold.'

'No problem getting in and out then?'

'No, none at all. I did bang my hand a couple of times but I don't think it's bruised.'

'Let's have a look,' said Geoffrey taking hold of her hand. 'You've taken a bit of skin off. I'll fetch a plaster.'

'How did you get on at the supermarket?' Janet asked.

'Fine. The croissants had just come in. They were still warm.'

'Shall I go and sit at the table on the terrace?'

'Yes, go ahead. The coffee's nearly filtered. I'll be with you in a minute,' said Geoffrey.

* * * * *

The landscape of *Fuerteventura* is a contrast of rocky coves, sandy beaches and volcanic contours, with *Pico de la Zarza* being the highest point at 2,664 ft above sea level. It is the driest of the Canary Islands, with over 3,000 hours of sunshine per year, and the closest to North Africa. There are two likely translations of the island's name. Ernest would doubtless argue the case for *strong winds*. Geoffrey preferred *good fortune*.

'Right. I've cleared the table and done the washing up. I'm going for a walk.'

'Going up that mountain to see the chipmunks, are you, Florrie?'

'Chipmunk Hill is a hill, not a mountain. Besides, it's a lovely morning and not much wind,' said Florence. 'What about you? What are you going to do?'

'Bit a weight training in the gym, perhaps,' said Ernest.

'Think you can find your way to the cave without getting lost?'

'I think so,' said Ernest. 'Anyway, I've got a tongue in my head.'

'Look!' said Florence, 'Why don't I walk you there and pick you up on the way back?'

'Yes, why not?' said Ernest, 'It'll save a lot of hassle.'

'Would you like to come for walk now, Janet?'

'No thank you, Geoffrey. I prefer the treadmill in the gym, if you don't mind.'

'Of course not. Hold my arm and I'll take you there.'

'That's nice. Then you go on your walk and collect me on your way back.'

'Sounds good. Let me know when you're ready,' said Geoffrey.

'I'm ready now if you are.'

Castillo Beach Club includes in its facilities *un gimnasio* where one can work out, take a sauna and have a massage. The Club does not mention that the gymnasium is in a windowless concrete bunker underneath the tennis court and 5-a-side soccer pitch. Once inside, Ernest had little trouble finding the multi-gym, the barbells and dumbbells. He decided to start with a pair of dumbbells.

'Ouch! Watch where you're going!' said a surprised Ernest.

'I'm sorry. Was that your foot?'

'Janet?'

'Ernie?' said a surprised Janet.

'Yes,'

'I'm trying to find the treadmill.'

'Hola! Señor! Señora!' It was the fitness instructor in charge of the gym. 'Uno momento, por favor. Voy dar las luces.'

'Do you know what he said, Ernie?' asked Janet.

'Hello Señor! Señora! I got that much ...' said Ernest.

'Inglés! Sorry. Please! A moment. I put on the lights.'

'What's your name?' asked Ernest.

'Manuel, Señor.'

'Well then, Manuel. Would you help this lady with the treadmill and then me with the multi-gym?'

'Si, Señor!'

* * * * *

'Hello, Geoffrey!'

'We meet again, Florence.'

'Where are you heading?' said Florence. 'The supermarket again?'

'No. Just out for walk,' replied Geoffrey. 'What about you?'

'A walk. Up the hill to see if any chipmunks are still there.'

'Mind if I join you?' Geoffrey asked.

'No. That would be lovely.' Said Florence.

Florence Broadbent and Geoffrey Walters met by chance attending a 20-week course in conversational Spanish run by the Workers' Educational Association for adults from all walks of life. They both came to look forward to the weekly evening class.

'So, are you staying here at the Castillo Beach Club?' Florence inquired.

'Yes, as a matter of fact we are,' said Geoffrey.

'So, we were on the same flight yesterday,' said Florence, 'and now we are in the same resort. What a strange coincidence!'

'Not strange really, Florence,' said Geoffrey with a slight smile.

'Is this your first visit?' Florence asked without noticing the odd look on his face.

'No. We came here last year. You've been here five times I believe.'

'Yes, that's right. How did you know?' said Florence with a surprised look on her face.

'Night school at the Tech. Remember? We had to talk in Spanish about our holidays.'

'So we did. I'd forgotten that. Did I tell the class we were coming here this week?'

'Yes, you did. So you see, Florence, our meeting is not entirely by chance. Shall we go and look for your chipmunks?' said Geoffrey.

When is a chipmunk not a chipmunk? When it's a striped squirrel. Chipmunks have stripes on their faces; squirrels do not. Chipmunks have cheek pouches for storing food; squirrels do not. A chipmunk runs with its tail held vertically. A squirrel runs with its tail parallel to the ground.

'There's one. Look! Over by that large rock.'

'Oh, yes, I see it now, Geoffrey. Let's sit here and see if it will come to us.'

'Why not. It'll give me a chance to take a close look at the view said Geoffrey.'

'Why are you looking at me, Mr. Walters?' said Florence. '*Caleta de Fuste* is down there. D'you know that *caleta* is Spanish for cove and *fuste* is a type of fishing boat. I've got a little book that says the horse-shoe beach is man made and the pale golden sand was imported. It must have cost a fortune.'

'D'you know you're a very attractive woman, Florence Broadbent?' said Geoffrey.

'Fuerteventura is the Canary Island closest to the North African coastline - sixty miles away,' continued Florence beginning to blush. 'It's too far over the horizon for us to see it from here even with binoculars.'

'Why should I look at the North Atlantic ocean when I can look at you?' said Geoffrey.

'Oh, look. Here he comes,' Said Florence. 'Look at that! He took that pistachio nut right out of my hand.'

'Did you know a chipmunk is a small striped squirrel (*una ardilla listada*)?'

299

'No, I didn't know that,' said Florence. 'I know *ardilla* is Spanish for squirrel.'

'If it hasn't got stripes on its face then it's not a chipmunk.'

'So I just gave a nut to...'

'A ground squirrel (*una ardilla moruna*),' said Geoffrey, gazing into her eyes.

'Look at the time,' exclaimed Florence. 'I'd better be getting back. Ernie will be wondering where I am.'

* * * * *

'Señor! Señora! Please. I close the gym now,' said Manuel.

'What's the time?' Ernest asked.

'12 o'clock, Señor!'

'How do I switch off this treadmill?' Janet asked.

'I will do it, Señora!' said Manuel. 'Please, I help you with your jacket.'

'Thank you, Manuel,' said Janet.

'De nada, Señora.'

'D'you mind if I take your arm, Ernie?' said Janet.

'Well, no, O.K. Actually I was going to ask you...'

'Señor! This cane is yours, no?' said Manuel.

'What? Oh, yes. Thank you,' said Ernest.

'Please. I hold the door open for you,' said Manuel. 'Adios!'

'Thank you. Crikey! It's hot outside.'

'Hmm, yes. I love to feel the sun on my face,' said Janet squeezing Ernest's arm.

'So where's your apartment, Janet?'

'It's by the pool, Ernie.'

'And mine. O.K. If we keep to this path we should get there.'

Manuel closed and locked the door of *el gymnasio* and watched admiringly as Ernest and Janet made their way up the path.

'Oh, dear. The gym's closed,' exclaimed Florence. 'I told Ernie I'd meet him here on my way back from my walk. I hope he's alright.'

'Why shouldn't he be?' said Geoffrey.

'You don't know my Ernie,' said Florence wryly.

'He probably gave up waiting and has gone back to your apartment. Where is your apartment exactly?'

'We're right by the swimming pool,' said Florence.

'So are we,' Said Geoffrey. 'Actually I was supposed to collect Janet from the gym. Perhaps she's gone back with your husband.'

'That'll be it. Yes, I'll bet that's what's happened,' said Florence. 'What a relief.'

'How about that?' said Geoffrey. 'My wife's with your husband and I'm here with you.'

'Geoffrey Walters! Were you flirting with me back there on Chipmunk Hill. Because if you were, you can stop. Stop right now,' said Florence. 'My Ernie can be a bit of a trial at times - especially since his accident - but he's my husband and I married him for better, for worse.'

301

'I apologise, Florence. I suppose I was being a bit of a flirt,' confessed Geoffrey, 'but you do know you are a very attractive woman. Will you forgive me?'

'I'm flattered,' said Florence. 'Of course I forgive you.'

'Friends?' said Geoffrey with a broad smile.

'*Amigos*!' said Florence. 'No more flirting. Agreed?'

'Agreed, mi amiga!' said Geoffrey.

'Alright then. Let's go and find our spouses.'

'You said Ernie had an accident...'

'Yes, it was a chemical leak from a fume cupboard in the lab where he was working.'

'What happened? Was it serious?' Geoffrey asked with genuine concern.

'Yes and no. He was lucky in one way, you know,' said Florence. 'He wasn't burned or scarred but the chemical he was working on was a neurological toxin. It affected his eyes.'

'What do you mean *affected his eyes*?' said Geoffrey uneasily.

'Ernie's blind.'

'Oh my God! He's blind?'

'Yes!' said Florence. 'Didn't I tell you?'

'No!' said Geoffrey. 'This is terrible. We've got to hurry.'

'Why? What's the problem? Your Janet's safe with him.'

'You don't understand. It's the blind leading the blind,' said Geoffrey.

'Your Janet's blind? She's blind too? Good gracious.'

* * * * *

'Well, Ernie, we've found the swimming pool. No doubt about that.'

'We certainly did, Janet, we certainly did. No doubt at all.'

* * * * *

Epilogue

In October 2005, following new Government rules, Thomas Cook Airlines allowed one blind person, travelling from Gatwick to the Canaries, to purchase an extra seat for their guide dog in the main cabin. The limit was just one dog with one blind person per flight. So one or other of my fictitious characters, Ernie or Janet, might have taken their guide dog on holiday if I had given them one and if I had endowed them with the patience to deal with all the rules and regulations of micro-chipping, anti-rabies vaccinations and EU Pet Passports.

Fuerteventura is popular with visitors wanting to avoid the more commercial tourism of Gran Canaria, Lanzarote and Tenerife. Aside from the resorts, the only man-made attractions are La Lajita Zoo and Baku Water Park. The Barbary ground squirrel was introduced to Fuerteventura in 1965 and became a pest, with numbers estimated at more than 300,000. Like the chipmunk, the squirrel is a rodent. For the sake of the tourist trade, these ground squirrels in Fuerteventura are, erroneously, called chipmunks!

The expression Where there's muck there's brass *– meaning that there is money to be made doing dirty, unattractive work - originated in Yorkshire, England in the 20th century. Brass is still slang for money and derives from the copper and bronze coins issued as long ago as the 17th century.*

The Workers' Educational Association (WEA) is the largest voluntary provider of adult education in the United Kingdom. Founded in 1903, it is now one of the biggest charities operating at regional and national level with over 450 local branches. The WEA runs over 10,000 courses, for relatively small tuition fees, each year for more than 110,000 adults.

* * * * *

Facts and Fantasies

Volume 4

A well polished apple

Michael C. Cox

Mimast Inc

THE APPLE CART

The small retailer has not yet been entirely driven to the wall by the supermarket chain. Some have survived as street traders in open markets which have become popular tourist attractions, e.g. Petticoat Lane in London and Albert Cuypstraat in Amsterdam. In our house here in Canada we still have knick-knacks from flea markets as far afield as the Canary Islands, France and Mexico. This story was conceived as a small tribute to the many stall owners we have encountered around the world. As my research and writing of it proceeded, this story became more importantly a tribute to my Canadian friends and SEARIC - their charitable Society for the Education and Assistance of Rural Indian Children.

* * * * *

The day began like any other Friday. Kavi Cheema switched off the alarm just before it could go off at 3 a.m. In front of the wall mirror above the hand washbasin in his bedroom he carefully trimmed his already close-cropped beard before he showered in the tiny cubicle in the corner. In the kitchen he had a breakfast of orange juice and Muesli (a breakfast cereal of wheat flakes, toasted oats, fruit and nuts) over which he poured some milk.

In the hallway he pulled on his overalls, tied his shoe-laces and put on his woollen hat and gloves. In his father's old Ford minivan he checked the shopping list on his clip-board, started the engine, checked the blind spot over his right shoulder and moved off. Kavi was a proud member of the Institute of Advanced Motorists and strove to maintain its high standards of driving. He arrived safely at 'London's Larder' just after 4 a.m. without breaking any speed limits or contravening any road traffic acts.

New Covent Garden Market, set up in 1961 on the site of the old locomotive works at Nine Elms, is the wholesale food & flower market controlled by the government. Kavi collected what his father would have needed from the companies he had dealt with regularly. As always, just like his father did, he left the apples until last. As always, he took his time to inspect each individual apple. He had become immune to the supplier's banter about his father's minivan.

'Old 'enry Ford made it 'ere then, Kev!' In the market everybody called him Kevin or Kev – never Kavi.

'Nah,' replied Kavi, mimicking their London Cockney accents, 'Ee packed up at Battersea an' I 'ad ter shove 'im the rest of the way 'ere, cor blimey.'

Kavi gave time for the laughter to die down then headed for Old 'enry Ford.

He was back in Southall and able to unload the van at his father's stall in The Broadway before 6 a.m. If the traffic warden caught him unloading after 6 a.m., when restrictions applied, he'd face a parking fine – known in law as a fixed penalty or penalty charge. Kavi knew it was not a criminal matter but in his position he could not afford even to break a local authority traffic regulation.

It was just after half past six when he parked Old 'enry Ford outside his parents' terraced house in Oswald Road and put the resident's permit on the dashboard. When he opened the front door Kavi heard the Panjabi radio broadcast coming from the kitchen. His mother was up. She was probably getting breakfast ready for Rajender, his 11 year old son who was just coming down the stairs. He was in his pyjamas.

Raj had been woken up by the noise of the minivan pulling up outside the house. Kavi still could not get used to the rattle of the engine and the squealing brakes. 'The BMW 5 series saloon, or any BMW car for that matter, would never make this noise,' he thought, as he slammed the driver's door three times before it finally shut.

'Kavi sat sree akaal,' said Mrs. Cheema as she poured glasses of orange juice for her son and grandson.

'Ma sat sree akaal,' he replied in Panjabi to his mother before saying in English to his son 'Good morning, Raj.'

'Hi, Dad,' his son replied in English with the slightest hint of a French accent.

'When is your maths test today?'

'First thing this morning.'

'Good luck. Come to the stall after school. You can give me a hand and tell me how you got on. OK?'

'OK, Dad,'

'Here's an apple for your teacher but don't give it to her until you've got your test result. I don't want to defend you against bribery and corruption charges.'

Kavi walked up Oswald Road to The Broadway to prepare the family stall for business just as his father used to do. 'Display all our fruit and vegetables so our customers can see what they are buying,' his father would say. Kavi did just that. He took extra care with the apples. Each one was individually polished before being arranged into a tall pyramid on a little wooden handcart at the front of the stall.

The cart belonged to Kavi's father who used it to sell fruit and vegetables door to door when he first came to England. When they opened their business in the Broadway, his father named the stall 'The Apple Cart' and kept his little handcart at the front as a reminder of their humble beginnings.

'Everything must be tip top and fair price,' his father insisted. 'Always be friendly and polite so the customers will be coming back again and again.' When Kavi's father died, many of his customers came to pay their respects and offer their condolences. Kavi often recalled his father's story about a Brahmin, who had an infinite supply of something that was absolutely worthless until he gave it away.

'What was it that the Brahmin had?' Kavi's father would ask. When Kavi pretended he didn't know, his father would smile and say, 'Kavi, the Brahmin had what I am just giving to you. You are receiving smile. Remember, Kavi, to be giving everybody smiles.'

* * * * *

When Kavi opened the stall at 7:30 a.m. he smiled at his first customer. As he was serving her, a small group of pupils from Beaconsfield School sauntered up and stood close to the apple cart. He was handing the lady her change when the group turned and ran as the pyramid started to collapse. Apples were falling off the cart and bouncing in every direction.

It happened so quickly. One minute there was a pyramid of polished apples. A moment later much of the fruit was lying bruised or broken on the floor. The worst of it was that Kavi saw his son, Raj, in the group running down the road. And he had an apple in his hand.

That Friday afternoon Kavi closed the stall early and at 3 o'clock marched down Oswald Street to Beaconsfield School. He was standing in the foyer when the bell signalled the end of school. 'There's yer dad by the door,' said Adil, 'and 'e don't look 'appy.' As soon as he saw him, Raj guessed his father was all out of smiles.

'Hi Dad!'

'Who are these boys?' asked Kavi.

'Adil, Sunil and Vijay. They're my friends.'

'Which one of you upset my apples this morning?' asked Kavi, glaring at the three boys.

Kavi hadn't actually seen Raj take the apple from the cart but he had seen him running away with an apple in his hand. 'Circumstantial evidence - two or more facts taken together to infer a conclusion about something unknown,' Kavi reminded himself.

'They didn't do it, Dad. I did. It was an accident.'

311

'What do you mean, it was an accident?'

'We dared 'im.' said Adil. 'We told 'im 'e 'ad to pinch an apple if 'e wanted to be in our gang. Vijay told 'im which one to pinch.'

'Vijay told 'im to grab the corner apple at the bottom. We didn't fink them apples would fall off the cart,' lied Sunil.

'We are very sorry, Mr. Cheema,' said Vijay.

'You don't look sorry, any of you.' said Kavi. 'Take those silly grins off your faces.'

'I'm sorry, Dad. I didn't think.'

'That's your trouble,' said Kavi, 'you don't always think. Those apples will come out of your pocket money. Let's go home.'

At that moment, Raj's class teacher appeared. 'Good afternoon Miss Kumar,' the boys chorused.

'Good afternoon Raj, Adil, Sunil, Vijay,' she said, smiling back at them. The attractive, dark-haired young teacher then looked at Kavi. 'Good afternoon! Mr. Cheema, is it?'

'Yes. Kavi Cheema. Good afternoon Miss Kumar,' he said, giving her his broadest smile.

'Will you be coming to the parents' evening next week?'

'Ah, yes, the parents' evening. Next week. I think so. Goodness me. Yes. Yes.'

'Good!' she said, 'It's our first meeting of the school year and the first chance for me to meet the parents of my pupils. I look forward to seeing you there, Mr. Cheema.' She smiled, this time at Kavi, and headed for the staff room.

Raj saw his dad's smile vanish as soon as Miss Kumar was out of sight. First the apples. Now he was in trouble for losing his teacher's letter about parents' evening. To make matters worse, he didn't think he had done his best in the maths test that morning.

As they walked home side by side, Kavi recalled how it had been when he misbehaved and let his father down. He remembered how his father forgave him especially when he owned up right away and didn't try to put the blame on somebody else. 'Kavi,' he would say, 'you are being foolish boy but I forgive you because you owned up and were sorry.'

'Rajender!'

'Yes Dad!'

'Why didn't I know there was a parents' evening next week?'

'It's my fault, Dad. I forgot to bring home the letter. I'm sorry. I just forgot.'

'I felt foolish when your teacher asked me if I was coming.'

'Sorry, Dad.'

'Well, alright. I forgive you. Don't forget again.'

'No, Dad.'

'Now about those apples... '

'Yes, Dad.'

'If I tell you how many were ruined, how much each apple cost me and how much a customer would have paid me for one, can you work out how many weeks it will take you to repay me if I deduct half your weekly pocket money?'

'Yes, Dad.'

* * * * *

Deeptikana Kumar was glad to sit down. It was the end of her fifth week in her first term in her first full-time teaching post. In front of her, on the small table in the corner, were the papers from the maths test that morning. Most of the teachers had already gone home. She had the staff room to herself. Correcting and marking her pupils' work was not her favourite occupation but it had to be done. What would her colleagues think if she didn't do any marking? She had yet to discover the value of what psychologists call immediate feedback.

Mrs. Frobisher, due to retire at the end of term, all too frequently commanded her pupils to change papers and mark one another's test. 'Strike while the iron is hot and make them learn from each other's mistakes,' the formidable lady would bark to justify her stratagem but never, of course, admitting that re-marking took much less of her time than marking!

Deeptikana entered the scores in her mark book and compared them with those of the two earlier tests. There were no surprises. Adil, Sunil and Vijay were near the bottom of the class and Rajender Cheema, her star pupil, was again top and the only one with full marks. Remembering her encounter with the four boys in the school entrance, she wondered why Mr. Cheema's clever son associated with those three mischievous, not-so-clever imps.' Perhaps she could broach the subject at the parents' evening. 'What,' she thought to herself, 'was Mr. Cheema saying to those boys this afternoon?'

'You are late, Deeptikana.'

'Sorry, Dad. I had a test to mark.'

'Please do not call me Dad.'

'Sorry, Father.'

'Your mother is just putting the food on the table.'

'Tell Mum I shall be there in a moment.'

'Please do not refer to your mother as Mum.'

Mr. Kumar sat with his head bowed and his eyes closed while Mrs. Kumar served first him and then her daughter. When she had served herself, she looked at her husband and then, shaking her head, glanced at her daughter. Prathamesh Kumar opened his eyes and without looking up he began to eat.

'So, Father - how was your day?'

'Please do not be bothering your father, Deep. We are having very bad day.'

'Is it Amal again?'

'No. It is not your brother.'

'It is problem with business. Please be eating your food, Deep.'

'Where is Amal anyway? Is he working late at the office again?'

'Amalesh is at the office where he should be,' said Mr. Kumar, looking up from his plate.

'What is he doing there, Father? What is wrong?'

'It is not your concern. Finish your food and help your mother in the kitchen.'

As her daughter loaded the dishwasher, Mrs. Ravinder Kumar put on her bright yellow kitchen gloves and started to wash up the pots and pans. When her father retreated into his study at the front of their large house, Deeptikana broke the silence and asked her mother what was bothering her father.

* * * * *

Prathamesh Kumar inherited the East India Woollen & Silk Carpets Ltd import business from his father, Parmesh. Had he bothered, Pramathesh could have traced his roots to Bhadohi in Uttar Pradesh. Located almost 300 feet above sea level, it is one of the oldest and largest carpet manufacturing districts in India.

315

His great-great-grandfather, Varesh Kumar, had been a master weaver in Bhadohi. His great-grandfather, Deepak Kumar, had learned the craft of hand-knotted carpets from his father, Varesh. Prathamesh's grandfather, Mahesh Kumar, had also become a master weaver in Bhadohi but he was not content just to weave someone else's carpets. He wanted his own business. So, through prudence, sheer hard work and the help of his three sons, Gagnesh, Parmesh and Bhuvanesh, he established his own workshop to produce carpets of only the highest quality.

When Britain declared war on Germany in 1939, Gagnesh, the eldest son, left his father's business to serve as a captain in the Army of India. He died fighting the Japanese in Burma. After the war, Parmesh came to England, married by arrangement the daughter of the owner of several large warehouses and became a British citizen.

When their father, Mahesh, died of a heart attack, Parmesh allowed Bhuvanesh, his younger brother, to take over the business in India and arranged for him to marry the daughter of a major carpet manufacturer in the nearby district of Mirzapur. Back in England, Parmesh formed the East India Woollen & Silk Carpets Ltd to import carpets from Uttar Pradesh.

When Prathamesh was born in Southall, Britain had already started down the road to post-war prosperity. Rationing was a thing of the past and people were beginning to buy their own homes. After India had proclaimed itself a republic in January 1950, thousands of Indians – many unskilled - came to Britain to find work especially in the Midlands. Pramesh wanted cheap flat weave carpets for these immigrants. 'Make as many dhurries as you can,' he told Bhuvanesh, 'and make them as cheaply and as quickly as possible.'

Pramesh's younger brother did as he was told. The loose weave, pile-less cotton and wool rugs became very popular in the Midlands. 'Make sure the dhurries are brightly coloured,' commanded Pramesh. 'These immigrants want something to cheer up their gloomy lives.' Again Bhuvanesh did as he was told. Why not? Pramesh was his elder brother and head of the family. And their export-import business was booming.

Almost as soon as he could walk, Prathamesh would go with his father to one or other of the warehouses. When he was a little older but still not at school, he would, if his father wasn't looking, sit astride a roll of carpet and pretend to be riding a horse. When he had started school and was learning geometry, Prathamesh became fascinated by the two-fold symmetry of the designs in the expensive carpets his father had started to import. He liked the floral and vine patterns but preferred the animal, bird and calligraphic ones. Prathamesh was also intrigued by the different kinds of knots used in hand-made carpets.

'Weavers came to India in the 16th century and taught us how to make hand-knotted wool and silk carpets,' said his father. 'A Persian knot – also called a Senneh or Farsibaff – is an asymmetrical single knot; the thread forms one loop around one of the two warps. There are other knots, of course, but what matters is the knot density – the more knots per square inch (kpsi) the better the quality and the more expensive the carpet. Our best carpets have more than 300 kpsi,' said his father with pride.

One evening after he had finished his geometry homework, Prathamesh showed his father sketches of four possible knots.

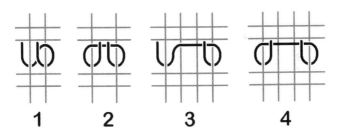

'Very good,' said Pramesh. 'Number 1 is a Persian knot. Number 2 is a Turkish knot. Numbers 3 and 4 are Jufti knots. Which Jufti is symmetrical?' Prathamesh was peeved that his father should even bother to ask him such a silly question but he just smiled, nodded and pointed to number 4. 'Well done,' said his father, not noticing the wry look on his son's face when he patted him on the shoulder.

Prathamesh joined his father's business after he had graduated and completed his articles to qualify as an accountant. He took over the company when his father, like grandfather Mahesh Kumar, died of a heart attack.

* * * * *

When Kavi and Raj arrived back at Oswald Road they were greeted by the sound of the radio and the smell of curry coming from the kitchen. Mrs. Cheema greeted them as usual. Raj said 'hello Gran' and ran upstairs before Kavi could reprimand him for not practising his Panjabi.

Kavi did not tell his mother what happened that morning. He knew it would upset her. Instead he told her that next week he would be going to the parents' evening at Beaconsfield School to see Raj's teacher and asked if she would like to go with him. She declined. She loved her grandson but accepted that she could never take the place of her late daughter-in-law. While his mother finished preparing the meal, Kavi sat in his father's old chair and looked at the advertisement he had placed in the local newspaper.

MANAGER WANTED
For 'The Apple Cart' Fruit & Vegetable Stall
in The Broadway, Southall
Must have current driving licence
Apply to Fosdyke, Cheema & Wong
tel: 020-7964-0469

When the food was ready, Kavi called Raj down from his bedroom to the table in the corner of the living room. Mrs. Cheema served her son and then her grandson before she sat down and served herself. 'Shukriya, Daddi,' Raj said to his grandmother. Kavi and his mother smiled at one another. 'That was right, wasn't it, Dad?'

Kavi nodded, thinking how lucky he was to have such a clever son who didn't say Dadda (grandfather) and remind his mother of her late husband. 'Can I help you at the stall tomorrow, Dad?' When Kavi frowned, Raj said, 'Sorry, Dad, may I help you tomorrow?' Kavi nodded and smiled at his son. He was indeed an intelligent boy.

Saturday came and went. They had sold out long before 5 o'clock. Raj handled the till all day while Kavi weighed and bagged the fruit

318

and vegetables for the customers. Raj cashed up and filled in the bank paying-in slip. Kavi swept the floor and washed the counters. On the way back to Oswald Road Kavi paused outside the bank so that Raj could pay the day's takings into the overnight safe. 'You did well today, Raj. I was proud of you. How would you like to manage your grandfather's stall?' He laughed out loud when Raj replied, 'Just as much as you would like to, Dad.'

Kavi, much to his mother's disapproval, had decided not to open the stall on Mondays. Business was usually slow and Monday was the one day when he could pop into the city, specifically to The Square Mile. He left Old 'enry Ford parked at Southall station – one of only two railway stations in Britain where the name on the platform is in both the Latin alphabet and the Gurmukhī script.

The 9.15 arrived at Paddington on time. During the 14-minute journey Kavi managed to glance at his weekly Gazette of the Law Society. The London Underground was busy as usual so it was standing room only on the Bakerloo line to Oxford Circus and on the East-bound Central line to Chancery Lane.

When he stepped out of the underground station and crossed High Holborn into Chancery Lane, there was a nip in the air. Leaves on the trees at Lincoln's Inn were turning colour and beginning to fall in the bright autumn sunshine. As Kavi walked through the Gate House and along a path strewn with dead leaves, he heard in his mind's ear Marie Claire, his late wife, singing her favourite song - Les Feuilles Mortes.

She always sang Jacques Prevert's lyrics to Joseph Kosma's tune. 'Non! Never shall I sing those words,' she would shout when Kavi,

319

pretending not to understand French, would start singing Johnny Mercer's lyrics for Autumn Leaves. When he reached the refrain she would sing loudly in French to drown out the English. Kavi would stop singing and laugh. Then he would hold her in his arms and whisper gently: 'Je t'aime beaucoup, Marie Claire. Je t'aimerai toujours.'

It was almost four years since a drunk driver ran over her on a pedestrian crossing but to Kavi it still seemed like yesterday. As he approached the four-storey building, a gust of wind swept away the dead leaves - les feuilles mortes - on the stone steps leading to the chambers of William S. Fosdyke, QC. and he recalled Johnny Mercer's final words of the refrain. Kavi did miss his darling Marie Claire most of all when the autumn leaves started to fall.

'Good morning, Bill.'

'Namastay, Kavi.'

'Nice try, Bill, but that's Hindi not Panjabi. Here's a present for you.'

'An apple?'

'Well spotted, counsellor. I hope our clients appreciate your razor sharp mind.'

'Is it from The Apple Cart?'

'Actually it's from New Covent Garden.'

'Is it fresh?'

'It all depends upon what we mean by fresh. May I respectfully refer you to the case of Jones v. Smith and the deep-frozen, smoked kipper hermetically sealed in plastic. Your Honour, I contend that my client had every right to ask if the kipper was fresh and that my client should not have been subjected to public ridicule.'

'Allow me to rephrase the question. On what day and at what time did learned counsel acquire said apple from New Covent Garden?'

'Last Friday morning at approximately 4.25 a.m.'

'I'm grateful to my learned colleague.'

'My pleasure. You realise I have just treated you to lunch?

'Lunch?'

'Yes. You know what they say? An apple a day...'

'keeps the judges at bay?'

'So, Bill, you wanted to see me?'

* * * * *

Mrs. Kumar finished the pots and pans, took off her yellow washing up gloves and led Deep into the sewing room at the back of the house. Before she sat down in her favourite chair - by the French windows that led to their large garden - Mrs. Kumar offered to make some tea but Deep knew her mother was stalling. She took a seat facing her mother and asked again what was troubling her father. Reluctantly, Mrs. Kumar sat down and tried to explain.

'Your father is worrying about business.'

'What has Amal been doing now to upset Dad?'

'Nothing. He is doing nothing.'

'That's what he usually does.'

'No, no. Amalesh is working hard.'

'So what has he been doing wrong?'

'Nothing. He is doing nothing wrong.'

'So what is Dad worrying about? Is he still upset because I teach and don't work for him in our family business?'

'No. Your father is very proud of you being good teacher.'

'So what is he worrying about?'

Deep's mother sighed. Just as she was about to answer, Deep frowned and looked towards the door thinking she had heard the sound of her father's study door opening. Her mother appeared to have heard nothing. She started to answer her daughter's question.

'It is your father's uncle, Bhuvanesh.'

'What has he been doing?'

'He is saying that he is doing what his brother, Pramesh, told him to do.'

'What did grandfather tell him to do?'

'He is saying that your grandfather was telling him to use children to make carpets.'

'Does he use child labour? Does Dad know he uses children to make carpets?'

'How can you be asking me such a thing, Deep?'

Before either of them could say any more, the door opened and Deep's father came in.

'Father! You don't look very well. Please come and sit down.'

'No thank you. I am very tired. I came to say goodnight. I am going to bed.'

The next morning Deep knocked on her brother's bedroom door and went in. Amal was still asleep. He looked so awful that she crept out, closed the door behind her and went down to breakfast. Her mother was already in the garden. She guessed her father was working in his study. She did not disturb him. She had her week's lessons to prepare so she worked at the kitchen table and waited for her brother.

Amal eventually appeared in his pyjamas and dressing gown. Deep noticed he was wearing the slippers she gave him for his birthday. She cleared a space on the table and put down a mug of coffee. Her brother yawned and flopped onto the kitchen chair opposite her. Before he had taken a sip of the hot black coffee she asked him what was going on.

'What d'you mean, what's going on?'

'This trouble with Dad's uncle?'

'Oh, that! I thought you meant...'

'Thought I meant what?'

'You know, the same old thing. Dad doesn't think I work hard enough.'

'Well perhaps you don't. He knows you'd rather be doing something else.'

'I would. I hate the warehouse and I'm sick of all those carpets.'

'Why didn't you come home for supper last night?'

'I was busy.'

'At the warehouse?'

'Yes, as a matter of fact.'

'What were you doing? Fiddling the cash book?'

'No. Never. Dad would spot it in a minute. You know what he's like with figures.'

'So you'd fiddle the books if you could get away with it?'

'You know I wouldn't. I do have some scruples. I'm a man of integrity.'

'So what were you doing at the warehouse.'

'Can you keep a secret?'

'Depends what it is?'

'I was applying for a management job in Southall.'

'Dad won't be pleased. That will be something else for him to worry about.'

'So what's old Bhuv been up to? Breaking the law?'

'It's possible. He may have been using illegal child labour to weave those carpets you import to keep us in the lap of luxury.'

* * * * *

Mandy, assistant to the Clerk of Chambers, teetered on her high heels into Bill Fosdyke's room carrying a silver tray on which was a pot of coffee, a jug of cream, two cups, two saucers, some sachets of sweetener and several chocolate biscuits. When she had teetered out and closed the door, Bill poured two coffees and selected a biscuit. Kavi refused cream and sweetener but accepted a biscuit. Black coffee and dark chocolate biscuits still reminded him of his days at Oxford. 'What,' asked Bill, raising his cup to his lips, 'do you know about child labour in India?'

'According to Section 24 of The Constitution of India (which came into force on the 26th January 1950) - Prohibition of employment of children in factories, etc.:

No child below the age of fourteen years shall be employed to work in any factory or mine or engaged in any other hazardous employment.

The Child Labour (Prohibition & Regulation) Act of 1986 broadened the scope of the ban on child employment by introducing

fines from 10,000 to 20,000 rupees per child employed and prison term penalties of up to two years.

In October 2006 the 1986 Act was amended to include a

324

ban on employing children under fourteen years of age as domestic workers or servants, in dhabas, restaurants, hotels, motels, tea-shops, spas and other recreational centres.'

'What are dhabas?'

'Road-side eateries,' said Kavi. 'Definitely not places for a gourmet such as yourself.'

'Are these laws enforced?'

'Not very effectively. There are few government inspectors with too much ground to cover to eradicate this age-old social evil as the Gazette of India Extraordinary called it.'

'How do you happen to know so much about this?'

'Marie Claire. She kept on to me to do something. "Kavi," she'd say, "you must stop these parents selling their children into bonded labour." I confess to my shame that I couldn't see that there was anything I could do. Anyway, what's brought all this on?'

'A client. He's been importing carpets from his uncle who is being charged with, among other things, trafficking of children, illegal use of child bonded labour and exporting carpets without a proper customs & excise licence. He came to see me on Friday. Has our client good reason to be worried?'

'His uncle might well have. What's his name?'

'The uncle?'

'The client.'

'Kumar. Prathamesh Kumar,' said Bill checking his notes. 'Name ring a bell?'

'A faint one perhaps but Kumar is the Indian equivalent of Smith. Rajender's teacher is a Kumar. Very attractive and intelligent to boot. Actually I shall be seeing her on Wednesday evening.'

'I see,' said Bill with a knowing look.

'You don't see at all. It's the school's parents' evening – the first this term. Anyway, it's time I was off.'

'Oh, I nearly forgot. Mandy took a phone call this morning. Someone's after your job.'

'My job?'

'Manager of The Apple Cart,' said Bill smiling and taking a bite out of his free lunch.

On his way to the Clerk's office, Kavi paused at an open doorway. David Wong looked up from his desk and asked when he should file bankruptcy papers for The Apple Cart. His grin turned to a look of alarm as a large orange flew at him. 'Well caught,' said Kavi to his squash opponent. 'I see you're keeping in shape ready for our next encounter – whenever that might be,' he said over his shoulder as he hurried down the corridor.

He knocked and opened the door just inside the main entrance to Chambers. 'Message for me, Mandy?' She nodded and told him that a Mr. Kumar had telephoned to apply for the job of manager of The Apple Cart. 'Not another Kumar! That's the fourth today,' said Kavi. A puzzled Mandy shook her head, consulted her notepad and told him that only one person had so far enquired about the position. He laid his broadest smile on her. 'Please telephone this Mr. Kumar and instruct him to be at the stall in The Broadway this Thursday afternoon - to meet the owner of The Apple Cart – at four o'clock sharp.'

* * * * *

Miss Kumar was sitting at her uncluttered desk when Kavi arrived at the open classroom door five minutes before his 7.15 p.m. appointment. He apologised for being early and asked if he might look around the room and see his son's desk. She nodded, smiled and pointed to the group of four desks near the fish tank.

A card, on which Raj had neatly printed his name, marked his son's desk. The other cards showed the other three desks belonged to another boy and two girls. Raj's desk was neat and tidy. Inside were some notebooks. In one of them Raj had started an essay entitled 'Upsetting The Apple Cart'. Kavi was starting to read it when he heard Miss Kumar inviting him to sit down.

'I'm sorry,' she said as he lowered himself onto the chair, 'these seats are not very comfortable or suitable for someone who is six feet tall.'

'Six feet three inches, actually, but please don't apologise. I've experienced worse.'

'Mr. Cheema, I must tell you that you have a very intelligent and very hard-working son.'

'That's good to hear, Miss Kumar.'

'In fact, Mr. Cheema, Rajender is my star pupil.'

'I hope you're not saying that because he bribes you with apples.'

'No, of course not,' she said with a puzzled look on her face.

'Just my little joke, Miss Kumar. Please forgive me. How did Raj do in his maths test?'

'Full marks. That's full marks for three tests in a row now.'

'What about his other subjects?'

'Again, he is usually top of the class.'

'And how are his social skills? That is the current jargon I believe.'

'Ah, I'm glad you asked that. Actually I'm a little worried by his choice of friends.'

'You mean Adil, Sunil and Vijay? I notice that you have seated them well apart from one another in the classroom.'

327

'Yes I have,' said Deeptikana, surprised that Kavi had remembered their names and had noticed they weren't sitting near one another. 'They get up to all sorts of tricks when they are together.'

'Boys will be boys, is that not so?'

'According to the headmaster of Narkover School.'

'Doctor Alec Smart – played by Will Hay - in the 1935 British mystery film entitled...'

'Boys will be boys,' said Deeptikana, glancing at her watch. 'I wonder why we never say girls will be girls.'

Hearing footsteps outside the classroom door and suspecting that the interview was nearly over, Kavi stood up and held out his hand. 'Thank you for seeing me. My son is fortunate to have you as his teacher.'

'I wish all my pupils were like Raj, Mr. Cheema.'

'Might that not be rather boring for you?'

'It might, Mr. Cheema. It just might be.'

'Before I go, Miss Kumar, I should like to ask you two questions if you have a moment.'

'Certainly,' she said.

'Did my son give you an apple before or after you marked his latest maths test?'

'Actually it was after. I remember it well. When everybody had left the classroom, he put the apple on my desk and said, "Cette pomme est pour vous, mademoiselle. Bon appétit." I had no idea he spoke French.'

'His mother was French. You might say that French is his mother tongue. However, his mother always claimed she was Parisienne rather than Française.'

'And your second question?'

'Would you consider it bribery and corruption if I invited you to have dinner with me on Saturday evening at my favourite restaurant?'

'No, not at all,' was all she said with a quizzical look on her face.

'Perhaps I should rephrase the question. Would you dine with me this Saturday evening?'

'Thank you, Mr. Cheema. I should like that very much.'

'Then I shall call for you at 7.15 p.m. if I may.' said Kavi giving her a broad smile.

* * * * *

Amal jumped when the phone rang on his desk in the corner of the warehouse. His father was in a foul mood and had just taken it out on his son. 'Hello,' said Amal. He completely forgot his father's instructions always to say Good afternoon. East India Woollen & Silk Carpet Import Company. How may I help you? The voice at the other end of the phone asked for Mr. Kumar.

'I'm Amalesh Kumar. Who is this please?' When he heard that it was Miss Amanda Winters of Fosdyke, Cheema & Wong, Barristers at Law, he held the phone closer to his ear and looked nervously around to see where his father was. On the other end of the line Mandy passed on the instructions for Amal to write down on his telephone notepad. 'This Thursday. O.K. 4 o'clock sharp at the stall. O.K. In The Broadway. O.K. I understand. Thank you. I'll be there.'

Raj gave the customer her change while Kavi put the two bags of fruit and vegetables into her wheel-along trolley. It was now 3.55 p.m. The only customer left was a young man dressed in a dark suit, white shirt and silk tie. His black leather shoes were highly polished.

Raj smiled. 'Good afternoon, Sir, what would you like?' Amalesh, clearing his throat, explained that he had come about the position of manager and believed that he was to meet the owner of The Apple Cart here at 4 o'clock. 'Dad! There's a man here to see the owner of this stall.'

Kavi emerged from behind some crates. 'And who might you be, young man?'

'Kumar. Amalesh Kumar. I have applied for the position of manager.'

'Ah! I see you're on time. One minute late and you would have been too late. You've passed the first test. So far so good.'

'Thank you, Sir. I am sorry but I do not know your name.'

'For now you can just call me Sir. Here's your next test. Serve this customer.'

'Excuse me?'

'Find out what Mrs. Joshi wants and serve her.'

'Very well,' said Amal. And with that he went up to the elderly lady, gave her a big smile and said, 'Good afternoon, Mrs. Joshi. How are you today?' When she gave him a puzzled look, he smiled again and said, 'Namastay, Smt. Joshi. Aap kaise hain?'

Raj gave Mrs. Joshi her change while Amal carefully put her fruit in a double bag.

'Excellent. You passed test number 2. Here's the third one. Help Raj close up the stall. He'll tell you what to do.'

None of this was what Amal had expected. He was enjoying himself. He removed his tie, took off his coat, rolled up his shirt sleeves and did what he was told. Sweep the floor. Wipe over the counters. Cover the unsold fruit and vegetables. Stack the empty crates. Count the cash in the till and record the exact details in the daily ledger. Pull down the shutters and secure with the padlocks. After he had secured the last padlock, Amal did up the buttons on his shirt sleeves and put back on his coat and tie.

'Did Mr. Kumar pass the test number 3, Raj?'

'Yes, Dad, he did.'

'Congratulations, Mr. Kumar. Just two more tests to go. Follow me to our headquarters.'

'Is that where my formal interview with the owner will take place, Sir?'

'Yes, I suppose so. Yes, if you pass test number 4,' said Kavi winking at his son.

* * * * *

With two chairs, his desk and the surrounding floor strewn with documents, Bill Fosdyke looked far from his usually unruffled self when David Wong arrived carrying his orange. Clearing a chair, David sat down. Bill took a bite from his apple and handed over a copy of The Children (Pledging of Labour) Act, 1933. David managed to read the note Bill had written on the cover page.

Raj (Hindi for reign) = British occupation and rule of India. Act banned all agreements whereby parents or guardians could receive payments or benefits in kind from employers for allowing any children below 15 (now 14) years of age to be used in any employment.

'We need Kavi's input on this,' said David. 'When's he returning to the fold?'

'Soon, very soon, I hope. Apparently, Marie Claire, kept India's child labour problem under his nose the whole time.'

'A lovely lady. Such a sad loss.'

'Yes she was. I think Kavi will want to be in on this one for her sake.'

'What did Kavi have to say on our client's behalf this morning?'

331

'He thinks our client's uncle – the one in India – could be in big trouble. But as for our client, we need to know more about his business relationship with his uncle.'

'D'you want me to look into that?'

'Would you mind?'

'No sooner said that done,' said David as he began to peel his orange.

'I gather from the orange in your hand that Kavi looked in on you this morning.'

'Nearly knocked my block off,' said David. 'He did not, I trust, throw that apple at you.' 'Certainly not. Unlike some I could mention, Mr. Cheema has proper respect for Head of Chambers. Now be about your business. Lunch is over,' said Bill dropping the apple core into his waste basket.

* * * * *

Kavi, Raj and Amal walked in the direction of the High Street, crossed over The Broadway and then turned into Oswald Road. When they reached Old 'enry Ford, Kavi asked to see Amal's driving licence. Satisfied that it did not restrict the holder to an automatic car, he gave Amal the keys of the minivan and told him his next test was to take them for a drive. 'What next?' Amal asked himself, as he drove them around the block and through the heavy homecoming traffic along the Broadway.

Just after they had passed it, Kavi asked him to explain the traffic sign close to their stall. Amal had no idea. Amal hadn't even noticed the sign. He was having a great time driving this old minivan around town. And he couldn't believe its colours: orange, pea-green and pineapple. It was like driving around in a bowl of fruit salad. His father would have been mortified. Cool! Real cool!

Back at Oswald Road, Amal parked the van, put the resident's permit back on the dashboard and managed to close the driver's door first time without slamming it. Kavi was impressed. 'You should consider taking an advanced motoring course, Mr. Kumar. I believe you would enjoy it? Incidentally, that road sign you missed gives the loading & unloading restrictions relating to the section of road and kerb marked by yellow lines. Now for the test number 5. Come and meet my mother. She speaks Hindi as well as Panjabi. By the way, you may now call me Mr. Cheema.'

Inside the house Amal heard the Panjabi broadcast coming from Mrs. Cheema's portable radio and savoured the aroma from the chicken kourma in the pot on the table in the corner of the room. He noticed that Kavi's mother had already set four places. Amal greeted Mrs. Cheema politely in Hindi and introduced himself. She smiled – first at Amal and then at Kavi. When they were all seated and tucking into the food, Raj asked Amal what he did for a living. 'In Hindi if you please,' said Kavi.

He began by telling them that he worked for his father as so-called manager of a carpet warehouse but that he was really just a general factotum: answer the phone, make the tea, sweep the floor and generally keep the place tidy. Kavi smiled to himself and refrained from pointing out that general is redundant because factotum means a person employed to do all kinds of work.

Realising that he wasn't helping his case, Amal tried to redress the balance by saying that, on reflection, he was more than just a dog's-body. In his father's company he was responsible for checking and

333

recording the delivery and dispatch of the carpets, keeping the day-to-day accounts, making up the weekly wage packets and controlling the petty cash. Raj wanted to know why Amal would want to run a fruit and vegetable stall but at that point he asked him, 'Do you love your father?'

'Oh! Nobody's asked me that before. You know what, I've never asked myself that. I often hate the way he treats me. Do this. Do that. Hurry up. Never please do this, Amal. Please do that, Amal. Thank you, Amal. And it's always Amalesh. Never Amal.'

'That's too bad,' said Raj, with a look that said my dad's not like that.

'Hey, and I always have to say Father. He gets really mad if I say Dad.'

'Perhaps,' said Kavi, 'your father thinks you're disrespectful by calling him Dad.'

'I hadn't thought of it that way, Mr. Cheema,' said Amal. 'My father's a brilliant man, you know. He's got a degree. He's a Fellow of the Institute of Chartered Accountants.'

'Do you like your dad?' said Raj.

'No. Yes. No, I don't always like,' said Amal, 'but I admire and respect him, I guess.'

'So why not stay in the family business?' asked Kavi.

'I want to make it on my own. And I'll never be able to fill Dad's shoes.'

'Do you live at home with your parents?'

'Yes, Mrs. Cheema, I do. I always have done.'

'The Manager of The Apple Cart would be required to live here. Board and lodgings would be part of the salary,' said Kavi. 'How would you feel about that?'

'Cool,' thought Amal but said aloud, 'that would be most acceptable, Mr. Cheema. When do I meet the owner for my formal interview, if I may ask?'

'You've met him,' said Kavi, 'and you've had it.'

When they saw the look on Amal's face, Mrs. Cheema and Raj started laughing.

'The job is yours if you want it,' said Kavi.

'Thank you,' said Amal, beaming broadly. 'Thank you so much. When do I start?'

'As soon as possible.'

* * * * *

Deep and Amal broke their news to their father on Saturday morning when they thought he was in a receptive frame of mind. They had told their mother earlier – Deep on Wednesday evening and Amal on Thursday evening. Amal was first to speak to his father. He was surprised, even a little hurt (he admitted to himself) but delighted that his dad didn't get angry. 'When do you take up your appointment?'

Amal told him it would be a week on Monday. 'Very well,' said his father, 'I shall promote Mukharjee and you will have a week to show him the ropes.' Amal told him that it was a live-in position but did not tell him where he would be working and living. His father did not seem to care. When Deep broke her news, she got an entirely different reaction.

'Who is this person you will be seeing this evening? What is his name and what does he do?'

'He is the parent of one of my pupils.'

'A married man! You are seeing a married man?'

When Amal heard this, he made a hurried escape to his room upstairs.

335

'No, Father, he is a widower. His wife died four years ago.'

'What does he do, this widower?'

'He sells fruit and vegetables.'

'He is a greengrocer! You know he is a greengrocer and you want to sit down and eat with him? No. I forbid it. The daughter of a merchant cannot eat with a greengrocer.'

'Father, we are British citizens living in England. The caste system doesn't apply here.'

'I am your father. I forbid this.'

'Father, listen. I do not wish to be disrespectful but the time is long past when Gandhi had to ask the Modh Bania permission to leave India to study law in England.'

'You know what Bania means?'

'Yes, Father, I know. Merchant. And Gandhi means greengrocer in Hindi. I know.'

'Prathamesh,' said Deep's mother, 'please be giving your daughter your permission.'

'I'm sorry, Mother, but I do not need his permission. I should like it,' she said, 'but I do not need it,' and flounced out of the room.

Turning to his wife, he raised his voice and asked, 'What is this greengrocer's name?'

'Mr. Kavi Singh ...'

'A Panjabi! A greengrocer, a widower and a Panjabi,' he shouted before she could finish.

As Mrs. Kumar settled in her favourite chair by the French windows she heard her husband slam shut his study door. He only reappeared for lunch and for afternoon tea. He was in his study when he heard Old 'enry Ford coming up the drive.

Deep didn't give Kavi a chance to switch off the engine and get out of the minivan. She was waiting on the front porch. She ran down the steps, wrenched open the passenger door, jumped in and slammed the door shut. Kavi, rather taken aback, asked if everything was alright. She nodded. 'Are you sure?' 'Yes!' she snapped. 'Please may we go.'

Her father saw everything through his study window. An old minivan! Bright green, orange and yellow! Making more noise than his drive-around lawnmower! The Apple Cart in large brown letters on the sides! And the greengrocer didn't even have the courtesy to open the door for the daughter of a merchant!

It was some while before Deep calmed down and realised how rude she had been. Kavi, for his part, couldn't get over how different she looked from the teacher he had seen at the parents' evening on Wednesday. She was beautiful. Her dark hair was so shiny. Her eyes – angry at he knew not what and framed by her dark eyebrows – were alight. Her pale-brown skin was smooth and unmarked.

She was wearing a dark green polo-neck sweater that went perfectly with the pale brown jacket and matching ankle-length skirt. 'I thought you wore glasses,' he said, keeping his eyes on the road and concentrating on his driving. Deep was impressed that he had remembered and explained they were for reading. 'And for marking test papers,' he said. She laughed and started to relax.

For the rest of the twenty minute journey she sat back and studied her escort. Kavi was wearing a dark brown suede leather jacket, beige-coloured casual trousers and dark brown suede shoes. His white silk shirt had a round collar that did not permit or need a tie. Deep noticed a hint of grey in his dark hair and neatly trimmed beard. She sensed in this man an inner confidence, a sureness of himself and of his abilities, together with an acceptance of his limitations. She also sensed a certain restlessness, an eagerness to know and learn from the people and the world around him. As Old 'enry Ford rattled to a halt outside Le Café Blanc Kavi said, 'I hope you like French cuisine.'

'Good evening Mr. Cheema,' said the Maître d'hôtel. 'We have not seen you for such a long time. Your table for two is ready. Please follow me.'

'Thank you, Henri.'

When they reached the candle-lit table in a nook by the stone fireplace, Henri pulled out a chair for Deep. 'S'il vous plaît, Mademoiselle!' he said, with a flourishing gesture that bade her sit down.

When they were both seated, Henri whisked the damask napkins from the table onto each of their laps then departed with another flourish: 'Bon appétit.'

'Good evening, Mr. Cheema,' said Claude, the wine waiter. 'Plum and grape juice for you, n'est-ce pas? Some wine perhaps for Mademoiselle?'

Kavi nodded then looked across the table at Deep who appeared even more stunning in the candle light.

'If it is non-alcoholic then I should like plum and grape juice, please,' said Deep.

'Bon! Chilled, oui?' said Claude who left before they could even nod their heads.

'I think,' said Kavi, 'that we should study the menu before the next assault. 'Would you like some help?'

Before she could say yes, the next wave arrived in the form of François. He introduced himself as their waiter for the evening and then rattled off the Chef's selection du soir.

'Merci, François,' said Kavi. 'We'd now like time to study the à la carte menu.'

'What do you recommend?' said Deep.

'French Onion soup – it has a melted gruyère crouton – as a starter followed by Poulet au Cidre Breton avec des petits pois et des pommes frites.'

'That sounds wonderful.'

'I suppose it does,' said Kavi. 'Chicken and chips with peas always sounds better in French.'

Deep laughed and Kavi noticed how white and even her teeth were.

'To finish, Mademoiselle, you must 'ave ze Crème Brûlée – ze spécialité de la maison, n'est-ce pas?' Just as Kavi said this in a mock heavy French accent, François returned.

'You are ready to order, n'est-ce pas?'

'Kavi and Deep looked at one another and burst out laughing.'

'So,' said Kavi, 'are you feeling alright now?'

'Yes, I am, thank you, Mr. Cheema.'

'Kavi! Please call me Kavi, Miss Kumar.'

'Only if you'll call me Deep.'

'Agreed but I thought your name was Deeptikana.'

'It is but I prefer Deep,' she said, wondering how he knew her full name.

'Well then, Deep, tell me how you knew about boys will be boys.'

'The Will Hay film you mean? Just one of those things. I like that kind of film. And before you even ask, Kavi, the answer is no – I do not like Bollywood movies.'

The soup was served. They both enjoyed every drop. Deep asked that they not talk shop, meaning she didn't want to talk about school. 'I understand,' said Kavi. 'You don't want to hear about the greengrocery business. You think fruit and vegetables boring.' When she tried to explain what she meant, Kavi held up his hand as she might have done to silence her class.

'Vegetables can be extremely interesting although not vegetables per se. Take these peas, for instance. How did they get out of their pods and end up here on my fork? Take these chips. Who peeled and cut up the potatoes? Might not the Le Café Blanc chef be exploiting young children labouring illegally in his kitchen?' Kavi immediately regretted his poor attempt at humour when he saw the look on Deep's face. 'I'm sorry,' he said, 'that was in bad taste. I've upset you. I hope I haven't spoilt your evening. Please forgive me.'

She shook her head. 'There's nothing to forgive,' she said, trying to put her father's business problem out of her mind. 'I nearly spoilt the evening before it started. It was my father, you see. It was so frustrating. He thought I needed his permission to dine with you. In some respects he is still living in the past. He went on about how Ghandi had to ask the Modh Bania permission to leave India...'

'...to study law at London University and be called to the bar at the Inner Temple,' interjected Kavi.

'Oh! Well, yes,' she said. 'I told him that we're British citizens and there's no caste system here.'

'Perhaps,' said Kavi, 'here in Britain it's called a class system.'

'Oh, I see what you mean. But there's no caste system like there is in India.'

'The Constitution of India of 1950 made the caste system illegal. So in theory there's no caste system in India. But as someone I know is fond of saying, the law is one thing – enforcement is another.'

François interrupted their conversation with 'Excusez-moi! Monsieur! Mademoiselle! Voilà – la crème brûlée. Bon appétit!'

'What exactly do you mean – the law is one thing – enforcement is another?'

'Let me ask you this,' said Kavi. 'What does this signify to you as a driver – a traffic sign with 50 in black letters on a white background inside a red circle?'

'A fifty mile per hour speed limit.'

'Correct. But what does it mean?'

'It means I should not drive faster than 50 miles per hour.'

'Correct. It is a limit. Unfortunately, the majority of drivers treat it as a target to be exceeded. They break the law and commit an offence. These offenders cause on average more than 100 deaths or injuries on the road each day.'

'Oh no,' whispered Deep under her breath as she remembered that Kavi's wife had been killed on the road.

'Oh yes,' said Kavi in an equally soft voice. 'The police (with the help of cameras) and the courts (by the application of fines, penalties and other punishments) try to enforce the law. Do you think they succeed?'

'No,' said Deep, 'I don't think they do.'

'Do you break the law?'

'No. At least I don't think so - not knowingly, anyway.'

'In the eyes of the law – not to be confused with justice - ignorance is no defence.' Then he paused, misunderstood the sad look on her face and said, 'I'm sorry, I'm riding my hobby-horse and starting to bore you.'

'Not at all,' said Deep. 'Please go on.'

François appeared once more to interrupt their conversation. 'Excusez-moi! Monsieur! Mademoiselle! Would you like to see the cheese board?' They shook their heads. 'Café?' Kavi ordered café noir. Deep order café au lait.

'Are you sure I'm not boring you?'

'No, Kavi, you're not, honestly.'

'Look, the law is a set of rules, often complicated rules, that we should all follow to live in peace and harmony with our neighbours in society. Justice is the exercise of authority in the maintenance of those rules. The task is to make everyone follow the rules and to punish those of us who don't.'

'But surely,' said Deep, 'the real task is to make us understand why we should follow the rules?'

'It sounds like you studied Dr John Dewey as well as Herr Friedrich Froebel when you were training to be a teacher.'

'How did you know I studied Froebel when I was at Maria Grey College?'

'Your qualifications on Beaconsfield staff register. NFF. National Froebel Foundation. Anyway, how did the story go now. Ah, yes, I remember.

A neighbour sees Dewey's son standing barefoot in a puddle.

The neighbour says, 'Shouldn't you make your son get out of that puddle, Dr Dewey?'

Dr Dewey replies, 'No, I should make him understand why he should get out.'

'What's wrong with that?' asked Deep.'

'Understanding why we should or should not do something does not mean that we will or will not do that something. In my experience, people do not always act according to their social conscience,' said Kavi somewhat angrily, thinking of the hit-and-run drunk driver who killed Marie Claire.

'How true,' said Deep somewhat sadly, thinking of her father's uncle in India.

As she drank her coffee, Deep thought how articulate and well informed Kavi was for – dare she share her father's prejudice - a greengrocer. Then she thought how expensive the meal would be and asked if they could share the bill. 'I appreciate your offer to go Dutch,' said Kavi, 'but this is my treat and not, as you agreed, a bribe.'

After Kavi had paid the bill, he asked the Maître d'hôtel if le Chef might spare a moment to have a word with him. A few minutes later le Chef arrived dressed in white and wearing his distinctive tall white hat. 'Jean-Paul,' said Kavi, shaking hands. 'Ça va?' Jean-Paul, grinning from ear to ear launched into a torrent of French.

At the earliest opportunity, Kavi introduced le Chef to Deep. Jean-Paul kissed the back of Deep's hand. and was into Enchanté, Mademoiselle. Je suis enchanté de faire votre connaisance, before Kavi interrupted. 'This is an evening of French cuisine but English conversation, mon ami.'

'Thank you so much. The food was delicious.' said Deep sincerely.

'But of course it was,' said Jean-Paul. 'That is why you come to Le Café Blanc, no?'

'Jean-Paul, please,' said Kavi. 'Of course the food is great. I dragged you out here because I want to know how the peas got out of their pods and onto my plate? How the potatoes got out of their skins and became the chips on my plate.'

'Peas? Non! Chips? Non! I, Jean-Paul, prepare only les petits pois et les pommes frites!'

'I know that, my friend,' said Kavi. 'What I don't know is who shells des petits pois and who peels the potatoes and cuts them into des pommes frites?'

'Ah. You think that I, Jean-Paul...'

'No, of course you don't shell peas and peel potatoes. But who does? Do you by any chance have children doing that?'

'Des enfants? Are you mad? Non. Pas du tout! I must go. A pleasure to meet you, Mademoiselle,' he said, kissing the back of her hand once more. 'Au revoir, mon vieux.'

Kavi said bonsoir to the Maître d'hôtel and led Deep by the arm to Old 'enry Ford.

It was just after 11 o'clock when Kavi brought the minivan as quietly as possible to a halt and walked Deep to her front door. The security porch light came on but her father's study remained in darkness. Her parents were already in bed. Her brother was watching television in his room at the back of the house. Kavi and Deep began to speak at the same time. They laughed. Kavi waited patiently.

'I have had a wonderful evening,' said Deep. 'Thank you so much for inviting me.' Kavi smiled, said what a pleasure it had been for him and hoped that they could do it again sometime in the not too distant future. 'I should like that very much,' said Deep, touching the sleeve of his jacket. Kavi smiled, kissed her on the forehead, said goodnight and walked down the steps to the minivan.

* * * * *

On the Monday, exactly one week after Bill Fosdyke had apprised him of Bhuvanesh and Prathamesh Kumar's possible involvement with child labour, Kavi and Raj took the train into town to spend the day in the South Kensington museums. Beaconsfield School was having a teachers training day. Raj tossed the coin. Kavi called 'heads' and lost.

344

So they went to the Science Museum in the morning – Raj's choice – and the Victoria & Albert in the afternoon – Kavi's choice. For the rest of the week it was school and The Apple Cart as usual.

On the same Monday, Deep did her best to concentrate on the teacher training but her mind kept drifting off, one minute to the evening out with Kavi and the next minute to her father's business problems, to child labour, the law and justice. She took note of what Mrs. Frobisher had to say on the subject of discipline in the classroom.

'As teachers,' said the femme formidable, 'we have a duty first to ensure that our pupils get into good habits. Respecting authority. Behaving themselves. Working hard. Doing their best. When they do the right thing as a matter of routine, then we have a duty to ensure that our pupils understand – as far as they can – the reasons for these good habits.'

This did not sound like the educational philosophy of Froebel or Dewey. Deep realised how much she would like to hear Kavi's comments on Mrs. Frobisher's views. For the rest of the week it was classes as usual.

On that same Monday, Amal was at his desk in the corner of the warehouse at 7 a.m. He was an hour earlier than usual and full of the joys of Spring in spite of the cold autumn weather. When Mukharjee arrived at a quarter to eight, he was surprised and somewhat disturbed to see Amal already at his desk. 'Ah, Mr Mukharjee, I see you have managed to drag yourself out of bed.' When Mukharjee said that he thought their meeting was for 8 o'clock, Amal said, 'Quite correct. 8 o'clock sharp. I am pleased to see you are early. You have passed the first test.' For the rest of the week Amal explained in detail to Mukharjee the business.

On that Monday when Kavi and Raj were travelling second class on the 9.15 train to Paddington, Mr. Prathamesh Kumar was travelling in a first class compartment two carriages away. His appointment with David Wong at Lincoln's Inn was for 10.15 a.m. He arrived some minutes early. At 10.14 a.m. Mandy took him to David's office, showed him to a seat and asked if he would like some coffee. He nodded. She left, saying that Mr. Wong would be along shortly. After what seemed ages but was in fact only two minutes, Mandy appeared with the usual tray of coffee, cream, sweeteners and chocolate biscuits.

At twenty past ten, David appeared. 'I'm sorry to have kept you waiting, Mr. Kumar. Ah, good. I see our Mandy has done her stuff. Now to business, so to speak. I'd like you to tell me about your relationship with Mr. Bhuvanesh Kumar.' When Prathamesh said simply that he was his uncle, David said, 'Yes. Yes, of course. What I meant was that I need to know everything about your business relationship with him.'

Prathamesh spent the rest of the week in his study either pouring over his books, contracts and other legal documents or talking on the telephone to his uncle in India.

* * * * *

'Do you need any fruit or vegetables, Mum?' I'm popping into The Broadway.' It was Saturday afternoon. Deep had finished her lesson preparations before lunch.

'Good! I am coming,' her mother said, 'Doctor Biswas said walking is good for heart.'

'You don't have to come. It's a bit windy this afternoon.'

'I am coming.'

They put on their warm coats, scarves, hats and gloves, waved goodbye to Prathamesh through his study window and set off arm-in-arm into the centre of what is known as Little India. Deep took the shortest route - past West Middlesex Golf Club where Mr. Kumar was a member – and within fifteen minutes of leaving their house they were window-shopping along the High Street and then The Broadway.

'That looks a good place for fruit and vegetables,' said Deep, pointing to The Apple Cart.'

'Yes, very good,' said her mother, suppressing a smile, and as they approached the stall, she let go of her daughter's arm.

'Good afternoon, Mrs. Kumar,' said Raj. 'How are you today?'

'I'm very well, Mr. Cheema. How are you?'

'I'm fine, thank you, Mrs. Kumar,' said Raj from behind the till.

Deep was speechless. She just stood staring at her mother until Raj said, 'Hello Miss. Come to buy some apples? They're fresh and juicy.'

Then Kavi appeared as if from nowhere and joined in. 'Mrs. Kumar. How nice to see you. Not too cold for you I hope.'

'No, not cold. It's nice to see you again. I believe you are knowing my daughter, Deep,' she said with a wry smile.

'I am privileged to say that I do know Raj's teacher,' Kavi said, looking at Deep and giving her his broadest smile. When he heard oh, oh, he turned towards his son and his smile vanished.

'I'm sorry, Dad. I forgot to give Miss Kumar your letter,' said Raj, reaching into his pocket. 'Sorry, Miss. It's a bit crumpled.'

Deep read the letter while Kavi and Raj served her mother with some guavas and papayas. Mrs. Kumar was impressed with how quickly Raj worked out in his head what she owed for the fruit and how confidently he handled the till, giving her the correct change from the ten pound note.

When she thanked him and addressed him as Mr. Cheema, Raj gave her his broadest smile. 'How like his grandfather,' she thought. 'He's going to be tall and handsome just like his father,' she said to herself, as she looked at Kavi and asked him in Hindi how his mother was.

Before he could answer, Ravinder Kumar heard a voice from the corner of the stall. 'Namastay, Smt. Kumar.' It was Mrs. Cheema. For the next fifteen minutes, the two ladies were engrossed in conversation and oblivious of anyone around them. During this time Raj hid behind the till while Deep answered Kavi's letter by saying how much she would like to go into London on Sunday for a pub lunch. Kavi was delighted and arranged to collect her at 10 o'clock sharp.

* * * * *

'What? She is going to a pub with this greengrocer? Today? In London?'

'Please be calm,' said Ravinder Kumar to her husband. 'He is very good greengrocer. Eat some guava.'

'How can I be calm? A merchant's daughter is going to eat and drink with a greengrocer. And in a public place!'

'Eat your fruit,' said Ravinder, 'and do not be worrying.'

Pramathesh sat and ate some of the guava his wife had prepared. He started to calm down. The fruit was excellent. He ate the rest and asked his wife if there was more. She gave him some papaya – his favourite. When he'd finished eating he was, she thought, more calm than she had seen him in a while. 'Excellent fruit, Ravinder. Thank you.'

'Please, Pram, now go to your study and read your paper.'

He was in his study all relaxed and enjoying his newspaper when at 10 o'clock precisely he heard Old 'enry Ford rattle to a stop outside the front door. Before her father could get up from his chair and look out of his study window, Deep was in the passenger seat and Kavi was driving out of the gate. As Pramathesh was watching the minivan disappear out of the gate, his study door opened and Ravinder came in. 'I am bringing you some more papaya, Pram.'

Kavi parked the minivan at Southall station and a few minutes later they were boarding the train to Paddington. It was the shortest journey he'd ever known. He sat opposite Deep and couldn't take his eyes off her. Her face glowed with vitality. She was wearing a smart fur hat and gloves. Over her tailored trouser suit she was wearing a fleece-lined jacket. Her shoes were smart. They matched her gloves and hat. Nevertheless, they were a sensible flat-heeled pair of suede shoes suitable for long walks.

From Paddington he took her on the tube following the same route he had used the last time he came up to town to Lincoln's Inn. When they stepped out of the station into the bright sunshine, he directed her across High Holborn and into Chancery Lane. Kavi was wearing a warm overcoat over his polo-necked sweater, sports jacket and trousers. He too wore gloves and sensible shoes but he had no hat so the crisp autumn air ruffled his hair as they walked.

'I love this part of London,' said Deep. 'Chancery Lane. Inns of Court. So much history and tradition. Have you read Bleak House? Charles Dickens writes of dinosaur lawyers walking up and down this smog-filled street. And an old lawyer blows his brains out in a coffee-house in Chancery Lane.'

'Old Tom Jarndyce.'

'Yes that's the lawyer. Have you read the book or did you watch the television serial?'

'Both, actually but I preferred the book.' Then leading her through the Gatehouse, he said, 'Let's see if we can find Lincoln's Inn Hall where according to Dickens at the very heart of the fog,...'

'... sits the Lord High Chancellor in his High Court of Chancery,' said Deep.

According to a tablet on the north wall, the Old Hall was built in 1492 after Henry VII came to the throne. However, from 1924 to 1927 it was dismantled brick by brick, stone by stone to straighten the five-centuries old wooden rafters and preserve the building. Kavi pointed to the numbers on some of the bricks. 'All the bricks and stones were marked when they dismantled the Old Hall,' said Kavi, 'so it could be rebuilt exactly as it was first built five hundred years ago.' When Deep asked what the Old Hall is used for today, Kavi said, 'As a compulsory dining hall during the four legal terms (Hilary, Easter, Trinity and Michaelmas) and as the High Court of Chancery out of term time.'

'What do you mean – compulsory dining?'

'Before you can be called to the bar,' said Kavi, 'you must attend twelve qualifying sessions which involve dining in Hall. You have to be in your place when Grace is said at the start and at the end otherwise the session doesn't count. It's a tradition going back to the time when a young barrister learned the law from older barristers over a meal and a glass of wine.'

'So nowadays if you want to become a barrister, all you have to do is dine in the Old Hall twelve times,' she said with a wry look on her face.

Kavi laughed. 'I don't think it's that easy. Shall we go?'

'Where to now? Another Inn of Court?'

Leaving the grounds of Lincoln's Inn, they walked south to the end of Chancery Lane, crossed Fleet Street and entered Inner Temple Lane. At the end of the lane they came face to face with Temple Church. Deep loved this round building. Full of enthusiasm, she asked Kavi if he knew that this round church had been built by the Knights Templar in the 12th century and what did he think of the grotesque carvings at the top of the stone pillars supporting the Norman arches.

As soon as she'd asked, she thought how much she sounded like a teacher on a school trip. She was relieved when he said that he hadn't really noticed the carvings until she had pointed them out.

'The Inner Temple is where Ghandi was called to the bar,' said Kavi, as they walked down the steps and through the beautiful landscaped gardens towards Broad Walk and Victoria Embankment. 'Did I tell you that there are four Inns of Court to select, train and call lawyers to the bar? Gray's Inn, Lincoln's Inn, Middle Temple and Inner Temple, of course.' When Deep asked how he knew so much about the

350

Inns of Court, barristers and the law, Kavi glanced at his watch and said, 'I don't know about you but I'm ready for lunch.'

'So much for your idea of a pub,' said Deep as they arrived at the George Inn – the last remaining galleried inn in London.

'It's a sort of old pub,' said Kavi. 'It was a 17th century coach terminus.'

'Dickens mentions it in his book Little Dorrit,' said Deep. 'I hope you don't want to sit outside.'

Kavi laughed. 'Not today.' And with that they went inside and sat in the corner on the bench just behind the door.

Over a lunch of cheese, home-made pickle, fresh home-baked bread, butter from a proper dish – not a little sealed plastic pot – and, to her delight, a glass of plum and grape juice, Deep told Kavi about Beaconsfield school's training day. They discussed Mrs. Frobisher's approach to classroom discipline. They talked about the films they had seen, the books they had read and the music they had listened to. The time flew by. Before they knew it they were on the tube to Paddington and on the train to Southall.

As Old 'enry Ford came to a halt outside her front door, Deep saw her father's face at his study window. When she asked Kavi if he would like to come in for a cup of tea, he smiled and said, 'Another time perhaps. Mother will be waiting to serve supper. I really enjoyed your company today. I hope you enjoyed our trip.' She answered by leaning over and kissing him on the cheek. Then she was out of the van and hurrying indoors.

* * * * *

At the end of school on Monday, the day after her trip to London, Miss Kumar gave Raj a sealed envelope with strict instructions to deliver it to his father or suffer the consequences. On that same Monday, Deep's father caught the early train to London to spend another day with his lawyers at Lincoln's Inn. Amal left the house early, actually before anyone else was awake. He was eager to be at

The Apple Cart before six o'clock – the time when Mr. Cheema said he would start teaching him the business. Mrs. Kumar left the empty house to join Mrs. Cheema for morning coffee at Oswald Road.

Kavi smiled when he saw Amal reading the detailed restrictions on the loading/unloading traffic sign near the stall. 'Good morning, Mr. Kumar. I'm glad to see you're here bright and early.'

'What time do they deliver your fruit and vegetables?'

'Oh,' said Kavi, 'everything is always unloaded and into the stall before 6 o'clock.'

'Is there ever any problem with deliveries? Our carpets didn't always arrive on time.'

'Ah, well,' said Kavi, 'you can't always rely on other people to do the right thing.'

'So how do we make sure your fruit and vegetables are here before 6 o'clock?'

'Good question. I'll let you in on our trade secret later. First, let's open up the stall and I'll show you how the morning normally begins.' And of course it began with Amal putting the wooden cart outside, polishing the apples one by one and carefully assembling them into a pyramid.

At about 11 o'clock, Kavi glanced at his watch. 'Time for another coffee break. You can close up and we'll pop back to Oswald Road. We shall need the van for our next task.' Amal's eyes lit up at the prospect of driving Old 'enry Ford again.

As they stepped through the front door into the hallway they heard voices coming from the living room. It was definitely not Mrs. Cheema's radio broadcasting in Panjabi. They hung up their outdoor coats and Kavi led the way into the living room.

'Good morning, ladies,' said Kavi. 'How are you both today?'

Amal was speechless when he saw his mother.

'Good morning, Amal,' chimed the two women. Then his mother said, 'Do not be being surprised, Amal. Mrs. Kumar is telling me about new job and all that. When will you be telling your father?'

Amal followed Kavi into the kitchen where they sat on stools and drank their coffee. 'So, that lady is your mother,' said Kavi, 'and your father imports carpets from India?'

'Yes,' said Amal.

'Do you by any chance have a sister?'

'Yes,' said Amal. 'She's a teacher. She's at Beaconsfield School.'

When they had finished their coffee, Kavi gave Amal the van keys. When he asked where they were going, Kavi said, 'your place to pick up your stuff. Starting today, you live here, remember?' Amal's mother refused their offer of a lift. She and Mrs. Cheema still had a lot to talk about and Dr. Biswas had told her walking was good for her heart.

When they returned to Oswald Road with the few things that Amal felt he needed, his mother had already left. Mrs. Cheema showed him his room. When they had emptied the van, they walked back to the stall in The Broadway. Later that afternoon Raj arrived at The Apple Cart and gave his dad the envelope from his teacher.

While Kavi read Deep's note, Raj showed Amal how to handle the till. When Amal asked about the float and how they handled the petty cash, he was impressed by how much Raj knew about the business. He hadn't known as much about the carpet business when he was eleven. 'Time to shut up the stall and go home,' said Kavi. 'We've an early start tomorrow.' Over the evening meal Amal learned the trade secret of the fruit and vegetable deliveries. 'Yes,' said Kavi, 'We'll get up at 3 o'clock and be at New Covent Garden Market by 4 a.m. Oh, and by the way, my name is Kavi – not Kevin or Kev – understood.'

Over the next four weeks, Amal and Raj proved their reliability, Amal as manager of the business and Raj as courier of sealed envelopes between his teacher and his father. Mrs. Cheema was glad of Amal's company especially when her grandson accompanied Kavi and Deep on

353

their Sunday trips to London. Sometimes she would help Amal at the stall. Raj helped at the till all day Saturday and for an hour after school during the week.

Kavi was gradually able to give more time and thought to the legalities of child labour in India. After the first two weeks, Kavi left Amal to cope on his own – The Apple Cart was now open six days a week – and went up to Lincoln's Inn for an 11 o'clock Monday morning appointment. It was Kavi's first one since his father had passed away.

* * * * *

'Mr. Cheema will see you now,' said Mandy.

'Please sit down,' said Kavi. 'May we offer you some coffee.' When his client shook his head, Mandy gathered up the tray from the desk and wiggled out of the room.

When the door had closed, Kavi looked up from the bulky file open in front of him and said, 'Your uncle may, I fear, be in serious trouble, Mr. Kumar, and in my professional opinion there is very little we can do to help him. The laws of England and India have much in common, of course, but it's really a matter of jurisdiction.'

'So,' said Pramathesh, 'there is nothing you can do for him?'

'No, I'm afraid not. I assume that he has consulted lawyers in Uttar Pradesh?

'Uncle Bhuvanesh thinks all lawyers are crooks – leeches to suck his blood – if you'll pardon me for saying so.'

'That's not uncommon amongst people who do not understand the complexities and subtleties of the law,' said Kavi, 'let alone appreciate the qualifications, training, experience and effort required of lawyers to interpret the law and plead a client's case. You are, I understand, a professional man yourself, Mr. Kumar. Do you share your uncle's view of lawyers?'

'No, I do not but I admit that we may always find a few rotten apples in a barrel be it one of lawyers or one of accountants.'

The two men smiled at one another in agreement then Kavi said, 'As regards your own position in this matter, I should like to clarify one or two points.' Turning over a page in the file on his desk, he asked, 'What was your official position in East India Woollen & Silk Carpets Ltd when your father died and you took over the company?'

'My father was the principal shareholder, chairman of the board and general manager of our private, family company. I was company treasurer. When my father died I inherited his shares and became the chairman.'

'Did Mr. Bhuvanesh Kumar ever hold shares in your company?'

'No. Never,' he said emphatically. 'Ours is a British business with no base in India.'

'Did your company ever employ Mr. Bhuvanesh Kumar in any capacity?

'No. Never. He has always worked quite independently of us.'

'Is Mr. Bhuvanesh Kumar a sole proprietor or a sole trader?

'He is a sole proprietor. He owns and runs a shop where his carpets are made. I suppose he could also be a sole trader because, to my knowledge, he only deals with carpets.'

'Mr. Bhuvanesh Kumar has never been under contract to your father or your company to make carpets just for your father or your company?'

'No.'

'So your father or your company could not instruct him to use child labour? And neither your father nor your company ever did issue any such instructions?' When the man sitting opposite him hesitated, Kavi said, 'Let me put this another way, Mr. Kumar. If your father had told your uncle to use child labour, would your uncle have had to do what your father told him? May I remind you that your father was senior to Mr. Bhuvanesh Kumar. He was head of the Kumar family and, by tradition, to be respected and obeyed.'

Pramathesh Kumar was beginning to feel uncomfortable. This tall, soft-spoken lawyer seemed to be cross-questioning him as though he were in the witness box and on trial. He knew his father had told his uncle to make the dhurries and the hand-knotted carpets as quickly and cheaply as possible. On the one hand, he could never believe his father would have told uncle Bhuvanesh to use children. On the other hand, he knew in his heart that children cost less than adults, that their fingers are nimble and that they need less light to work by. What he didn't know – or perhaps didn't want to know – was that these children usually became severely ill by the time they were adults, suffering eye damage from the poor light and lung diseases from the dust and carpet fluff.

'My father was an honourable man. He would never have done such a thing.'

'Did your father ever visit his brother in Bhadohi?'

'He saw my uncle when they attended my grandfather's funeral.'

'Have you ever visited your uncle?'

'No. I never seemed to have had the time.'

'Does your uncle have a large family?'

'He has three sons and two daughters.'

'Does he have any grandchildren?'

'I think so. I'm not sure. Why are you asking me these family questions?

'Many employers of child labour use a loophole that puts family members outside the protection of the law. In addition to using their own sons and daughters, grandsons and granddaughters, cousins, nephews and nieces, these employers often claim as family the young children they buy – and even steal – from parents and guardians.'

Pramathesh looked aghast. 'That's criminal.'

'Indeed it is,' said Kavi. 'So you see, I need to know more about your uncle's operation and, more importantly, how much you and your father may have known.'

Pramathesh looked at his watch. 'Do you have any more questions? I'm feeling unwell.'

'Just one more for now,' said Kavi. 'Do your imported carpets carry the RUGMARK trademark?'

'I'm sorry,' said Pramathesh, 'I don't know what that is. I've never heard of it.'

'RUGMARK. A voluntary program launched in 1994 to certify Indian carpets made without the use of child labour. I suggest you look into it,' said Kavi, getting to his feet.

'Thank you. I shall.'

'Whatever your uncle has been up to, you and your company may have nothing to worry about legally at the moment,' said Kavi, opening the door, 'but we're not out of the woods yet. I bid you good day.' As Pramathesh walked away down the corridor Kavi said softly under his breath, 'If you've any heart at all, Mr. Kumar, you should have plenty on your conscience.'

* * * * *

It took four weeks for Pramathesh, Amal and Kavi to make up their minds and decide what to do. All three men decided to take action on the very same day – on the Sunday – after they had talked things over with their confidantes.

For the first time in a very long time Pram sat across from his wife in her sewing room. Even at this time in the year there was some colour in their garden. No, not their garden – Ravinder's garden. The deciduous trees were preparing for winter by losing their leaves. The evergreen shrubs – the laurels and holly – would hold onto their tough waxy ones and display their berries in spite of any frost and snow. Pram began to see why his wife loved to sit in her room and look through the French window at such a restful, tranquil scene.

'What are you wanting to tell me, Pram?'

'It's about the company, Ravinder. I want to sell it and retire.'

'I am thinking that this is good thing to do. I am very happy to hear this.'

'I also want to take you on a voyage of discovery to India.'

'That would be very nice, Pram. Thank you. Will you be telling Amal?'

'Yes, of course, and Deep.'

Ravinder smiled to hear him call their daughter Deep instead of Deeptikana – his beam of light. 'Please be telling them this morning. Amal is coming soon to collect more things from his room. Deep is going out again.

'With the greengrocer, I suppose,' sighed Pram. 'I am going to my study to read the paper. Let me know when he arrives.'

'I think you will be hearing him,' she said with a smile. 'Would you like some guava?'

358

In spite of encouragement from Mrs. Cheema, Amal was still rather nervous as he approached the front door of his parents' house and parked Old 'enry Ford on the drive in sight of his father's study. He hadn't lied to his father. He was the business manager. He did manage the stall. And he was enjoying every minute – even, to his own surprise, getting up at 3 o'clock in the morning. The pay wasn't great but, as he'd come to realise, money isn't everything. When he got out of the van and walked up the steps towards the front door, he caught sight of his father looking out of the study window. He waved. To his astonishment, his father waved back.

'Hello Dad!'

'Amalesh! What are you doing with that van?'

'I'm using it to collect some of my stuff,' said Amal with a smile.

'That's the greengrocer's van, isn't it?

'Yes Dad.'

'So why are you driving it?'

'Because I'm the greengrocer now.'

Pramathesh fell back into his big leather chair and listened while Amal told him how he got the job, how hard he was working and how much he was enjoying the work.

'Amal,' said Pramathesh, using the name his son preferred and always wanted his father to use, 'I am selling the company. I am going to retire and take your mother on holiday to India.'

'Good for you, Dad. You both deserve it. Mum's always wanted to visit India.'

'Would you like to come with us?'

'I'd like to Dad but I am too busy right now. Thanks all the same.'

'Would you like me to help you with your stuff?'

'Thanks, Dad. Cool!' And it was especially cool when his mum helped as well.

When Old 'enry Ford had disappeared noisily out of the gate, Pram and Ravinder sat in her sewing room to enjoy the peace and quiet.

Deep wanted to clean and tidy her room before washing her hair and getting ready to see Kavi. Over the noise of the vacuum, she hadn't heard Amal's voice but at one point she happened to look out of her bedroom window. There was The Apple Cart minivan parked in front of the house. She panicked as she imagined the confrontation of merchant v. greengrocer.

Deep dropped the vacuum and dived into the shower. She dried her hair as quickly as possible and was just putting on some casual clothes when she heard the noise of the minivan. When she looked out of her bedroom window she saw Old 'enry Ford's rear end disappearing through the gateway at the bottom of the drive.

'Hello, Deep,' said her father, as she dashed into her mother's sewing room.

'Was that The Apple Cart minivan I saw leaving here a minute ago?'

'Yes,' said her mother, 'but it wasn't your greengrocer friend driving. It was Amal.'

'Amal! Amal was driving it?'

'Yes, Deep,' said her mother. 'Did you know he's the manager of the stall now?'

'Amal's the manager of The Apple Cart? Would you believe it! What do you think of that, Dad?' she said, forgetting herself. Before he could answer, the three of them heard the front door bell. Deep dashed back upstairs to tidy her hair. From her bedroom window she saw a car parked on the drive.

360

She was surprised. Nobody had heard it arrive. Amal could have told her it was a BMW 5 series saloon.

Her father who saw it from his study window could have told her it cost a lot of money. Mrs. Kumar put down her sewing and went to answer the door. When she saw who was standing in the porch, she smiled and said, 'Please come in.' Then she knocked on her husband's study door, opened it and said, 'There's a gentleman to see you, Pram.' Ravinder smiled to herself as she retreated and closed the study door behind her.

'Good morning, Mr. Kumar,' said Kavi. 'I have come to plead the case for a greengrocer who wishes to become engaged to your daughter.'

* * * * *

Epilogue

The characters, the East India Woollen & Silk Carpets Ltd and the events in my story are fictional but the poverty and the exploitation of children in India are matters of fact.

India has more than 1 billion people. 250 million are below the poverty line and three-quarters of the poor are in rural areas. More than 40% of the population over the age of 15 are illiterate. Of the 33 million or so children under 14 years of age at least 300,000 are estimated to work in Uttar Pradesh mostly in its hand-woven carpet industry spread over 2000 sq. kms. The Indian government estimates the number of child workers in all industries to be 12 million but other NGOs (non-government organisations) estimate numbers as high as 20 million. Child labour in India is deemed necessary for poor families to earn an income.

*On the 25th July 1995, Congressman Dan Burton, testified before Congress on The Exploitation of Child Labour in India. He reported that child labour is a main component of the carpet in*___*at many children are separated from their families to work 12* ___ *day with only short breaks for meals of minimal staple and that* ___ *(against employing children under age 14) is rarely followed and does not apply to the employment of family members. Congressman Burton also testified that employers often circumvent the law by claims of hiring distant family and that in rural areas there are few enforcement mechanisms and the punishments for violation are minimal or non-existent.*

The Anti-Slavery Society, formed in 1983, is a public charity and one of many such organisations seeking to relieve the suffering of child bonded labourers. It promotes 'Rugmark' hand-woven carpets which carry a guarantee against the use of child labour. World Vision International is 'a Christian relief, development and advocacy organisation dedicated to working with children, families and communities to overcome poverty and injustice.' It promotes sponsorship for the education and welfare of children.

SEARIC is the registered charitable Society for the Education and Assistance of Rural Indian Children established in 2006 in Edmonton,

362

Alberta by a small group of individuals initially to provide financial support for a rural school in Andhra Pradesh. In the early years of its formation I served as Secretary. My wife and I are now life members.

* * * * *

ACROSS A CROWDED ROOM

On the 6th of August 2010, on the cruise liner Celebrity Constellation, Maureen and I celebrated our Golden Wedding Anniversary. This is the story of how I met my wife. Some of my scientific friends suggest we travel through life encountering people haphazardly as particles collide according to Einstein's mathematical theory of random walk. Maureen and I met by chance they say. Some of my non-scientific friends suggest otherwise. It was kismet they say. Whatever the case, of one thing I can be absolutely sure, I am glad we met.

* * * * *

Maureen and I went to the same school. Well it was almost the same one. I went to Merrywood Grammar School for Boys. Maureen went to Merrywood Grammar School for Girls. The two school buildings were mirror images of each other, linked at the front by an archway leading to an open courtyard. The design of the two buildings and the vigilance of the teaching staff kept most of the boys and girls apart most of the time. This, and the fact that I entered and left the school three years before Maureen, certainly kept us apart. I never met Maureen at school.

In 1952 I went up to the University of Bristol Faculty of Science to read Chemistry. Three years later Maureen went up to the University of Bristol Faculty of Arts to read French. When I graduated in 1955 I still had not met Maureen. So what quirk of fate brought us together?

* * * * *

From my first day at university, or perhaps even before I went up, I resolved to work hard and play hard. The lectures and laboratory practicals guaranteed the hard work. It was up to me to choose the hard play. I played basketball and eventually became secretary of the men only basketball club. I attended the student chemical society lectures and eventually became secretary of the Student Chemical Society (otherwise known as the Chem. Soc.). You could be forgiven for thinking that neither activity would bring Maureen and me together. I should be inclined to agree with you if I did not know otherwise.

I know the basic steps of the waltz and at one time I managed the basic steps of the quickstep but I have never been good at dancing or particularly fond of that activity. Nevertheless, I resolved to attend one formal Ball each year. I did. They were grand black bow tie affairs. On each of the first two occasions I escorted a young lady from Merrywood Grammar School for Girls. She was not Maureen.

My first year of research for my PhD was spent in Holland. In my second year of research back in Bristol I became engaged. It was not to Maureen. And the engagement was not to last. When I began my third year of research, now disengaged, I was fully occupied with my experiments and my duties as Student Chem. Soc. Secretary.

In my first undergraduate year, I dutifully attended not only the Chem. Soc. Lectures but also the Chem. Soc. Christmas Party. It was a shameful affair. It was held in a pub. Almost none of the female undergraduates came. Those that did were, I believe, suitably revolted at the sight of lecturers, including some senior lecturers, rapidly becoming drunk and bringing up their boots. I left early. I believe the like-minded students did too.

The second and last Chem. Soc. Christmas Party I attended was five years later when, as Secretary, I felt duty bound not only to attend but also to persuade the committee not to hold it in a pub. Foolishly overestimating my influence on the Chem. Soc. President, I called a meeting of all undergraduate and postgraduate chemistry students.

It was well attended especially by the female students many of whom were, I fear, persuaded by my vow to prevent the Christmas Party from becoming a drunken affair held in a pub. To my utter shame and dismay I failed. The party was held in a pub. It was a drunken affair. My sober friends and I left very early that Saturday. On the Monday I called another meeting.

* * * * *

At this second meeting which was well attended mainly by the students, male and female, who shared my disgust at the previous Saturday night's fiasco, I apologised for letting everybody down and invited all present to come to my Christmas Party at which there would be dancing and games, food and drink but NO alcohol. I was overwhelmed not only by the numbers wanting to come but also by their insistence on sharing the cost of hiring the hall and providing the food and drink. An undergraduate in his third year and working in my laboratory on his honours project was especially helpful.

Jack persuaded me to drive him into the countryside one evening after dark so he could cut holly from a hedgerow and shin up some trees and pick bunches of mistletoe. I thought Jack was slightly potty but I had to admit that the holly and mistletoe added significantly to the Christmas decorations which he helped me to hang around the hall. Jack offered to help me in another way.

367

'Would you like me to ask my girl friend to bring a girl friend along for you?'

'There's no need,' I may have said, thinking that I would be too busy acting as MC.

'I know she has a friend who would like to come,' said Jack.

Our party took place on the Saturday following the disastrous Chem. Soc. Booze up. We held it in the Co-operative Society Hall not far from where I lived with my parents and six other students. The hall was rectangular, quite big and much longer than it was wide. At one end was a raised platform upon which I, the master of ceremonies stood almost the whole evening. At the other end, and to the side, was a single door – the entrance and exit.

As the revellers arrived, mostly in pairs, they were invited to collect a sheet and move around the room to play the first game - name the products from the advertisements pinned on the wall. We had of course cut the words out of the adverts. Jack was one of the last to arrive. He was accompanied by two female students. One had dark hair. The other had fair hair.

* * * * *

In 1947 James A. Michener won the Pulitzer Prize for his book Tales of the South Pacific. In 1949 Richard Rodgers composed the music and Oscar Hammerstein wrote the lyrics for one of the greatest Broadway musicals – South Pacific. In 1950 the musical won the Pulitzer Prize for Drama. Songs such as Bali Ha'i, I'm Gonna Wash That Man Right Outta My Hair, Younger than Springtime and I'm in Love with a Wonderful Guy became smash hits. My favourite was, and still is, Some Enchanted Evening.

That Saturday became my enchanted evening when I saw the stranger across that crowded room. I certainly knew I should see her again and again. I had found my true love and I felt her call me across that crowded room. So I flew to her side to make her my own because I did not wish all through my life to dream alone. Actually, what I did was to abandon my post on the raised platform to speak to Jack.

368

He introduced me to the student with the fair hair. Her name was Annette. It was his girl friend's friend! Maureen was Jack's girl friend! I returned to the platform and might have stayed there for the rest of the evening if Maureen had not asked me to dance. The party was a great success. Afterwards Jack, Maureen, Annette and a few close friends came back to my house to chat and play a few more games. I walked Annette home – she lived quite nearby – and apologised for having spent little time with her that evening.

* * * * *

The Christmas holiday came and went. On Wednesday the 1st January 1958 the European Economic Community Treaty came into force. I never noticed. On Saturday the 4th January, after ninety-two days in orbit, the Russian satellite, Sputnik 1, returned to earth; it actually fell to earth. I never noticed. On Monday the 6th January, I returned to the lab. When Jack arrived, I wished him a happy new year and asked how his girl friend was.

'She's not my girl friend anymore,' he said. 'We've split up.'

'Oh, too bad,' I said trying to sound sympathetic but failing utterly because in the next breath I said, 'What's Maureen's telephone number?'

Once I had found her, I never let her go.

* * * * *

Epilogue

The Co-operative Society Hall could be hired for a modest sum but no alcohol was permitted on the premised. The party was a success and nobody felt the need to drink in order to be merry. Needless to say, it was the most significant event in my life. I can still see in my mind's eye Maureen entering the hall and feel my heart beating faster. I forever thank my lucky stars for my wife, my closest companion and my dearest friend for more than fifty-four years.

* * * * *

THE DISAPPEARING CHEMISTRY TEACHER

The central incident in this story occurred in 1960 during my first year of full-time teaching and is described as accurately as my memory will allow. I have given fictitious names to the school and the people involved just in case the long arm of the law could stretch 50 years back in time and instigate prosecutions under the 1974 Health and Safety at Work Act.

* * * * *

News, especially bad news, travels fast anywhere. In the school where I began my career as a chemistry teacher in Britain, the rumour of Dr Harold Dainton's mishap travelled so fast that my colleagues in the Physics Department questioned Einstein's theory that nothing can travel faster than the speed of light. I had assembled most of the pieces of the story several days before I was able to speak to Harry himself.

The Laboratory at Bishop Moncton

The teaching laboratory I shared with Harry was on the far side of the school at the end of the main science corridor. The only door in and out was directly opposite the steps down to the basement corridor that led to the prep room and the laboratory technician's hideout.

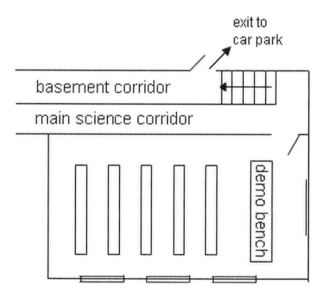

On the right, at the bottom of the steps, was the fire exit to the school car park. There were five laboratory benches for the pupils who faced the teacher's demonstration bench and the blackboard on the wall behind it. The blackout curtains were usually drawn across the three windows on the pupils' right (the teacher's left) to keep out the sun. Harry and I invariably kept the laboratory door open during our lessons. The Friday afternoon in question was no exception.

The Laboratory Technician

It was Friday afternoon and school had finished for the day. I put my nose round the door of the laboratory where our technician was clearing the mess on the demonstration bench. 'Sorry to trouble you, Bert,' I said. 'Have you seen Dr. Dainton?'

'He's gone I think, Sir.'

'Really? That's a nuisance. I wanted a word.'

'Well, I think he's gone, Sir. I'm pretty sure it was him dashing out the fire exit a few minutes before the bell. In a devil of a hurry he was.'

'The demo bench looks a bit of a mess, Bert.'

'No worse than usual, Sir, on a Friday afternoon when Dr Dainton's been enjoying himself. When he first started here, about thirty years ago, he...'

'Sorry, Bert. Can't stop. See you tomorrow morning.'

The Head of Chemistry

Dr Jacob Fothergill was Head of Chemistry and a man with strong views on what to teach and how to teach it. He was particularly keen on exciting demonstrations to capture the boys' interest and frequently referred to *Lecture Experiments in Chemistry* by George Fowles. The copy on his desk was signed by Fowles himself.

Dr Fothergill had started his meteoric career under George Fowles at Latymer Upper. On my first day at the school Dr Fothergill introduced me to the man I could turn to for help with demonstrations – Dr Harry Dainton. This introduction, as I later discovered, served at least two purposes. First, it placed me under the supervision of someone other than Dr Fothergill himself. Second, it re-ignited Harry's enthusiasm and innovative spirit.

Before my first class on Saturday morning I encountered Dr Fothergill in the corridor outside his office.

'Ah, Michael. Glad I caught you. Have you seen Harry?'

'No, sorry. As a matter of fact I was about to ask you that.'

'Bert seems to think he dashed off early yesterday afternoon. Before the bell! Very odd! That's not like Harry. He usually hangs around after school trying out some new experiment or other. Which reminds me,' said Dr Fothergill, 'What did you think of those competition reactions he showed us yesterday lunchtime?'

'Excellent. I'm going to demonstrate them to my Upper Fourths on Tuesday,' I answered.

'Make sure you give Bert a chitty today. He'll want plenty of notice to get the chemicals ready for you.'

'I've already seen Bert. Yesterday afternoon as a matter of fact.'

'Good man. Bert's pretty efficient but I suggest you weigh out the quantities yourself just to be on the safe side.'

'I've already told Bert to weigh out the metal powders and oxides on separate pieces of paper so I can check the weights and make up the mixtures in front of the class. I'm going to get one or two of the boys to assist.'

'Good idea.'

'By the way,' I said, 'I liked Harry's idea of using lead oxide with zinc, aluminium and magnesium as the first three mixtures and then using copper oxide with zinc, aluminium and magnesium in that order for the last three. The zinc with lead oxide was pretty tame but that magnesium copper oxide was something else.'

'It certainly was,' said Dr Fothergill. 'I noticed Harry only used a small amount of the mixture but I felt the heat on my face when it went off. I'm glad I was standing well back'

'I believe Harry did those demonstrations in the last double period yesterday afternoon. I wanted to ask him how they went.'

'There's the bell,' said Dr Fothergill. 'See you in the staff common room at break.'

The Chemistry Class

Saturday morning school came and went. There was no sign of Harry who, incidentally, was a bachelor living with his mother. On Saturday afternoons he often came to watch one of the school rugby matches even though, in deference to his years, he was no longer required to coach a team or referee a match. Nobody saw him that Saturday. He was not at the morning or evening service in the school chapel on Sunday. On Monday there was still no sign of him when the bell rang for the start of the first period. As it happened I shared a class with Harry as well as a laboratory.

'Good morning, Sir.'

'Good morning, boys,' I said to the class that Harry had seen for the final double period of school on the Friday afternoon.

'Be seated.' They sat down rather noisily.

'Less noise if you please, Gentlemen,' I said, as I started to hand back their notebooks.

'Sir!'

'Yes! What is it, Smithson?'

'Have you seen Dr Dainton, Sir?'

'Why do you ask?'

'Well, Sir, it's about his lesson last Friday.'

'What about it?'

'Well, Sir, you see, he sort of vanished in a cloud of smoke.'

'What do you mean, vanished?'

'Well, Sir, he was showing us some composition reactions...'

375

'Competition reactions, Sir,' piped up Hadrill, the boffin in the class whose father was the Director of the Ministry of Defence Chemical Research Establishment at Porton Down. 'He was demonstrating how a metal can displace a less reactive metal from its oxide.'

'That's what I said, Hadders,' retorted Smithson.

'No you didn't,' said Hadrill. 'You said composition not competition, you twerp.'

'Thank you, Gentlemen. I can do without this bickering. Perhaps you would be kind enough to tell me what happened, Hadrill.'

'Certainly, Sir. Well, Sir, Dr Dainton put six different mixtures of a metal powder and an oxide on fireproof asbestos mats on the demonstration bench,' said Hadrill looking at a table in his rough notebook.'

metal powder	metal oxide	observations	conclusion
zinc	lead oxide	flame – powder turned yellow then white later	Zn > Pb
aluminium	lead oxide	flame – mixture glowed hot	Al > Pb
magnesium	lead oxide	mixture flashed – heat given out	Mg > Pb
zinc	copper oxide	green flame – fluffy white powder formed	Zn > Cu
aluminium	copper oxide	mixture flashed – green flame – lots of heat	Al > Cu
magnesium	copper oxide		

I walked over to where Hadrill was sitting and looked at his book.

'Neat work, Hadrill, but where are your observations for the magnesium powder and copper oxide mixture? Didn't Dr Dainton do that demonstration?'

'Oh, yes, he did that one, Sir. It was the last one he did.'

'It was the last one he did alright, Sir,' piped up Smithson.

'Oh shut up!' said Hadrill. 'Sir, Dr Dainton did do all six reactions. I drew a diagram of the demonstration bench.'

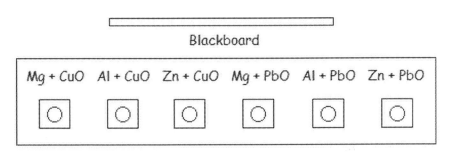

I looked at his diagram and asked the class, 'Why did Dr Dainton spread the mixtures out along the bench? Yes, Smithson!'

'For safety reasons, Sir.'

'Yes, Hadrill.'

'He didn't want one reaction to set off the one next to it, Sir. He didn't want to start a chain reaction.'

'Very good. Did Dr Dainton demonstrate the reactions in order from right to left as you look at the bench?'

'Yes, Sir,' said Hadrill. 'He did the Zn and PbO first and the Mg and CuO last. The reactions went much as we predicted. Copper oxide was more reactive than lead oxide. Magnesium was more reactive than zinc.'

'Sir,' chimed in Smithson, 'The last one – the magnesium and copper oxide – was brilliant. I felt the heat from back here on the third bench.'

'Please, Sir,' said Beechwood, a timid, bespectacled little fellow, 'Smithson's right, Sir. That last reaction was fantastic. And, Sir, Dr Dainton disappeared, Sir.'

377

'What do you mean by disappeared, Beechwood?'

'Well, Sir. When he lit the last mixture, there was a terrific flash and a huge cloud of smoke, Sir. When the smoke cleared, Dr Dainton had disappeared, Sir. He'd vanished!'

'That's right, Sir,' said Smithson. 'We haven't seen him since.'

The Chemistry Master

When Dr Harold Dainton turned up at school on the Tuesday morning he was looking exceedingly the worse for wear. From a distance he looked like a boiled lobster wearing white goggles over his eyes and a bandage over his large right claw. Close up I could see that his normally pale face was burned as though he had been out in a dry desert for a week under a fierce noonday sun. His sandy-coloured eyebrows had gone. His hairless, red face was in sharp contrast to the top of his head. His scalp was its normal pale colour and still sparsely covered by a layer of wispy, sandy-coloured hair. 'Harry! Where have you been? What have you been up to?'

'All my fault, old boy. I should have known better.'

'I gather it was your competition reactions. I had our Upper Fourths yesterday. According to Beechwood, you vanished in a cloud of smoke.'

'I suppose that's what it would have looked like to them.'

'So what happened?'

'My fault. You remember those reactions I showed you and Jacob at lunchtime last Friday. Well I thought they'd be a bit more exciting if I doubled the quantities. The first five reactions worked a treat. Great fun! The last one was the problem.

It wouldn't start. So I held a burning wax taper to the mixture. It went off like a bomb. I felt the heat on my face. I knew I was in trouble, so I dashed straight out the door, down the stairs to the basement exit, jumped in the car and drove straight to the hospital. The boys couldn't have seen me for smoke dust, you might say.'

'How come your eyelids and the skin around your eyes aren't burnt?' I asked.

'Saved by my Woolworth spectacles,' he said, handing them to me. The glass in the frames was scarred, deeply pitted and even melted in places.

'Crikey, you were lucky, Harry,' I said. 'Without these you would probably have lost your other eye.'

'Quite likely, old boy,' he said with a laugh. 'Anyway, the boys won't easily forget those demonstrations, will they.'

* * * * *

Epilogue

On the 31st July 1974, the Health and Safety at Work Act came into force. Its aim was to (a) secure the health, safety and welfare of persons at work, (b) protect others against risks to health or safety in connection with the activities of persons at work, (c) control the keeping and use and to prevent the unlawful acquisition, possession and use of dangerous substances, and (d) control certain emissions into the atmosphere.

Schools, colleges and universities came under the act, being regarded as places of work even if, in the opinion of some teachers and professors, the inactivity of pupils and students sometimes indicated otherwise. As a result, the one-eyed Dr Dainton and his like have become relics of a by-gone age. Many of the demonstrations that excited me as a pupil and that I performed as a chemistry teacher have been banned or confined to video clips to be watched on a computer screen.

I have a confession to make. Throughout my entire teaching career I continued to demonstrate many hazardous and exciting chemical reactions but I always took every possible safety measure. And I always made sure that my pupils understood the precautions I was taking and the hazards we were facing. More than seven thousand people, many of them school children, died in traffic incidents annually in the 1950s but no teacher or a pupil, to my knowledge, was ever killed by a chemical demonstration.

* * * * *

AN ALARMING BUSINESS

This story is set in Broadstone, Dorset, where I lived and worked from the Easter of 1971 until I moved to Canada in December 2000. The characters and their goings-on are figments of my imagination but inspired by certain events in which I was involved and by some people whom I held in high regard and about whom I should not, nay would not intentionally write a libellous word.

* * * * *

As Police Constable Donald Norton walked up the weed-free garden path between the shrub border on his right and the well-kept lawn on his left, the front door of the house was opened by Mrs Mavis Dudridge. Her steel-grey hair was as neat, if not neater than the miniature conifers on sentry duty either side of the porch. Her cheeks were flushed and her eyes red-rimmed and watery. She was wearing a check-patterned apron and wiping her hands in a matching tea-towel. PC Norton took off his helmet and followed her into the hallway.

She was obviously distressed so he skipped the formality of showing her his warrant card. He put his helmet on the hallway table and followed the lady of the house into her living room. The constable had just taken his notebook and pencil from the top pocket of his uniform when Mr Dudridge, wearing slippers and an old gardening coat, came in from the kitchen. 'Oh, Frank,' said Mavis, 'this is Constable Norton. He's come about the break-in.'

'It was a burglary, Mavis,' said Frank. 'It happened last night while we were asleep. It's housebreaking in the daytime, isn't it, Constable?'

'That's what we used to call it, Mr Dudridge, but the *1968 Theft Act, Section 9(1,2)* did away with the distinction. It's all *burglary* now even if nothing is actually stolen. Have you made your list of what's gone missing?'

'Mavis! Where did you put that list?'

'On the desk in your study, Frank. Hang on. I'll go and fetch it.'

'How did they get in, Sir?'

'They forced the back door. Follow me. You can see for yourself,' said Frank, leading the way into the kitchen. 'We'll need a new door and frame now. That'll bump up our insurance premiums.'

'Here you are, Constable,' said Mavis, joining them in the kitchen.

'Thank you, Madam,' said Donald, 'this will be very helpful.'

'What are your chances of catching these thieves, Constable?' asked Mavis.

Before Donald could reply, Frank turned to Mavis and said, 'You can kiss goodbye to that silver tea-service your Gran left you. They'll probably melt it down and turn it into tiny bits of metal for teenagers to stick through their nose and other places I don't care to mention.'

When Mavis started to cry, Donald decided it was time to leave. As he put on his helmet, he said to them, 'You might want to consider having an alarm system fitted.'

'Bit late for that. Closing the stable door now the horse has bolted,' retorted Frank.

'Actually it isn't,' said Donald. 'In the next month you are statistically twelve times more likely to be victims of another burglary than your neighbour who hasn't been burgled yet. You should get expert advice on making your home more secure.'

Donald closed the garden gate, put his bicycle clips around the bottom of his trouser legs and rode away in the direction of his married sister's house.

'What a nice young man,' said Mavis, drying her eyes. 'He got here pretty quickly.

'Waste of time,' said Frank. 'I'd better get on and sort out that kitchen door.'

'I'll make us a nice cup of tea first,' said Mavis. 'You fill in the claim form for the insurance before you start messing about in the kitchen.'

* * * * *

Broadstone had changed in the years since the first house of any size was built there in 1840. The railway line was long gone and the station, built in 1872, had been replaced by a fitness and leisure centre, complete with a 20-metre swimming pool. The population of the parish had increased to more than ten thousand souls and the number of

383

crimes had risen accordingly. Donald cycled past all the banks, estate agents and shops in the busy main street, Lower Blandford Road, – still locally known as 'the village' – and headed downhill to the Derby's Corner roundabout and the local police station where he made out his report.

When he signed out at 4 o'clock he decided to drop in on Dorothy, his younger married sister, who lived with his brother-in-law, Ronald, just around the corner in the Waterloo Estate. His boots crunched on the weed-infested path as he walked to the kitchen door at the back of the house. His sister waved to him through the window as he leant his bike against the wall.

'Any chance of a cup of tea, Dot?'

'I put the kettle on as soon as I heard your big feet on the gravel drive. Sorry I can't offer you a chocolate biscuit. Ronnie had the last one last night and he hasn't given me this week's housekeeping money yet.'

'Still keeping you short, is he? What's he up to now?'

'He went to some meeting or other last week and came back all excited about how he's going to make us rich. He kept going on about MLM but I didn't pay much attention. When I said it sounded like a pyramid selling scheme, he got quite upset.'

'I can tell you, Dot, that multi-level marketing is definitely *not* the same thing as pyramid selling. MLM is a legitimate business operation that *could* make you a lot of money but it's not easy. I don't think it will suit Ronnie. It's too much like hard work. Speaking of work, when's he going to cut the grass?'

'You know Ronnie. He hates gardening. I'd suggest buying a goat to eat the grass and give us milk but he'd probably take me seriously and come up with another of his money-making schemes.'

'Where's the mower I gave him? He hasn't flogged it, has he?'

'No. It's in the shed. At least I think it is. I never go in there.'

'Right! Thanks for the tea,' said Donald, taking off his coat and rolling up his sleeves. I'll see if I can find that mower,'

Ronald Meeks appeared at the shed door just in time to watch Donald finish winding up the hover mower's electrical cable. The lawns, front and back, were now neatly cut and the mower was clean and oiled. Police Constable Norton didn't bother to point out to his brother-in-law that the lawns needed feeding and weeding. It would be a waste of breath. Instead, he asked him what he'd been up to lately. That was all Ronnie needed to launch enthusiastically into a detailed description of MLM and the wealth it promised.

'Did you know that multi-level marketing, or network marketing as it is now called, evolved over a 20-year period prior to the second world war? The biggest and longest established network marketing company operating worldwide is Amway - a contraction of the American way. In MLM you recruit people into your network and earn commission primarily from their sales and *not* from their recruitment or from selling them business support materials, etc. Network marketing is a legitimate operation and *not* a pyramid scam like a no-product scheme where recruits pay you money when they join and when they recruit others to join. And it's not the same as a product-based pyramid scheme where recruits may or may not pay you money to join but they buy your products for re-sale if they're lucky.'

'So what are you going to do, Ronnie? Become an Amway distributor?'

'Not likely. No, I'm going to start my own *bona fide* network marketing operation from scratch.'

'If you don't want me nicking you, Ronnie, make sure you're not starting a pyramid.'

'No chance of that. I won't charge people for joining and training – well not very much anyway. And we'll sell something. You know, we'll distribute a product. I just haven't decided what.'

'Just make sure you stay within the law. Oh, and by the way, give Dot her housekeeping.'

'You know me, Don. Honest Ron they call me. Thanks for mowing the lawns by the way.'

'That's alright. If you'd only feed and weed, they'd soon look like the lawn I saw this morning in West Way. Immaculate that was – just like the whole house.'

'What were you doing there?'

'An elderly couple were burgled last night. The thief or thieves got away with some family silver - the wife's grandmother's tea service. Worth quite a bit I imagine. Usual story. Poor locks, no bolts and no alarm system.'

'That's it!' said Ronnie.

'What? What is it?'

'My product,' said Ronnie. 'I'm going into the home security business. What was the number of that house in West Way?'

* * * * *

Mavis Dudridge was flattered that the owner of Watchdog Securities himself was calling personally to advise them just a week after the burglary. Ronald Meeks had polished his own shoes for once. Dorothy thought he was going down with something. He put on a clean white shirt, dark socks and his best suit and tie – actually his only suit and tie. Dorothy let him have her late father's black leather briefcase. He filled it with stationery he'd had printed and various catalogues he'd picked up locally. Dorothy straightened his tie, adjusted the lapels of his coat and sent the owner of Watchdog Securities out of the front door with a good luck kiss.

'It's so good of you to come personally, Mr Meeks,' said Mavis Dudridge.

'Think nothing of it, Mrs Dudridge. I felt it was the least I could do when Constable Norton happened to mention your misfortune. What dreadful times we live in. Who can you trust these days?' When Frank

Dudridge came in from the kitchen, Ronnie leapt to his feet. 'Good morning, Sir. Mr Dudridge, is it?'

'That's right. I suppose you're the bloke come to sell us an alarm system we can't afford.'

'No, Frank,' said Mavis, 'that nice policeman told him we needed advice and Mr Meeks has come round personally to help us.'

'Quite right, Mrs Dudridge. No, Sir, I'm not a salesman. I own Watchdog Securities and we do supply alarm systems but I'm here just to offer some advice.'

'And what's this advice of yours going to cost me?'

'Frank! I do apologise for my husband, Mr Meeks. He can be a bit blunt.'

'No apology needed, Mrs Dudridge. I prefer a man who speaks his mind.'

'Would you join us in a cup of coffee?'

'Thank you, if that's not too much trouble. Not too strong. Milk but no sugar.'

While Mavis was in the kitchen Ronnie complimented Frank Dudridge on his front lawn and asked how he kept it so weed-free. That launched Frank into an account of the fertilisers and herbicides he used, including how and when he applied them. He had just started to describe his two different lawn mowers and the various heights of cut he used according to the time of year and the weather conditions, when Mavis came in with the coffee and a plate of biscuits. Ronnie made sure that Frank and Mavis had taken what they wanted before he selected a chocolate-covered orange cream wrapped in gold foil.

'I wish I had your green fingers, Mr Dudridge, I really do,' said Ronnie. 'My wife says I'm the angel of death when it comes to plants.'

'You just need time and patience, that's all. Mind you, it helps if you're retired. It wouldn't be the same if I were working full-time running a business like yours.'

'Now then, Mr Meeks, in your expert opinion, what should we do to make our little place more secure?' asked Mavis.

Ronnie had done his homework. He started with the obvious and the inexpensive. Put bolts on the outer doors and also a chain on the front door. Fit locks inside all ground floor windows. Then he moved on to the slightly more expensive.

Replace the spring tumbler lock on the front door with a minimum 1-inch deadbolt. Mount bright lights, activated by motion sensors, high on the walls at the front and back of the house. Replace the carriage lamp in the front porch by one activated by a motion sensor. Put a decoy/dummy bell box high up on the front of the house to fool thieves into thinking the house has an alarm.

And then, in response to Frank's question, Ronnie described the components of a full interior alarm system (control panel, infra-red motion detectors, magnetic door and window contacts, etc.) and discussed the pros and cons of installing wireless versus hard-wired systems.

When Ronnie walked down the garden path to the gate, he had a substantial order – the first of many - in his briefcase. Mavis and Frank Dudridge had persuaded him to take their order along with a second cup of coffee and another foil-wrapped chocolate biscuit. The first recruit into his network would be an old school pal, Tommy Fielding, who was a Do-It-Yourself enthusiast and a qualified electrician. Ronnie knew he'd never recruit his brother-in-law into his business but he planned to get his help.

PC Donald Norton called on Mr and Mrs Dudridge in the evening, the day after their alarm system had been installed and activated. As he opened the gate, a floodlight came on and nearly blinded him.

'Good evening, Mr Dudridge. Constable Norton, Sir.'

'Course you are,' said Frank. 'Everything alright, Constable?'

'Just passing by. I thought I'd check to see how you are. Looks like you've made your place more secure.'

'Yes, thanks to you,' said Mavis, who had come to the door. 'Watchdog Securities did a good job.'

'Cost a pretty penny,' said Frank, 'but we reckon it's worth it. Thanks again.'

* * * * *

Over the next twelve months Ronnie, and two more old school pals he recruited, visited homes recently burgled and listed as such in local neighbourhood watch bulletins. They offered a *Free Home Security Audit* and, as a result, usually took substantial orders for alarm systems that Tommy expertly fitted. Ronnie's most fruitful visits were always to homes that his police constable brother-in-law, Donald, had visited in response to the report of a burglary. Ronnie knew Donald never recommended his or any other security firm to the home owners. That didn't matter. What mattered was that Ronnie knew about the burglary before any rival firm. The knowledge gave him the chance to be first on the scene, so to speak.

Ronnie soon registered his business as a private company. As Tommy the installer became more experienced and proficient, Watchdog Securities Ltd started to offer a wider range of alarms and services. One day Tommy suggested they should put in monitored alarm systems.

'How would that work?' asked Ronnie.

'Well,' said Tommy, 'if someone breaks in, a silent alarm goes off and the police will come running to catch the thieves in the act.'

'I'll have a word with my brother-in-law about it,' said Ronnie.

'You still haven't cut your lawn, Ronnie,' said Donald.

'Too busy. I've got a company to run.'

'Going well, is it?'

'Mustn't grumble. Anyway, if I did, nobody would listen. Look, Don, I need your help.'

'What is it this time? Want me to mow your lawn?'

'No, nothing like that. I want to pick your brains. How do we go about getting you blokes to monitor the alarm systems we're installing?'

'I haven't a clue. Getting a bit ambitious, aren't we?'

'Look, this is important. Can you look into this for me? We've been asked for a monitored system a couple of times now. Mustn't let our customers down.'

A few days later Donald cycled to his sister's house and left a note.

Ronnie,

The alarm should conform to the Association of Chief Police Officers (ACPO) Unified Intruder Alarm Policy. A remote signalling alarm should be hardwired, maintained in accordance with an appropriate British Standard and, when registered with the police, identified by a unique reference Number (URN). Watchdog Securities Ltd would be subject to inspection by independent organisations identified in the police policy.

You might want to tell your customers that the police may not respond if they have competing urgent calls or they are short staffed. If an alarm triggers a lot of false calls in a year, it will be given a lower police response priority.

Don

* * * * *

It looked as though Ronnie had found his niche. His marketing network never grew but Watchdog Securities Ltd was doing quite well. Ronnie made himself chairman. He made Dorothy secretary so she could claim her housekeeping as expenses. Tommy was treasurer. Ronnie's other two former school pals stayed as independent distributors and took a commission on sales.

Insomniac, their silent monitored alarm system, was beginning to worry their competition – the other local security firms. All would have been well if only Ronnie had not started reading some of these 'improve your small business' books. The 'Guru' who threw the spanner in Ronnie's works wrote, *No business stagnates – it either grows or it dies.*

The five members of Watchdog Securities sat around Dorothy's kitchen table, drinking her coffee and eating her biscuits. Ronnie called their informal meeting to order.

'We're stagnating,' said Ronnie. 'If we're not careful the business is going to die.'

'How do you make that out?' asked Tommy.

'We've had the same number of orders each month for the last three months,' said Ronnie.

'What's wrong with that?' chimed the two distributors in unison. 'Our orders are not going down.'

'That's not the point,' said Ronnie. 'They ought to be going up.'

'So what you're saying is,' said one distributor, 'we should be on the telephone cold calling or out there knocking on doors? *Good morning, madam, could I interest you in a security system? Oh, and by the way, we have a special on double glazing this month.*'

'If you want telephone cold calling, you can do it yourself,' said the other distributor.

'And I'm not knocking on doors at random,' said the first distributor.

'Unless the number of burglaries increases, Ronnie,' said Dorothy, 'you'll have to be content with the business as it is.'

'You've got a point there, my love. Meeting closed,' said Ronnie. 'Tommy! I'd like a word with you in private?'

* * * * *

Over the next six months, business picked up. Sales increased little by little. Watchdog Securities Ltd was no longer stagnating. It was growing. One afternoon, just before Donald was due to sign out, the station sergeant called him over to his desk. The sergeant wanted the opinion of the station's *neighbourhood watch liaison officer* on the small but steady increase in the number of local burglaries he had noticed in the station reports. According to the sergeant, two things didn't quite add up.

First of all, in most of the cases, there was very little damage and nothing was stolen. Second of all, this increase coincided with an increase in the number of neighbourhood watches being set up locally. Donald had to agree that it was curious but he could offer no explanation. Just as he turned to leave, the sergeant asked him if he'd investigated the recent noise complaint.

'Yes, Sarge. It was the major's trip flares going off late at night. I didn't file a formal report'

'Trip flares? What's all that about?'

PC Donald Norton explained.

'Some ex-army major strung a series of trip wires criss-crossing his rear garden backing onto what used to be the old railway line. He's been burgled three times in the past two months. They always came through the garden and used a jemmy on the kitchen door or window. First time the major's wife lost most of her jewellery. Second time they lost their silver dinner-service. Third time was the last straw. They took the major's medals and smashed his prize marrow.'

'So the thieves tried for a fourth time and set off these flares?'

'Hard to tell, Sarge. More likely it was a fox on the prowl. The neighbours got fed up being woken up in the middle of the night by all those loud bangs and flashes. I've had a word with the major. He didn't like it when I pointed out that he might be hounded by the Wildlife Protection Society or sued by a would-be burglar for damage to his ears and eyes. Anyway, I hung around until he'd turned his assault course back into a normal garden. The neighbours have probably heard the last thunderflash but not the last of the major.'

About two weeks later Donald was instructed to attend an evening meeting of a group of residents in the major's locality. It was not a gathering to complain about late night thunderflashes. The meeting was in the major's house to agree the formation of a neighbourhood watch. Donald attended in his capacity as neighbourhood watch liaison officer. It was almost a waste of his time. He handed out a leaflet but had little to say. The major was firmly in command and his night ops were clearly forgiven and forgotten.

The minutes of the meeting showed they unanimously agreed that (a) the major would be the new neighbourhood watch representative, (b) his telephone would receive from the police their recorded messages of local incidents and their alerts of criminal activities and (c) he would arrange through the local council to put an official sign on a nearby lamppost.

It was 10:55 p.m. when Donald put on his helmet and left the major's house to cycle home. A few minutes later he received on his two-way radio a message that a silent alarm had been activated in a house twenty yards down the road. He called back and informed the duty officer that he would investigate. Just before he reached the house, Donald switched off his front lamp and leant his bike quietly against the neighbour's garden wall. Then, torch in hand, he moved as quietly as his boots would allow to the house.

The front gate was open. Donald stepped onto the front lawn and crept up to the front door. He switched on his torch long enough to establish no sign of a forced entry there. Keeping to the lawn, he moved as quietly as possible to the rear of the house. It was in complete darkness. Just as he was about to shine his torch on the back door, he heard a faint sound from inside.

Somebody or something was moving around in the kitchen. The back door was open. He risked his torch again. The door was open. He tiptoed forward and stood alongside the door with his back to the wall. 'Patience is a virtue,' PC Donald Norton thought to himself. And sure enough, it was.

After a minute that seemed more like an hour, a figure crept out through the open kitchen door. 'Gotcha!' said Donald, grabbing the arm of the intruder's black tracksuit top. At 175lbs in weight and 6ft 3ins in height plus another 3ins of police helmet, PC Donald Norton's word was his command. 'Alright, my lad, let's take a look at you,' he said to his captive who was a mere 118lbs and 5ft 4ins tall. Donald shone his torch onto the intruder's face. 'What the...? Oh, Lord! What have you been up to?'

Donald quietly pushed the back door shut and without waking the occupants, left the property with the would-be burglar. With one large hand on the handlebars of his bicycle and the other firmly holding his captive's arm, he marched in the direction of the police station. When they reached Derby's Corner, he hesitated and then turned towards the Waterloo Estate. When they reached his sister's house, they went inside and sat down to face one another across the kitchen table.

'So,' said Donald, 'are you going to tell me what this is all about?'

'Watchdog Securities Ltd.'

'I might have guessed. How long has this been going on?'

'I'm not sure. Quite a while I suppose. I'm sorry. This must be a bit awkward for you.'

'You can say that again.'

'I really am sorry. It's just that the business wasn't growing and we thought...'

'You'd help it along.'

'Look, I never took anything and I did as little damage as possible. What happens now?'

'By rights I should arrest you and you'd be charged with burglary.'

'It wasn't my idea. You know that don't you?'

'Yes, I do. You'd never come up with such a hair-brained scheme yourself.'

'And you can guess why I did it, can't you?

'Yes, I can. You did it out of loyalty.'

'Well, yes that too I suppose. But really, I knew if he did it, he'd be caught the first night. I mean, he can't even mow a lawn.'

'Alright. Here's what I'll do. I'll report that there was no sign of an intruder when I arrived at the house and that the silent monitored alarm may have been set off by a cat.

'One of our competitor's alarms, was it?'

'No. As a matter of fact it was one of your own. Didn't Tommy tell you he'd installed it?

'No. But I usually don't know what's going on.'

'Anyway, I'm going to let you off with a caution but you must swear to me that tonight was your last attempted burglary.'

'I swear, Don. Never again.'

'Right, that's that then. I'd better be off. I've the early shift tomorrow,' he said heading for the door.

'Never again, Don. I promise.'

'Fine. Goodnight, Dot. Sleep tight.'

* * * * *

Epilogue

In 1982, the United Kingdom of Great Britain and Northern Ireland saw the launch of satellite TV, the start of the Falklands War and, in the sleepy village of Mollington near Chester, the formation of the first neighbourhood watch. One of the villagers brought back the idea from a visit to the USA and Canada. By 2007 there were more than 170,000 neighbourhood watch groups in the UK with over 10 million members.

The reduction in crime and increase in the sense of safety generated by the scheme underlines the value of knowing and getting on with your neighbours. I was instrumental in forming the neighbourhood watch in the cul-de-sac where we lived in Broadstone. I was our representative and our telephone received those recorded messages from the police. Our friendly neighbours referred to me as 'Colonel of the Watch.'

When we moved out of that cul-de-sac, we sold our house to, surprisingly enough, a real Colonel. He was only too willing to take command of our little neighbourhood watch. Shortly afterwards, my wife and I moved to Canada where, equally surprisingly, we have yet to be part of an official neighbourhood watch. I did try to form one but... well that is another story.

* * * * *

Keep reading for an excerpt from Michael C. Cox's novel

Once Upon A Term

available in paperback and electronic book form from Amazon

* * * * *

"The writing of solid, instructive stuff fortified by facts and figures is easy enough. There is no trouble in writing a scientific treatise on the folk-lore of Central China, or a statistical enquiry into the declining population of Prince Edward Island. But to write something out of one's own mind, worth reading for its own sake, is an arduous contrivance only to be achieved in fortunate moments, few and far in between. Personally, I would sooner have written Alice in Wonderland than the whole Encyclopaedia Britannica."

Stephen Leacock (Sunshine Sketches of a Little Town)

INTRODUCTION

"Truth is stranger than fiction, but it is because Fiction is obliged to stick to possibilities; Truth isn't." Mark Twain

* * * * *

This story is fiction but not pure and simple. Beaumont Abbey School does not exist. The activities of its staff and pupils are products of my imagination but not entirely so. In my experience of teaching in the independent, private sector, in England, facts have proved stranger than fictions. However, all the companies, events, organisations and places in this book are either the product of my imagination or used fictitiously.

The names and characters are figments of my imagination and any resemblance to actual persons, living or dead, is entirely coincidental. Now, should any former colleagues think I have included them in my story and, heaven forbid, portrayed them unfavourably, may I point out that more often than not the law seems to benefit the lawyers rather than the litigants.

* * * * *

Beaumont Abbey I imagine to have been founded by Sir Athelstan de Beaumont in 1587, during the reign of Elizabeth I, as a Public School, meaning, of course, a private school. I apologise to my friends in North America for the confusion. Some four hundred years or so later, I

398

imagine the school is still private and independent of the state school system.

In my imagination, the school would be located on the border of the northern counties of Cumbria, Durham and Northumberland. Its ancient stone buildings would be listed to protect them from man but not the elements. Its modern buildings would contrast sharply.

The academic staff would be highly qualified, all men, individualistic and bordering upon the eccentric. Many, but not all, would themselves have been educated at an all-boys private boarding school. Their pupils would be sent to Beaumont, from the British Isles and other parts of the globe, to be similarly educated and become steeped in tradition.

The headmaster or principal - I call him the High Master – would be responsible to the board of governors and, in theory, overall in charge of the school. The deputy head or vice-principal – I call him the Second Master – would be responsible to the headmaster and, in practice, overall in charge of the school. The Housemasters would be members of the academic staff and responsible for the boys in their boarding houses.

The Bursar – often an ex-serviceman - would be responsible to the board of governors and in charge of the financial management of the school and the non-academic staff with, of course, the exception of the headmaster's secretary who is often a law unto herself.

This story concerns the third and final term in the academic year, the summer term - I call it the Trinity Term – in which the school is on the brink of becoming co-educational.

* * * * *

CHAPTER 1

"Childhood has no forebodings, but then, it is soothed by no memories of outlived sorrow." George Eliot - The Mill On The Floss

* * * * *

Dr Llywelyn Pugh-Jones gently tapped the shell of his soft-boiled egg in time with the music emanating from his radio, precisely and almost permanently tuned to the BBC Radio 3 Breakfast Hour programme. He sat alone in the kitchen. Louise, his wife, had taken her breakfast tray and Daily Telegraph newspaper into the relative peace and quiet of the sunroom. If she had broken her routine and stayed in the kitchen, perhaps the High Master of Beaumont Abbey might have paid attention more to his wife than to the music Sergei Prokofiev composed for the film *Lieutenant Kijé*. If she had eaten her breakfast at the kitchen table he might not have had two ideas, one of which nearly led to tragedy.

Reginald Thomas De Vere, MA (Cantab) covered the hot porridge with cold milk, added a sprinkling of granulated brown sugar, glanced at his wrist watch and began the Times crossword. Eighteen minutes and 23 seconds later he had finished the crossword but not the porridge. He poured himself a second cup of coffee from his *cafetière à piston* before selecting a croissant from the woven silver basket on the breakfast table. Reg, as he was fondly known to his colleagues, had been a widower for almost four years. His wife, Madeleine, whom he had met in Paris and who had been three years his junior when they wed, had died of a brain tumour when she had just turned fifty. She had given him the silver cafetière on their 25th wedding anniversary. He had given her the silver basket. They owned a small holiday cottage on the Dorset coast. All being well, Reggie, as his wife fondly called him, planned to retire there after four more years as Second Master at Beaumont Abbey.

Anthony Parker-Smythe, purportedly a former major in the Royal Army Pay Corps, had finished his porridge, his kipper, his cooked breakfast of two eggs, bacon, sausage and mushrooms and was halfway through his second slice of toast and marmalade when Elsie, his housekeeper came to clear the dining room table. His mouth was so full he could only nod in the direction of his china cup and saucer. She poured him some more coffee then disappeared before he could attempt a smile of gratitude, not that he ever smiled or was grateful. At the kitchen sink, Elsie began washing the dishes and resolving to hand in her notice at the end of the week. She had had enough of her employer, the Bursar of Beaumont Abbey, real name Tony Smith who, according to her late husband, had only risen to corporal in the Army Catering Corps.

Gregory Watson had, as usual, been for a 5k run, showered, shaved and changed into his gym kit and track suit before joining his wife, Kathy, and their two young children, Mark and Tracy, at the table for his bowl of cereal and glass of orange juice. He came to Beaumont Abbey straight from Loughborough University after gaining a joint honours degree in Geography and Sports Science and completing his teacher training. He was in his third year at Beaumont and expected to become Head of Physical Education when Walter Barnes retired at the end of the year. Greg looked forward to modernising the PE curriculum and Kathy looked forward to receiving more house-keeping money. Neither gave thought to the possibility of unforeseen difficulties.

Colin Harper overslept. It had been another disturbed night of bad dreams he might, with professional help, have erased from his mind. His colleagues in the Mathematics Department at Beaumont seemed not to notice or care about the dark rings around his puffy eyes and the bags underneath them. Had Dr Klaus Heilbronn, the Head of Maths, ever noticed or cared, he might have assumed his assistant, whom he had placed in charge of the computer room, was spending too much time staring too closely at too many screens. One strikingly good-looking boy not only noticed but also really cared.

Rupert Jardine had inherited his angelic good looks from his English mother, an actress of good repute, and his devilish ways from his American father, an entrepreneur of ill repute and head of a corporation specialising in computers and software engineering. He was flying business class from JFK airport to London, Heathrow where a chauffeured car would be waiting. He had mixed feelings about returning to Beaumont. Only two members of staff really liked him; the rest tolerated him. He knew he had overstepped the mark with his last prank; he was only being allowed back because the member of staff involved had not been seriously injured and because Randolph Jardine was a very wealthy man.

It was Saturday morning. The summer term was about to begin. At 10 o'clock sharp the staff of Beaumont Abbey would assemble in the Long Room for the High Master's words of welcome, for the Second

Master's notice of any changes affecting staff and for the Housemasters' lists of pupils flying in late from far flung regions of the globe or arriving on time but with a leg broken whilst skiing in the Alps. After the Chaplain's reminder that evensong in the chapel would begin at 7 p.m. on Sunday, the meeting would finish. The High Master would retreat to his study. The Second Master and staff would retreat to the Common Room for coffee or tea, biscuits and gossip. School would begin in earnest immediately after chapel on Monday morning. For most, the coming weeks would be hectic but normal. For a few, the summer term would be very hectic and not normal at all.

* * * * *

CHAPTER 2

"Meetings are indispensable when you don't want to do anything." John Kenneth Galbraith – American Economist

* * * * *

He was deep in thought and chewing thoroughly the last fragment of his second piece of toast when his wife returned to the kitchen from the sun room.

'Good morning, Llew,' she said. 'How was your breakfast?'

'Fine, thank you Louise,' replied Dr Llywelyn Pugh-Jones, the High Master of Beaumont Abbey. 'Lacking in taste but healthy and nutritious. Just what my doctor ordered.'

'Not that bad, surely?' said Louise.

'Let me think for a moment. One half of a fresh grapefruit - *no sugar*. One soft-boiled egg - *no salt*. Two thin slices of *whole grain* toast - *no butter*. One small glass of orange juice – *unsweetened*. Oh, yes! *No coffee. No tea.*'

'Sounds delicious,' said Louise. 'In fact it was delicious. I had exactly the same.'

'Really? *Exactly* the same? No sugar on your grapefruit?'

'No! I did *not* sprinkle any sugar on my grapefruit,' Louise said haughtily, knowing her husband would not notice the pot of honey on her tray. 'Anyway, I'm not the one with a heart condition.'

There was a history of heart problems in the Pugh-Jones family. Llywelyn's grandfather was forty-six when he died. Llywelyn's father was forty-nine when he died. Both men had heart attacks. Both deaths were blamed on the men being overweight, heavy smokers and Welsh coal miners. Llywelyn believed he had already outlived his father by two years because he had never worked down a coal mine, he had never smoked and he was not overweight. At his last medical examination, the High Master of Beaumont weighed 174 pounds, stood 6ft 3in tall in his cotton socks and measured 35 inches around his waist. His body mass index (BMI) of 21.7 was exactly in the middle of the normal range. He felt he was in good physical shape for a man of his age but Louise made him go for a medical when he returned from a staff meeting complaining of a pain in his chest.

'Before you ask,' said Llywelyn, 'yes, I did take my blood pressure tablet. Thank you for putting it on my tray.'

'Will you be back here for lunch?'

'Hopefully but I must have a word with the Bursar after the staff meeting,'

'What's Nosey Parker been up to now?' said Louise. 'Nothing illegal, I trust.'

'You're not very fond of our Major Anthony Parker-Smythe, are you?'

'No, to be honest. Something not quite right about him. Too smarmy for words if you ask me,' said Louise.

'I think you're being a trifle harsh, my dear,' Llywelyn said, knowing full well his wife was a pretty good judge of character. 'The major knows how to handle Beaumont's finances.'

'Now *that* I don't doubt for one moment,' Louise said, with a wry look on her face.

* * * * *

The chapel, the walled garden and parts of the main building date back to 1587 when the school was founded by Sir Athelstan de Beaumont. Some of the trees in the extensive grounds are even older. The Long Room is actually more square than oblong. A little daylight filters through the narrow windows high above the tall oak panelling covering the walls but even when all the lights are switched on, the room remains gloomy. Ronald Beech, the head caretaker, was in the Long Room when the Second Master arrived.

'Good morning Mr De Vere.'

'Good morning Ron. Everything ready for the meeting?'

'Yes, sir,' said Ron. 'Tom and Dolly were in here first thing this morning. I just popped in to check they had finished. Tom buffed the floor while Dolly did the dusting.'

'How long have the Browns been with us now?' asked the Second Master.

'Must be going on for ten years now,' said Ron. 'Worth their weight in gold.'

'Yes indeed.'

'Tom will keep watch as usual,' said Ron. 'When he sees you leave the Long Room, he'll let Dolly know the meeting is over so she'll have the coffee in the Common Room for when the staff arrive. Now, if you'll excuse me, sir. I must be getting along.'

The door into the room was in the far corner of the shorter wall. Near the door and just inside the room, were two rectangular tables placed end to end and parallel to the shorter wall. Six more tables, in two sets of three, were placed end to end and parallel to the longer wall. The names of past pupils were carved on these eight heavy oak tables and bore witness to the age of the school.

On the two tables by the door was a green baize cloth, creating the illusion of one large table, and a silver tray bearing a jug of iced water and two glasses. Behind each half of the table, and close to the oak-panelled wall, was a chair with a carved high back and a padded seat. On the table in front of the chair furthest from the door, Reg placed the walnut gavel and block that had belonged to his great-grandfather. Dr Pugh-Jones mistakenly believed the Second Master's great-grandfather had been a judge. The Second Master was never afraid to correct the High Master when he was wrong but on this point he kept his own counsel. His great-grandfather had simply been an auctioneer. Reg glanced at his watch then strolled outside to await the arrival of the staff.

'Good morning, Second Master. Nice morning,' said Gregory Watson.

'Good morning, Greg. Been for our morning run, have we?

'Oh Yes. Too nice a day to stay in bed,' said Greg. 'Am I the first?'

'Only if you exclude me as a member of staff,' said Reg, with a smile.

'I stand corrected. I'm the second,' said Greg. 'If you'll excuse me, I'll go on in.'

Heavy oak chairs, with low backs and no padding, had been placed on either side of the long tables (two sets of three) running parallel to the longer walls of the room. These hard chairs were for the staff. There were, however, four high-backed, padded chairs, one either side and at the head of the long tables and nearest to the baize-covered table. These padded chairs were for the housemasters. Greg sat on the hard chair next to the padded chair nearest to the door because he wanted to be seen by the High Master and the Second Master. He also wanted to be first out of the door when the meeting ended.

It was three minutes to ten when Colin Harper came scurrying up the path.

'S-S-Sorry S-Second M-M-Master. Am I late?'

'No, Colin. You cut it fine. I see the High Master heading our way. Get inside before he sees you.'

'Yes. R-right. Th-Thank you, s-sir.'

'Good morning High Master,' said the Second Master. 'How are you this morning?'

'Fine! Never felt better,' said Dr Pugh-Jones. 'All present and correct?'

'Yes. Everyone is here.'

'Good. Let's get started. Lead the way.'

* * * * *

When the Second Master entered the room, the staff stood up. Then the High Master entered the room and took his seat behind the baize-covered table. When the Second Master had taken his seat alongside the High Master, the staff sat down. The Second Master poured two glasses of iced water and placed one in front of the High Master. Even though the only sound in the room was the ice tinkling against the sides of the High Master's glass as he sipped his water, the Second Master struck the walnut block three times with his walnut gavel. It was exactly ten o'clock. The High Master cleared his throat.

'Good morning, gentlemen. Welcome back to Beaumont Abbey. I hope you all enjoyed your Easter break and are ready for the Trinity term. I am sure I need not remind you that the first half is a crucial time for the Upper Fives and Upper Sixes. Good examination results are not of course the be-all and end-all - *pause for a sip of water* - but at this time in a boy's life they will decide what options he may have for his future. It is up to us to see that every boy gives of his best. Beaumont has built up a reputation for academic excellence that should be reflected in the examination results. The future of the school may depend on them. I, as do the boys, put my trust in all of you. Thank you.'

As the High Master turned to leave, all the staff (except Geoffrey Rusbridge who was engrossed in the Financial Times) stood up and stayed standing until he had left the room and closed the door behind him. The Second Master sat down, drank some iced water and used his gavel again. David Peters stood up and said the delay of a flight from Singapore would mean five boys from Armstrong house might not be back in time for Sunday evensong. Some younger members of staff seated at the back of the Long Room sniggered when they heard the Housemaster read out the names in rapid succession: Chin, Chin, Kung, Fu and Woo.

The Second Master managed to keep a straight face and called upon the Housemaster of Burdett. Ralph Abrahams leaned forward out of his seat, said he had nothing to report and sat back down. Alan Radford reported for Gower that Morris Minor might be late. Before he could explain, someone at the back of the room whispered audibly *engine trouble* and caused more sniggering. The Second Master used his gavel. The Housemaster of Gower then explained the boy was recovering from influenza.

'Wedgewood,' said the Second Master, looking at E. Gordon Hamilton.

'Thank you, Second Master,' said Hamilton rising slowly to his feet, blithely unaware of the restless shuffling of some feet at the back of the room. 'I have six boys delayed on the same flight to which Mr Peters referred.'

'The flight from Singapore?' said the Second Master.

'Yes!' said Hamilton, a modern linguist.

'Your Chinese contingent?'

'Yes!' said Hamilton.

'How's their English coming along?'

'They speak English almost as well as they speak Cantonese and Mandarin,' Hamilton said somewhat tetchily. 'May I read out their names?'

'Yes, of course,' said the Second Master.

'Chén, Chéng, Liú, Wáng, Yáng and Zháng.'

'Thank you Mr Hamilton,' said the Second Master. 'Since some of us do not have your ear for the four tones of Chinese - the first two sounded the same to me - would you spell those names.'

'If you wish,' said Hamilton, again ignoring more restless shuffling of feet. After he had spelled each name carefully, including the accents over the vowels, he remained standing.

'Do you have anything else, Housemaster?' asked the Second Master.

'Just one question, if I may,' said Hamilton. 'What has the High Master decided to do about Jardine?' No more shuffling of feet or nervous coughing. The room was silent.

'He is being allowed back to complete his year in the Lower Sixth. No decision has yet been made about his continuing into the Upper Sixth.' The murmurs around the room masked Colin Harper's sigh of relief at the news.

407

'When, may I ask, were we to be informed of this decision?'

'Today. Mary Cranborne sent a note to you, and the Heads of Maths and Physics, for a meeting with the High Master and myself this afternoon at 2 p.m.'

'Will Jardine still be denied privileges, Second Master?' asked Gregory Watson.

'That's something we shall be discussing this afternoon. We'll try not to deny the First Eleven its opening fast bowler.'

The Second Master looked around the room, glanced at his watch, picked up his walnut gavel and said, 'Coffee awaits us in the Common Room. Is there any other business, gentlemen?' No hand was raised and heads were shaking, so he struck the walnut block a resounding blow and declared the meeting closed.

* * * * *

Dr Llywelyn Pugh-Jones closed the Long Room door quietly and walked slowly from the portico out into the sunshine, unbroken by the few wispy clouds in a pale blue sky. Directly ahead of him was a concrete path leading straight to the main building and the Bursar's office. To his right was a gravel path, bordered on both sides by well-tended beds of assorted evergreen flowering shrubs – azaleas, japonica, rhododendrons, skimmia and viburnum – that would lead him first to the walled garden. He hesitated just for a moment then turned right onto the gravel path.

His doctor advised a brisk walk every morning. Llywelyn was a good patient and usually took his doctor's advice but not this morning. He was in no hurry to see Nosey Parker, as his wife Louise called the Bursar, Anthony Parker-Smyth. Llywelyn pretended he was just out for a stroll. It was after all a beautiful morning. He savoured the fragrant scent from the tiny white flowers of the skimmia and viburnum and feasted his eyes upon the purples and reds of the azaleas and rhododendrons. A thrush, hiding in the shrubbery, suddenly stopped its flutelike song when it heard Llywelyn's footsteps on the gravel path.

Perhaps the birdsong reminded him of the music on the radio that morning. Llywelyn began to hum Prokovief's sleigh ride tune, Troika, and to recall that in a short story by Vladimir Dal and published in 1870, Kijé was an imaginary officer brought into being by a bureaucratic blunder. Emperor Paul I of Russia promotes Kijé to lieutenant, captain and eventually to colonel. When the Emperor asks to see the colonel and the bureaucrats realise their original blunder will be discovered, they inform the Emperor that Colonel Kijé has died. The whimsical thought, of bureaucracy creating an imaginary person that the authorities treat as a real person, was going through his head when he arrived at the Bursar's office. Dr Pugh-Jones smoothed his thinning ginger hair, tousled during his stroll, drew himself up to his full height, knocked once and strode briskly into the room.

'Ah, High Master! Good morning, sir,' said Nosey, putting down his coffee cup and rising to his feet. 'Beautiful morning! You're looking extremely well this morning, if I may say so. How is Mrs Pugh-Jones these days?'

'She is very well. Thank you for asking, Anthony.'

'May I offer you some coffee?' said Nosey, reaching for the jug on the tray on his desk.

'I should refuse, doctor's orders and all that, but on this occasion I *will* say yes to a small cup,' said Llywelyn. 'Milk but no sugar if you please.' Having committed this minor transgression, he sat down and, while his coffee was being poured and he was attempting to prepare his opening remarks, he noticed Nosey also poured himself a whole cup of coffee and added two spoonfuls of brown sugar and a generous helping of full cream.

'Here you are, High Master,' said Nosey, reaching across his large mahogany desk to hand Llywelyn his half cup of coffee. 'I hope you like it. It's made from the *arabica* bean. They're a bit more expensive than the *robusta* bean but the coffee is more aromatic, has more flavour but only half the caffeine of coffee made from robusta beans.

'Only half the caffeine, you say? Very interesting.'

'May I offer you a chocolate biscuit?' said Nosey.

'Thank you, no,' said Llywelyn. 'Not good for the cholesterol and lipids in the blood, so I'm told.'

'Actually,' said Nosey, 'these are Belgian biscuits. Thin wafer coated in dark chocolate which, I am told, is good for you. Please try one.'

'Oh, very well. Just one. Thank you.'

The two men sat facing one another in silence, a silence broken only in their heads by the crunching of a chocolate biscuit and the swallowing of arabica coffee. His secretary, Mrs Susan Taylor, had reminded the Bursar that the High Master would be dropping in but had been unable to tell him the reason for his visit. Nothing in his visitor's manner so far led

Nosey to believe he had anything to be nervous about. He kept calm and tried not to think about accounts and financial records. The High Master had instructed his secretary, Mary Cranborne, to tell the Bursar he would come to see him on Saturday morning straight from the Long Room. When Mary wanted to know the purpose of his visit in case Susan asked, Llywelyn told her to say it was just to say hello. 'No, Sue,' said Mary, 'Dr Pugh-Jones didn't say why he'll be dropping in. Probably just wants to chat. Nothing serious. Nothing specific.' But of course Mary Cranborne, BA. had worked for the High Master long enough to know that he would never chat, that he was always serious and that he would have something quite specific in mind.

'You wanted to see me, High Master?' said Nosey, breaking the silence.

'Yes, Anthony,' said Llywelyn. 'It's about money, I'm afraid.

* * * * *

Made in the USA
Lexington, KY
20 July 2019